"Action-ac ...
want to read ... of
Crichton, the military teen know-how of Clancy, and the
spine-tingling intensity of Koontz, allow me to introduce
you to Gregg Andrew Hurwitz. You're going to love
Minutes to Burn."
Jan Burke, Edgar Award-winning author of *Bones*

"The science is fascinating, the story is exciting, and the
plot moves with the unstoppable precision of a SEAL
team mounting an assault."
Robert Crais, author of *Demolition Angel* and *Hostage*

"Vivid . . . engrossing . . . A rousing actioner reminiscent
of *Jurassic Park, The Dirty Dozen, Lord of the Flies,* and
maybe even *Beowolf* . . . Hurwitz demonstrates once
again that he is a thriller writer to be reckoned with."
Kirkus Reviews

"Gregg Andrew Hurwitz captures the warrior spirit of the
past and takes us to a future where science unleashes
discoveries that society has yet to comprehend."
Richard Marcinko, *New York Times* bestselling author of
Rogue Warrior®

"Gripping action . . . a deft recombinant blend of
a thriller . . . This page-turner keeps a satiric edge,
while Hurwitz proves he is perfectly at home with
toothy creatures on the rampage and a thrilling array of
soon-to-be-FX."
Publishers Weekly

"Hurwitz's crew in *Minutes to Burn* are the hardest,
orneriest, funniest soldiers since *The Dirty Dozen*. The
novel has a breakneck drive, chilling realism, and
graveyard tension. Hang on to your hat.
James Thayer, author of *Terminal Event* and *Five Past Midnight*

Also by Gregg Andrew Hurwitz

THE TOWER

Available in Hardcover

DO NO HARM

GREGG ANDREW HURWITZ

MINUTES TO BURN

HarperTorch

An Imprint of HarperCollinsPublishers

HARPERTORCH
An Imprint of HarperCollins*Publishers*
10 East 53rd Street
New York, New York 10022-5299

Copyright © 2001 by Gregg Andrew Hurwitz
Excerpt from *Do No Harm* copyright © 2002 by Gregg Andrew Hurwitz
Maps by James Sinclair
ISBN: 0-06-101551-2

First HarperTorch paperback printing: August 2002
First Cliff Street Books hardcover printing: August 2001

HarperCollins ®, HarperTorch™, and ❦™ are trademarks of Harper-Collins Publishers Inc.

Printed in the United States of America

Visit HarperTorch on the World Wide Web at www.harpercollins.com

10 9 8 7 6 5 4 3 2

For Jess Taylor

and

Adriana Alberghetti
Brian Lipson
Dawn Saltzman
Tom Strickler

Acknowledgments

My Crew:

Matthew Guma—the champion of M2B, and my editor extraordinaire

Diane Reverand—my publisher, a woman of great vision

David Vigliano and Dean Williamson—for their support

Marc H. Glick and Stephen F. Breimer—for holding it all together

My Consultants:

Ross Hangebrauck—former member of SEAL Team EIGHT, and one cool Johnny

Cynthia Mazer—entomologist, Conservatory Director of Cleveland Botanical Garden

Joshua J. Roering—Professor of Geological Sciences at the University of Oregon

And also:

Tim Tofaute—former member of SEAL Teams FIVE and EIGHT, and of the Naval Strike Warfare Center

Jack Nelson—beachcomber, international yachtsman, owner of the Hotel Galápagos

Dr. Amanda Schivell of the Biology Department at the University of Washington

Robert Kiersted—professional traveler

Sean D'Souza—Ecuadorian Peace Corps guru

Byron Riera Benalcázar and Pablo Leon—for showing me real Quito

Ron Cohen—Professor of Earth and Planetary Science at Berkeley

Fredie Gordillo, Alex Montoya—for introducing me to some off-the-beaten-path Spanish

Barry Brummer, M.D., Vani Kane, Chuck O'Connor, Andy Sprowl, Geoff Smick, Anne Trainer, Bret Peter Nelson, David Schivell, Kristin Baird, M.D., and the fabulous Laura Tucker

All mistakes result directly from my inability to listen to them better.

And of course:

My parents, my sister

The booksellers who have shown me such wonderful support

Kristin Herold for putting up with me throughout

MINUTES TO BURN

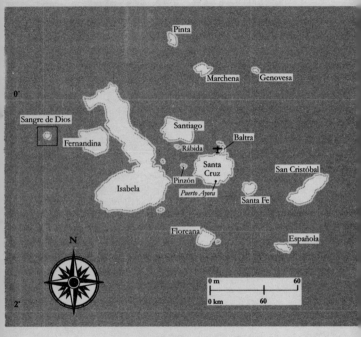

Galápagos Islands

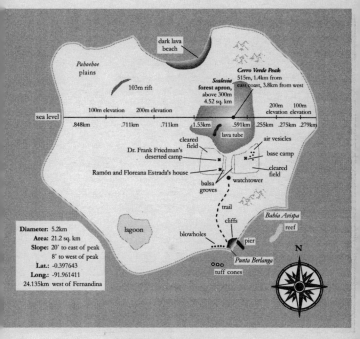

dark lava beach

Pahoehoe plains

103m rift

Cerro Verde Peak
515m, 1,4km from
east coast, 3.8km from west

Scalesia forest apron, above 300m 4.52 sq. km

200m elevation   100m elevation

sea level

100m elevation   200m elevation

.848km   .711km   .711km   1.53km   .591km   .255km   .275km   .279km

cleared field

lava tube

air vesicles

base camp

Dr. Frank Friedman's deserted camp

Ramón and Floreana Estrada's house

cleared field

balsa groves

watchtower

trail

Bahía Avispa

cliffs

reef

blowholes

pier

lagoon

Punta Berlanga

tuff cones

Diameter: 5.2km
Area: 21.2 sq. km
Slope: 20° to east of peak
8° to west of peak
Lat.: -0.397643
Long.: -91.961411
24.135km west of Fernandina

N

Sangre de Dios

A faint cry carried into the house, distracting Ramón Lopez Estrada from the plate of fried pork. He froze, fork raised halfway to his mouth. The noise had probably come from the livestock pens at the edge of his property, across the rows of crops. It was slightly different than the usual, restless mooing of the cows—it was more like a frightened whinny. Dismissing it to the wind, he took a bite and loaded up another generous forkful. He ate hungrily; he'd worked on his farm from sunup until dusk, clearing another section of forest to free the volcanic soil for crops.

Soil was a rarity in Galápagos, islands formed of basaltic lava. It took hundreds of years for the barren rock to soften, turning to brick-red clay as its iron oxidized, then to topsoil as roots and rain intervened. Over millennia, dense *Scalesia pedunculata* forests emerged and flourished, the trees stretching as high as twenty meters in the air. Only the most elevated regions of the highest islands had undergone the process in its entirety, catching clouds that passed aloof and withholding over the scorched lowlands.

Floreana, her belly rounded beneath her apron, stopped behind Ramón and rubbed his aching shoulders. She paused to pluck a twig from his hair and tickled his cheek with it until he lovingly shooed her away.

They'd had one child already, a boy whom Ramón had sent to Puerto Ayora to find work and play. Ramón had chosen his boy's happiness over his own need for a second pair of hands around the farm, permitting him to discover life in the small port town on Santa Cruz. However, that meant more time for Ramón in the fields, clearing the forest, building pens for his livestock, planting his crops with a meticulousness based on the seasons and his own islander's sense.

Because of the earthquakes, the supply ship had stopped passing by last month. Without any gasoline or oil, the town had slowed down, like a wind-up toy losing steam. The chainsaws no longer roared in the mornings, the gas stoves were used only as countertops, the houses fell dark after dusk—even Ramón's prize tiller sat in the field collecting rust while he worked the ground with a spading fork.

Sangre de Dios had been a sparsely populated island to begin with, and the new conditions had driven the other farming families away. Though few had admitted it, many had also fled because of the strange things that had been happening around the island. Dogs and goats missing, changes in the behavior of the wildlife. The girls who used to live one farm over told stories about the tree monster with glistening fangs. And then Marco's little girl had gone missing. After a week of frantic searching, they'd given her up for dead, and Marco had taken his family and moved to the continent.

Ramón and Floreana were now living on a deserted island. In their haste to leave, one of the families had stolen their boat. But it didn't matter—Floreana was too pregnant to travel anywhere until she delivered, and an oil tanker still passed by the island every other month.

Ramón finished his meal and pulled his wife into his lap. He groaned, pretending to be crushed by her weight. She laughed and pointed to her stomach. "This is your fault, you know," she said. Her voice was high and lively; she spoke a rapid, chattering Spanish with the accent of the Oriente, though she'd been born in Galápagos. She'd been named for the island of her birth.

Ramón raised a hand to her cheek and leaned forward to kiss her, but Floreana playfully pushed him away, wiping a smudge of *ají* from his lip with her thumb and clearing his plate. She pointed to the stack of logs in the corner of the humble box of a house. Built of porous concrete blocks cemented with a thick, messy mortar, the walls were cracked and skewed by the numerous earthquakes that wracked the small island. A cooking fire danced in the hearth, which was little more than two absent blocks backed with plywood and opened to the Pacific air above.

Ramón groaned, lowering his head to the table with a thump. His fork and knife jangled. With a sigh, he rose and crossed to the fireplace. Picking up the ax, he twirled it as he stood a log on end on the dirt floor. Suddenly, a loud bleating split the air. Floreana dropped the plate, which shattered across the counter, and the ax slipped through Ramón's hand, giving his index finger a deep nick. The bleating rounded out into a moan, and Ramón realized it was an animal bellowing in pain. The cry, an intensified version of the one he'd heard minutes before, was rife with panic. Instinctively, Floreana circled the table toward her husband, her eyes on the small hole of the window.

The sound was coming from the livestock pens, across the rows of crops. Ramón squeezed his wife reassuringly, but his hand was trembling. He stepped for the door, ax swinging by his side, blood curling around his finger and dripping to the floor.

The nights were growing warmer and the air outside was thick and moist. The *garúa* was settling into the peaks of the forest, crowning it with ribbons of mist. The cry came again, this time with more urgency, and Ramón imagined he felt it rattling through his bones. He passed through the low castor oil plants, the wide-leafed flowering guavas, the tall stands of *plátanos*. Beside him hung the bunches of fruit, hard-sheathed and ridged. He thought of the panicked looks in the eyes of his neighbors who had fled, the foolish stories that had been told around the village. The tall tales seemed more real in the darkness.

The cry elevated into an almost human scream, undulating unnaturally, like the wail of a child seized and shaken. Its pitch, except when wrenched high with pain, was low and broad, issuing from some large creature. There was more bleating, more sounds of struggle. Though the air was cool, Ramón felt his shirt clinging to his body, moist and limp. He tightened his grip on the ax, thinking of his over-under shotgun in the small house and cursing the ammunition shortage, and reached a hand out cautiously to part the fronds.

Something lay up ahead, wheezing in the tall grass of the westernmost livestock pen. A large creature, lost in the shadows, the darkness, and Ramón's own intoxicating fear, was retreating slowly to the brink of the forest. At least three meters tall, it seemed to walk upright like a man, the grass shushing around its swollen body. Unhurried, it reached the edge of the *Scalesia* forest and faded from sight.

A renewed cry brought Ramón's attention back to the injured beast. It was one of Ramón's favorites, a thick brown-and-white spotted cow. He stepped forward, trying to focus on her, but his mind was slow and unresponsive, having followed the thick majestic creature through the mist and into the forest.

The cow bleated again, but its cries had none of the fearful edge of before. Its side was raked open in two diagonal strips, the torn flesh revealing a crushed tangle of ribs and tissue. Her breath rattled through the holes, fluttering the fur surrounding the gashes. Her hind leg was snapped back under her body, and her head rested at a painful angle to her neck, as if she'd been raised and dropped, or thrown a short distance in frustration.

As if something had bitten off more than it could chew.

Ramón lowered the ax to his side, breathing hard. There were no bears here, no large cats or crocodiles. As far as he knew, the largest natural predator in the entire archipelago was the Galápagos hawk.

The cow moaned and Ramón crouched over her, caressing her flank. Her mouth was sprayed with froth. He noticed that the back of her neck had been attacked, scraped or gnawed through to the thick plate of the scapula. The flesh was ribboned across the wound, glistening with blood and a foreign, clear, viscid liquid that looked like saliva. Ramón reached out and touched the wound, drawing his hand back sharply as pain shot through the cut on his index finger. He wiped the excess blood on his jeans and instinctively put his finger in his mouth to clear the wound. He spit into the grass, a red-lined glob thick with mucus, and rose.

The cow rustled in the grass, her head trembling above the ground. Ramón picked up the ax, again cursing the fact that there were no shells for his shotgun. With a nervous glance at the band of forest into which the large creature had vanished, he raised the ax back over one shoulder and swung downward at the cow's neck.

Chapter 1   Cameron leaned forward, resting her elbows on the steering wheel of her Cherokee. The horn blasted, startling her back in her seat, and several of the children on the playground turned and glanced in her direction. She waved, but none waved back.

The timing was less than perfect.

Though not beautiful, Cameron had neat, pretty features. Her blond hair was badly cut—thirteen dollars at Super-Cuts—yet it somehow added to her casual good looks. It was short, up off her shoulders in the back and blunt along the sides. She was solid through the hips and broad across the shoulders. She was not a petite woman.

In the twenty minutes she had been watching, children had overrun the small playground. She found something vulgar in their exuberance—the exaggerated swinging of their arms, the open screaming mouths, the tint of their rosy cheeks. A stocky girl tripped a smaller boy, and he went down with a yelp. He stood, bawling, the knees of his jeans marked with dirt.

Cameron noticed that she was nervously jiggling her hand, so she set it on her knee. She examined her fingers, thick and strong like a man's, free of jewelry, the nails cut short. She kept her wedding ring as a pendant on her necklace. The ring, a handsomely sized sapphire surrounded with diamond chips, served both as an engagement and wedding ring. It had cost Justin approximately twenty percent of his life savings. At first, Cameron had valiantly tried to wear the ring on her finger, but it was a constant hazard, catching in trigger guards and rip cords. She had finally given up, as Justin later had on his wedding ring, which he kept around his watchband. Moving the ring to her necklace, Cameron had resigned herself to yet another abnormality in her abnormal life.

The chanting of girls jumping rope called Cameron's attention back to the playground. The thin girl in the middle was beautiful, with curly hair bouncing across her perfectly smooth cheeks. She held her flowered dress down when she jumped, Marilyn Monroe style. When she was finished, a boy ran by and goosed her. She ignored him brilliantly, and he lingered in the shadows by the handball wall, sheepish and sullen.

For the first seventeen years of Cameron's life, every part of her had felt large and unwieldy—her solid breasts, her size-ten feet, her stomach ridged with muscle from as early as she could remember. She'd always felt thick and horsey next to other girls. Her strong hands and broad shoulders seemed all the more undainty beside their thin elegant fingers, their frail necks and girl-skinny arms. In high school, other girls always seemed busy with makeup and dating and first kisses. Cameron, on the other hand, never even bothered to get up when the phone rang. Until she met Justin, she'd been convinced she was meant to spend her life alone.

She shook off her thoughts and checked her watch. She'd have to be home soon for dinner. In the four years of their marriage, Cameron and Justin had seen less and less of each other. The timing of their tours was almost always unfortunate; one of them would leave a few days after the other returned home. And those days together were hardly blissful—last time she'd arrived home with her back thrown out and twenty-one stitches laced up her forearm, and she'd spent the hard-won three days with her husband eating microwave popcorn and watching a James Bond marathon on TV.

She and Justin had fallen in love the quiet, old-fashioned way, with unspoken assurances and soft yieldings of vulnerabilities. Cameron had sworn always to recognize their relationship as a necessity and an enchantment; together, they had sworn to always put each other first. Because of that, they'd recently resolved to restructure their lives so that they could spend more time together. They'd dropped from active duty, choosing to remain on call as reserves. The transition from full-time soldier to weekend warrior was not an easy one, and they were still trying to adjust to their new lives. The time requirements were not taxing—one weekend a month to maintain proficiency, two weeks a year active duty.

Cameron found she missed the order of the military, the rules and codes she'd kept around herself like armor. With civilian life came much more freedom, and she found herself unraveling without the imposed pressure holding her together. Justin was having an easier time with the transition, but then he'd never been the soldier she was.

They'd started looking for other work this week, and both had been startled by how useless their skills were in the real world. They'd return from days full of interviews, spent and discouraged, and sit side by side on the couch sipping beer in the dark. She'd stopped opening the bank statements.

The timing was less than perfect.

Last week, a day care building had collapsed in Oakland after only a 4.2. Cracks in the foundation from previous tremors that no one could even see. Would've gone down in a strong wind, the structural engineer had said. Seventeen kids had died, and four more were in intensive care. The photograph in the *Bee* focused on a bright yellow jump rope on the front lawn, framed by the majestic ruin of the building in the background.

And they were only catching the secondary quakes here, the spent distant rumbles of the East Pacific Rise, which grew shallower and quieter as it twisted its way north into San Andreas, sending ripples up to Sacramento. In South America, riots followed the seismic activity up the coast from Ecuador into Colombia, but UN troops had quelled the outbreaks.

A siren blared, so piercing Cameron could feel its vibration in her teeth. Kids scrambled off the jungle gyms and swings, off the monkey bars and tetherball courts. They hit the ground, curled up in balls, hands laced over the backs of their necks. They stayed like that for a few moments, frozen little animals. The siren stopped as abruptly as it had begun, and the children resumed their activities.

Cameron glanced down at the small wand of the pregnancy test on the passenger seat, the "+" sign glaring at her in red.

The timing was less than perfect.

21 DEC 07

Chapter 2   The barking bulldog woke him up, just as it had every morning that week. William Savage groaned and shifted in bed, releasing his death-grip on the empty bottle of Jack Daniel's. It clattered on the concrete floor, momentarily drowning out the dog. Mumbling angrily, Savage pulled the pillow over his head, fighting the onslaught of light from the window.

Savage was fully clothed from the night before, though one of his boots was missing. His reddish-brown hair was amply streaked with gray, held off his face with a blue bandanna he kept tied around his forehead. His long hair, in concert with his thick beard and ripped navy cammies, made him look as if he'd just stumbled in from a tour of duty. Strapped to his calf was his favored knife—a Lile "Death Wind."

The apartment was little more than a room, a small box on the third floor of a run-down building. The ceiling was buckled with water damage and cracked on the north side from a recent earthquake. When the wind was strong, drafts through the closed window stirred the paper shooting-range targets on the floor. A wooden gun cabinet, the only piece of furniture in the apartment aside from the small bed, leaned against the far wall. A Congressional Medal of Honor served as a coaster for a half-drunk cup of coffee on the kitchen counter.

The bulldog's barks continued, adding to the pounding in Savage's head.

"Shut the fuck up!" he yelled, his voice still glazed with sleep.

A truck rumbled by down on the street. The dog let loose with a fresh flurry of barks. With a grunt, Savage swung his legs over the edge of the bed and sat up. The room swam around him, but he fought it back into focus. It felt as though the bulldog were inside his head, each bark echoing against the walls of his skull.

Savage rose and stumbled to the window. He tried to slide it open, but it wouldn't budge. Outside, the wind sucked at the pane. The street and buildings were drab gray, as if bled dry. To the sides of the road rose drifts of snow sheathed in ice, spotted with mud and brown splashes of road water. The joys of Billings, Montana, in the winter.

Standing guard on a porch three houses up the block, the bulldog stared at Savage, tongue lolling. Savage eyed the dog angrily. "That's right. Just shut up. Lemme go back to sleep."

The dog bolted forward, straining against its metal chain and howling.

"Goddamnit!" Savage yelled. He banged the sash, but that only caused the dog to bark even louder. "YOU GET THAT DOG TO SHUT THE FUCK UP!"

A beefy man strode through the front door of the house, stopping just behind the frenzied bulldog. "What's your problem, pal?"

Savage yanked the window, but it slid up only a few inches. He leaned over so he could shout through the small gap. "That fuckin' dog has woken me up every morning this week! You'd better—" He threw his weight against the window, but it refused to budge any further.

The beefy man threw his arms up in the air. "It's eleven-thirty!" he shouted.

Savage leaned over and dug through the pile of clothes beside his bed until he unearthed his alarm clock. It read

11:17 A.M. He threw the clock against the wall and returned
to the window. The dog was practically bouncing up and
down at the guy's feet.

"I don't give a shit what time it is!" Savage yelled. "Get
your dog a muzzle or I'll shoot the thing!"

The beefy man held out his arm and slowly extended his
middle finger, then turned and headed back inside his house.
Angrily, Savage returned to bed, pulling the pillow back
over his head. A wave of nausea swept his stomach, and he
realized he desperately had to piss. The bulldog's barks were
even louder now that the window was edged open. They
penetrated the pillow, his head. He tried pressing his hands
over his ears, tried humming loudly, tried tying an old
sweatshirt around his head.

Finally, he snapped upright again, hurling the pillow at
the wall. He crossed the room quickly, throwing open the
doors of his gun cabinet and removing an air rifle. The
ammo drawers were stuffed with different rounds. He
started digging. A bunch of .22s clattered to the floor like
brass rainfall. Buried beneath a stack of Sig Sauer cartridges
was a box of tranquilizer darts, left over from an elaborate
prank he had pulled during downtime on a tour of duty.

He slid a dart in the chamber, stormed to the window, and
smashed the left lower pane with the end of the air rifle. He
took careful aim. The bulldog snarled and growled,
bounced and barked. Savage sank the dart into its neck and
waited. The bulldog swayed on its feet, then collapsed flat
on its stomach, the bloom of the dart waggling in the
breeze.

A moment later, the beefy guy came out to investigate. He
crouched, leaning over the fallen dog. Savage couldn't resist
a smirk.

When the guy rose to his feet, his eyes were lit with rage.
"You motherfucker!" he screamed. "I'll rip your fuckin'
eyes out, you stupid—"

With a grimace, Savage slid a second dart into the chamber. He snapped the rifle up against his shoulder, eyed the

sites, and fired. Beefy guy looked down at the dart in his thigh with shock. He stepped forward once, paused, and stepped forward once more. He fell to his knees, then slumped over next to his dog.

Savage returned the gun to the cabinet, relishing the silence of his apartment. After a satisfying piss, he stuffed a sweatshirt in the broken pane, filled a coffeepot with water and drank from it, then fell back on his bed and stared at the ceiling. He closed his eyes. The peace was divine.

He was just drifting off when he heard the sirens.

22 DEC 07

Chapter 3   Rex Williams banged through the screen door into his front yard with his white pajama pants aflutter, a mobile satellite phone pressed to one ear, and a nine-foot rainbow boa constrictor wrapped around his left leg. "Do you really think we need that many people?" he barked into the phone. "Three, four, maybe, but I mean, seven soldiers! What am I, Salman Rushdie?"

His lank, jet-black hair hung medium-length, darting down to the back of his shirt collar, and swept hastily to one side in the front. His eyes were almost hypnotically intense, a dark brown that looked black in dim lighting. As usual, he was unshaven, an even sprawl of stubble covering his cheeks and his too-strong chin.

Donald Denton chuckled on the other end of the phone. "They only travel in groups. I guess it's a half platoon, the smallest unit they use for international outings. I still can't believe we're getting you down there at all."

Rex was the preeminent complex plate margin ecotectonicist specializing in South American sites. The New Center for Ecotectonic Studies, of which Rex and Donald were Co-Chiefs of Research, focused on the interaction of tectonic movements and ecology, examining how earthquakes impacted flora and fauna. It had been established to contend with environmental fallout from the Initial Event, a massive earthquake that had occurred on March 3, 2002. Registering 9.2 on the moment magnitude scale, the quake had ruptured the tectonic plates near the Ecuadorian coast along a 307-kilometer length. The resultant high rates of plate motion, unprecedented since the Precambrian era more than six hundred million years ago, accounted for massive and recurrent aftershocks.

For the last five years, the region had been plagued with earthquakes in excess of the usual frequency and intensity, perturbing other stress fields and causing rumblings for thousands of miles in every direction. In Ecuador, an earthquake registering approximately six on the moment magnitude scale occurred on average once a week, with $M^w=3$ or $M^w=4$ events registering almost daily. This scale, which measures both the energy release and amplitude of earthquakes, replaced the Richter in the early 1990s.

The fourteen large islands, six small islands, and forty-some islets that compose the Galápagos Archipelago—Rex's principal area of expertise—could not have been more precariously located given the increase in seismic activity. Nine hundred and sixty kilometers off the coast of Ecuador, the Galápagos sit dangerously close to the triple junction of three tectonic plates. Perched high on the north edge of the Nazca plate a mere one hundred kilometers beneath its junction with the Cocos plate, the islands had been regularly rattled by the earthquakes that accompanied the upwelling magma from the rift. The sea floor continued to spread along this seam, the Galápagos Fracture Zone, driving the Nazca plate southward. To further complicate the tectonic regime, a north-south running chain of undersea mountains, the East Pacific Rise, spread the ocean floor in similar fashion one thousand kilometers west of the Galápagos, pushing the Nazca and Pacific plates apart and shoving the Nazca plate east beneath the South American continent. There had been six centimeters of eastward displacement in November alone.

Rex and Donald's colleague, Dr. Frank Friedman, had gone to Sangre de Dios, the westernmost island of the Galápagos, at the end of October, prompted by troubling reports of increased microseismicity from the island.

He had not been heard from since.

Due to the elevated earthquakes in the area and the resultant social unrest, travel to Ecuador and the Galápagos had since become restricted by the U.S. military, the airports closed off to civilians. The scientists, like everyone else, were fleeing the Galápagos, leaving behind antiquated equipment that yielded low resolution data. What little information the New Center now received came in from what remained of the Charles Darwin Station in Puerto Ayora.

As the New Center's remaining field ecotectonicist, Rex needed to lead an expedition to Sangre de Dios, to complete the survey Frank had presumably begun, and to outfit the island with Global Positioning Satellite units. These would allow the New Center to monitor coseismic and crustal deformation on Sangre de Dios from afar.

As the westernmost island in the archipelago, Sangre de Dios held a vital geographic position—it stood to be the first and most accurate bearer of bad news concerning earthquakes along the East Pacific Rise. Getting the proper geodetic equipment in place to measure its surface deformation would enable the New Center to predict earthquakes within the entire tectonic regime—both on the mainland and the islands—sometimes as much as forty-eight hours in advance. Rex and Donald could alert the government leaders down there, evacuate communities, and save lives.

However, without a trained military team to escort and protect him, Rex couldn't so much as board a plane headed for Ecuador. He'd spent weeks sifting through mountains of red tape, trying to secure military support before the December 24 departure. A few days ago, realizing he'd been making little progress, he'd finally forgone the bureaucratic route and called in an enormous favor from Secretary of the Navy Andrew Benneton.

"I told you I could get it done," Rex said as he crossed the front lawn, heading for his mailbox. "Did you doubt me?"

"Well, our correspondence with that captain last week wasn't so promising."

It was true. The Commander of Naval Special Warfare Group One had rejected their request in an e-mail, describing the new riots sweeping through Quito, the organized crime in Guayaquil, and how American troops were already overextended dealing with social deterioration and natural destruction throughout South America and domestically. He'd closed by stating he saw little reason "to drop everything to lend out a squad of highly trained, high-demand operators to transport scientists interested in secondhand reports about minor rumblings on a barely populated island in the middle of the Pacific."

"He changed his tune rather quickly once Benneton got involved." The boa nosed its way up into Rex's crotch, and he shoved its head away. His was one of the larger boas around, even bigger than the behemoth the receptionist kept in her desk drawer at the vivarium in Quito. " 'Preemptive' is a term largely missing from jarhead terminology. The military gives no consideration to how we could alleviate potential political or social problems down there. Always running around expending all their energy on secondary effects."

In the house across the street, a middle-aged woman watched Rex through the kitchen window, one soapy dish frozen midway to the sink. Rex waved and she turned away in horror. He glanced down and noticed that the boa's head was protruding from between his legs like a living penis. He opened the mailbox, but it was empty. The boa tightened around Rex's leg until it started to tingle. "How do you like those myths coming back from Sangre?"

Donald laughed. "I suppose it makes sense. In hectic

times, people are more prone to project the uncertainties of the world onto something tangible."

"Monsters."

"Indeed. The Galápagos are a land of strange creatures to begin with. It's already in the cultural unconscious."

"Darwin's backyard," Rex proclaimed melodramatically.

"Indeed. Don't underestimate how much people love to believe that creatures dark and dreadful evolve there on a daily basis."

Rex snorted. "What we shouldn't underestimate is people's ignorance."

Donald sighed. "You rarely do."

The boa eased around Rex's stomach, sliding its tail up over one shoulder. It tensed and relaxed, an orange-spotted band of black moving about him like a pulse. Rex stopped in the middle of his lawn, turning his face to the rising sun. The boa wrapped a coil around his throat, and he felt the firm edges of its skeleton beneath the sleek surface. A minivan drove by, five faces peering at the window. It drifted to the side of the road, then veered sharply to avoid hitting a telephone pole. Rex did not notice.

"I'm just eager to throw down permanent benchmarks and get the continuous GPS units up around Sangre," Rex said. "It's about time we got more concise data on the rates of deformation and reduced the guesswork. In fact, that's what Frank should've been doing down there—scouting equipment locations. I bet he wasted his time collecting butterflies. Like when he spent two days observing that strain of mutated frogs outside Cuyabeno. He was so distracted he barely got the geochemical sensors in place."

"The ecos versus the tectos. Like the raging geology-geophysics rivalry when I was coming up. And I thought the Center was too young to be divided by factions."

"It's no longer divided," Rex said, "now that Frank has been sensible enough to pass on." There was a long silence and Rex glanced at the phone to make sure it hadn't cut out. "Just a little humor, Donald. Don't be a bore."

"Frank is a great loss," Donald replied defensively. "Aside from you, he was the nation's most prominent field ecotectonicist."

"Oh, come on, Donald. Frank wasn't prominent. Just loud and fortuitously published."

Donald heaved another deep sigh. "Some things . . ."

"And all that referring to himself in the third person. God that was awful. 'In attempting to witness the tireless mastications of the *Rhicnogryllus lepidus*, the author found himself in the middle of a magnificent rain forest glade.' " Rex groaned. "His phrasing was second only to that stupid *Gilligan's Island* fishing cap he wore everywhere like a yarmulke."

"Well," Donald said, a note of offense in his voice, "he's gone now."

"The fact that he's dead does not raise him in my professional estimation. But that's neither here nor there. What time are we meeting with the GI Joes Monday?"

"Nine o'clock."

The boa stretched itself out in the air, then swooped back toward Rex. He kissed it on the face. "I'll be there with bells on."

Chapter 4 Cameron regarded the large wicker cornucopia bulging with plastic fruit that sat on the glass table smack in the middle of the waiting room. The cornucopia had stubbornly remained through her six years of checkups, gathering dust, the reds and oranges fading on the waxy peels. Particularly unsubtle decor for an OB/GYN's office, she mused.

Spread on a stand to her left were all the magazines that people only read in doctors' offices—*Redbook*, *Psychology Today*, *Prevention*. And on the lowest part of the rack, accessible to little hands, a neat row of *Highlights for Children*. How she hated that magazine. Along with crayons, decorative Band-Aids, and minivans, *Highlights for Children* was beyond Cameron's domain; it belonged to that vast and clannish group of people she had always regarded with something more than curiosity, something bordering on irritation. Some envy as well, perhaps.

The clicking of a woman's footsteps approached, and Cameron waited to see which door concealed them. Justin leaned forward and coughed uncomfortably as the door to the right of the waiting room opened. A girl, who couldn't have been older than sixteen, came out, a nurse trailing her by a few steps.

The nurse was a short, stocky Italian woman with the darkest rings around her eyes Cameron had ever seen. She was always there, that nurse, behind the door, escorting them in, escorting them out. Her back was humped with age, and when she smiled, her teeth protruded at all angles.

Though Cameron had never seen her up close, she would have bet the woman had wisps of facial hair. She recalled the street lady from that Tennessee Williams play with all the sex in it, the one who kept muttering, "flores para los muertos." Cameron cleared her throat softly and shifted in her chair. She would be seeing the woman up close soon enough.

In hands curled like talons, the girl clutched a cheap leather purse in front of her, as if concerned that someone might snatch it right in the waiting room. She looked shaken, her cheeks a puffy red that suggested she'd been crying a short time ago.

Smiling her sickening smile, the nurse pulled the door shut behind the girl, leaving her to face Justin and Cameron uncomfortably for a moment before she scurried from the waiting room. Cameron realized she was tense through her shoulders and neck.

Justin caught her eye and smiled. Reaching over, he pulled

the clasp of her necklace around to the back so that it wasn't visible. A calming ritual. The ring dangled out of view beneath her shirt, a small bump in the fabric.

The thick wooden door to the right led back to the abortion suite. Cameron had always found it shocking that day surgery emptied into the same room where women waited for their postpartum checkups. It seemed wrong.

She'd spent enough time in the waiting room to be able to predict which door the other women were going to be beckoned through for their appointments. The doors even looked different. The door to the "proper" OB/GYN suite was painted a cheerful yellow, a large smudge-free window taking up most of the top half. The door that led into the dilation and curettage rooms was dark, solid, ominous. It didn't even have a peephole.

Younger girls in the waiting room, with dark half-moons under their eyes, were a shoo-in for the wooden door, especially when they were alone, or with only their mothers. When accompanied by both parents, they often headed through the happy yellow door, disappearing into the stream of light behind the window. Women who looked like teachers went through the yellow door, as did women with baby barf crusting on old sweatshirts proclaiming the names of cities and vacation spots. Women in smart navy blue business suits always went through the dark door. For these last women there were, to date, no exceptions. Navy blue was the color of death.

Feeling Justin's thigh pressed against hers, Cameron leaned forward, elbows on her knees, and studied the individual strands of the orange carpet. The navy blue suit women always seemed calm and assured while they waited; Cameron felt neither.

She suddenly felt her transmitter vibrate, a gentle tugging beneath the flesh of her deltoid. Turning her head, she spoke into her shoulder through her shirt, activating the unit.

In '04, subcutaneous transmitters had replaced saber radios, which had headsets that allowed soldiers actually to listen through their jaws. The transmitters were better protected than the bone phones and impossible to lose. The soldiers' day-to-day movements powered the units, kicking a tumbler back and forth and recharging a minuscule battery—self-winding watch style.

Cameron disliked using her transmitter in public; often it drew strange looks from people who thought she was talking to herself. It had been some time since she'd been paged.

Justin glanced over, eyebrows raised, then whispered a command to activate his transmitter as well. A click sounded in the room, indicating that the transmitter had switched from silent mode to audio. "Kates," Justin said. "Public."

Lieutenant John Mako had called in on the primary channel so that he could speak to them both at the same time. His disembodied voice issued through their transmitters. "Cam and Kates, Mako. I think I got you kids an assignment. You with Cam?"

Justin rested his hand on Cameron's knee. "No, sir, a redhead about five seven with a vacant smile."

"What do you mean, 'you kids'?" Cameron asked. "We're working together?"

"Do I have a speech impediment of which I'm not aware?"

"No, sir. It just seems a little . . . odd. Isn't that breach of—"

"I need bodies," Mako said. "And I need them quickly."

"What kind of time frame are we looking at here?"

"Briefing Monday, depart Monday night. I need you to babysit a scientist, take him down to Ecuador and make sure nothing gets his tape measure in a tangle. He's an earthquake guy, wants to check out an island down there. It's a short, easy mission. You'll be back in a week."

Justin groaned. "Sounds thrilling."

"You'll be surprised how much things have deteriorated down there. Might rustle up some excitement after all."

Justin leaned back in his chair. "I'll be sure to wear my spurs."

"How big's the platoon?" Cameron asked.

"It's a half. Seven, eight."

"Isn't that a bit vague given we're lifting out Monday?"

"You know how things are right now. Besides, this is hardly a black op."

"Who's the LT?" Justin asked.

Mako paused for a moment before answering. "Derek Mitchell."

Justin looked at Cameron nervously. "Do you really think that's a good idea, sir?"

"Do you really think you want to question my judgment?"

"Is Derek active again?" Cameron asked.

"He'll come off emergency leave. I'm pulling the rest from reserves."

Justin cleared his throat nervously. "But has he . . . recovered?"

"Enough. This mission will get him back into the swing, get his mind off things. It's exactly what he needs. Ask your wife. She's his ex–swim buddy."

"Yeah," Justin said, "but after what happened to his baby."

"Don't forget, it wasn't *him* who..." Mako's voice trailed off.

Justin gritted his teeth. "If you say so, sir."

Cameron leaned back in the chair. A flash of Derek on their last mission. Riding shotgun in a humvee, foot on the dash, tongue pressed into his cheek as he jammed M-4 mags. Miles of desert stretching around the vehicle in all directions. Without looking up, Derek handing her the last gulp in his canteen the minute she reached for hers. Knowing hers was empty before she did. "Who else?" Cameron asked.

"Some familiar faces."

"Like whose?"

"I did mention that the briefing was Monday?"

"Yes, sir."

"And you are aware of the purpose of a briefing?"

"Yes, sir."

"Then I'll assume there are no more questions at this time. Is that a fair assumption, Cam?"

Cameron flashed an unamused smile, letting it fall quickly back into a grimace. "Yes, sir."

"I'll be in touch with information about the briefing. In the meantime, see if you can contain your curiosity." Mako clicked out without waiting for a response.

The old nurse pushed open the wooden door, which creaked softly on the hinges. She leaned forward into the lobby, a plastic clipboard in her hand. Her voice was deep, textured like a smoker's. "Kates. Cameron Kates. The doctor's ready for you."

Cameron looked up at the nurse. "How long will this take?"

The nurse shrugged. "Probably about fifteen minutes."

"Jesus," Justin said. "That's longer than it takes to *make* a baby."

"Yeah," Cameron said with a faint smile. "I wanted to talk to you about that." She glanced back at the nurse. "And I can be up and on my feet after?"

"You'll have to take it easy for a couple of days."

Cameron turned to Justin, her frustration evident. "I wanted to get this over with."

"If we're lifting out Monday . . ." Justin raised his hand, then let it fall to his knee. "You can't really risk being sore."

"God*damnit*." Cameron pushed herself back in the chair, then slumped down.

The nurse waited, tapping the clipboard against her thigh, her breath a rattle in her throat. Justin faced his wife, speaking gently. "It's only a week, honey. That'll even give me time to knock you up again."

Cameron's frown lightened, almost imperceptibly. "That's not how it works."

"Oh yeah," Justin said. Reluctantly, Cameron pushed herself up in her seat. Justin turned to the nurse. "I think we're gonna have to reschedule."

"Talk to the receptionist," the nurse said before disappearing behind the door.

"She's pleasant," Cameron muttered.

"I'm surprised she didn't call you 'dearie.' "

Justin stood, but Cameron didn't budge. He took her hands in his and pulled her up from the chair. She rose with melodramatic slowness, and he looped his arms beneath hers to hold her up. She kissed him softly on the mouth before turning to leave.

"Christ," she said over her shoulder. "No wonder they don't want broads in the military."

Chapter 5   His gold scraggly coat spotted with brown and draped sheetlike over his gaunt frame, the feral dog paused at the edge of the field facing the *Scalesia* forest of Sangre de Dios. A *garúa* haunted the curves of the forest, lurking in the trees' rounded domes.

Shrubs and plants tangled the forest understory, and the tree branches were draped with moss and festooned with twisting vines, giving the forest a massy thickness from ground to treetop. Usually white, but sometimes a surprising red or orange, the lichen on the tree trunks broke up the greens and browns of the forest.

Hunger had driven the dog up into the highlands; the departure of most of Sangre de Dios's farm families meant fewer compost heaps to raid outside the rugged houses. The chickens left behind had already been slaughtered in their coops by a fortunate pack of dogs, but they had driven him away when he'd tried to sneak in on the kill. He had returned the next day, but little had been left aside from a few blood stains on the wooden planks, which he had licked until his tongue bled. Managing to unearth a couple of tortoise nests in the fallow fields that had been cleared beside the forest, he'd eaten a few eggs, but that had been the previous week, and he'd found no food since then.

He moved forward between the trees, his eyes glinting yellow. A stone lodged in the pad of his front foot made his gait awkward, but as he hit the soft ground of the forest, his trot smoothed into the effortless glide of a predator.

He sensed movement up ahead and caught a whiff of something when the wind shifted. Something living. His nose twitched, his lip drawing back from his teeth in a silent snarl that gleamed in the night. Dark streaks of dried mucus trailed from the corners of his eyes.

Slinking forward, the soft pads of his feet sinking in the mud, the dog lowered his head, his skin rippling in waves of coarse hair. He crept past a cluster of trees, the long trunks lost among the leaves and stalks of lesser plants. The path widened into a clearing, trees lining the edges of a mud wallow like sentinels. Wind whispered through the dead sprays of elephant grass.

Abruptly, the dog halted, sensing an odd blend of danger and opportunity. One foot raised above the ground and angled back like a pointer's, the other three sunk in the mud, he stopped breathing. His eyes were wide, but he didn't turn his head. The rise and fall of his ribs beneath his coat died. He was still. He was almost invisible in the night.

Suddenly, a plant right beside him sprang to life, lunging at him with two raptorial legs. The spiked appendages folded back on themselves, snapping shut around the dog's midsection. The dog emitted a pained grunt as he was lifted into the air. He struggled in the grasp of the massive clamp, yelping. The strike occurred in a fraction of a second.

A triangular head full of sharp, quivering mouthparts lowered to the dog's skull. The dog's yelp was cut short when the creature chewed through his neck.

The dog twitched in the jagged legs as the creature devoured him, nibbling through his neck to get at the nourishing tissues packed inside the chest cavity. The dog provided good sustenance, but it was not nearly large enough. The creature's appetite was growing. The supply of dogs and goats on the island was dwindling, and the cows had proved too heavy for it.

It discarded the paws and the head, as well as a long segment of the dog's intestines, which dropped to the ground like a length of rope. It rarely ate off the ground.

After it finished, the creature dipped its head, cleaning chunks of flesh from the spines of its legs and wiping its face in deft, catlike motions. Then it stepped back into line with the trees, undulating until it mimicked perfectly the movement of the surrounding foliage in the breeze. It swayed with the trees, all but disappearing from sight.

23 DEC 07

Chapter 6   Water was dripping somewhere nearby. The window didn't cast enough light through Savage's cell for him to see the water dripping, but he heard it. He glanced up at the small square of blue, split three times with steel bars, and saw that there wasn't a cloud in the sky. Probably a busted pipe somewhere, he thought, some faulty plumbing. Probably did it on purpose, those bastards. Chinese water torture.

He walked to the front of his cell, resisting the urge to grip the bars like some yahoo criminal in a Western. He was still missing one of his boots, and the ground felt moist through his sock. He'd been arrested on a Friday, and they'd taken their time processing him, ensuring he'd have to wait through the weekend for a Monday arraignment. It had been a peaceful two days.

Across the way, a pale, fleshy prisoner was sitting on the floor, legs kicked wide like a child's. Across the chest of his shirt, *FIN* was written with a black marker. Probably got hauled in drunk and naked last night. He was rubbing himself through his jail-issue pants.

"Lovely," Savage said.

"Hey, buddy, you trying to steal a free peek?"

Savage went back to his bed and flipped it over, dumping the thin stained mattress on the moldy floor. He leaned the narrow frame up against the wall, hooking two of the legs on the ledge of the window. He climbed on top of the frame, threading his legs through the aluminum bed slats, and leaned back down the incline. Some of his reddish-brown hair fell loose from the bandanna.

Fin was on his feet, staring across the dim corridor into Savage's cell. "You trying to break out, buddy? You think you're goin' somewhere?" He laughed, a high-pitched cackle. "I'm in the big leagues, you know. Got me a little girl, cut her up like a paper doll."

Savage tuned him out and began his incline sit-ups, trying to move his shoulders directly toward the ceiling to increase the strain through his stomach. Once he was well into his set, he began grunting slightly with the exertion.

Fin started grunting along with him, drawing the grunts out into moans. When Savage finished his set and rolled back over his shoulders to the ground, Fin continued his moaning, elevating to yells and hip thrusts. He squealed loudly through a fat grin and shuddered, as if he'd come. When he finished, he bounced on his toes and laughed a flat, atonal laugh.

Savage stared at him, unimpressed. He leaned forward into a handstand, placing his legs barely against the wall. He started doing push-ups, moving his body directly up and down. The cell was so cold he could see his breath.

"I wish I was over there, buddy," Fin called out. "You bouncin' up and down like that, it's givin' me a little tingle in the tummy. Make me wanna—"

Savage could hear him making some kind of furious gesture, but he ignored him, straining through his final push-ups. The strain in his triceps intensified, and he lowered himself from the wall and extended his arms straight out before him to loosen the knots.

"Bet you'd like to think that, huh, buddy? That I wanna fuck you? Well, I ain't no faggot. Have me a lady on the outside. I don't go in for no backdoor action, if you catch my drift. I ain't no queer." Fin slapped his chest with a fist, and it sent a ripple clear down to his stomach. "I don't want no piece of you. No sir."

Savage glanced up at him. "I don't remember making you an offer."

Fin ran a hand along the sallow skin under his chin, pushing it to one side. "I saw you lookin' at me. When I had my hands on myself. I know that look. I broke people's faces for less. Got in a brawl one time down south, outside of Ciudad Juarez . . . ."

Savage ignored the drone from the other cell and crawled back up on the bed frame, beginning another set of sit-ups. He was not surprised, halfway through his set, to hear Fin mimicking his grunts again. Not a broad range of material. He finished his sit-ups and regarded Fin blank-faced as he enacted another orgasm, this time accompanied by screams and bar rattling.

"Thanks, buddy," Fin said through a beefy grin. "I liked that one even better."

The door down the corridor opened and two guards approached, flanking a young, clean-shaven law officer. Savage noticed the khaki uniform as the officer drew nearer and realized he was a Montana Park Ranger. The three men paused outside Savage's cell.

"William Savage?" the park ranger asked. Savage stared back at him.

"Yup, that's him," Fin shouted. "That's him I bet."

"I'm Ranger Walters. You're coming with me."

Savage studied the stains on the ceiling. "Where to?"

"You let me worry about that." Walters signaled one of the guards to unlock the door. He started to slide it open, but Savage pulled it shut with a bang.

"Thanks," Savage said. "But I prefer to do my own worrying."

"Oh man, buddy!" Fin groaned. "You gonna take that? You gonna take that from this shitty-ass bastard?"

Walters tried to appear calm, but Savage saw the corners of his jaw flex out. "All right, fine. We can just leave you in there." He stepped back and crossed his arms, evidently quite pleased with himself.

Savage raised his hand, formed a gun, and aimed it at the empty air of his cell. "Bam!" he said. "I just killed your hostage." He spread his arms and turned around once, slowly. "I like it in here. Got my three squares a day, john in the corner, view of the sky. You gonna threaten me with something, you'd better make it something good. And until then . . ." Savage sat on the floor, Indian-style. He raised his eyebrows until they almost disappeared beneath the line of his bandanna.

Walters opened his mouth, then closed it. He uncrossed his arms.

Fin burst into a wheezing laugh, spraying the floor with saliva. "Oh fuck, buddy. Oh man, this guy's *askin'* for it. For a good beatin', like the kind—"

"Shut up!" Walters barked.

Fin covered his mouth with a hand, his face turning red as he theatrically held in his laughter.

Walters turned to one of the guards. "Shut him up. *Now.*"

The guard banged his baton against the bars of Fin's cell, and Fin held out his arms, spreading his hands. "Hey buddy, no problem. You want quiet, all you gotta do is—"

The guard drew back his baton again as if to strike, and Fin shut up. He pretended to zip up his mouth. He crossed his cell and threw the imaginary key in the toilet. He flushed the toilet. He busted a fat grin like this was the funniest thing he'd ever seen.

Walters turned back to Savage, a pulse beating in his temple.

"Now," Savage said calmly. "Like I said. Where to?"

No sound save the dripping water somewhere down the dim moldy corridor. Walters pulled his head to one side, as if to relieve a kink in his neck. "Sacramento."

Savage still refused to rise. "Why?"

Walters's jaw flexed again. Savage leaned back on his hands, kicking his legs out in front of him. With effort, Walters relaxed his face. He didn't raise his voice, but he still conveyed anger by shaping his words into hard, compact syllables. "Briefing on a mission. The details are confidential."

"There now," Savage said, standing up. "That wasn't so hard."

The guard slid the door open, and Savage stepped into the corridor, brushing the dirt from his sleeves.

"That's it?" Fin shrieked. "You're gonna let him go? Whaddaya mean a mission? I could fight a mission. I could fight a mission better than this weasel. You should hear him moan during push-ups. Like a bitch. Just like a—"

As Savage passed Fin's cell, he reached through the bars, bunching Fin's shirt in his fist. With a sudden sharp movement, he recoiled his arm, jerking Fin's head forward into the bars. Fin buckled and went limp in his grasp. Savage released him and stood facing both guards and Walters obediently before the clang had finished echoing up the corridor. Fin slumped to the ground, bent awkwardly over his legs. The two guards glanced at each other, then back at Savage, but Savage remained perfectly still, his arms at his sides, wearing an expression of total compliance.

Behind him, Fin's body shifted, his torso tilting over onto the floor. He began to draw air in slow, rasping breaths.

"Well," Savage said, gesturing down the narrow corridor. "Shall we?"

"CONFIDENTIAL, HUH?" Savage rolled a cigarette from one side of his mouth to the other, leaning back out of the open door of the camouflage Blackhawk so he could feel the cold wind whipping across his face. His foot rested on one of the skids, still covered only with a sock. "Must be important for them to pull me out of the clink."

Walters snickered. "Yeah, they only use felons on missions of the utmost importance."

"I can imagine I'm probably a distant second to someone with *real* military training. Like, say, a park ranger."

Walters didn't reply.

Savage toed the small mound of supplies Walters had loaded in the back of the helicopter—rope, canteens, climbing gear. "We've been heading northwest for a while now. Last I remembered, Sacramento was due southwest of Billings."

"Your briefing's not until tomorrow A.M. I'm just in charge of picking you up and dropping you off. I have a mission of my own here in the meantime."

"Helo shortage?"

Walters nodded. "And everything else. The chopper's due in Sac end of the day. They weren't exactly gonna make a special outing to pick up a jailbird. Since I was headed out anyway, I landed the lucky task of transporting you. But first, we're making a detour. You get to wait."

Savage nodded ever so slightly. He glanced down and wiggled his big toe, protruding from a hole in his sock. "Any way you could see about getting me a boot?"

"Like I said, you get to wait."

The helicopter pulled in tight to the land, running along the top of an elongated gorge. Below, rivulets trickled along icy banks. Through the thick forest, Savage could make out only occasional spots of ground, white splotches showing through the patchwork of trees.

Walters scanned the forest with a pair of high-tech binoculars. They whirred, electronically focusing as he swung them back and forth. "Glacier National Park. We had three campers killed here last week by a grizzly sow. One guy survived the attack, staggered back to a logging camp. Severe head wounds. Said he was batted around like a soccer ball.

He did the smart thing though—curled up, covered his vitals, refused to panic." Walters lowered the binoculars, and Savage was surprised by the intensity in his eyes. "Said he could hear the grizzly's teeth clinking against his skull." His top lip pulled up in the start of a sneer. "Park ranger stuff."

Savage feigned a shudder, though his face kept its sardonic cast. "Bad news bear."

"It's a different kind of death," Walters said. "Wild animal. At least in a war, you know what you're getting. Bullet to the head, grenade in the gut—you go down and out. Not like this. Not like being eaten."

Savage looked at the rifle across Walters's lap. A .300 Win Mag, single action, equipped with a 10x scope; the weapon was a punisher—one of the few that had the stopping power to drop a full-grown grizzly. "Fought a lot of wars, have you?"

Walters ignored him, leaning forward to set the rifle on the deck by his feet. "The governor of Montana personally sent two trackers into the woods to hunt down the problem bear last week. One returned after four days with no sighting. We lost contact with the other. Presumed dead." He formed a fist and tightened the fingers of his other hand around it. "They needed it handled. Call went in to me. I booked the chopper, even promised I'd drop you off in Sac personally to make sure I got it." He ran his tongue across his teeth. "Figured we'd use the last place the second tracker established radio contact as the center point, then sweep the area in an expanding spiral."

Savage took a long drag off his cigarette and flicked it out the open door. He watched it fall, a red glowing dot twirling in the wind. "Good thinking," he said, just the right amount of sarcasm easing its way into his voice.

Below, a river fought its way around bends and over boulders, finally cascading down a twenty-foot drop. Savage couldn't hear the noise of the waterfall over the rotors of the Blackhawk, but he imagined it perfectly, sensing the pulsing water as if it were running through his veins.

Just a few hours ago, the guards had signed him out in full. Battery, cruelty to animals, assault with a deadly weapon, possession of illegal firearms—they'd all vanish if he agreed to participate in the mission, whatever it was. He had known that there was a shortage of U.S. troops with all the trouble down south, but until now, he'd had no idea how serious it was. He'd been in the Gulf, but the last war he'd seen action in was Nam. He hoped that he'd been targeted for his record; if they were trolling county jails indiscriminately for anyone with military training, then they were in a lot more trouble than he'd imagined.

The pilot swooped the helicopter so sharply Savage had to grab the rifle to keep it from sliding out the door. He handed it back to Walters silently, noticing the pilot's smirk in the reflection off the windscreen. The helo plunged again.

"Picked her up," the pilot said, a hint of excitement creeping into his voice. "She's heading south."

Walters raised his binoculars and located the grizzly sow. She was loping along the ridge about twenty yards back from the gorge. Her legs as thick as cannon barrels, she moved with astounding quickness, hammering over fallen trees and crashing through underbrush.

"Goddamnit, don't lose her," Walters said. He leaned forward, his hands clutching the pilot's seat.

"She hears us and she's hauling ass," the pilot yelled, his hands fisting the control stick, desperately trying to keep the bear in sight.

Walters pushed Savage aside and peered out the open door. He took aim, the rifle bobbing as the helicopter swooped and turned. He fired once and cursed, then struggled to unbolt the rifle.

Savage calmly leaned back against the side of the helicopter, spotting a distinctive gray patch on the bear's flank. Walters wobbled in his shooter's stance and fired another shot, reeling from the kick.

Savage sighed. "You planning on doing this thing anytime soon?"

"I can't get a clear shot through the fucking canopy!" Walters yelled.

"There's nowhere to set down," the pilot said.

Savage picked up a SPIE rig harness and went to work on it, pulling his large knife from the ambidextrous pouch sheath he kept laced over his right calf.

Chambering another round, Walters turned back to face Savage, who was slipping the harness over his shoulders. "What the hell are you doing?" he shouted. Catching another glimpse of the sow, he hastily raised the rifle and fired.

Savage tied the harness to a thick, braided rope that was coiled on the floor beside him. The other end of the rope was secured to a carabiner, which he clipped to the helo rigging. Pausing to light another cigarette, he looked at Walters. "To kill a grizzly, you gotta hit it the right way. Face, lungs, or heart. Even the top of the head won't cut it. Got a skull like plate armor. You need a clear shot, and it ain't gonna happen with meatstick up there swooping like a kite and the bear in full sprint beneath the tree cover."

"You heard the pilot—we can't set down anywhere. This is the best angle I'm gonna get."

The Blackhawk pulled to a midair halt, quivering beneath the whirring rotors. "I lost her," the pilot said. "Fuck. I lost her." A blast of wind hit the helo, wobbling it.

"Do I have to do everything here?" Walters yelled. "You people only give me a twelve-hour window on the Blackhawk and now I'm supposed to navigate the thing too?" He threw the rifle down on the floor. Savage picked it up and angled it, eyeing the scope.

"Keep going south," Savage said softly.

The pilot looked over at Walters, unsure if he should obey the order. "What the fuck are you talking about, Savage?" Walters said. "We need to circle in and find her."

Savage dragged deep and dragoned twin streams of smoke through his nostrils. "We have about three minutes to head south to where that gorge ends in a cliff. That's the direction she was heading, and she's gonna follow the ridge. Now you can sit here like the pencil-pushing cocksucker that you are, or you can act like the man you wish you were. Just try to make up your mind sometime in the next ten seconds so I have at least a small chance of getting in position."

Walters bit the inside of his lip, staring at Savage. Savage returned the glare. "All right," Walters finally said. He waved a hand at the pilot and settled back in his seat. "Give the felon a go at it."

Savage set the rifle down and pulled himself up to a crouch. "I want you to trace the line of this gorge until it falls away at the cliff face. Pull about twenty yards off the lip when we hit it and hold steady."

"All right," the pilot said. "I'm not dipping lower than the top of the tree line, though. We're gonna have problems with the wind against the cliff, and there's nowhere to land down there if we need to back down."

"Just let me worry about that," Savage said.

The helicopter tilted forward and thundered down the gorge. Walters searched the woods for the bear but saw nothing except the waving firs. "I hope you know what you're doing, Savage," he said.

Savage tightened the modified harness around his shoulders and slid one arm loophole down over his waist as the helicopter shot along the ridge.

They passed the cliff and were suddenly out several hundred yards above a stone basin cut by a rushing river. The pilot swung the helicopter to face the line of trees at the edge of the cliff. Nothing was visible but foliage.

"How the fuck are you gonna get a shot here?" Walters said, his anger intensifying. "It's all foliage from this angle and we can't drop the helo any lower!"

Savage smiled around his cigarette and leaned backward out of the helicopter, grabbing the Win Mag with one hand. His tattered sock was the last thing to disappear over the side of the Blackhawk. Until the carabiner pulled tight on the rigging, it seemed from the helicopter that he'd gone over in a suicide dive.

Falling the twenty-foot length of the rope, Savage snapped to a halt. Flat on his stomach, he floated in a sniper's stance. Below him, the drop stretched for an eternity to the snow-dusted boulders. The rifle was positioned on his shoulder before he even completed the fall, his left eye on the scope.

The lower vantage opened up his line of vision tremendously; he could see a good distance into the forest between the trunks of the trees. The light was magnificent, filtering through the needles in thin, twinkling shafts.

He didn't doubt the Blackhawk; he knew from the Gulf that it could pull eight thousand pounds' suspension. He and the .300 were child's play.

The crosshairs waited patiently, lined just above the peak of a small hill on which the sow should appear. It was a little over a quarter mile away from him.

Savage counted under his breath. "Five . . . four . . . three . . . " The head of the grizzly appeared, and she looked ahead, rearing up to her full seven feet when she saw the helicopter. Savage spit the cigarette out the side of his mouth. "You're early," he growled, pulling the trigger.

The bullet caught her right through the roaring mouth, but Savage couldn't see the impact because the kick from the rifle sent him swinging back beneath the Blackhawk. He kept his eye on the scope though, checking for the slumped body on his backswing.

He dropped the rifle, bearing its weight on the sling around his neck, and started climbing hand over hand up the rope. He got a leg on the skid, then pulled himself into the helicopter. Walters and the pilot stared at him, speechless.

Savage lit another cigarette, snapped his lighter closed, and made it disappear into one of his many pockets. "Well," he said, raising his head. "What the fuck're we waiting for?"

Chapter 7   The forest-green Blazer flew up the freeway through the suburbs of Sacramento, country music blasting from the speakers. Justin was driving over ninety, singing along with the radio. He pulled off his T-shirt and grabbed his camouflage top from the back seat, the Blazer swerving as his attention lapsed. Calmly, Cameron reached over and steadied the wheel.

"So we'll make an appointment right when we get back?" she asked. "I want to get it over with."

"Absolutely." Justin reached over with one hand and rubbed her neck. She put her hand over his and squeezed it once, impatiently, then pulled it off. Staring out the window, she watched the trees fly by along the side of the road.

Brooks & Dunn came on the radio and Justin sang along, grabbing an unloaded pistol from the glove box and using it as a mike. At the high part of "My Maria," he took his voice up into a yodel. Cameron knew he could see her smile in her reflection in the window. "A gun is not a toy," she said.

"See? You're your old self already."

Justin exited the I-5 at Q Street and headed east. Cameron noticed the small cluster of soldiers as the Blazer rounded the corner at Ninth. The soldiers were hard to miss in their ripstop woodland cammies. Didn't exactly blend into the stucco that fronted the New Center building.

Justin slowed as the car neared the group, a smile creeping across his face. "Szabla, Tank—Holy shit, is that Tucker?"

"Who's that other guy?" Cameron asked, gesturing to Savage, who leaned against the building, apart from the others.

"Don't know. The guy must be fifty. Looks like Uncle Dicky with a hangover."

Savage leaned forward and shot a loogy at the P Street sign. It hit dead center and oozed down, dripping from the bottom like a yellow stalactite. Szabla was facing the building, shadowboxing and talking to herself under her breath, and Tank stood perfectly still, arms crossed over his massive chest.

Justin parked, and he and Cameron got out of the car, heading for the others.

Tucker noticed them first and waved self-consciously. With a strong, all-American jaw, clear blue eyes, and straight blond hair, Tucker looked like either a sunglasses model or an SS officer, depending on the severity of his expression. He had grown up in boys' homes from age twelve after his parents deserted him at a truckers' stop. A small dimple in the lobe of his left ear remained where he'd pierced it years ago with a ten-penny nail. He'd dropped from active duty a little over a year back and fallen off the radar. Cameron had always found something slightly vulnerable in his shy smile, a flash of a grin that seemed oddly unassuming given his good looks. She'd often wondered how he was doing.

"Hey, guys," Tucker said. The same easy Alabama drawl.

As she neared, Cameron noticed that Tucker looked different somehow, not quite sickly but weary, as if he'd just come out the far side of a harrowing dream. He smiled. "Hey Tucker," Cameron said, as Tank gathered her up in an immense hug.

A building of a man, Tank kept his blond hair cut in a flattop, giving his head a rectangular appearance. Cameron and Justin both suspected that he harbored an enormous crush on Cameron; in noncombat situations, she was the only person he allowed to touch him. Supposedly, he'd been at the top of his class through BUD/s in Coronado, and he'd gone on to be a sixty gunner with Justin on Team EIGHT, his bulk allowing him to tote the larger M-60. No one knew much about Tank's past, but it was rumored he once played center for Notre Dame.

Tank didn't talk much.

"Szzzaaabbbllaaa!" Justin growled through a smile. The "S" in "Szabla" was silent, giving her name a rhyming beat that the other soldiers drew out like a swear word used affectionately—*Za-bla*. The name, along with a 110-pound rottweiler named Draeger, was left over from a short-lived early marriage.

Szabla turned to Justin, still in a fighter's stance, and feigned two jabs at his face. A black woman with well-defined, even features, Szabla was striking, though hard in appearance. Her arm muscles were better defined than those of most of the male soldiers; Justin maintained that he could rest a beer on the shelf of her triceps. As always, she wore a sleeveless top to show off her build; today it was an army-green tank. Since she wore her brawn over her intelligence, it was easy to forget that Szabla was ROTC, MIT, Phi Beta Kappa. She'd been a structural engineer as an undergraduate, and after she graduated, she had been one of the first women through BUD/s. Though she remained in the Special Forces reserves, she was an architect full-time at a downtown Sacramento firm.

"Droppin' off the little lady?" she asked.

"Nope," Justin said. "I'm your corpsman."

Szabla drew her head back, her forehead lining with wrinkles. "Hubby and wife? This ain't no Amway convention."

Cameron shrugged. "I don't know what's going on. Mako told us both to report." She walked over to Savage and extended her hand. "Cameron Kates."

Savage glanced down at her hand, then looked away. She lowered her arm, electing not to comment since she couldn't determine his rank from his ripped cammies. As she stepped back, she noticed that he wore only one boot.

Savage followed her eyes down to his sock. "Tough night," he said.

Cameron turned to Szabla, who raised her eyebrows. "Far as I can see," Szabla said, "he ain't gonna join in any reindeer games."

Cameron smacked Tucker in the chest. "We got something of a reunion going on here, huh?"

Tucker shifted on his feet and smiled his nervous smile, his eyes darting to the pavement. "Yeah. Guess so. I been . . . I sorta fell off for a while there, you know." He laughed a short stuttering laugh, and Cameron noticed his eyes were ringed with faint black circles, like fading bruises. "You know how it goes."

"Who's our OIC?" Szabla asked.

Justin turned to her, eyebrows raised. "You haven't heard? Derek."

"Mitchell?" Szabla whistled, one dying note.

"He'll be fine," Cameron said defensively. Justin rested a hand on her back, but she stepped away ever so slightly, not wanting to have any personal displays before the other soldiers.

Szabla snorted. "Listen, girl. After going through something like he went—"

Derek rounded the corner, pulling off his jacket. "Sorry I'm late." At six foot four, Derek was surprisingly unintimidating, especially for someone built like a linebacker and trained extensively to kill other people. Barrel-chested, arms stretching his shirtsleeves at his biceps, he tapered in, almost impossibly, to a slim waist before expanding again through his powerful quads. His full cheeks would have made him look young were they not generally covered with stubble.

He nodded at Justin and hooked Cameron's neck with a hand, yanking her forward on her toes. "It's good to see you, Cam." His eyes drifted, then focused. "Really good to see you." He turned to Justin with a smile. "So how do you feel about me stealing my old swim buddy here back for the mission?"

Justin shrugged. "Take my wife, please."

Derek turned to Cameron and winked. "You should get yourself a real man."

Justin laughed. "That's what I keep telling her."

Derek nodded at Tucker, then smacked Tank on the shoulder. Tank didn't move.

"Hey, LT." Szabla leaned over, offering her hand to Derek. He slapped it, and they locked hands for a moment.

Derek strode over to Savage and glanced him up and down. Savage didn't bother to meet his eyes. "Why don't you introduce yourself to the platoon?"

Savage ignored him. Derek leaned in close until his face was inches from Savage's. Savage met his eyes evenly. Leaning back against the wall, he made no effort to rise to a more protective posture. Finally, his eyes flickered to the others. "We got seven men." He looked at Cameron, then at Szabla. "Make that five. That ain't a platoon. That's three shy of a half."

"For all practical purposes, it's a squad, and I'll run it as such." Derek paused, straightened up. "I gave you an order."

Savage ran his tongue along the inside of his bottom lip, his blue eyes hard like bits of sea-washed glass. "Savage," he said. "William Savage."

"Are you shitting me?" Justin said. "*Savage?* Yeah, okay buddy." He turned to Derek. "If he's Savage, then I get to be Harddick."

"And I wanna be Dickwrench," Szabla added. "Or something."

"You already are," Justin smirked. Szabla flipped him off.

"If you're having trouble with the name," Savage said, running a hand over the stubble beneath his beard, "I can carve it on your forehead for you."

"Yeah, try not to knock over your walker as you head over here," Justin said. He laughed, shaking his head. "*Savage.* That's great. That's fucking brilliant."

A mother walking with her two kids saw the group of soldiers up ahead and ushered her kids across the street to avoid them. They turned into Roosevelt Park and the children sprinted ahead onto the soccer fields, laughing.

Savage reached out, sliding his fingers down behind Justin's ear before Justin knocked his hand away. Savage rubbed his fingertips together, then smelled them. "Still a little wet."

"Oh?" Justin said, slightly flushed. "Not up to par with your Civil War comrades?"

"Vietnam. Team ONE, Bravo Platoon, sixty-gunner."

"I thought we'd forgotten about all the Vietnam vets," Szabla said. "Wasn't that national policy?"

"You fuckin' candy-ass whore—"

"Candy-ass whore." Szabla whistled. "Nice, this is nice. Where'd you find this one, LT? Recruiting in prisons?"

"Actually, yes," Derek said. A thick silence settled over the soldiers. Savage grinned vengefully.

"Fuck," Tank said.

Cameron tapped Derek on the arm. "Can I have a minute here, please?" Derek followed her across the street to the park. Cameron slowed down near the playground, setting her foot in the bucket of a swing. "What's going on, Derek?" she asked.

He didn't respond, so she just looked at him, hard and steady. Finally, he sighed. "It's a low-priority mission."

"That seems to be something of an understatement. We're a shooter short, Tucker looks like death warmed over, and Mako sprang a jailbird."

"Look, Mako doesn't have the men, but he was getting leaned on from up top. I guess one of these New Center guys predicted an earthquake in Santa Cruz, gave the residents twelve hours' notice to evacuate. Saved some lives, including—"

"That of our very own Secretary of the Navy, Andrew Benneton," Cameron said with a grimace.

"Favors, like shit, flow downhill. You know the drill: Secretary of the Navy calls the Commander, who calls the Team

THREE CO, who calls our favorite Operations Officer, John Mako, who, with little notice and a big headache, needs to field a SEALs squad."

"So he scraped together reserves and pulled you back from leave."

Derek nodded. "His ass is covered as long as he provides BUD/s-trained soldiers. We're just here to dog-and-pony. The best I could do was request old platoon-mates. No one wanted this. It's a jerk-off of a mission—keep the slipper in one piece and get him home as quickly as possible. If it's feeling a touch half-assed, that's because it is."

Cameron let her breath out in a whistle. She glanced at the kids running over the lawn. The girl attempted a cartwheel and landed flat on her back. "How's Jacqueline?"

Derek bit his lip, turning his face to the breeze. "You never know just how tough you are until something like that happens. Just how much you can stand." His face looked narrow and displeased, as though he'd bitten into something sour. He murmured, "You have no idea what it's like to lose a baby."

Cameron averted her eyes, uncomfortable. "No. No I don't."

Derek shook off his thoughts like a chill and turned back, all business again. "I'm gonna run the squad like they used to run half platoons before they kicked the fulls up to sixteen. Szabla's next in rank as an 0-2, so she'll be the AOIC. Believe me Cam, I'd rather it was you."

Cameron wasn't really sure what to make of his rapid mood swings—she figured they were bumps in the road of his mourning process.

"At least we don't have any screaming seamen on board," Derek continued. "You five are all E-4 and up, though Savage and Tucker haven't kept up proficiency training in some time. Like I said, low-priority mission."

Cameron grimaced. "What a squad."

"Hey!" Szabla yelled from across the street. "You about done with your little tea party?"

Derek waved for her to shut up and nodded at Cameron. "Ecuador's in a martial law state—first time since '78, I think. Heavy UN influence. There was some talk upstairs about having NATO move in so we could have more control, but the French weren't having it. We'll have to cut through a decent amount of red tape at Guayaquil, but it should be clear sailing once we hit the islands."

"Is Guayaquil that dangerous?" Cameron asked.

"Hell no," Derek said. "The city center's cordoned off— it's basically a UN camp. Outside of that, there's still a lot of random crime, as always, but things are up and running. I suppose it's no place for a civilian, but it's hardly Borneo. These scientists are just freaked out because that last guy went missing."

"Or they're using us to cut through the red tape."

"Probably a little of both." Derek formed a fist and held it out. "Gonna need your level head and your bad Spanish."

Cameron tightened her hand and Derek brought his down on top of hers. He smiled, and a few faint wrinkles fanned through his cheeks. Cameron noticed a patch of stubble on his chin that he'd missed while shaving and felt a sadness move through her. Derek had aged a decade since she'd seen him last month. "Are you sure you're ready for this?" she asked. "It's hardly been six weeks."

"I know. But this is a cakewalk of a mission. It'll get my legs back under me." He smiled almost bashfully. "Mako leaned on me pretty good. I didn't want to do it at first. Didn't think I was ready."

"What changed your mind?" Cameron asked.

"When he told me you were signed on." Derek looked down and studied his thumbnail for a moment. When he raised his head, his eyes were steeled with resolve. "Let's get this goatfuck on the road."

DONALD FACED Rex across the oblong disk of granite that served as the New Center conference table. Charts and diagrams hung about the room, and information seemed to jump out from the walls—the darkened hues of bathymetric maps, the curving arrows of oceanographic currents, the jointed lines of surface temperatures climbing hesitantly upward. No fewer than five computers were currently running, though Rex and Donald were the only ones sharing the office on the top floor. The other scientists worked in cubicles below, or in the basement lab.

"I'm impressed you were able to get here on time," Donald said. A slightly rounded short gentleman with kindly eyes and a shock of white hair that sprayed up from his head at all angles, Dr. Donald Denton stubbornly refused to yield to comb or brush. He wore only linen—linen shirts of all shades and patterns, linen dinner jackets at formal events, linen slacks so wrinkled they resembled corduroys. His skin had an enthusiastic reddish sheen to it, as if he had just finished some weighty task that involved a great degree of physical exertion. The truth of the matter was that he loathed physical exertion. Fortunately for him, as the President of the New Center, and the more academic Co-Chief of Research, the closest he got to exercise was a few swings of a rock hammer.

Still breathless, Rex pulled off his bicycle helmet and tossed it in the corner. "Well, it's not every day one gets his very own team of trained SEALs."

Donald leaned over, exhaling audibly, and pulled two jars filled with red-tinted, brackish liquid from a padded box. He set them on the table before Rex.

"Alien urine specimens?" Rex asked.

"Water samples. From Frank. Dated the twenty-seventh of October. The mail from Ecuador, as you can imagine, has all but ground to a halt. They came in on a cargo plane late last night, and were waiting for me here when I arrived this morning."

Rex took one of the jars and held it up to the light. Particles swirled in the cloudy liquid.

"One from Santa Cruz, the other he took first thing after landing on Sangre de Dios. I guess he sent them back with the boat that dropped him off. I'll run them down to the lab after the meeting, see what I come up with. Oh, and I almost forgot." Donald leaned forward, pulling a folded sheet from his back pocket. He handed it to Rex. "Take a look at this."

Rex took the sheet and glanced at it. "Sixty-four hundred bucks!" He whistled. "What the hell's that for?"

"Evidently, Frank ordered one of those solar-powered specimen freezers delivered to him on the island. Some shady shipper threw it on an oil tanker out of Manta, got it to him in two days." He snatched the bill back from Rex and read from it. " 'Expedited delivery—four hundred dollars.' " He shook his head. "I just don't understand what he would've needed a freezer that large for."

Rex shrugged. "Maybe he didn't. Maybe he didn't know what he was ordering. Maybe they sent him the wrong size to rip him off. Us. To rip *us* off. Did he clear the expense with you?"

Donald waved him off. "Please. You know Frank. He was never in touch on a survey. Hated to be distracted from his work. He couldn't be bothered with lugging communications equipment."

"Ah yes. His Thoreau routine."

Donald rubbed one eye with the heel of his hand. "That's why it took me so damn long to realize he was missing." He drummed his fingers on the granite. "I have to confess, I'm glad you'll have a military squad looking after you. I was assured they were the best."

A loud single knock hit the door, and Donald rose to his feet. He opened the door to reveal Savage, standing slightly crooked in one boot and one torn sock. Beside him, Tucker jiggled his hand back and forth, watching it closely.

"Hello," Donald began. "I'm—"

Savage knocked Donald's shoulder as he passed him. Tank followed Tucker into the room, banging his head on the door frame. Derek emerged from the rear, holding out his hand to Donald. "Derek Mitchell. I'm the OIC of this platoon."

Donald took his hand with some hesitation. "OIC?"

"Officer in Charge."

Szabla curled her arm across her chest, rotating her fist so the ball of her biceps slid back and forth. Donald turned slowly to face Rex, who remained blank-faced, leaning back so the chair cocked under his weight.

"Well," Rex said, staring at the ceiling. "Let the games begin."

After the introductions were made, the squad gathered around the conference table. Derek sat at the far end beside Rex and Donald, facing the soldiers. Cameron was relieved to see that he looked more steady than before, more professional.

Rex studied Derek, a hint of a smile on his lips. "Sure we don't need more men?"

"Two of us are women," Szabla said. "And, in keeping with the finest naval tradition, prefer to be referred to as either broads or dames."

Rex laughed, but Derek shot her a stern look. Donald rose, folding his hands across his generous belly. "Now, I've already gone over the itinerary with Lieutenant Mako."

"I'm up to speed," Derek said. "There'll be plenty of time for me to brief the others before we lift out tonight."

"Good," Rex said. "Because it's bad enough there's going to be seven of you. But I certainly can't get through an expedition of this importance—"

"Of this importance," Szabla repeated.

Rex stared at her. "What the hell does that mean?"

"It means that with the current state of affairs, I don't think a scientific outing is of the utmost—"

"I'm handling this, Szabla," Derek said.

"—importance that we need to dispatch top-notch soldiers—"

"Szabla," Derek said, his voice raised in warning. "Which part of 'I'm handling this' did you not understand?"

"I think 'handling,' LT. She has trouble with gerunds," Justin said, turning a sweet smile to Szabla before she back-handed him. He caught her hand at the wrist inches from his nose.

Cameron almost told Justin and Szabla to shut up but restrained herself, not wanting to undermine Derek. She placed her hands between her knees, pressing them together.

"Top-notch?" Rex asked rhetorically. Savage dug his fingernail beneath a small scab on the back of his neck and scraped it off, examining it before flicking it onto the floor. He ran his hand across the sore, then wiped the blood on his pants.

"Rex," Donald said softly, his voice tense. "I don't think—"

Derek stood up and leaned over the table, facing his charges. "Let's get one thing straight. We are escorting Dr. Williams because that's our mission." He turned to Rex, who gazed up at him from his chair, seemingly awed by his considerable size. "But *you* don't have to make things more difficult than they need be."

"I'm merely taking issue with the choice of 'top-notch' as an adjective." Rex pointed at Savage. "That guy looks like he crawled out of a sewer."

Savage waved. He went back to relacing his boot, which was resting on the table.

"The only thing that matters," Cameron said, "is the mission objective."

"Who brought the girl scout?"

"*Szabla*," Derek said. "I'm not fucking around here."

Donald removed his small spectacles and polished them nervously. "I'd like to . . . if it's okay, I'd like to discuss—"

Rex bounced forward in his chair. "We're flying into Guayaquil, need to stop there for the night. How? I don't know. That's your department. Obviously we're not taking United. We get to spend Christmas night in Guayaquil, lovely polluted industry town and cultural hub of the universe. We're picking up Dr. Juan Ramirez, a professor of ecology at Universidad de Guayaquil, who will be assisting me in my objectives. Then we're flying to Baltra, which houses the only operating airport in Galápagos. It's a former U.S. Army base, so that should float your respective boats."

Savage belched. Rex elected to ignore him.

"Then we'll need to establish our telemetry gear at the Darwin Station on Santa Cruz, scold whoever's left in the seismology department for letting their operation go to shit, and we're on our way to Sangre de Dios where I'll be undertaking the extraordinarily ambitious and impressive task of outfitting the island with geodetic trinkets and toys—six Global Positioning Satellite units, to be precise."

"What's the terrain?" Cameron asked.

"Quite varied. From scorched lava to dense forests."

"We bringing NVGs?" Szabla asked.

Rex shot Derek a puzzled look. "Night Vision Goggles," Derek explained. He turned to Szabla. "No. It's not triple canopy, and we're setting the GPS units during the day. We don't need to be tricked out for combat—it's not exactly a hot area."

Szabla leaned back in her chair, placing her arms behind her neck and flexing. "How do the units work?"

Rex said, "They measure the rates of the land's deformation. We need six to form a network. They'll relay information to the Darwin Station, and the scientists there will, in turn, forward the information to us via computer."

"Why don't you just have the information relayed directly here?"

"Unfortunately, the telemetry equipment isn't that sophisticated. It only relays information along line of sight. The distance from Ecuador to Sacramento is great enough that the curvature would throw off the transmissions."

"Curvature?" Tucker asked.

"The earth is round," Rex said, with a sardonic grin.

Tucker pressed his lips together. "Oh, yeah."

Derek leaned forward, resting his elbows on the table. "I understand transportation around the islands is a problem?"

"Yes, but I've arranged it all after we hit Baltra—it's just the airports that are tangled in military red tape. Boating between islands is a logistical pain in the ass, but not a political one." Rex turned to face the others. "In all, it's an eight-day trip—two days transport out, four days on Sangre, one day back. If all goes well, we'll be back for New Year's. Your job is to make sure I don't get shot, stabbed, or drawn and quartered in Guayaquil, to get me through the airports without any cavity searches, and to help me blanket Sangre de Dios and get the gear in place."

"Aren't there scientists out there already who can do this?" Cameron asked. "And save us the trip?"

"That's a very good question, Miss . . ." Rex looked at her expectantly.

"Chief," Cameron said. "Kates. But Cameron will do just fine. And a straightforward answer without the condescension."

Rex whistled. "Lo siento mucho."

"No problema."

Rex suppressed a smile as he leaned forward. "All right, Cameron. The reason the scientists there can't take care of it is because their funding, as you can imagine, has gone to even further shit as a result of the economic turmoil, and they can barely afford upkeep, let alone cutting-edge technology. Shipping's gone to hell, so we can't send the equipment down to them. We can hardly get through via phone, fax, or E-mail just to find out what the hell's going on. On top of all that, they're fleeing the islands in droves."

"Why?" Cameron asked.

"Because they're not as courageous as we are." Rex smiled. "Or as stupid. 'The few, the proud . . .'"

"That's the Marines," Szabla said.

Rex waved her off. "Same difference."

Tucker was listening intently. "Why's Sangre de Dios so important?" he asked.

"Because it sits over a network of fissures running south from the Galápagos Fracture Zone and, more significant, fissures running inland from the East Pacific Rise—it's near the source of both major forces that affect movement of the *entire* Nazca plate."

Tank watched Rex blankly. When Rex finished speaking, Tank turned to the others. "English?" he said.

"It's near where shit is the most fucked up," Szabla replied.

"Because of that," Rex continued, "it's our canary in the coal mine." He noticed that Tucker was jotting notes in a small pad. "That's C-A-N-A-R-Y."

Tucker looked at him self-consciously, then slid the pad back into his pocket. "Just thought it would help keep me up on things," he said.

Rex flashed a grin. "Indeed."

"I'm sure you're all aware of the severe ozone deficiency in that region." Donald stood and crossed to a large cabinet, pulling it open. "You'll need to take every precaution down there. Protective contacts, SPF one hundred lotion." He pulled out several tubes of sunblock and waved them at the soldiers. "Get it everywhere—webs of your fingers, insides of your ears; if you part your hair, rub it along the exposed line of scalp." He held the tubes out to Derek, but Derek waved him off.

"We're covered," Cameron said. "Customary operating supplies for missions in ozone-poor regions."

Derek clapped his hands once and rose. "We'll be lifting out at 2300 from the base. Any other questions?"

"Yeah," Savage said, thunking his bootless foot on the table. His voice was gravelly with phlegm, so he cleared his throat and spit in the corner. "You think we could see about getting me another boot sometime soon?"

CAMERON WALKED out of the women's room on the third floor of the New Center and headed down the hall toward the stairs, her boots loud on the tiled floor. Sealed with yellow police tape, the elevator doors were now used as a bulletin board. Cameron stopped for a moment and glanced at the flyers advertising lecture series and research trips.

One section of the doors was dedicated to the tropical ozone problem. Her eyes flickered over the papers, trying to condense the information.

Evidently, tropical regions had always suffered the highest penetration of UV radiation. Since the Initial Event, ocean surface heating from tectonic activity had only compounded the problem. It had spawned hurricanes that, in combination with aberrant weather patterns, had evolved into hypercanes, massive hurricanes that were so tall they reached into the stratosphere. Because of their elongation, hypercanes pumped water from the ocean surface directly into the stratosphere, introducing massive amounts of HO and HO_2. This accelerated the hox catalytic cycle, a natural process that broke down ozone and removed it from the stratosphere. It took a full year for the ozone balance to normalize after a hypercane, and one had been occurring every three to four months. For the past five years, the flyer warned, people, plants, and animals near the equator had been absorbing unprecedented amounts of UV radiation.

A tear sheet listed the effects of ultraviolet B on organisms—reduced shoot length and average leaf area in plants; decreases in rates of photosynthesis; structural damages to light-sensitive plankton; corruption of bird, reptile, and insect eggs; reduced proportion of healthy hatchlings. But the reported effects on humans were the most disturbing. The ten percent reduction in equatorial stratospheric ozone had led to a forty percent increase in the incidence of basal cell carcinoma, and a sixty percent increase in squamous cell carcinoma in Ecuador, Colombia, and northern Peru. The study also reported a rise in the number of cataracts, and a condition described cryptically as a general weakening of the immune system.

Cameron looked down and realized she was clutching her belly. She stared at her hand, laid protectively over the greens and grays of her camouflage shirt, tense and spread-

fingered. Suddenly feeling light-headed, she leaned against
the elevator doors, holding her stomach. Her eyes caught on
a small sign posted among the ozone bulletins that cheerily
announced, "We're living in the warmest climate to exist in
millions of years!"

A door opened down the hall, and Cameron straightened
up quickly when she saw Rex heading her way. She wiped
the sweat from her forehead with the back of a sleeve.

"I love a woman in uniform," Rex said, snapping her a
mock salute. A flicker of concern crossed his eyes when he
took note of her expression, and she was surprised by it.
"Everything all right?"

"Yeah," she said, turning to the stairs. "Swell."

Chapter 8   Cameron had always found the ritual of
preparing for a mission comforting. Cleaning and lubing the
guns, rolling the socks back into themselves, putting fresh
batteries in the weapons lights. One rule was never broken
on the teams: Always pack your own gear. That included
everything from filling the canteens to jamming the mags.

She shoved down on the kit bag so she could get the zipper closed. When she finished, she was straddling the large
olive-drab duffel, her bare feet cold against the floorboards.
Pausing, she took in the small living room. One yellow
couch sitting at a slight tilt due to the missing leg, an empty
gun mag resting atop a TV on the floor, a ripped Kings
schedule on the wall—they lived as if they were still in college. Until recently, they had been home so infrequently it
never seemed worthwhile to spend the time and effort to
get the house more comfortable. That would change when
they got back. She'd start looking in some of those cata-
logs, the ones with lots of beiges and candles, and order a
few things to get the place looking like it was inhabited by
adults. Once they found regular jobs, maybe they could

even have some friends over for dinner. If they made any friends.

Wearing a towel around his waist, his hair still wet from the shower, Justin walked into the room, his handsome, even smile texturing his face with wrinkles. "You ready?"

Cameron shrugged, then patted her stomach. "Not so pleased about bringing a hitchhiker."

Justin crossed the room and stood beside her. She embraced him around the legs, and he hugged her face to his stomach, her cheek warm against his flesh. He lifted her hair up in the back and gently rubbed her neck.

"You know," Cameron said, her voice slightly muffled by his stomach, "we're going to have to be professional on this mission. Like we're nothing more than fellow soldiers." She turned her head slightly and began kissing his stomach. "I don't want our judgment to be impaired by the fact that we're married."

"Mine never is," Justin said. "Ask the mail lady." He crouched and kissed her gently on the forehead, then high on her neck, right where it met the corner of her jaw.

"I'm serious," she said.

"Relax, babe. We're part of the most notoriously casual trained fighting force in the world. I forgot how to salute."

"You didn't have to fight for the right to join the teams," Cameron said. "Not like I did. I'm not gonna fuck this up for other women. So let's remember that it's going to be like we're not married. Rules of conduct are important. We can't show each other any favoritism, can't put the others at risk because of emotional entanglements."

Justin tilted her head back, looking into her eyes. "I hate emotional entanglements," he said. "I'm just looking for a quick lay here, lady."

Cameron pulled him toward her. They kissed, long and slow.

He stood. The towel dropped to the floor.

* * *

TANK BANGED on the front door and Cameron opened it. A cluster of green plastic canteens hung together like grapes from her kit bag, and her M-4 was slung across her shoulders. She'd outfitted the gun with some extras—a night vision scope, a laser designator, and an M203, 40mm grenade launcher. She was dressed in full cammies and black jungle boots. Justin scrambled behind her, grabbing his last few things.

Tilting his head, Tank indicated the van behind him, engine running. "Four and a half minutes late," Cameron said, smiling. She could see that Tank wanted to help her with her gear, but he knew better. Instead of offering, he nodded and headed for the van. When he climbed back in the driver's seat, the vehicle seemed to settle a bit on its chassis. Tucker swung open the passenger door and hopped out, his green, long-sleeve T-shirt pulling tight across his chest. He met Cameron halfway up the walk, his eyes tracing the cracks in the concrete. "Hey, Cam," he said.

"Hey Tucker."

He reached out to take her weapon, but she shook her head. "I got it," she said.

Tucker followed her silently to the back of the van. She swung the door open and tossed her bag in on top of Tank's and Tucker's. Derek, Szabla, and Savage were going to meet them at the base.

Cameron slammed the back doors and leaned against them, staring up at the dark sky. "Sunset was blood red today," she said. "Did you see it?"

Tucker nodded. "Earthquake weather."

He pushed up his sleeves, crouched and lit a cigarette, pinching the filter and letting it swing between his legs. For the first time, Cameron noticed the shadow of healed needle tracks running up the insides of his arms. Thin dark skids, most of them ending in the dot of a faded bruise. His flesh looked red in the glow given off by the brake lights. The asphalt was still shimmering from the afternoon rain.

Tucker inhaled deeply and sent a cloud of smoke down toward the pavement. It rose, clinging to his body. He glanced up and noticed Cameron's eyes on his arms. Protectively, he crossed his arms, pulling them to his chest. Cameron looked away uncomfortably, but when she turned back, Tucker's eyes were still on her.

Slowly, he uncrossed his arms, revealing again the pattern of scars. "Been a long road back," he said. He looked down at the asphalt, as if he could see his reflection in it. His voice wavered a little bit when he spoke again. "It's good to get a second chance."

Cameron pushed herself up off the van. Tucker did not look up. "You're a good soldier, Tucker," she said, though she wasn't sure why.

His head bobbed a bit with what she guessed was a smile. "You ever had something you loved?" he asked. "So much you couldn't give it up?"

He flicked the cigarette butt, and it sizzled out on the moist asphalt.

"No," Cameron said.

Justin came out onto the porch, closing the door behind him, and Tucker rose and circled back to the passenger seat of the van.

**25 DEC 07
MISSION DAY 1**

Chapter 9   The C-130 banked and finally began its descent into the airport at Guayaquil. It circled twice, then made its approach from the east, sweeping low over the stretch of river where the Río Babahoyo flows into the Río Guayas. Cameron unbuckled and stood, leaning against the wall so that she could peer through the small round window out past the two prop engines on the wing. The water was muddied and thick with sediment, a wide rippling stream of rich brown. The earthquakes had induced landslides and rockfalls, which had clogged the river network, especially the drainages to the coast.

Square patches of factories and warehouses checkered the countryside, and up ahead, Cameron could make out the smog wreathing the city. Two of the runways were out of commission, having been split with large fissures, and men in orange vests ran back and forth between construction trucks, barking commands.

Derek and the others were applying sunblock and putting in their extended-wear, UV-protective contact lenses. Cameron sat back down and followed suit. Tank ran the lotion through his flattop like conditioner, rubbing it into his scalp. The soldiers also Velcroed solar cells to the shoulders of their cammy shirts, the flat batteries positioned like tiny officer shoulder boards.

The plane screeched to a halt on the tarmac, bouncing them slightly in the red webbing of the cargo seats. Derek stood, slapping his hands to his thighs. "Szabla, you guard the pallets once we unass."

She nodded, grabbing the M-4 by her side as the other soldiers disembarked. Red lettering stretched across the main wing of the terminal—*Aeropuerto Simón Bolívar Guayaquil*. The dead tufts of grass around the taxiway were baked brown and yellow, nodding in the breeze. The air was thick and slightly moist; Cameron could feel the humidity through her lungs when she inhaled.

Though it was still early morning, a wall of heat hit them when they stepped clear of the plane's shadow. "Holy Christ," Savage said. "Don't this fuckin' beat all?"

Rex removed a Panama hat from his bag, unrolled it, and placed it with a slight tilt on his head. The sun glared off the tightly woven straw. The combination of the hat and his clothes—white shirt with twin pockets, khakis—gave him the distinctive air of a rubber baron in Malaya. In addition to a brown leather briefcase, he carried several circular nylon bags, padded and zipped shut.

Cameron was grateful for the fifty-percent nylon ripstop cammies—they were light and breathable, and the long sleeves provided protection from the sun.

Rex glanced over at her and Szabla. "Hey, Thelma and Louise," he said. "Get your sun hats on." He pointed to an orange electronic billboard situated on top of one of the hangars: *Minutos para Quemarse—4:30*. The translation was written beneath: *Minutes to Burn*.

Szabla grimaced and headed to the ramp to join Tank in unloading and unbuttoning the aircraft pallets, which held the cruise boxes, kit bags, and comms boxes full of Rex's GPS hardware. The cruise boxes, 3 x 2 x 1.5 foot collapsible cases of sheet metal, stored the general-purpose gear.

A U.S. army private jogged out from the airport, heading for the squad. In addition to his regular uniform, he wore the light blue beret and blue elastic belt of the United Nations. Derek walked forward, waving off the private's salute. They spoke for a few moments, then Derek signaled the squad to follow him.

The airport was in complete disarray, filled with uniforms and a few clusters of civilians. When Cameron stepped through the cracked glass doors onto the sidewalk, she was surprised by the crowd and the congested traffic. Though the earthquakes' effects were evident in the uneven pavement, buckling walls, and heaps of rubble, the life of the city went on. She realized she'd expected to find doors and windows hammered shut with planks like in some bad late-night movie about a plague.

A teenage boy scrambled forward and attempted to grab the weapons box Szabla and Tank were carrying, but Szabla turned, quickly slinging her M-4, and side-kicked him, hammering the bottom of her boot just beneath his ribs. The boy collapsed on the pavement, moaning. A nearby policeman, a clean-shaven man with a front tooth that was turned sideways, sprang forward and began screaming at Szabla in Spanish.

"You'd better back off before I straighten out that fucked-up tooth of yours," she growled.

Rex, who'd been punching the numbers on his sat phone in frustration, trotted over and exchanged a few heated words with the Ecuadorian policeman. The policeman threw up his arms. Szabla set the box down, peering at the police-man over Rex's shoulder. "I got more if you want some, you mother—"

Cameron drew Szabla back so Rex could finish dealing with the policeman. When Tank moved over and stood silently behind Rex, the policeman quieted down a bit. After helping the boy to his feet, the policeman stormed off. Rex turned to face Szabla, his mouth tight. "He was just trying to help you with your things. Trying to get a tip."

"He wants a tip?" Szabla said, pointing at the box. "How about: Don't touch my fucking ordnance. I don't give a shit where we are. These are M-4s."

"There are different rules down here."

"No," Szabla said, stabbing a finger in Rex's face. "There are different rules *here*. When we get to the science shit, you can run the science shit, but for now, keep your mouth shut and your ass out of my way."

"Next time, before you kick," Rex said, picking up his bag, "try 'no gracias.'"

"Sorry," Szabla said. "I only speak French."

"Then try 'non, merci.'"

Derek walked through the doors with Tucker and the pri-vate at his side just as a *chiva* pulled up to the curb. The pri-vate pointed at the open bus with its thatched roof. He took one look at Derek's expression and shrugged apologetically. "We're overbooked on military vehicles, and the UN takes priority."

They loaded the gear and sat on the edges of the *chiva*, M-4s lazing outward on cocked arms, pointing at the open sky. The weapons were high-speed versions of M-16s, shooting 5.56 rounds, thirty rounds per magazine. Most of the squad had tricked them out with flashlights, scopes, and other trinkets.

Savage glanced down at the M-4, much smaller than the M-60 to which he was accustomed. "Fuckin' pea shooter," he grumbled.

"I wouldn't complain," Derek said. "It's a step up from a shiv."

The city was gray and run-down, and the driver drove a mad winding path through blocks filled with warehouses and shabby buildings. It took Cameron a few moments to realize that the meandering path was actually strategic; the driver was seeking out the streets that were still intact. The amount of construction under way was astounding. Everywhere she looked, Cameron noticed building crews, orange cones, yellow cranes, and trucks. The hot smell of asphalt made the pollution all the more oppressive.

A little boy made a gun with his hand and pointed it at the *chiva*. Savage lowered his gun jokingly, aiming it at the boy, and Derek slapped it to the side.

Rex was trying not to appear nervous around the weapons. He sat beside Cameron, his feet up on the split plastic seat in front of them. "Lovely, isn't it?" he asked. "Two and a half million people living on converted mangrove swamp."

The driver turned a hard right, barely avoiding a large divot, and suddenly they were on a street filled with highrises. Vendors pushed carts, and bicyclists flew by on both sides of the *chiva*, so close Cameron was amazed they didn't nick the bumpers. They turned up a street that ran along the west bank of the Guayas, and Cameron craned her head, checking out the different military outfits overseeing construction and running vehicle checkpoints. A platoon of *iwias*, Ecuadorian specialty troops, gathered by the river's bank. Farther along, a UN tank was stopped beside a large statue of two men shaking hands, the white and sky-blue flag rippling against the backdrop of the river. A number of

French soldiers sat around the tank, legs dangling over the sides, eating sandwiches and drinking Coke from bottles. The tall, chain-link fence of the cordon loomed ahead.

A major stepped forward as they slowed at the checkpoint. He examined Derek's military ID, tilting it to check the holograms. "Mitchell, huh?" he said. "Team reserves?"

"Yes, sir."

"Nice ride."

Derek took a moment before answering. "Thank you, sir."

The major bobbed his head, the faintest beginning of a smirk crossing his lips. "Got a call this morning regarding your mission." He pulled off his soft, blue beret and ran a hand up the back of his bristling gray hair. He tapped the end of Derek's M-4 and Derek lowered it. "No weapons out past checkpoint. We have the city center secure." He glanced at the squad in the *chiva*. "Last thing we need is a bunch of . . ." He stopped short, clearing his throat.

"Soldiers," Tucker said. "We're soldiers."

"How long are you here?" the major asked Derek, ignoring Tucker.

"Lifting out tomorrow," Derek said. "0700."

The major handed back the ID. "I don't want to see any of you carrying within my AO. You're to keep all weapons *and* ordnance under watch at the hotel. Do I make myself clear?"

"Yes, sir."

The major knocked the side of the *chiva*, and it pulled through the checkpoint. Savage snapped the major a crisp, exaggerated salute. The major looked over and Savage winked at him, clearly enjoying the major's expression as the *chiva* turned the corner. "Christ on a stick," he muttered. "What an asshole."

The *chiva* cut inland and pulled up to the hotel, a decrepit colonial-style high-rise on Calle Chile. Two guards at the entrance held pump-action shotguns, and wore red berets and pressed navy blue pants with yellow piping down the seams. They nodded at Derek and Rex as they passed inside. Cameron waited behind with the others, guarding the gear.

A mother pushed a baby in a carriage up the street toward the hotel, pausing beneath a torn green store awning.
The window, shattered but protected with bars, was filled
with knockoff Nikes and Levis. Leaving the carriage, the
woman inched up the street to examine a pair of jeans
stretched out at the side of the display. Cameron caught herself staring at the baby carriage. Cheap, black-painted metal,
wobbly back wheels, blankets arranged lovingly around the
inside as cushions.

A horrible squalling suddenly issued from the carriage.
Cameron ran over and gazed down at the baby. A band of
sunlight had worked its way through the torn awning above,
falling across the baby's plump thigh. It had already red-
dened.

Adjusting her gun on her back so it dangled from the
sling, Cameron leaned over and picked up the baby, holding
it awkwardly out away from her body. She tried to shush it,
bouncing it up and down in a way she thought might be
soothing. The others stared over at her, puzzlement across
their faces. A cigarette dangled from Savage's lips, a tendril
of smoke curling up between his eyes.

The mother came scurrying over, holding up her sweeping red dress as she ran. Cameron handed off the baby
roughly. "El sol," Cameron said, pointing at the ripped
awning, then at the baby's leg. The mother thanked her pro-
fusely before heading off, comforting the baby softly.

Feeling self-conscious before the others, Cameron found
Justin's eyes, and he smiled at her reassuringly.

"Hey there, Mother Goose," Szabla smirked, holding one
boot up before her. "I think I stubbed my toe. Would you
mind kissing it to make it better?"

Cameron knocked Szabla's boot away. Szabla stumbled
backward into Tank, who caught her under the arms and
hauled her to her feet.

Derek and Rex emerged, and Derek signaled the squad to
grab the gear. Szabla climbed up on the roof of the *chiva* and

began lowering the cruise boxes and duffels to the others. Across the street, two men leaned up against a building, watching them unload. One of them, a tall, handsome *guayaquileño*, wore an unbuttoned shirt to show off a dazzling array of gold chains. He watched Szabla bend over and blew her a kiss. His friend, a shorter man with his hair pulled back in a ponytail, laughed. Szabla squared herself on the roof of the *chiva*, facing them, and grabbed her crotch. The shorter man cheered and she curtsied before sliding off the roof.

Rex tried to lift one of the cruise boxes and couldn't get it off the ground. With a smirk, Szabla hoisted it up and motioned Rex ahead of her. "Why don't you be a gentleman and get the door?" she said.

Inside, the wallpaper was bubbled and peeled, the maroon carpet worn thin around the front desk. Savage stopped beneath a particularly gruesome sculpture of Christ on the cross, nailed to the wall beside reception. He ran a finger across the crown of thorns and rubbed his fingertips, as if expecting the blood to come off on them.

The squad followed Derek up the stairs, hauling the gear. They circled up in the first bedroom of the third floor, stacking the gear in the corner.

Derek opened the lid of the weapons box, revealing the foam interior. Removing the magazine from his M-4, he placed the gun inside, tossing the mag in a nearby cruise box, where it landed on one of the two spare ammo crates. He gestured for the others to do the same. "Make sure you clear and safe your weapons," he said. "Sigs too."

Rex looked up in disgust at the vents. "An ozone hole the size of Mars and the air conditioner's running full blast." He started for the dial on the wall, but Szabla blocked him.

"Not in this heat, you don't," she said. "CFCs be damned."

"It's precisely that kind of—"

Derek cleared his throat. "We'll take the rooms in buddy pairs. Me and Cam'll stay here. Szabla and Justin, you guys are straight across the hall. I want Savage and Tucker next door to you, and Rex and Tank in the next room down."

"I think I can manage alone," Rex said. "Tempting as it sounds, I don't think I'm really in need of a 'buddy.' "

Derek ignored him. Tank sat down on one of the beds with a grunt, pulling off a boot. He snapped his fingers, and Justin pulled a can of Tinactin from his kit bag and tossed it to him.

When the others had finished putting away their M-4s and 9mm Sig Sauer p226s, Derek counted the mags in the cruise box, making sure they were all accounted for. Since he was standing watch, he kept a loaded pistol in his belt.

The sound of a crying baby issued through the thin wall. Derek stiffened, his face blanching. Cameron coughed loudly to draw attention away from him. The crying continued. Probably the baby that got sunburnt.

Rex punched a number into his sat phone. He hung up and dialed again. "A recording says the north part of the city's still out. I tried before from the airport."

Some of the color was returning to Derek's face, but he still looked unsteady.

"So the north part of the city's out," Szabla said. "Who gives a shit?"

"That's where Dr. Ramirez's lab is."

Szabla looked at Rex with irritation. "Need I repeat my question?"

"I haven't had an opportunity to inform him of our departure time tomorrow. If he's going to meet us at the airport for the flight, he needs to know when it is."

"So go tell him."

"It's through the UN cordon."

"Now we're an escort service," Szabla said.

"Doubt you'd get many bookings in that line of work," Rex said. "Look, someone needs to accompany me. Why don't you take a vote or something?"

"This is the navy," Szabla said. "We don't vote."

*   *   *

"I'll go," Cameron said. "Me and Tank. That okay, LT? LT?"

Derek snapped from his trance. The baby's cries had stopped. "What?"

"Me and Tank'll accompany Rex to find Dr. Ramirez. That all right?"

Derek nodded. "With all the attitude we're running into, I want you to keep it low-key around the UN troops. Change into civies and keep your Sigs out of view." Opening the weapons box, he pulled out two pistols and tossed them to Cameron and Tank. He slammed the lid, locked both padlocks, and looped the keychain around his neck.

"Anyone finds out you're carrying and it's my ass. If you run into trouble with UN or domestic, flash ID; with the element, retaliate reasonably. I'm assuming you'll be fine. It's broad daylight, and I'm pleasantly surprised by the stability of the city, even beyond the checkpoints. We'll wait for you here, and see about dinner later." He flipped Cameron a rubber-banded wad of sucres, bluish-green on one side, red and orange on the other.

Cameron wedged the money into her front pants pocket, safe from pickpockets. The baby next door let loose with a scream, and she saw Derek's face tighten, as if he were bracing for a punch. He regained his composure quickly. No one else seemed to notice.

"The lab is out by Julian Coronel," Rex said. "It's not the nicest part of town."

Tank laid an enormous hand on Rex's shoulder, guiding him toward the door.

"Don't worry," Cameron said. She stole another glance at Derek before turning to follow. "You're in good hands."

Chapter 10 The paper crackled as he inhaled, the orange ring of the cherry inching its way down the length of the joint toward his generous lips and well-manicured mustache. Diego Byron Rodriguez held the burn in his lungs for a moment, his chest stretching the fabric of his cheap Darwin Station T-shirt, and surveyed the mess around him.

A filing cabinet lay with its top smashed into his desk, a webbing of cracks working their way from one end of the fine oak surface to the other. Supporting a slender laptop, a dissecting microscope, and a coffee can full of pencils, was a makeshift second desk, humbly erected from four fallen cinder blocks and a piece of plywood. A screensaver—flying marine iguanas—blinked across the computer, and the power cord plugged into an orange heavy-duty surge protector on a cable that threaded its way through the detritus and out the broken window to functional outlets in the Protección building next door. Amid the shattered glass from the two picture windows fluttered fallen papers and posters, diagrams of fire ants, the wings of stiffened insects in broken cyanide jars.

On the wall hung two photos, frames cracked and glass shattered from their many falls, of Stephen Jay Gould and Niles Eldredge—an homage to Diego's heroes.

Diego's dark brown hair was sleek, his short ponytail seeming of one piece. His face was youthful, though traces of wrinkles remained for a few moments after he smiled or frowned, as if his face, coming into its fourth decade, had developed an aversion to change. His long hair seemed at odds with the neatness of his mustache, his faded T-shirt with his suit-bottom pants, the tassels of his Miami-bought Italian loafers with the stripes of bare, dusty skin visible at his ankles.

A pair of his boxer shorts was drying on the antenna of

the PRC117 Delta satellite radio. Because he'd fried it two weeks ago by overloading the circuits, he now had to use an old-school, high-frequency PRC104 that the *ejército* had dropped off on their last swing through. The rigid, ten-foot whip antenna that stood up like a coat rack from the low-tech PRC104 only permitted regional transmissions.

Leaning back on the ripped cushion of his leather couch, Diego exhaled, watching the jet of smoke unravel. He propped his feet up on a fallen TV and stared at the two items on the coffee table before him: a telephone, and the last box of .22 rounds on the Isla Santa Cruz. He ran his tongue over his teeth, leaned over, and tried the phone for the fourth time. Miraculously, the call went through.

A gruff voice answered. "Guayaquil Shipping. Tomás aquí." Though Diego had never met Thomas, he knew him well enough from the fat gringo accent and the self-assured cadence of his words—another American entrepreneur moved down to Guayaquil to play buccaneer and make a fortune off Ecuador's problems. Diego thought about switching to English but decided to humor him.

"Thomas, Diego Rodriguez. Acting Director, Darwin Station."

"Sí, sí. ¿Hombre de ecology, no?"

"I'm gonna make this quick because we could get cut off any minute. My Protección Department has mostly deserted, we have feral animals overrunning two of the islands, and I'm shit out of .22s."

Thomas's chuckle made Diego grimace, but at least he switched to English. "That's right, you got wild dogs and goats and shit eating up all the butterflies."

"Something like that."

"I remember 'cause we used to ship you guys out sodium monoflor-acetate—enough to poison the cast of *Cats*, if memory serves. But why are you handling eradication now? Isn't that supposed to be the Park's job?"

A noise of disgust escaped Diego's throat. "El Parque.

The Park officials split after the first tremor. Me and my staff have been handling everything." He looked around his empty office. "Small staff."

"Well, I can get you anticoagulants. Brodifacoum, klerat, more ten-eighty."

"The goats have become finicky, like cats. We've got to get ahold of more bullets."

"Even if I could get my hands on .22s, what makes you think you could afford them?"

"Maybe I have deeper pockets than you realize."

"Well, bullets are one commodity that even I can't locate. You know that."

Without domestic manufacture of bullets, Ecuador was dependent on imports from the United States and Israel. Ever since the Initial Event and the resultant social unrest, the U.S. had severely limited the export of bullets to Ecuador. The few attempts to make bullets in any quantity within the country had been abandoned by the organized crime leaders in Guayaquil due to earthquake disruptions.

Diego sat up, tugging at his ponytail. "Even on Santa Cruz, the goats are destroying the topsoil, eating what's left of the vegetation, digging up tortoise nests. And they're reproducing like rabbits. If you don't help me, these islands are gonna be what they started as—barren mounds of magma. Española's already been irreversibly damaged, chewed down to the rock. I know you have connections in the States. There must be bullets around Guayaquil. If you can get me even two, three cartons, it could make a big—" Realizing that he was pleading, Diego paused, trying to regain his composure. So this is what it's come down to, he thought. An island for a carton of bullets.

"Diego, buddy. There's nothing I can do. The ammo I do come across brings high prices you scientists can't pay. With all the rioting, the military, the armed guards . . . you should see it here."

"I *need* more bullets."

"Everyone needs, my friend. The home owners need for their armed guards, the military needs for the soldiers, the robbers need for the robberies. I don't have any bullets, but if I did, I'll tell you what I'd do. I'd have a big auction. Right in the middle of Parque Centenario."

"Your priorities are to be commended."

"Please. There are no priorities in times like this."

"There are always priorities. Especially in times like this."

"Even if I could get bullets, which I can't, and even if you could afford them, which you can't, how the hell would I get them to you? We haven't had boats out of here or Manta in three weeks, and—you forget—TAME stopped running all flights last Sunday. The only thing we see of Galápagos anymore are its citizens washing up on the coast in pirated fishing boats, broke, stinking, and looking for somewhere to sleep."

There was a long silence. Diego relit his joint.

"I am sorry, my friend," Thomas said. "But such is life."

Either the line cut out or Thomas hung up. Diego toked, held the burn.

A fourteen-year-old boy ran up to the building and addressed Diego through the open window. He wore a T-shirt tied around his head, draped down over his neck foreign-legion style.

Diego instinctively lowered the joint to his side so that the boy wouldn't see it, but then he gazed about the ruin of the office and raised it in offering instead. The boy shook his head and Diego shrugged. Desperate times call for desperate measures.

"Pablo left," the boy said.

"What do you mean, he left?" Diego's words were clouded with smoke.

"He left. As in, hopped a fishing boat to the mainland. Like everyone else."

Diego cursed under his breath. "Who do we have in Protección?"

"Pablo *was* Protección. There's no one left. Except you."

"There must be. What about the other departments? Plantas y Invertebrados?" The boy continued shaking his head. "Bio Mar? Proyecto Isabela?"

"Look around, Señor Rodriguez. The Station is empty. Even those earthquake guys who took over the Bio Mar building are gone. The fat guy left yesterday morning with his wife, took the new computer with him." The boy scratched his hair behind his ear. He was an odd-looking child, with a round, squat head perched precariously atop a slender neck. The T-shirt tied around his head only served to accent its width all the more. "Just the locals are left. And you."

"I'm not a local?"

The boy laughed. "The closest you can get, I suppose."

Diego took another toke. He mashed his tongue up against his teeth. It felt large and unwieldy. He stubbed out the joint, vowing to quit. "So what's the bad news, Ramoncito?"

"How do you know there's bad news?"

"Because you're only around when there's bad news. You're like a vulture. Or the paparazzi."

"Paparazzi?"

"Never mind. Tell me. Not more nonsense tales from Sangre, I hope."

"There's no one there to tell tales anymore. Just my parents." The boy paused, and Diego braced himself for bad news. "Carlos just got back from Floreana, and he said he saw the Menendez family loading up on an oil tanker headed for Manta."

"Goddamnit, I hope they killed the livestock."

Ramoncito shook his head. "Pigs. Loose everywhere."

"¡Chucha madre!" Diego sprang to his feet. "They'll go after my turtles."

For seven years, Diego had worked tirelessly to revive the dwindling Pacific green turtle population. The process had been slow; he first had to wait for the turtles to mate in captivity so that he could incubate the eggs indoors, safe from the devastating UV rays that so easily compromise the integrity of the shells; then he'd nurtured the hatchlings, keeping them in darkened boxes for the first hours of their lives to simulate nest conditions. He'd moved them to rearing pens and indoor pools as they grew, waiting for their shells to harden sufficiently to withstand the onslaught of radiation they'd meet back in the wild, and giving them time to reach sexual maturity. Only last May he'd released them off the shores of Floreana, eagerly anticipating their return to their nesting grounds at Cormorant Point.

Diego ran his hand back and forth across the front of his slacks. "If this nesting period doesn't yield offspring . . . if those pigs get out there . . . we've got to . . . I'm going to . . ." Pulling another joint from his pocket, he lit it with a soggy match. He paced, stepping carefully over the debris on the floor, before returning to his seat on the couch. He twirled a pen around his finger and tapped it against the table, sometimes holding it against the wood. Tap tap hold tap. Tap tap hold. Hold tap hold tap. Hold tap hold.

Ramoncito laughed. "Did you just spell 'fuck'?"

"Huh? I don't . . . yes, I suppose I did. How do you . . . ?"

"Maybe I listen to your lessons better than you think."

Diego held the pen against his full lips, leaning back on the couch. Accustomed to his moods, Ramoncito watched him, waiting for him to return from his thoughts.

Before the Initial Event, Floreana, like most of the other islands in the archipelago, had a few inhabitants. As it became clear that the aftershocks would be intense and unremitting, more and more settlers had elected to move to the mainland rather than try their lot on volcanic islands caught over a hot spot near the intersection of three tectonic plates. For the most part, the exoduses had been panicked, illadvised ventures. A few spots would open up on a fishing boat, or an oil tanker would pass nearby, and families would pack the belongings of a lifetime in a frenzied twenty minutes and crowd expectantly onto docks and into *pangas*. Parents kissing children goodbye, husbands embracing wives. And when families were fortunate enough to find space together, their houses and farms were left as they were—ket-

tles on stoves, doors banging in the breeze, goats and pigs
nosing their way out of pens.

If the Menendez family had left a herd of pigs behind on
Floreana, given the absence of indigenous predators, the
population growth would be astounding. A dozen or so feral
animals could quickly grow to hundreds. The island of San-
tiago was already a lost cause—over 100,000 feral goats had
turned it into a virtual wasteland; having exhausted the native vegetation, the goats had outlived their food sources and
were dropping of starvation in tremendous numbers. Diego
had sailed past the island en route to a survey on Pinta last
month, and the stench from the goat carcasses reached him
almost a kilometer offshore. He was determined not to let
Floreana meet a similar fate.

Since arriving in Galápagos to conduct research for his
masterado, Diego had developed an intense, almost obses-
sive commitment to the islands. They embodied the very
essence of life, of selection and design. Each island to Diego
was a wonder of ecological balance, a monument to the ability of species to persist, endure, adapt, and even thrive. The
fragility of the islands was so extreme as to be frightening;
an island's entire ecology could be irreversibly altered by
the arrival of a single ant, or one wasp hitchhiking in a bait
bucket on the deck of a boat. The examples were endless: six
wild dogs had attacked a colony of Isabela land iguanas in
June, leaving over four hundred bodies to rot; black rats that
had stolen rides to the islands in the bellies of ships had
quickly outcompeted endemic rice rats, causing their extinction on four islands; quinine trees cut reddish swathes into
Scalesia forests on the Santa Cruz highlands; *lantana ca-
mara* shrubs metastasized through the nesting areas of the
dark-rumpled petrel on Floreana, choking the birds there out
of existence. Changes borne of carelessness, of expediency,
of shortsightedness. To oppose them, Diego had his scientific training, an extensive background in ecology, herpetol-
ogy, and the eradication of introduced species. He had the
rapidly diminishing staff and resources of the Darwin Sta-

tion. He had determination, stubbornness, an uncompromising commitment to the life of the islands. And he had one carton of .22s.

Diego flicked the joint on the floor and rose, grabbing the ammo.

Ramoncito regarded Diego suspiciously. "What are you doing?"

Diego unearthed a rifle from beneath a pane of crumbled Sheetrock and rested it against his shoulder. "Looks like I just added animal control officer to my list of jobs." He wedged the carton of bullets into his pocket and headed out. When he slammed the door behind him, it left the hinges and continued right into his office.

Chapter 11   The creature drew herself to her full nine feet, rearing up on her hind legs. Pigmented a leafy green and dappled with dusty brown highlights, she picked up the hues of the *Scalesia* forest, blending with the crisscross shadows of the branches.

She was segmented into three major parts: a head with antennae, a thorax, and a long, full abdomen heavy with eggs. Her brown forewings, the tegmina, were leathery, covering and protecting her delicate underwings.

The creature was for the most part slender. Her abdomen and wings, which made up most of the length of her body, ran parallel to the ground. When she raised her head, her thorax swooped upward from her abdomen like the torso of a centaur, giving her a remarkably human erectness and orientation. Her abdomen, normally the breadth of two oil drums, was swollen even wider with her eggs, striking a contrast with her lean muscular thorax and four spindly rear limbs. A series of holes ran along her abdomen on each side, spiracles through which she drew air.

Her enormous raptorial forelegs protruded from the top of

her thorax, just beneath her head, and they were usually held close to her body. The insides of these legs were furnished with sharp spines, those on the femurs angled in the opposite direction from those on the tibias so that they'd snap shut on prey like a bear trap. At the end of both tibiae were two curved hooks that served to rake her prey to her.

Rotating her head nearly 180 degrees to face behind her, she tried to detect something in the rustling bushes. She twisted her thorax and it bent easily, pivoting her jagged front legs. Her head was shaped like an inverted triangle, with her eyes forming the top corners and her mouth the apex. Two long, thin antennae protruded from her head between her eyes like wayward wisps of hair. She cocked her head to one side, her antennae straightening to pick up odors and subtle vibrations in the air.

A male hesitantly emerged, following her through the thick brush. Because of her compound eyes, the female could see several directions at once, but she focused on the male's approach, watching him like a mosaic in the many facets of her eyes.

Significantly smaller than the female, the male regarded her warily, his large eyes protruding like bulbous growths from the top of his obcordate head. One of his hind legs was slightly smaller than the others, having regenerated after being lost in a molt. His antennae bobbed as his sharp mouth-parts quivered with curiosity.

He fixed the female in a gaze, but she broke eye contact and moved slowly away, weighed down with her unfertilized eggs. In a gait that was at once halting and graceful, the male stalked her, drawn by the sexual pheromone she excreted from two shiny protuberances near the tip of her abdomen. Occasionally, she turned her head on her elongated neck, taking note of his progress.

After about an hour of this strange and delicate ritual, the male spread his wings and curled his abdomen to attract her attention, but she turned and kept moving away. He pursued her again, launching into an even more rigorous sequence of abdomen movements. His folded wings rubbed against his cuticle, the hard exoskeleton, producing a high-frequency courtship song.

She slowed. Gathering his courage, the male approached her, drawing near as if to smell her before fading back. Extending her forelegs, the female responded with a few pumps of her abdomen. The male watched her against the backdrop of the trees, cutting back and forth before her with terse motions. She spread her raptorial legs in front of her, as if offering an embrace. He took a few tentative steps forward and she stroked his front legs. Finally, in a quick burst, he mounted her.

His legs were a flurry of movement around her as he bent the end of his abdomen in a sinuous motion to explore her genital area. He lowered his head, distracting her by rattling her antennae with his own. Twisting his abdomen to one side, he joined the tips of their bodies and began to copulate. She stayed still for a few moments as he labored, then calmly turned and bit into the armor covering the back of his neck.

As she chewed through his head, the male convulsed, continuing to pass sperm cells from his body to hers. With steady palpitations, she gnawed her way down through his neck and into his prothorax, contorting herself so that she could strip tissue from him as his genitalia continued to pulse away.

The sperm cells safely deposited in the spermatheca in her abdomen, the female wriggled forward, shedding the male's body like an unwelcome piece of clothing. On the ground beside her lay his head, the antennae still twitching.

Though his main nerve ganglia were severed, the headless male stumbled forward, spreading his wings in a futile attempt to fly. With a lightning flash, she snapped her raptorial legs around him. The body trembled in her grasp.

She bit into his choicest abdominal segment and pulled his body apart with a moist pop. His corpse, skewered on her spines from both sides, would serve to nourish the lives taking shape inside her. She tore off chunks of his abdomen, strips of tissue dangling from her mandibles. When she finished, she began the elaborate process of cleaning herself.

Her body was functioning at a rate much quicker than that for which her instincts were programmed. Though she had just mated, her eggs would be ready to be laid by nightfall.

The creature drew her front legs together, folding them like a jackknife. They curved up under her chin, positioned in an attitude of prayer.

She swayed, and she waited.

Chapter 12   As Cameron left the hotel with Rex and Tank, she noticed the man with gold chains who had harassed Szabla earlier. He seemed to recognize her despite her civilian clothes. A sat phone raised to his ear, he blew her a kiss before ducking into an alleyway.

Rex led the way north a few blocks on Calle Chile. Along the way, shoe shiners called out from the pavement, smiling through crooked teeth and pointing to Tank and Cameron's scuffed jungle boots. A man stepped out from a shop across the street and scooped water from a bucket onto the sidewalk, using a detergent bottle with the top cut off. Dust mingled with the water, running off the fractured curb into the street.

"It's amazing, isn't it?" Rex said. "The resilience of these people. They're used to having no control over anything." He started to sit on a bench to get his shoes shined by an old man with no front teeth, but Cameron grabbed his sleeve and kept him moving.

"Getting your shoes stroked isn't the mission today," Cameron said.

A boy followed them with a shoe shine box, chattering away, tugging at Tank's pant leg and pointing to his boots.

Cameron had a hard time keeping up with the Spanish; it was a more rustic form than she had studied, the consonants blurring together.

"If you didn't want a shoe shine," Rex said, "you should've worn sneakers."

On the corner, Otavalo Indians were still setting up for the day, stuffing T-shirts into metal racks bolted into the walls and scattering trinkets carved from Tagua nuts on blankets on the ground. Cameron found a street sign cemented into the wall of the corner building: *Avenida 9 de Octubre*. A number of American fast-food joints crowded the block. One franchise building had crumbled into the street, but the rubble had been bulldozed to one side to allow traffic to pass. Fragments of the red and white sign lay on top of the mound. One of Colonel Sanders's eyes was missing.

They waited for a break in the traffic, then sprinted across the street. The banged-up cars driving by or broken down roadside were built of mixed and matched parts, some of them tricked out with familiar emblems and gold steering wheels. A bus shuddered to a stop in front of them and a scrawny driver hopped out, removed his shirt, and crawled underneath with a wrench. They cut one street over and kept heading west. Rex bowed to a group of uniformed school-girls, removing his Panama hat, and they giggled and called out greetings in bad English.

A wide band of sweat darkened the lower half of Tank's shirt. Stopping on a corner, he pulled a tube of sunblock from his back pocket and smeared lotion liberally across his wide cheeks, which were already beginning to redden. Cameron felt her pants clinging to her legs. An orange electronic billboard flashed nearby: *Minutos para Quemarse—3:40*. She took the tube from Tank.

Cameron flashed ID at the UN cordon, and they headed into a dismal neighborhood. The street was bare and cracked, lined with deserted warehouses. Here the fallen buildings were left as they were, no construction crews in evidence. A man pissed against a wall, and a passing woman and child paid him no mind, stepping over the rivulet of urine on the sidewalk. Cameron kept in the lead.

After a few more blocks, Rex halted outside a brown box of a two-story building dotted with graying, cracked windows. A large section of asphalt had tilted up, leaving a two-foot lip in the middle of the sidewalk, and the building had settled unevenly across the hump. Rex rang the doorbell beneath a placard that read: *Dr. Juan Ramirez.*

Above their heads, a security camera rotated down so it was pointed at them. Then the door swung open, revealing a man with a hoop dangling from his nose, like a bull's ring. What was supposed to be a dragon peered out from his biceps, but it looked more like an obese lizard. He regarded Tank suspiciously, then spoke in rough-accented English. "What do you want?"

"Dr. Ramirez?" Cameron asked.

"That's not him," Rex said.

"No, I'm not el doctor. I just come to shut off la electricidad. He leave to wander around." He made a sweeping gesture with his arm, indicating the surrounding neighborhood.

"Well, it's extremely important that we find him tod—" The door slammed shut in Rex's face. He turned to Cameron. "O-*kay*. Now what?"

"What are our choices? We search for him. You know what he looks like, right?"

"Yes," Rex said, regarding the shady neighborhood around them tentatively.

"We'll sweep the area block by block, checking the bars and parks."

They tediously searched the neighborhood, sticking together, walking up and down the decrepit streets, peering at the faces of passing men. Cameron called in to Derek on her transmitter, updating him on the situation and obtaining clearance to return late.

They passed a junk heap and a burning car. Up ahead,

three shirtless men, their skin baked dark brown, were sitting on an overturned bathtub, throwing beer bottles at a wounded street dog. The dog lay on its side across the street, bleeding from a gash in its neck. Cameron noticed the dog's broken back leg, bent at a ninety-degree angle midway up the femur. She quickly fought away her anger.

"Here's where you earn your keep," Rex said, stepping between Cameron and Tank as they headed toward the men. The men, busy tormenting the dog, ignored them.

"¡Oye, perro callegero!" one of the men cried, hurling a brick at it. The brick shattered on the ground near the dog's head, sending splinters across its face. The dog struggled to move away, whimpering.

Tank clenched his jaw, his hands tightening into fists. Noticing the change in his demeanor, Cameron placed a hand on his back, moving him forward. "Not now," she said. "This isn't on our list of concerns."

The men were digging in the rubble for more bricks to throw. Cameron glanced nervously at Tank. She could see his arms were flexed even through his shirt. Rex had also taken note of Tank's growing anger. He fiddled nervously with his Panama, rubbing the rim with his thumbs.

As they passed the three men, Tank turned in time to see another brick flying at the dog. It struck the dog in its stomach, and it let loose with a series of pained yelps, unable to crawl away. Tank broke from Cameron and Rex and faced the men. Cameron grabbed his shoulder, but he shook her loose.

"What are you doing?" Rex yelled after him.

The men turned to face Tank, smacking their hands together to rid them of dust. One of them pulled a makeshift blade from the back of his trousers. When Tank was about fifteen yards away from the men, Cameron caught up to him, blocking him with her body.

The men howled with laughter, doubling over, clearly amused by the sight of an enormous man being restrained by a woman. One of the men imitated Cameron, standing with his hands on his hips and adding in high-pitched nagging for good measure.

Tank glared at Cameron, the first time he'd ever looked at her angrily. Anyone else he might have struck. "You're not gonna let this go, are you?" she said, her voice eerily calm.

Tank moved to step around her. Cameron pulled her Sig Sauer from the band of her pants and he stopped dead in his tracks.

She raised the pistol at the dog, took careful aim, and delivered a bullet to its skull. The crack of the gunshot echoed up the empty street. The dog stopped whimpering. The men were silent.

"This is *not* our objective," Cameron said, her voice tight. She turned, grabbed Rex around one biceps, and proceeded up the street.

"SOMEONE'S GOTTA shut that baby up," Savage muttered. He lay on his back on the bed, playing with his knife, the hefty Death Wind. With a formidable six-inch blade of D2 steel and three-sixteenths-inch stock, it was an impressive killing tool. But it was also beautiful, at least to him. Eight ounces, an eleven-inch stretch from butt to tip. Black Micarta handle, tapered tang, no teeth to detract from the line of its edge. It was smooth on the way in, sliding through flesh like water. Of all his weapons, the Death Wind was his favorite. There was a rawness to killing with a knife, something lost in the pull of a trigger. The ultimate stealth tool. He'd even anodized the blade so it wouldn't glint.

Savage sheathed the knife and glanced over at the others. Derek traced the lines of discoloration on the glass, his forehead pressed to the window. Justin looked at Derek, then shot Szabla a look, his eyebrows drawn together in concern. She leaned back against one of the twin beds, kicking her legs out in front of her, and shrugged. Tucker sat Indian-style on the carpet, pretending he wasn't eyeing the minibar.

Savage tuned out the baby next door, who squealed on like a stuck pig. Five high-demand shooters holed up in a hotel on a field trip—the room reeked of bad mood. Boredom and restlessness usually led to trouble when there were Navy SEALs involved.

The baby finally quieted, and Savage could make out the mother's cooing voice.

Tucker grabbed the ashtray from the night stand and arranged two books of matches in it to form a miniature pyre. He moved back to his former position, sitting cross-legged on the carpet, and using his thumb, flicked matches at the ashtray. The first two missed and burned out on the cheap carpet, but the third hit and the ashtray ignited, sending up a three-inch flame that flared briefly before dying. Justin cleared the ashtray unceremoniously, like a father taking an unsafe toy away from his child.

"Explosives," Szabla said. "The game the whole family can play."

"I thought that was incest," Justin said.

Tucker pulled another matchbook out of his sleeve. With a snap of his fingers, he spun the book around and laid a single match across the friction strip. Flicking his thumb, he lit the match, holding the flame before his eyes. He watched its familiar dance. Probably lost in thoughts of spoons and needles, C4 and trip wires.

Savage knew the type well—loved having their hands in the plastics, being able to assemble what they could from wires and det cord and boosters. It was like assembling death. Like opening up Pandora's box and tinkering around inside. They got off on it all—the rigging, the detonating, the blasts so bright you'd think you saw the eyes of God.

"You always been a breacher?" Savage asked.

Tucker nodded slightly, his eyes on the small flame. "Started when I was twelve, you could say. Firecrackers in

mailboxes, bottle rockets in pipes, cherry bombs down toi-
lets. Useful skills growing up in and out of boys' homes." He
whisked a finger through the flame and back, then licked the
black residue. "First night in my third home, an 'older
brother' beat me unconscious with a sockful of quarters. Next
day, I rigged his shoe, blew off half his big toe." His smile
sprang up quick and goofy. "No one fucked with me after."

Derek slid his fingers down the pane to the sill, streaking
the glass. Still spaced out.

"You all a remnant of a platoon?" Savage asked.

Szabla nodded. "Mostly. Me, Cam, Derek, and Tucker
were platoon buddies in THREE off and on for four, five
years. Justin and I have buddied before, but he and Tank
came up mostly on Team EIGHT. Dick for action, but pretty
Danish girls." She jerked her head in Justin's direction.
"Ain't that right, sunshine?"

"Beats desert and diaperheads."

"What does? Shit detail teaching Norwegians how to rig
C4?" She snorted. "At least we got world ops, not endless
scrimmaging."

The match burned down to Tucker's fingers, and Tucker
threw it on the floor. He stuck a finger in his mouth, then
pressed it on the glowing match head. It sizzled out, sticking
to his finger when he raised it.

Savage pulled out a pack of cigarettes from one of his
front pockets.

"You mind?" Tucker asked, gesturing to the pack with his
eyes.

"No," Savage replied. "Not at all." He lit the cigarette and
enjoyed a long drag, shooting the smoke out the side of his
mouth. "Why don't you go back to watching that minibar,
son? You're outta matches."

"Fuckin' prick," Tucker muttered, bending over to tighten
the laces on his boots.

Savage leaned up a bit from his recline on the bed. "What
did you say?"

"I said, 'Fucking prick,' " Tucker answered, enunciating clearly. "Park your attitude somewhere else. Things have changed just a touch since Vietnam."

Savage laughed, then his eyes went cold. "What the fuck do you know about Vietnam?"

"Not much," Szabla said. "Heard it was some fucked-up shit."

"You heard right," Savage said. He grinned, the glint in his eyes matching the cherry of the cigarette. He glanced at Szabla. "How old are you, princess?"

"Twenty-six."

Savage shook his head, making a humming noise. "We were out of there before you were even born."

"You're old," Tucker said.

"I'm experienced."

Justin glanced over at Derek, as if unsure of what to make of him. He looked back at the others. "Look, why don't we—"

"Experienced at what?" Tucker snarled. "Slaughtering villagers? Raping women?"

"What are you, boy? A fuckin' dove?"

"No, I was just trained with a military code of ethics. Some of the shit you guys pulled . . ." Tucker's voice trailed off with disgust.

Savage nodded calmly. "I seen some things," he said, as if agreeing. He raised his cigarette, lodged in the fork of his fingers, and pointed it at the track marks on Tucker's arms. "Bet you have, too."

Tucker sprang to his feet, but Savage leaned forward quickly on the bed, yanking his knife from his ankle sheath and setting his feet on the ground. He flipped the knife once, caught it by the handle, and smiled. Tucker stared at him a while then looked down, almost shyly, and walked out of the room. Over at the window, Derek still didn't move.

"You lay the fuck off," Justin said to Savage.

"You know what they say." Savage leaned back on the ripped pillow. "If you play with fire . . ."

Justin stood and began to change into civies. "We need to get the fuck out of here."

"Where the hell are we gonna eat?" Szabla said. "Anyone speak Spanish?"

"I only know three words," Savage said. "Casa de putas."

"What's that mean?"

Savage smiled. "Look it up."

Justin crossed to Derek and laid a hand on his shoulder. "We're gonna grab Tucker and find somewhere to eat," he said.

Derek turned slowly from the window, his eyes blank. "I'll take weapons watch." He stood and stepped out onto the small balcony, pulling the chair with him.

"Any time you want us back?" Justin asked. "LT?"

Szabla leaned forward, lowering her voice as she spoke to Savage. "Is it true?" she asked. "Did you really rape women there?" Her face was calm, but her eyes were excited.

Savage shrugged, enjoying the web of intrigue that he'd spun around himself. The new breed of soldier, raised with ethics books and dry-cleaned LTs, always expressed a certain disgust at anyone involved in the Vietnam mess. It had angered him at first, but he'd come to realize that the disgust was a form of respect. They knew he'd seen things that they'd never see, not in the push-button, long-range sniper world they lived in now. They knew he'd done things.

He sucked hard on the butt. "I was eighteen," he said. "It got lonely."

Szabla leaned back against the bed. She ran one of her hands up the curve of her arm, gripping her biceps. Justin had overheard Savage's remark. "You sick bastard," he muttered. "Rape, that's admirable."

Savage cocked his head, looking into Justin's handsome blue eyes. "Who ever told you war was admirable?"

* * *

THE SUNLIGHT was dwindling, the brief equatorial dusk already under way. Tank and Cameron flanked Rex. Cameron was grateful to Rex for quietly letting the matter of the dog go. Frustration was setting in—they were beginning to realize just how difficult it was to locate one man in this neighborhood of dark streets and broken buildings. If they didn't find Juan to alert him of the take-off time tomorrow, Rex's survey would be compromised.

Cameron shooed away beggars as they approached, and watched for eyes darting to her boots so that she could thwart advancing shoe shiners. A woman walked by peddling newspapers—*El Comercio*'s headline announcing another 120 dead in a Quito landslide.

They stopped at a vehicle underpass before Julian Coronel, a thoroughfare with four lanes of quickly moving traffic. Across Coronel, an enormous white wall ran in both directions for as far as Cameron could see, broken only by large arches with locked metal gates. Ahead and to the left stretched a white pedestrian bridge, which Rex indicated with a gesture. "Might as well try there."

Underneath the bridge, colorful advertisements for ice cream were peeling from the concrete in strips. One strip ran through the smiling face of a light-skinned woman.

Steering wide of a group of homeless men, they climbed the pedestrian bridge and walked over the busy thoroughfare. When they got halfway across, the land on the far side of the wall became visible, and Cameron gasped out loud. It was perhaps the most breathtaking sight she had ever seen. Against the backdrop of several small hills, white marble gravestones, tombs, and mausoleums stretched up into the air, forming what appeared to be a miniature city. Some of the tombs were so extravagant that they resembled residential buildings with distinct floors, each one featuring gates for the ornate caskets. A few others were domed, fronted with immense tinted-glass doors with polished metal handles. Paved walkways ran between the tombs, some of them as wide as small streets. Shrines, statues, and trees gave the cemetery a jagged skyline. Only a couple gravestones had fallen over; for the most part, the cemetery had been resistant to the tremors. It almost glowed in the darkening air, a small forest of white stone.

Even Tank stopped dead in his tracks.

"They call this 'La Ciudad Blanca,' " Rex said. "The White City." He grinned. "For obvious reasons."

Rex walked down the far set of stairs, descending down into the cemetery. It was almost nightfall, and Cameron glanced ahead at the rows of tombs, the myriad hiding places for muggers and thieves. Tank felt for the pistol in the back of his pants, so Cameron knew he was thinking the same thing.

"This is the history of Ecuador," Rex said. "Every important name, every important date, is here. Buried, gilded, commemorated."

As they walked through the grounds, Cameron noticed the family names carved into the white marble. Palm trees lined a slender, marble-paved lane, the trunks painted white. The silhouette of a man appeared in the middle of the path. He was genuflecting, staring up at the humbler monuments dotting the dark hillside.

Rex drew closer. "Juan?"

The man rose and threw his arms wide in greeting. He was an ugly man, with wide, uneven features, his cheeks deeply pocked. His skin was dark, his arms covered with hair. "Dr. Williams," he said in heavily accented English. "You are here in one piece, no?" He nodded to Cameron and Tank. "And the soldiers. A pleasure to meet you. Thank you for your offer to escort us."

"Offer?" Tank said, but Cameron elbowed him in the ribs.

"You might have waited at the lab," Rex said. "We've spent hours searching for you."

"I am sorry. It is hard for me to be in the lab now, you see." Juan fiddled with his wedding ring nervously, rotating the gold band around his thick knuckle. Despite his warmth, he exuded a gentle sadness. "I do not know how much longer it will exist. There is no funding. I've had to let go my assistants. Many of the experiments will not be finished. And the islands are in bad shape, my friends. I was doing a longitudinal study, tracking a population of masked boobies on Española . . ." He shook his head. "But with the feral goats taking over the past few years . . ."

"They're bad?" Cameron asked. "The goats?"

"Animals aren't good or bad. They're just sometimes in the wrong place. If they don't belong, they can threaten the entire ecosystem. Galápagos are especially fragile. Many of the animals evolved on the islands with no enemies, so they have no way to contend with predators if they arrive. And man has brought many predators, most of them seemingly benign, protected by their very . . . how do you say? . . . banality. Puppies and kittens, hamsters . . . all killers. All capable of wiping out whole populations of endemic species. Like the goats on Española with my masked boobies . . . eating the eggs, the chicks . . ." He sighed heavily. "All dead. I received a report from a friend at the Darwin Station telling me not to bother coming back." He tapped his hand against the corner of a nearby gravestone, his wedding band making a soft clicking noise. "There's so much we've lost." He looked away, his eyes growing moist.

Tank dug something out of his teeth with a finger.

"We really should get back," Rex said.

Cameron reached out and touched Juan gently on the sleeve. "I'm sorry," she said.

Juan's smile was a faint, dying thing. He looked back up at the hillside. "Those graves up there, those are the graves of the poor." Evidently, the families of the dead buried on the hills couldn't afford marble; the gravesites were decorated with bright fabrics and flowers. A number of these plots were recent additions, with dark, freshly turned soil. "So much death, so quickly."

"Let's be honest," Rex said. "This is nothing new. Life has always been cheap here. Children succumbing to preventable diseases, poisonous snakes in the Oriente, buses colliding on windy pueblo roads. Death happens here."

Juan shook his head, studying the fresh graves in the hills. "Not like this."

A church bell tolled somewhere in the distance, and Rex glanced down at his watch. "I need to get back and check in with Donald." He shoved a slip of paper with the flight time and survey procedures into Juan's hand. "See you tomorrow."

Juan nodded and walked off a short ways, sitting on the ledge of a particularly broad mausoleum. Cameron found Rex's abruptness in the face of Juan's grief to be offensive. "Tank'll escort you back," she said. "I'll be along in a minute."

Tank followed Rex into the darkness. Cameron walked over and pulled herself up on the ledge beside Juan. The echo of the church bells lingered in the darkness. The air was thick, humid, foreign. It smelled sharply of bark, burning wood, and stale food.

"I come here often at night," Juan said softly.

Cameron gave him the silence, listening to the rush of cars beyond the high cemetery wall.

Juan pulled off his wedding band and set it on his knee. He regarded it for a few moments. "I lost my wife," he finally said. "And my baby girl. I was teaching at *Universidad* when the apartment building collapsed. That was . . . that was almost three years ago, but still I feel it sharply on quiet nights like this." He picked up the ring, tilted it so that he could catch the blur of his reflection in the gold, then slid it back on his finger.

When she realized that he was crying, Cameron wasn't sure what to do. She popped a stick of gum in her mouth and worked it over, waiting uncomfortably through the silence. Juan finally wiped his cheeks and raised his head.

"I am sorry. You do not need this. There's just something in your eyes, some softness that lets me talk where I haven't before. That's unusual for Americans. They often come down here and see our ways and the violence, and think us primitive." He shook his head. "Death is part of our culture. During the conquest, half our population was killed by disease, civil war. But no country can endure this kind of disruption, this kind of . . . " With a sweeping gesture, he indicated the cemetery before them. "Loss."

A man stumbled by, his head lowered, carrying an armful of flowers. When he passed Cameron and Juan, he paused and looked up at them. Cameron couldn't make out his face, because he was wearing a hat pulled low over his eyes. "No, gracias," she said, waving him away.

The man spoke back to her in a soft but angry voice. He gestured at her several times, and she felt for the pistol, just to make sure it was still there.

"What did he say?" she asked Juan when the man finished speaking.

Juan slid off the ledge onto his feet. "He asked that we get off his family's mausoleum, that he can lay the flowers there for them."

He nodded an apology at the man and headed back toward the footbridge.

Chapter 13 Rex leaned over the hotel phone as Tank stretched out on the bed. He had to dial three times before the call went through. Donald picked up on the first ring. "How is it?"

"Lovely as always," Rex said. "Puts Paris to shame."

"Some interesting news. Remember that seawater that Frank sent back?"

"Of course." Rex pulled off his shirt and turned so that he could see his back in the mirror. He pressed his hand to the back of his neck, and the white imprint of his fingers lingered a few moments before fading.

"I finally got it under a microscope. The sample from Sangre de Dios was highly unusual. Most of the plankton were dead. Clumped together. Mostly unicellular phyto-plankton—dinoflagellates were most prevalent, but a lot of them I didn't recognize."

"Really?" Rex said. "Species *you* didn't recognize?"

"My guess is that they were nonviable mutations. Re-member, plankton are extraordinarily sensitive to UV-B."

"Yes," Rex said, pulling a *Natural History* magazine from his bag and perusing the back cover, "but they live at depths that screen out most radiation."

"Ah," Donald said. "But this was a surface sample. So my thought was, seismically motivated shifting currents pushed them upward, and their composition was altered by UV ex-posure. But the range of the mutations was staggering—they couldn't be based on radiation alone."

"So?" The phone line cut out. Rex looked over at his sat phone, still charging at the outlet, cursed, and dialed again. This time, the call went through on the first try.

"So," Donald said, picking up right where they'd left off. "I did a gas chromatography mass spec to check for DDT, but that came back negative, so I isolated some dinoflagel-late DNA, and ran a gel."

Donald checked his watch. His linen shirt was creased and wrinkled across the front, dotted with sweat. He'd spent the entire morning in the lab. The work required a precision that had quickly become tedious. First, he'd centrifuged the water samples, placing them in a rapidly spinning test tube so that the denser dinoflagellates would settle at one end of the tube. Then, he'd made genomic preps to isolate the DNA strands, cut specific segments, and ran those segments through ethidium bromide-soaked agar to see how they'd settle. When they did, their banding patterns were visible under UV light, and ready to be compared to the control.

From past studies, Donald was familiar with the banding pattern of dinoflagellate DNA from around Galápagos; gen-erally it banded from three to five kilobases down to ten base pairs. The DNA from the island of Santa Cruz matched this banding pattern. However, the sample from Sangre de Dios was irregular, with several of the DNA segments remaining at the top of the agar, barely traveling downward.

When Rex heard the results, he sat down on the bed. "Holy shit," he said. "What are you thinking?"

"Those segments are swollen with something to be moving that slow," Donald said. "I'm guessing a virus got ahold of them, finding its way through the UV-weakened cell walls and inserting its own DNA into their structures."

Rex whistled. "Well, viruses are phenomenally bountiful in H_2O."

"That was my understanding. But this is well out of our field. I'd like you to take plenty of water samples on Sangre de Dios. In the meantime, I've sent the sample off to Everett at Fort Detrick."

"Samantha Everett?" Rex rubbed his forehead. "Are you sure that's such a good idea? I've heard she's a little . . . " The line cut out. "Unpredictable."

FORMER CHIEF of Viral Special Pathogens Branch at the Centers for Disease Control in Atlanta and current Chief of the Disease Assessment Division at the U.S. Army Medical Research Institute of Infectious Diseases at Fort Detrick, Maryland, Samantha Everett was decked out in a blue full-body space suit, complete with neoprene gloves taped to her sleeves. The droning air circulation unit inside the space suit was mesmerizing, forming a low-pitched symphony with the other sounds of the Biosafety Level Four lab—the constant one-way airflow, the blowers situated near the doors to ensure negative pressure, the HEPA filters working double-time overhead. To maintain her sanity, Samantha sang "Itsy Bitsy Spider" to herself, substituting her own lyrics where she forgot the words.

A short woman—five foot two in sneakers—Samantha had the slightly frazzled air of a mother of three. Having neglected the wash for the past month and a half, she'd shown up to work wearing her daughter's T-shirt featuring the five smiling faces of NVME's members. Fortunately, she also fit into her six-year-old son's shoes—green Velcro Adidas with asphalt marks on the white rubber outsoles—as she'd run from the house barefoot that morning only to realize it when she'd pulled up to base. She'd found the Adidas in the back of the minivan, buried in a mound of camping equipment from a trip into the Catoctins that, having been planned for two months and canceled three times, had almost come to fruition the prior weekend, only to be interrupted by the emergency at hand. A pair of wire-frame John Lennon–style glasses perched on her nose, the thin metal arms disappearing back into her curly brown hair.

Having little use for a husband, she'd adopted all three of her children over the past nine years. Earlier in her career, she couldn't have even considered being a mother. She'd been dispatched for months at a time on various projects— bleeding horses in rural Costa Rica for Venezuelan equine encephalitis, chasing Machupo virus up the eastern slope of the Andes, trekking through mosquito breeding grounds in the Nile Delta. But after her stint at CDC in Atlanta, she was given an offer to run DAD at USAMRIID, and she'd vowed to attempt some form of a domestic life. Being a mother, she'd found, had toughened her considerably more than being a major and running a division of testosterone-poisoned, military-sanctioned control freaks. But she liked Fort Detrick nonetheless, and the seasons in central Maryland.

The stark modern USAMRIID building looked as if it had been dropped into the middle of the base from orbit, so out of place did it look among the conservative, faded-brick buildings. Inside, the sleek, tiled floors and fluorescent lights countered the battleship-gray walls. All work with infectious agents was undertaken in one section, divided into four units, each of which was in turn split into four "hot suites." Each hot suite employed a constellation of blowers, vents, and pressure systems to ensure that airborne pathogens could not leak from the area. The filters killed any atomized biohazard before laboratory air was released to the outside. Everywhere in the building, the airflow was directed inward.

It was precisely this inflow of white noise that Samantha sought to combat with her singing. "The itsy bitsy spider . . ." Her voice, soft and high like a child's, activated the small microphone that allowed her to communicate with her lab technician, who wore a space suit similar to her own. ". . . contracted a new strain of aerosol-infectious Bolivian hemorrhagic fever . . ." She leaned forward over the cadaver. She'd already made a Y-shaped incision to open the chest and abdomen. Her arm throbbed slightly from the latest battery of inoculations; because of all the shots she received in her line of work, her deltoids were usually sore.

She gestured with her scalpel at the lab tech. "Retract the small bowel so I can get at the root of the mesentery." The abdominal cavity was always difficult because it was so full; with all the coils of bowel, there was less room for maneuvering. She reached down and poked at the fattened stomach, knowing from experience it would be filled with clotted, foul-smelling liquid. Unfortunately, the respirators did not screen out odors.

"Down came the virologist, and washed the virus out," she sang.

The lab tech leaned forward and secured the squishy bowel in his gloved, slightly unsteady hands. "Don't cut me," he said.

"Oh really?" Samantha replied. "Well, there go my plans for the week. I was hoping to watch the effects of the disease take hold in one of my colleagues."

Starting at the mesentery, she cut away excess tissue and muscle attachments so that she could pull out the organs. The procedure was crassly referred to as "the pluck." One "plucked" out first the thoracic organs, then the abdominal organs.

"Hemorrhaging around the gums, yellow sclera, bloody stool, ecchymoses, petechial hemorrhages, blood in the urine . . ." Samantha grasped the enlarged heart, pulling gently, and began singing again. "Out came the sun and dried up all the rain. . . ."

The tech nervously regarded the nearby formalin, ready to plunge his hand into the sterilizing agent at the slightest nick. But Samantha's hands were completely steady. She trimmed neatly around her assistant's fingers, humming the next bar from the children's song as she sliced through tissue. She stopped suddenly. "Aha! Look at this."

The pleural cavity was filled with fluid, and the lungs were scattered with hard patches of red. She took a sample, placing it in a small vial and screwing the lid on tightly before scrubbing the outside with a disinfectant.

"Condom," she said. Another lab tech stepped forward, holding open an unfurled, nonlubricated Trojan. They'd had to be slightly inventive with their equipment; the last shipment from the supplies company in San Diego hadn't arrived due to a train derailment outside Vegas. Samantha dropped the vial into the condom, and the assistant knotted the end of the latex, placing it into a nylon stocking and lowering it into a tank of liquid nitrogen. He hooked the end of the stocking on the lip of the tank, careful to keep his hands clear of the liquid, which was 195 degrees Celsius below zero.

Samantha turned back to the body. It was a gruesome specimen. A prominent Baltimore businessman had returned six days ago from Cochabamba, Bolivia, in his Gulfstream VII. Previous to his flight, he'd been febrile, with myalgias, weakness, and chills. Though the symptoms had quickly become gastrointestinal—he'd been beset with abdominal tenderness and diarrhea—he'd decided to fly anyway. After takeoff, the man had been stricken with vomiting, and spontaneous bleeding from his nose, gums, and the whites of his eyes. Johns Hopkins Hospital received warning while the plane was midair, the pilot calling ahead to have an ambulance waiting at the airport. The reports worsened as the plane approached Baltimore, and the Chief of Staff at Hopkins had reached Samantha at her campsite in the Catoctins. They'd agreed to have the plane diverted to a stretch of Highway 15 near Fort Detrick, so that the businessman, and his wife, pilot, and flight attendant, who were showing early symptoms, could be quarantined at Level Four.

Samantha had raced home to treat them, but the virus had reached high titers in the businessman's blood, and the coagulopathy had already been far advanced. The antiserums they stored in the banks that counteracted other forms of BHF were not working on this mutated strain, nor had ribavirin.

Samantha had taken fluid and tissue samples from the businessman while he was still living and inoculated cell cultures with them, allowing the virus to replicate until the cell cultures contained viral antigens. The pilot's and flight attendant's condition continued to deteriorate, but the wife had recovered from her fever on the second day, which meant she'd probably produced antibodies that had fought off the virus. Sure enough, her serum showed the presence of immunoglobulin G antibodies, indicating an older infection from which she'd previously recovered. The IgG had enabled her body to combat her reexposure to the virus.

Samantha drew blood from her to isolate these antibodies, then spun down the blood in a centrifuge to separate the antiserum. The antiserum was added to the inoculated cell cultures, then washed down to remove everything that didn't specifically bind to the antigen. Next, she'd added specially tagged antibodies that allowed her to see, under ultraviolet light, that the antiserum had indeed bound to the antigen, strongly indicating that the antibodies in the wife's blood were manufactured to combat this specific virus.

Samantha had managed to isolate enough of the antibodies to fight off the virus in six of seven rats she'd infected. Each of the surviving rats had replicated the antibodies, which she'd been able to extract from them, isolate in larger amounts, and, using advanced genetic manufacturing techniques, replicate on an even larger scale.

Samantha was now awaiting clearance to passively immu-
nize the pilot and flight attendant with the experimental antiserum. Top brass from PHS and the FDA were meeting next
door, deciding whether or not to approve the experimental
plan of treatment. If the patients had to wait for the antiserum to clear the usual PHS paperwork labyrinth, they
would surely die within the week.

Samantha forced herself to concentrate on the task at
hand—performing a full autopsy on the body of the businessman, who had died that morning. She tried not to think
about the decision being made next door that would determine the fates of two people. The body on the autopsy table
was grotesque. Old, fading lesions peppered the armpits,
and the gums were a bloody, suppurating mess. The mouth
was caked with blood.

Samantha dug into the open cavity with renewed vigor.
She continued to sing; her lab tech continued to sweat.

"So the itsy bitsy spider climbed up the spout again. . . ."

A woman in a white lab coat tapped on one of the windows. "Sammy!" she called out.

Samantha couldn't make out what the woman was saying,
so she set down the autopsy instruments and shuffled to the
window, awkward in her space suit. "What!?"

The woman leaned forward and shouted something, but
Samantha couldn't hear over the hum of the air blowers. She
leaned forward until her hood was inches from the glass.
"What?" she mouthed.

The woman shook her head in exaggerated fashion.
"They voted no," she yelled, enunciating each word for
Samantha's benefit.

Samantha closed her eyes tightly. She tried to count to ten
to quell her rising temper, a device her youngest had learned
from his kindergarten teacher and in turn imparted to her,
but by the time she reached four, her mind was rife with images of the fever that was sure to befall the pilot and flight
attendant. The sweats, the shaking, dappled bruises taking

shape under the surface of the skin. Because of legal concerns, the PHS and FDA were going to send them to their graves, wrapped in red tape.

Samantha turned to the lab tech. "Take over," she said. She banged on the glass. "I'm scrubbing out."

THE UNIFORMED and suited men and women sat around a large conference table, sipping coffee and talking. A plate of Krispy Kremes sat untouched on a silver tray. Folders were stacked around the pitchers of water, and a single telephone sat at the end of the table, before an older woman in a gray Chanel reproduction. The others were just rising to leave when Samantha banged through the doors, a metal briefcase balanced on her hand like a cocktail tray.

She slammed the briefcase down on the table and opened it. Two syringes filled with liquid lay in the spongy bedding.

The older woman stood, her expression hardening. A rose blush colored her cheeks one shade short of absurd. "Samantha, we knew you'd be difficult about this, but we can't be expected to approve a treatment of this magnitude for humans based on animal experiments alone. There are precedents, legal complications. Maybe next week, we'll be able to get the results back from the autopsy and run some experiments. . . ." Her voice faded as Samantha unbuttoned and rolled up her shirt sleeve. "What are you . . ."

Holding the first syringe vertically before her, Samantha smiled sweetly. "Bolivian hemorrhagic fever," she said. "New strain." She bit the tip protector off the needle and spit it onto the floor.

Two women fell back into their chairs. "Jesus Christ," one of the men cried, covering his nose and mouth with his tie.

Samantha deftly ran the needle into her arm, sinking the plunger.

"Goddamnit," the older woman cried. "Where's her senior officer?"

Two people crept around the table, backs pressed to the walls, and fled the room.

Samantha raised the second syringe. "My antiserum," she said. She shot it into her arm, just below the mark the last shot had left.

The older woman's lips were quivering with anger. "Well, you've done it this time," she said. "This cowboy routine of yours is going to land you in a heap of trouble."

"Yippee kay yay," Samantha said.

The woman leaned over and hit a button on the phone. "Get her in the slammer."

THE SLAMMERS, run at Biosafety Level Four, were in the medical section, just beyond the hot suites. Two-room units with locks only on the outside, the slammers each had two beds. Crash doors led to small operating rooms; in the event of a medical emergency, doctors could enter the slammers in full space suits. The survivors of the Bolivia trip had been individually quarantined in three of the units since their arrival at Fort Detrick.

As the slammers' main function was to isolate and observe people who'd been exposed to hazardous agents, each featured an enormous window running the length of one wall. A cluster of technicians and virologists crowded around the Slammer Two window. Inside, Samantha sat on the bed, humming to herself.

One of the virologists, an overweight man with a bushy beard, clasped his hands and shook them in the air. "All right, Sammy!"

She stood and bowed, and went to the far wall and pretended to run against it, like a hamster on a wheel. The crowd outside cracked up. Then, she grabbed a coffee mug from the counter and ran it across the length of the window, as if drawing it across prison bars. More howls. Finally, the crowd began to dissipate, but not before her colleagues called out their good-byes.

Samantha sat on the bed and lowered her head into her hands, thinking of the week before her. She'd been instrumental in developing a new test that could detect early BHF-specific antibody response in twenty-four hours—a test she'd soon take. If it showed that the antibodies were present in her blood, they'd have to clear the antiserum for use on the pilot and flight attendant. Even so, they'd need to hold Samantha for at least a week to be certain that the antibodies had cleared the virus from her body. She felt fine so far, but it was way too early to tell anything. Placing the palm of her hand across her forehead, she closed her eyes. The antiserum would work; she was convinced her methods were sound.

She glanced down at her watch and shot to her feet when she noticed the date. December 25. She had three children and a nanny waiting for her at home by a half-decorated tree, and she wouldn't be out of the slammer until New Year's. A sudden rush of guilt flooded through her. They hadn't had time to unwrap gifts this morning, and she'd promised she'd be home before dinner. How could she do this to her children?

Crossing to the telephone on the counter, she asked the operator to patch her through to home.

KIERA ALMOST didn't hear the phone ringing over the blare of her stereo. She lay on her stomach sideways across her bed, flipping through *Cosmo Girl*, kicking her one leg lazily in the air behind her. Her skin was dark, betraying her Guatemalan heritage, and a chevron scar remained on her abdomen from the liver transplant she'd received as a five-year-old when she'd first entered the country nine years ago. Her walls were adorned with colorful posters: Timmy Mandalay sulking on a rocky shore; Daddy Trippilicious decked out in gangsta garb; the Ebola virus blown up to 10Kx magnification.

The song ended, and she heard the shrill ring of the phone.

She stood, hopped over to it, and answered, having first to unearth it from beneath a mound of clothing. "Yeah?" The expression on her face changed to one of weary irritation. She lowered the phone, pressing the mouthpiece to her shoulder.

"Mom's in the slammer again!" she shouted.

Chapter 14   The creature felt something moving within her; it was time. Turning her head, she scanned the dark forest for a suitably protected location. She rustled through the understory of the *Scalesia* forest, twigs whispering against the smooth hard shell of her cuticle. The ground dipped slightly, the blanket of trees following the contour of the slope.

Suddenly, the ground moaned and vibrated beneath her feet, but she did not rear up on her hind legs; she was accustomed to the sound. The lava tube that ran beneath the stretch of the forest was catching the wind and sucking it along its innards.

About 350 meters in length, four meters wide, and five meters high, the tube had been formed centuries ago when lava had spread quickly out of a volcano crater. The surface of the lava had cooled quickly and hardened, but the inner flow had continued to rush downhill. When the lava flow ceased, an empty tube had been left behind, ringed with a hardened crust. Additional lava flows over the years had buried the tube, except for the two ends, which broke through the forest floor like gaping mouths.

Her front legs hanging before her, the creature nosed her way through the ferns shielding the southern entrance of the lava tube. They fell back into place after she passed through, camouflaging the hole.

She all but filled the entrance, her antennae brushing the ceiling. Inside, the tube was cool and damp. Water dripped against the black lava floor, the sound amplified up and down the tunnel. A few thick *Scalesia* roots twisted into the cave at the entrance, running along its mouth. She moved forward, pulling her swollen abdomen to the base of the wall.

Though she was close to nine feet tall, the creature was not tremendously heavy; most of her height was in her long, spindly legs and neck. The significant length of her body made up most of her mass, but it too was light, enabling an efficiency of movement.

Grasping an outcropping of lava with the hooks of her forelegs, she tugged on it; it would hold her weight. Moving with quick halting motions and using the claws at the ends of her legs, the creature pulled herself up the wall until she was dangling upside down from the roof of the cave. She twisted her abdomen in tight circles, and a light frothy substance began to emerge from the appendages at the tip.

As she turned her abdomen in continuous spirals, she formed the ootheca, the translucent case for her eggs. Two antennae-like protrusions on the tip of her abdomen combed the froth as it emerged. Applying discreet doses of the white material, she built a structure five feet in width, enmeshed along the length of the thickest tree root. Then she began the laborious task of inserting her eggs inside the structure, each egg laid at the base of its individual chamber. The chambers would protect her offspring from predators and desiccation; they were bordered with pockets of insulating air and topped with one-way valves that would permit the fragile larvae to emerge without damaging themselves.

The creature labored with the unremitting energy of a machine, twisting through her arcane, instinctual dance. The chambers of the ootheca that were laid first began to harden. The female finally egested the last bit of froth, pinching it off neatly into a final chamber. There were eight individual chambers in the ootheca. Her abdomen swayed again, straining, but nothing more emerged.

Still upside down, she curled up, grooming excess froth from the tip of her abdomen with her mouth. If the froth hardened, it would prevent her from being able to excrete wastes, and she would die prematurely. Rolled in a complete circle, she looked like a huge green bud sprouting from the roof. She cleaned herself meticulously, her mouth worrying over her lower extremities. Finally, exhausted, she crawled back to the ground.

The creature pulled herself from the cave, breaking through the veil of ferns into the open air. A pair of smooth-billed anis lifted from a tree to her left, and her head pivoted automatically to watch them depart. They called to each other in distinctive whining whistles, as they faded into the foliage, black dots with streaming tails.

The creature moved forward, tired but oddly strengthened. She was hungry.

Chapter 15   Cameron was disappointed not to find her husband back in his room. She and Justin had done well maintaining a professional distance, but it was more difficult than she would have thought. Until now, she'd never realized how accustomed she was to small, affectionate exchanges—exchanges not overtly emotional but quietly attentive, like how he'd pull her shirt down in the back when it came untucked.

Tucker and Savage's room was empty, save Tucker's good-luck charm, a thermite grenade, which rested on top of the small minibar. Cameron peeled back the top pocket of her cammy pants, glancing at the digital face sewn inside—2107. The others had probably gone out for chow. She paged Szabla to ascertain everyone's location, then knocked on the door to Tank and Rex's room.

Tank stepped out into the hall. He looked at the ground as he sometimes did when he was around Cameron, as if schoolboy-nervous to look her in the eye. "Uh . . . Cam." He cleared his throat. "About the thing with the dog . . ." He scratched his hair above an ear.

"Apology accepted," she said.

He nodded a little, then raised a hand halfway to her face, as though he wanted to touch her. He withdrew his hand and gestured. "You have a, uh, a hair in your mouth."

She brushed the wisp of hair aside, hooking it behind an ear, and headed to her and Derek's room. At first, she thought it was empty, and she was angry that the weapons had been left unguarded, but then the door to the balcony banged in the breeze and she crossed and saw Derek sitting out there alone. There was no sound of the baby next door.

"Cam," he said without turning around.

"Yeah?" She pulled the mag from her Sig and tossed it in the cruise box.

Without looking at her, Derek pulled the key chain from around his neck and handed it to her. She unlocked the two padlocks on the weapons box and set her pistol next to Tank's on the foam. "I might need a little time alone tonight," he said when she handed him back the key. "Would you mind bunking in with Justin and Szabla? I figured you wouldn't mind sharing a bed, given he's your husband."

Cameron leaned against the door to the balcony. "Well, I don't . . . I don't know that that's appropriate. . . . Why don't—"

"I'm the OIC," he murmured. "I decide what's appropriate."

Cameron took a moment to digest the rebuff before speaking. "I paged Szabla. She said they're out at a restaurant down by the river. Savage took off somewhere." She paused, deciding how to phrase her next sentence. "I know everyone's antsy, but you gotta rein them in. We can't be scattered all over the city like this."

"I know," Derek said.

"Maybe I should go round them up."

He nodded slowly but still did not turn around. She

watched the back of his head for a moment, then reached out and set her hand on his shoulder. He did not seem to notice. She removed her hand, backed out of the room, and closed the door quietly behind her.

Derek sat trance-like after she left, gazing over the rooftops as the minutes smeared into one another. The streets within his view were empty. The construction crews would be back in the morning, hammering things together—streets, buildings, sidewalks—readying them for the next wave of destruction. The noise of a guitar being badly played carried to him, and occasional high-pitched voices and peals of laughter. The night never faded in these towns, these South American towns; it just eased into daylight.

He closed his eyes for a moment, felt the humidity on his cheeks, the tropical scent of life and rot in the air. Cameron was right; as the LT, he had to buckle down and keep things under better control. It would be some time before he felt as though his thoughts and emotions were put away where they belonged instead of sliding around inside him like broken glass. The baby next door certainly wasn't helping. Though it hadn't cried in a while, he could still hear it, gurgling and cooing.

Down below, a couple walked up the street, holding hands. The man stopped and helped the woman over a wide fissure in the sidewalk. A vivid image caught Derek by surprise—Jacqueline late in her pregnancy watering the roses out back, her belly a globe beneath a yellow dress, her smile wide and drifting, full of secret thoughts.

He ran his fingers over the bump of the transmitter—his bug. Ever since Jacqueline had been committed to the institution, he'd awaken in the night, listening for the soft rasp of her breathing or the cry of the baby beneath the crickets, and the hum of the electric clock. But then he'd remember they weren't there. It was just him, just him and the crickets.

He'd stopped by to say good-bye to Jacqueline before leaving on the mission.

Her Haldol dosage had been increased again, the antipsychotic medication making her face fight itself—stretching, biting, popping like a carnival clown's. She'd stopped washing again; he'd noticed a thin line of dirt at the base of her hairline.

As soon as Derek had gotten within her reach, she'd dug a finger painfully into his ear, searching for bugs. She'd twisted her nail so hard he'd had to check his ear for blood. She believed *they* were planting bugs on their minions—a conviction exacerbated or maybe even caused, he feared, by the penny-sized transmitter that stood out from the curve of his left anterior deltoid. She thought he'd been bugged under his skin.

He had stood in the small, sterile hospital room, gazing at the woman who was his wife with tragic disbelief. In the hospital parking lot, he'd sat in his wife's old Subaru, pressing his forehead to the top of the steering wheel, a keen sense of loss moving inside him like a sharp-bladed tool. He hadn't been in his wife's car since Before; he'd only driven it that day because he'd banged his truck against a tree the night before coming home from a bar. Her car had echoed with memories of the unintelligible cooing, sounds that wouldn't quite form themselves into words or laughter. Before driving off, he'd ripped the bright pink-and-white cushioned car seat from the upholstery and hurled it away.

It had been a long road since the wedding five years ago. Jacqueline had been nineteen years old then, just a baby, her rich brown hair pulled back in a French braid. She used to wear a pair of round glasses that made her look like a librarian. Bad genetics, his friends from the teams would joke, referring to her bad eyesight, but they wouldn't have joked if they'd known how right they were.

Since her father had asphyxiated himself on the fumes of his '77 Dodge Ram in the garage two days after she'd turned eleven, Jacqueline had been raised by her mother alone. By the time Jacqueline began high school, her mother was already having delusions, and around Jacqueline's sophomore

year, she'd started hearing the voices of the three monkeys
and was moved to the Whitehill Psychiatric Institution.
Jacqueline had been raised in Utah by a stern spinster aunt.

It had been difficult for Derek to admit that his wife
needed to be institutionalized. He'd fought the reality for
months and it had cost him everything. He'd never forget the
morning he finally drove through the wrought-iron hospital
gates and left her there with the battered brown suitcase
she'd packed with three dresses and a rain slicker when
she'd fled Utah for college. Now, one continent and nearly
four thousand miles away, the images still maintained their
vise-grip on him. It felt pretty barren now, his life, and it
didn't look as if it would be changing anytime soon.

He was snapped from his thoughts when the building
lurched, throwing his chair to the side. He grabbed hold of the
balcony railing to steady himself, but it pulled free from
the stucco and plummeted to the street. He staggered inside
the hotel room, falling over and banging his head on a cruise
box. His Sig Sauer fell from his belt. One of the walls was
undulating so fiercely, he thought it might buckle. Pulling
himself to his feet and wiping the blood from his forehead,
he fought his way to the weapons box, the floor shuddering
beneath his feet. He double-checked both padlocks, then
turned, lurching out into the hallway in time to see Tank rush
Rex to the stairs. The woman from next door flashed down
the stairs to safety, the baby cradled to her chest.

Rex was grinning a madman's grin. "Feel those compres-
sional waves?" he yelled.

Derek pointed Tank down the stairs and Tank yanked Rex
along with him. The stairs seemed to be swaying from side
to side. The three men crashed through the lobby and stumbled onto the street. The quake finally subsided.

"Here," Rex said, pulling them into an arched stone doorway across the street. People ran past in both directions.
Shattered glass was strewn across the sidewalks, and a few
fingers of asphalt had risen in the street, but no buildings had

gone over. The hotel guards were arguing with a construction worker at the end of the block.

Derek felt for his gun and noticed it missing. "Fuck!" he barked.

Eyes glowing with excitement, Rex didn't seem to hear him. "We're practically sitting on the epicenter," he cried, banging his fist into his palm. "Those roller coaster waves—those are the shear waves. Usually there are all sorts of heterogeneities by the time they reach you, but those fuckers were clear as day." He leaned out the doorway to look up the street, but Derek forced him against the wall, his forearm pressing into the top of his chest. "That must've been a six!" Rex crowed, straining to see over Derek's arm.

They huddled together until some of the commotion settled on the streets. Soon it was quiet, save the long, wailing moans of a woman somewhere in an apartment nearby. Derek stepped cautiously from cover. He glanced up an alley alongside the building and realized that it was the same side street his room overlooked. He located his balcony and saw a man frozen in the window, looking right at him. He was the man they had seen earlier, the handsome *guayaquileño* with the unbuttoned shirt and gold chains. They stared at each other for a moment, then the man bolted from the window and Derek sprinted for the lobby.

A worker tried to restrain Derek at the door, but Derek sent him flying with a straight-armed shove. He was up the stairs two at a time, and he kicked through the door to his and Cameron's room, splintering one of the wooden panels. The cruise box holding the two spare ammo crates and all the jammed mags was empty, and Derek didn't see his pistol on the floor. The weapons box and the other cruise boxes were banged up, some of them flipped over, but they all seemed to be intact.

Cursing, Derek leapt back through the doorway and glanced in both directions. At the far end of the hall, a large window, newly shattered, looked out onto Calle Pedro

Carbo. Derek sprinted the length of the hall and stuck his head out, cutting his hands on the bits of glass stuck in the bottom of the frame. Holding the last ammo crate, the man with the gold chains ran to a waiting truck. The back was covered, but through the flap, Derek saw the other ammo crate, and a bag he assumed held the Sig and M-4 mags. The man turned back and laughed, spreading his arms. He blew Derek a kiss, jumped in the passenger seat, and the truck was gone.

Derek stood for a moment leaning in the direction it had gone, breathing the heat, watching the truck's exhaust fade into the air. Behind him, a bare bulb dangled from a wire, its protective casing smashed. Light danced around the narrow hall as the bulb swayed from an aftershock. When Derek shifted his weight, he noticed the glass digging into his palms, so he lifted his hands from the sill. Turning, he sank to the floor, leaning back against the wall. He raised his hands to his face and pushed back the skin of his cheeks until his eyes slanted.

There was a momentous rumble from the stairs, then Tank ran down the hall toward Derek, Rex following close behind. Tank stopped before Derek, breathing hard. "What?" he asked.

Derek lowered his hands. His cheeks were smeared with blood from his palms, two crimson marks like war paint. "The ammo," he said. "They got the ammo."

THE SQUAD convened at the hotel immediately following the earthquake, Cameron having successfully rounded up the others. Derek sat in the wooden chair, the soldiers circled silently around him. The cuts on Derek's hands were superficial; Justin had easily picked out the glass, then applied antibacterial gel. They all stared at the boxes, which Derek had already opened and inventoried.

"At least they didn't take the geodetic equipment," Rex said.

Szabla's smooth cheeks drew up in a squint. "The black marketeers will be devastated."

"I contacted Mako, who put me in touch with the UN colonel who runs this AO," Derek said. He spoke in a soft, angry voice. "As you can imagine, the colonel was less than helpful in fielding my request for replacement ordnance, despite the fact that this happened in their fucking backyard. The UN does not seem to be making us the highest priority, which in light of the ammo shortage down here, puts us somewhere worse off than shit out of luck. They did promise armed transfer to the airport tomorrow."

"Whoopee," Szabla said.

Tank started checking the weapons to see if anyone had accidentally left a round chambered. "Nothing left?" Tucker asked. Tank shook his head.

Derek said, "Both crates and the mags. They got it all. We're essentially without weapons."

Savage thunked his boot down on the edge of Derek's chair. He pulled up the leg of his pants and yanked his blade from the ankle sheath. "Not really," he said.

"Yeah," Justin said. "I'm sure we could take on an army with that bad boy."

Derek knocked Savage's foot off his chair. "That's the good news," he said. "We don't need to take on an army. We lift out tomorrow morning, and the islands are a docile environment."

"How do you know that?" Rex asked.

"Guayaquil's basically a docile environment," Szabla said.

"Yeah, you guys seem to be breezing through this leg of the mission."

Szabla stiffened. "Look, you fuck—"

"I have been assured that the islands are not hostile," Derek said, "aside from the obvious seismic complications against which weapons will hardly be useful. Our mission is to assist you in distributing the GPS gear, which we can accomplish without ordnance."

"I'm just nervous about bandits, or random . . ." Rex stopped, looking around. "Well, it is a concern. The situation in Galápagos has gotten increasingly desperate."

"I think you'll find the seven of us adequate bodyguards," Derek said.

Szabla held up a hand, fingers spread. "One of us would be an adequate bodyguard." She rose from the bed. "But remember your request for a massive misallocation of resources? You see, to impress you and all the contacts you called in—"

"Szabla," Derek said, his voice raised in warning.

"—we all have to waste a week and wave guns around so you feel like you're well taken care of in a city less dangerous than New York on an average Saturday night."

"Szabla!" Derek barked. She looked down, fuming.

Rex applauded her performance. "Love the drama," he said. "And you're right, Guayaquil is much safer than New York City, if you ignore all the minor details of life here, like, say, those four journalists who were found two weeks ago with their dicks cut off and rammed down their throats. Hey, Guayaquil has even more advantages over the Big Apple. More of the cab drivers speak English . . . there's no Andrew Lloyd Webber . . ."

Szabla lunged for Rex, but Cameron stepped in her way. Szabla stopped before bumping into Cameron and stared at her, but Cameron didn't meet her eyes. "Why don't we all take a time-out here?" Cameron said softly, looking down at her boots. After a moment, Szabla took a step back. Cameron continued, "We no longer have weapons but, as Derek said, they're not essential for our mission objectives from this point. We'll get an armed escort to the airport tomorrow and from there, we can easily bodyguard Rex and Juan, assist in positioning the equipment, and get home."

"So everyone stow it and get some sleep," Derek added.

They grabbed their kit bags and headed for the door.

"Feliz fuckin' Navidad," Justin said.

Chapter 16   Dusk had thickened the air by the time Diego steered *El Pescador Rico*, a converted twenty-two-foot fishing boat, to the waters just off Cormorant Point on Floreana. Already, he saw a herd of pigs bickering on the soft, white-sand beach, and he felt his stomach drop as he realized what the pigs were fighting over.

He pulled the Zodiac from its withered repose near the stern and heaved it in the water, engaging the dive bottle of compressed air secured on its transom. As the launch inflated, he debated pulling his speargun from its mount on the polished wood but decided that reloading it after each shot would take too long. Kicking off his loafers and tossing his rifle ahead, Diego leapt over the side of his boat into the Zodiac and headed for shore.

In the water ahead, he noticed a shadowy mass, and he cut hard to avoid hitting it. As he passed, the dark shape took form as two turtles—a small male mounted on top of a female, clinging to her with his flippers as she paddled to keep them afloat.

Diego cranked the throttle, landing the Zodiac hard on the beach. The pigs acknowledged him with grunts as he splashed toward them through the surf, yelling and cursing. The turtle nesting ground, the twenty-meter stretch of sand that crested the top of the beach, was trampled and uprooted, the pocked and mounded sand resembling the site of an archaeological dig. Snorting and rooting into the sand, the pigs were enjoying a lavish feast of eggs and hatchlings. Whatever eggs may have remained buried in the nests were surely crushed.

A spotted sow gobbled up a soft, pale-green sea turtle hatchling as it struggled toward the surf. Diego took off the top of the sow's head with his first shot. He hit two pigs dead in the chest with his next shots before missing, and they spit blood, their legs stroking the air like broken pistons as he paused and regarded the width of the herd.

When he stepped, his feet pulled from the sand with a sucking noise. Inland, a scattering of rocks gave way to low scrubby brush, broken only by the path leading back to the lagoon. The mineral crystals in the sand gave the beach a subtle, green cast that, with the darkening sky and the carnage ahead, made the events unfolding around Diego seem dreamlike.

He felt his chest tighten with grief and rage and he fired and reloaded, fired and reloaded even through the spray of blood, the wet and wounded snorts, the wriggling bodies that layered the sand. Pieces of hatchlings lay discarded on the beach, flippers and heads and peels of flesh dusted with sand. Halfway through the carton of bullets, Diego realized he was crying. He cursed the pigs as he fired, cursed the yolk and shell dripping from their sticky snouts, cursed their curled tails protruding from holes and their forked feet trampling the sand. Then he cursed the farmers who'd left them behind to roam the island. Despite the crack of the rifle, the pained squeals, and the stench of death emanating from the blood-drenched sand, the pigs refused to spook. They remained, rooting and chomping and falling dumbly, torn through with bullets.

There were at least ten pigs dead or wounded, but their numbers seemed inexhaustible; every time a pig dropped, two more seemed to spring from its shadow, running tight, excited circles in the sand. Seemingly oblivious, a large turtle was bedded down in the middle of the ruckus, continuing to lay her eggs, even as a piglet ate them right out of her body. Diego took aim with a blurry eye and fired, but the hammer clicked down on nothing. He dug through the carton, found it empty, and cast it aside. The turtle squeezed out another egg, directly into the waiting mouth of the piglet. Cocking the stock of the rifle back over one shoulder, his scream an echo from the pit of his stomach, Diego charged into the fray.

Chapter 17 Ramón stirred in the night, feeling oddly
uneasy. It had been hard adjusting to living on a deserted island, just he and Floreana. He had caught himself talking to
one of his cows again today, and though he had laughed it
off, it was increasingly difficult to deny that it was very
lonely on Sangre de Dios.

He rolled over on the mattress, resting his hand on his
wife's rounded belly. The *bloque de hormigón* walls of the
small house were slightly aglow with the embers from the
fireplace. He lay on his back, staring at the soft orange tint of
the ceiling for a few minutes, counting the cracks and trying
to wipe the feeling of discomfort from his mind. The cut on
his index finger had healed, leaving a smooth strip of a scar.

Floreana murmured something in her sleep, her hand moving to rest atop his, though she didn't wake. He leaned over
and kissed her softly on her temple, damp with sweat. It used
to be cooler up in the highlands, but ever since the large hurricanes that damaged the skies, it had grown hotter, even in
the night. He still made fires, but only for cooking and light.

Ramón stood and crossed to the sink, his feet bare on the
dirt floor. The door rattled slightly in the wind, loose against
the frame. He doused a towel under the spigot and returned
to his wife's side, lying beside her and gently wiping her
forehead. The feeling of unease returned, and finally he sat
up in bed, staring around the small room. The fire was dwindling now, but a few stubborn coals persisted, staring out at
him like demon eyes.

He looked at the small stack of firewood in the corner, the
ax leaning on its side, the humble wooden table, the black
hole of the window. Something caught his eye in the window—a tiny glowing point, one of the embers reflected back
into the house.

His breath caught in his throat, but he let it out evenly, not wanting to make a sound. He felt blood go to his face in a rush. There should have been nothing outside that window, only an open field.

Beside him, Floreana nuzzled into her pillow, and the pinpoint reflection shifted slightly, as if whatever was out there had tracked her movement. Ramón's mind ran back through the countless stories he'd heard over the past few months, and he pictured the tall, thin creature he'd seen that night in the *garúa*.

He fought the darkness, straining his eyes to distinguish the outline of the thing in the window. He'd never believed in monsters, not even as a child, but right now in the night, his beliefs seemed far away.

The last ember died, and Ramón waited for the darkness to ease all through the room. His eyes adjusted, and he saw it just barely—a large triangular head, tilted slightly to one side. The ember had been reflected back in one large, glassy eye, an eye that now seemed riveted on him and his sleeping wife. Ramón held his breath, praying his wife would not stir. He shifted his eyes to the ax in the corner, careful not to turn his head, gauging its distance from the bed. He looked back at the window, losing himself in the liquid black eye.

The thing turned its head slightly, taking in the room in a long, slow sweep, then pulled back, fading into the darkness.

Ramón waited a moment, then let his breath out sharply. He ran a hand across his chest and it came away slick with sweat. Beside him, his wife rolled to her side, facing away from him. He leaned over and kissed her softly between the shoulder blades with trembling lips.

He lay quietly for a few minutes, but every time he almost drifted off, he'd snap to, his eyes on the window. Finally, he rose and retrieved the ax from its recline in the corner.

He fell asleep with the blunt edge of the ax head pressed against his cheek.

Chapter 18 At dawn, the ootheca began to squirm. The individual chambers wriggled until the ceiling of the lava tube looked alive.

A crackle echoed down the shaft as the ootheca strained and trembled. A small bright-green head pushed through the papier-mâché-like egg case exterior, making use of the special exit valve in the chamber. Encased within a membranous sac, it wiggled forward like a worm, a thin body following.

Rather than dropping to the ground, the larva eased slowly down, suspended by a fine silk thread produced by a gland in its abdomen. As it descended, other larvae began to break free and fall as well—writhing, slime-covered packages dropping from the roof of the cave. They were visible through their translucent surrounding membranes. Three of them clumped together, dangling from their lifelines and spinning in the air.

Blood pressure pumped into the first larva's head, causing the membrane to split. It wriggled, shaking off the nursery-cowl and falling to the ground. About two feet in length, the larva resembled an enormous grub or caterpillar. With a fat, curved eruciform body composed of a long abdomen and smaller thorax, and a well-developed head, the larva was smooth and cylindrical. It had six true legs—tiny, pointed extensions, each one ending in an apical hook. The true legs were paired, each set protruding from one of the three segments of the thorax—the pronotum, mesonotum, and metanotum. The abdomen was also segmented, into nine parts, but instead of true legs it featured prolegs, fleshy stumplike appendages. The larva used its overgrown prolegs to inch along in something like a crawl.

Most startling about the larva's appearance, however, was its head, which seemed oddly animated due to its size and the precise placement of its features. Unlike most larvae, which had clusters of ocelli rather than true eyes, it had large glassy eyes, one on each side, and a mouth that darted in a line beneath a sloping bump of a nose. Though the thorax was a mere half foot to the abdomen's ten inches, the head took up a full eight inches of the larva's length.

Three thin gills quivered on each side of its head as it breathed. Two antennae, each segmented into three parts and terminating in a long filament, extended from the top of the larva's head. A pair of spiracles on each abdominal segment permitted it to draw air.

Heads began to poke from the other membranes as the larvae shook themselves free, scrabbling with their tiny true legs and puncturing the sacs. Once loose, the prolegs waved in the air like blunted human hands. The larvae landed and eased forward, rippling their bodies and gripping the ground with their prolegs.

Up in the ootheca, a runt larva flailed partially out of its chamber, air squealing through its cuticle. Wriggling forward in its sac, it tried to pull its lower body free. The other larvae gazed up at the squawking runt, their heads instinctively going on point.

With a final, struggling shriek of air, the runt pulled itself free of its chamber. Even through the membranous sac, one true leg caught in the ootheca and tore off with a wet ripping sound. The runt flailed as it descended slowly on its mucuslike strand, air rushing irregularly and audibly through its spiracles. It managed to push itself partially free of its sac, but two of its true legs remained pasted to its side. Its cuticle, like that of the other larvae, was almost transparent, a soft, green sheath stretched over the network of hemolymph and organs pulsing beneath.

The other larvae, crawling with slow awkward movements, gathered beneath the descending runt, watching expectantly. Wriggling its remaining five true legs, the runt neared the circle of its siblings. The mouths of the other larvae peeled open, each revealing two opposing dark mandibles. The mandibles were heavily sclerotized, pointed and arced like jagged moons. At first conforming with the head, they were now spread, exposing a front labrum and lower labium, fleshy and flaplike, that worked together like toothless gums. The runt fell into the ring of the larvae's upturned faces, air screeching through its spiracles as their mandibles began to saw through its still-fragile cuticle.

The larvae fell on it ravenously, sawing and nipping as it writhed and squealed and slowly died. They concentrated on the plump abdomen, fighting over the richest mouthfuls. When they finished, their faces were covered with a moist sheen, the greenish paste of the dead larva's insides.

They crawled away from the kill once they finished eating. The runt's body was almost entirely gone; only a portion of its head and the sharp mandibles remained. The larvae eyed one another suspiciously, like boxers in a ring, but they all were of equal strength. There would be no more meals without a fight.

Overhead, one of the ootheca's chambers remained stubbornly closed, devoid of movement within.

A first larva struck out for the forest, pushing through the wall of ferns at the mouth of the lava tube and turning its head from the sunlight that assaulted its eyes. The air was filled with alarming sounds—the call of a yellow warbler, the howl of a feral dog, the wind rustling through the leaves. The fronds fell back into place around the opening, again enclosing the other larvae in darkness. A second larva resolutely followed, the other four trailing behind.

With their prolegs and rippling contortions of their abdomens, they crawled off in different directions, disappearing into the lush vegetation. Fronds rustled around the last larva, then stilled.

The forest was quiet.

Chapter 19   Even compared to Guayaquil's, the airport at Baltra was in bad shape. One of the runways was decimated with cracks and fissures. Cameron stretched her legs as the C-130 came in evenly on the one remaining strip of intact pavement and eased to a halt.

The flight had been smooth. Difficult getting out of Guayaquil, but once they'd been airborne, it had been an easy hour-and-a-half glide over miles of blue ocean. The pilot would rest, fly back to Guayaquil, and return to pick them up in five days.

The tension within the squad seemed to be even worse. Szabla was furious that Derek had breached protocol by ordering Cameron to bunk in with her and Justin, and Justin had made things worse by cracking threesome jokes all night. At four-thirty in the morning, Savage had woken the entire hall screaming from the depths of some nightmare, and Derek had had to kick in the door to see what was wrong. It had taken two of them to awaken Savage. Tucker had gotten the sweats in the middle of breakfast, and after one look at him, Justin had removed the morphine Syrettes from his trauma bag, wrapped them in a sock, and hid them at the bottom of the weapons box.

At least Juan seemed to be getting along with everyone—at the Guayaquil airport, he'd greeted the squad with a half bow, telling them how pleased he was to be along on their mission. Szabla had scooted over, letting Juan sit beside her for the flight.

Derek had been quiet since takeoff, standing by one of the windows and gazing out across the water. He looked as if he hadn't slept at all.

Rex had filled the uncomfortable silences on the flight, providing a geology lesson and pointing out the window at the islands as they passed. Born of volcanic eruptions—

fierce plumes of magma shot through the earth's crust—the Galápagos, he said, had spent much of its ten-million-year existence in flux, its islands undergoing a continual process of reshaping and reforming through eruptions and earthquakes. Rising from the Galápagos Platform, a basaltic submarine plateau some two hundred to five hundred fathoms beneath the sea, the islands were arranged chronologically, aging as they moved east. The shadowy ghosts of islands past lurked beneath the waters east of the current island chain, victims of erosion and the erratic movement of the earth's crust.

Española and Santa Fe, the oldest existing islands at 3.25 million years, were less volcanically active than their westernmost cousins, Fernandina, Isabela, and Sangre de Dios, which at seven hundred thousand years still experienced marked fits and growing pains. Because the islands were formed of basalt, a low viscosity magma that flowed and spread easily, the volcanic peaks rose less steeply than their continental counterparts, whose silica-laden andesite magma permitted more conical protrusions. The product of gentle, effusive eruptions, the Galápagos were broad and mildly sloping islands that resembled the domed backs of the tortoises for which the archipelago was named.

The islands floated amidst seven oceanic currents, which carried with them marine life from as far away as Antarctica and Panama. The confluence of these currents, warm and cold, northern and southern, gave the archipelago a climate uncharacteristic of the equator. In most aspects, Rex pointed out, the Galápagos were anomalous: the lumbering reptiles; the smattering of penguins and flamingos among the more traditional pelagic birds; the albatross that clattered their way through their elaborate mating dance and threw themselves from cliffs to become airborne.

Cameron had listened to Rex intently, but she'd thought the others seemed bored.

The sun in Baltra was much more intense than in Guayaquil. Their faces slick with sunblock, the soldiers ex-

ited the plane. Cameron felt the heat of the concrete through
her boots. A *Minutes to Burn* electronic billboard flashed
2:50 on the runway. Two Kfirs were parked on the far edge
of the apron, where they sat in the hot sun, still linked to tow
tractors—Israel had been kind to the Ecuadorian army.

Two French soldiers met them on the tarmac, their uniforms adorned with UN trimmings. One of them jogged out
to direct the taxiing plane. Szabla conversed with the other
in French and gestured to the squad to follow them inside.

The terminal was all but deserted. A flat open building
with visible rafters and three-quarter-height walls composed
of large porous brown slabs. The west wall had fallen over,
but since it wasn't directly connected to the ceiling, it had
dragged nothing else down with it. It left an open block of
air, looking out over low, scrubby vegetation. Dirt had blown
in, scattering across the concrete floor. The emptiness, in addition to the barren landscape and abandoned souvenir
shacks, made the place seem haunted. The squad walked
silently through the building. A wooden sign with grooved
white lettering hung on the nearest wall: *Bienvenidos, Parque Nacional Galápagos, Ecuador*. To its left was a crudely
painted blue map of the archipelago. Poorly drawn pictures
of turtles, iguanas, and an impossibly elongated flamingo
hung on the walls. A thin film of red dust covered everything.

Cameron stepped forward, kit bag slung over one shoulder. An enormous cardboard cutout of a short, stubby penguin lay on the ground, the beady black eyes staring up at
her dumbly. Savage put his foot on its beak. Setting a boot
on one of the dilapidated benches, Cameron glanced at the
old jitney terminal behind the airport. Just beyond it, a metal
dolphin with chipped blue paint had fallen on top of a tortoise sculpture, giving the distinct impression that it was
humping it.

Savage flipped a cigarette into his mouth and lit it, taking
in the scene around them. "This place is a fucking zoo," he
grumbled.

The French soldiers went behind the disused TAME ticket counter and Szabla waved the squad over. "Let's get our shit down on the manifest and head out of here."

The soldiers lined up and filled out the information, each listing name, rank, and company, completing a Park form, and showing the French soldiers military ID. Savage dawdled over by the wall, gazing at the cardboard cutouts. He put his cigarette out in a tortoise's eye. Tank and Derek loaded the gear onto a dolly they'd found in a back closet.

The two-mile road to the Itabaca Channel was split with scarps, earthquake wounds where the ground had cracked and then clamped shut again. They'd have to heft their gear over felled telephone poles and wires to get to the dock. Cameron gazed at the strip of water. It was apparent that the channel had been created by water filling the crack of a seismic fault.

Rex tapped her shoulder with the clipboard, and she took it from him. He pointed to a small, flat-bottomed *panga* moored at the dock. Stretched out on the pontoon, a man slept in the shade afforded by the makeshift *ramada* of palm fronds that he'd propped overhead using two fishing poles. His hat was over his face, Huck Finn style. "The seismologists at the Station said they'd have someone waiting," Rex said. "I arranged it a few weeks ago." He smiled, pleased with himself. "The roads across the channel are a mess, so we're going to have to take the panga around the island to Puerto Ayora."

He noticed Tucker mishandling a comms box and scurried off. The others had already headed out behind the airport and circled up, waiting for them. Cameron finished at the clipboard and handed it off to Savage, the last one left. He took it with some hesitation, and when Cameron glanced back, he was still standing over it, an uncomfortable expression on his face. He stared at the form, chewing the end of the pen. He set the pen down and followed Cameron, but the French soldier called out in heavily accented English, "This not eez complete."

Cameron backtracked and checked the forms. Though he'd

written his basic information in the manifest, Savage had left the complicated Park form blank. He took out another cigarette, coughed into his fist, and put the cigarette away.

"You gotta do this shit," Cameron said. "We don't want a hassle."

Savage shrugged. "Fuck it." He raised a hand and ran it over his bandanna. His face softened a touch, and Cameron thought she caught a glimmer of vulnerability in it.

"Move it!" Derek yelled from outside.

Savage cleared his throat. "Just a touch rusty, that's all," he said.

Cameron looked at his handwriting more closely. She glanced from his dyslexic scrawl to his face and picked up the pen. "Come here," she said. "I'll help you."

Chapter 20   Samantha lay back on her bed, resting her legs straight up the wall. Lagging behind a guided tour of the facilities, a four-star general paused at the slammer window, double-taking at Samantha's posture. He stopped, crossing his arms in disapproval. Out of the corner of her eye, Samantha saw him looking at her. Thrashing around on the bed, she feigned a seizure, rolling her eyes and moaning. The general quickly turned and scurried away.

She sat up on the bed and rubbed her face. Suddenly, she recognized her children's laughter down the hall, and she rose and crossed to the window, waving as her three kids made their way toward her.

Iggy, her six-year-old, led the charge, running toward the slammer. Adopted from an orphanage in Kaliningrad, he had almost white hair which he wore in a bowl cut, his bangs a straight line across his forehead. His smooth cheeks were accented with nearly perfect circles of rosy red. Kiera limped behind him, still having trouble with her new prosthetic leg, which she'd only had a few weeks. She was growing so quickly, it seemed she was always adjusting to a new prosthesis. Maricarmen, the nanny, hurried behind the two older children, holding Danny, the three-year-old, on one hip.

Danny was emitting a long, steady moan, his voice garbling with each of Maricarmen's footsteps. He finally stopped and giggled explosively. Iggy reached the window first and banged on it. Samantha held her hand flat against the window, pressing it against the outline of his. "Hey, baby," she said. "I'm sorry I missed Christmas. But you have a ton of gifts to open the minute I get out."

Down the hall, Kiera tumbled over. A passing soldier stopped to help, but Kiera got up herself, adjusting her prosthesis and picking her backpack up off the floor.

Maricarmen set Danny down and he ran to the window. Iggy had to pick him up so that he could see over the sill. Samantha kissed the glass, then realized that probably wasn't such a good idea and wiped her lips.

"I brought the air ticktacktoe!" Iggy cried, setting Danny down. He unrolled a thin, transparent plastic board against the window, and it clung in place. He pulled out a magic marker and made an "X" in the middle. Samantha pointed to a slot, and he penned in an "O."

"How are things going, Maricarmen?" Samantha asked.

Maricarmen rolled her eyes and ruffled Danny's hair. "He's no eating," she said, with her distinctive accent. "I make him peanut butter, but he refuse. And Iggy's no brushing his teeth."

Kiera reached the window and leaned against the glass. "So *that's* where my shirt went," she said.

Samantha gazed down at the NVME T-shirt. "I think the blond one's a cutie."

"*Mom!*" Kiera rolled her eyes. "You are *so* embarrassing."

"You'll have to buy marshmallow fluff for the peanut butter," Samantha continued to Maricarmen, "or else he won't—"

A lab technician approached and knocked on the glass. "Sorry to bother you, Sammy, but I wanted to let you know we finally got the shipment. Everything looks fine. Oh—and there's new gloves for the hood lines. Latex hands bonded to neoprene sleeves. Less slippery. Also, Tim's having problems with the Machupo rats. He can't get a safe handle on them."

"No!" Samantha said. "You can't use those gloves. We had them once before—"

"Mom!"

Samantha pointed at a slot, and Iggy penned in another "O." "And the latex separates from the sleeves. They leak like hell. Send 'em back and tell admin that their insistence on lowest bidder is going to have someone vomiting blood."

"Gross," Iggy said. "Your turn."

Maricarmen picked up Danny again, and he yanked on her necklace. Samantha turned back to her. "Brush. And pick up that glittery kid's toothpaste that comes out shaped like an elongated star on the toothbrush." She tapped the glass to get the lab tech's attention. "Tell Tim to grab the rats by the tail and lower them onto a wire cage. When they pull away, their necks are exposed and it's the perfect scruff-grabbing angle."

Kiera pulled a folder out of her backpack. "I brought the flashcards. I'm sending them through the pass-through box," she said.

Beside the window was an autoclave that could be opened from both inside and outside the slammer. One side always remained sealed. Inside, extremely strong UV killed off any germs. Before an object was moved out of the slammer, it first had to sit in the box under UV light for fifteen minutes, then be sprayed down with disinfectant for further decontamination.

Samantha grabbed Kiera's folder as Iggy cried, "Three in a row!" and wiped the marker off the board with his sleeve.

"No, don't . . ." Samantha shook her head, looking at the black smudge on Iggy's sweatshirt. He started a new game, drawing another "X." "I'm sorry they're being difficult, Maricarmen," she said, pointing at the board to take her turn. She pulled out an enlarged photograph from the folder and pressed it against the glass. It was a fuzzy black-and-white enlargement of long slender threads that curved around themselves.

"*Ea-sy,*" Kiera groaned. "Filovirus."

"Good, baby," Samantha said. She waved at Danny with one finger. "How's my little blowfish?" she asked. He laughed and puffed out his cheeks. Samantha turned to Maricarmen with pleading eyes, holding another photograph to the window. "I should be out in a week. I've already contacted day care—they can take them days. Do you think you could . . . ?"

Kiera gazed at the photograph, which featured spaghetti-like rods curved in shepherd's crooks. "Marburg," she said. "Causes disseminated intravascular coagulation."

Maricarmen waved her hand. "Of course. I will maybe have to reschedule some things, but if you are busy saving the world . . ."

Iggy laughed. "My mom saves the world," he said.

"Not quite, honey."

Iggy banged into Kiera with his rear end, almost knocking her over. She leaned over, unstrapped her leg, and smacked him across the head with it.

"*Kiera!*" Samantha said. "We talked about that kind of attention-getting!"

"Well—"

"No 'wells.' Are you going to act like that when you're a senator? Well? Are you?"

"I'm not gonna be a senator. I'm gonna be a virologist."

"You can be both if you stop whacking people over the head with your prosthetic limb. Now . . ." Samantha pulled out another enlargement and pressed it to the glass. Round particles containing small grainy bits.

Kiera bent over, strapping her leg back on. "Arenavirus," she said.

"Excellent." Samantha tapped the glass and Iggy penned an "O." He blocked her move with an "X."

The lab tech returned. "I took care of the gloves," he said. "And you got this from Donald Denton at the New Center." He pulled a test tube, containing the Sangre de Dios dinoflagellate DNA pellet, out of a padded box. "He thinks the plankton are virus-laden. I'm sending them through." Not wanting to damage the DNA, he clicked a switch to deactivate the heat and UV light inside the autoclave before placing the test tube inside. The precautions were only a necessity when moving materials from inside the slammer to out.

Opening the autoclave from her side, Samantha pulled out the test tube and held it up, then glanced at her microscope on the counter. She looked back at the kids.

"I know, I know," Kiera said. "You have to get to work now. I recognize when your mouth gets like that."

Danny shook his head back and forth furiously. "I don't wanna go yet."

"Honey, I'll be home soon," Samantha said. She tapped the window with a blunt fingernail. "I promise."

"Yeah, right," Kiera said.

"Honey, please. Give me a hand here."

"Well, I can't spare a leg."

Samantha set her hands on her hips. "Maricarmen, why don't you take the boys to the car? I'll send Kiera out in a moment."

The boys kissed the window, and Samantha cringed but refrained from scolding them since she'd set the example. Maricarmen took the boys by their hands and led them out. Kiera played with a hole in her jeans.

"What is going on with you?" Samantha asked.

"Why are you in here?"

"I just . . . I needed to . . . I got exposed to . . ."

Kiera sighed. Loudly. "I read what you did in the newspaper. Maricarmen cut out the article, but I saw the blank square and knew it would be something good, so I dug it out of the garbage."

"Don't dig in the garbage, honey."

"That is *not* the point!" Kiera said, her nostrils flaring.

"Honey, you know how my work is. We've talked about this. I sometimes have to take risks to help other people."

"Well, what am I supposed to tell Danny if you end up with . . . with hantavirus pulmonary syndrome or something? Then what?"

Samantha pressed her lips together to keep from smiling. "How old are you again?"

Kiera's face remained angry. "It's not just you anymore, you know," she said. "It's us too."

Stunned, Samantha sat down slowly on a nearby chair. She felt as though she'd just had the breath knocked out of her. The test tube was cool in her hand. "I know," she said. "You're right."

Kiera chewed her bottom lip. "Well . . . just don't let it happen again."

"Okay," Samantha said. "I won't." She stood again and crossed to the window. She reached out to touch the glass, then lowered her hands in frustration. She'd never wanted to hold her child so much. "Honey, you kids are the most important thing to me in the world. I hope you know that."

Kiera's face softened. "I do." She looked up at her mother. "I'd better get going. Maricarmen's waiting."

Samantha leaned against the glass, watching her daughter until she turned the corner at the end of the hall. She sat back down in the chair and leaned forward, her elbows on her knees. She didn't move for a long time. Then she rose and walked over to the microscope.

Chapter 21   With all they had seen on their respective tours—men drinking cobra blood in Snake Alley in Taiwan, the diffuse orange sunset over Hagia Sophia in Istanbul, decapitated frogs still breathing in Vietnamese markets—the soldiers had never encountered a place like the Galápagos.

The water was postcard-blue and calm, lapping against the *panga*. The soldiers sat up along the pontoons, the gear stacked between them. The *panguero*, who smelled of *aguardiente* and wore jeans cuffed in wide bands, navigated admirably, despite the fact that the outboard was straining under the load. Cameron leaned over the side, running her fingers through the clear water and praying the little boat wouldn't sink under the weight of their gear. She stole a look at Justin, who winked at her. His face was streaked with sunblock that needed to be rubbed in.

The island of Santa Cruz loomed before them, a low-lying black bulge on the surface that sloped upward and lost itself in mist. Overhead, frigate birds circled, black streaks against the sky. When they caught the sun, they reflected a greenish sheen. Their tails deeply forked for maneuvering, they dipped and turned, their long slender wings spread wide. Rex pulled his Panama hat low over his eyes to cut the blazing sun.

A white bird with gray wings and bright blue feet swept low over the stern, crying out in a nasal honk. It banked high and then folded its wings to its side, plummeting toward the water like an arrow. Cameron pointed and the other soldiers watched as the bird hit the water hard and vanished. Even Savage glanced over, though he pretended not to be interested. "The blue-footed booby," Juan said. "The great plunge diver of Galápagos. It can go up to ten meters beneath the water."

After a few moments, the bird popped to the surface, then took to the air. One of the iridescent frigate birds chased her, closing quickly to attack her in flight. She squawked and flailed, disgorging the fish, and the frigate bird used its long hooked beak to snatch the fish from her mouth. With a defeated squawk, the booby headed for land.

The *panga* approached the sleepy town of Puerto Ayora, which was stretched along a rocky inlet on the southern shore of Santa Cruz. Pulling into Academy Bay, a small anchorage split by a damaged cement pier, the *panguero* cut the engines, drifting until the boat nosed up against the massive black tires guarding the dock. The Bay was almost empty. A few dinghies floated despondently near a set of white buoys and a weathered rowboat, but there was only one boat of any size—*El Pescador Rico*. A number of bloated fish drifted on the surface, forced upward by a recent swell until their air bladders had exploded through their mouths. Cameron wrinkled her nose at the stench.

A pelican skimmed low with its huge bill angled toward the water. It dipped, hitting the water with a splash, and surfaced with several gallons of water distending its pouch. As it began to drain its pouch, a brown noddy flew over, landing on its chestnut-brown head, waiting eagerly for fish scraps to wash out.

The coastline was composed of thickets of red mangrove and jagged, low-lying lava rocks spotted with tide pools. Rusted and broken, abandoned bicycles were chained on the railing that ran the length of the pier. Nailed to a kiosk was a cardboard *Minutes to Burn* sign. Crude numbers hung on pegs beneath it—*2:10*.

Avenida Charles Darwin, a road cobbled with red composite blocks and lined with shops and restaurants, curved parallel to the coastline heading east. Many stores had boards nailed across the doors and windows, but a few still remained open.

The soldiers disembarked and stacked their gear on the dock. Derek stuffed a roll of sucres in the *panguero*'s pocket and said, "Justin and Szabla—you guys stay here with the gear while we go find the Darwin Station. We'll rotate shifts later so you can grab a bite." He'd removed two of the unloaded Sigs from the weapons box; he tossed one to Szabla and stuffed the other in his belt. "In case you need to bluff."

Szabla raised her index finger and twirled it in the air.

Rex pointed at one of the boxes marked TELEMETRY. "We need that one."

"Then carry it," Savage retorted.

Tank stepped forward and grabbed both handles, hoisting it up with a grunt.

The *panguero* was busy unmooring the boat from the pier. A swell lifted the *panga* suddenly, and he fell over. Szabla and Savage laughed, and Tucker looked down with a smile. The man glared at them, his mouth drawn tight with indignation, then shoved off.

Leaving Justin and Szabla behind, the squad fell into line with Rex heading east along the road toward the Darwin Station. The effects of the earthquakes grew increasingly apparent. A few of the buildings had toppled over, leaving large blocks of space between standing shops. On one side of the road, a half-built boat had fallen off its blocks, the unfinished wood on the bow rent nearly in two. Up ahead, two sturdy boards were lain over a four-foot rift in the street, so that people could bicycle and walk across. A red Chevette had evidently tried to make it over as well; it lay smashed and angled into the split earth, its taillights sticking up into the air.

Though almost all the scientists and visitors had fled the islands, many of the *colonos* had stubbornly remained. An old man had fallen asleep sitting in a wooden chair outside his store, one arm swinging at his side, his face tilted back and covered with a venerable Panama hat. Cameron watched nervously as a shirtless young boy jumped on the trunk of the Chevette, fanning his arms wide to keep his balance as he walked across.

A few men were blasting a chunk of raised concrete that reared up from the sidewalk like an angry animal. They were arguing about where to set the TNT. The seal of the Ecuadorian army painted on its side, the crate of TNT sat open, revealing a tangle of assorted blasting caps and detonators.

"The military dropped off explosives?" Cameron asked.

Juan nodded. "The *ejército*. For the roads and fallen buildings."

Tucker stopped beside the men and pointed. "There," he said. "That's your stress point." They looked at him uncomprehending, so he took the red block and positioned it on the concrete. He made a sound like an explosion. The men stared at him as if he were psychotic. "You'll see," he said.

Juan explained to them in Spanish, and one of them nodded. They backed up and blew the concrete. It severed almost perfectly at road level, crumbling onto the pavement. Tucker made a gun with his hand and blew the invisible smoke from the barrel of his finger. The men laughed and nodded their thanks as the soldiers headed up the road.

Clusters of people sat at tables on the sidewalks, laughing and drinking from large brown bottles labeled *Pilsener*. They watched the squad as it passed but did not seem particularly interested or intimidated. A truck lumbered by, weaving expertly to avoid cracks and potholes. To the right, water sneaked through lava rocks to lap against the concrete sea wall protecting the street.

Cameron nodded at a group of teenagers hanging out in the back of a diesel-guzzling blue truck, parked at the curb. A little girl sat in the driver's seat, playing with a pair of handcuffs that had been decoratively hooked around the rearview mirror. The teenagers waved and smiled, calling out in Spanish, asking if they were movie stars.

Eventually, the road forked into two dirt roads. Juan continued to the right, heading between a cemetery studded with raised white blocks of caskets and a bent sign featuring a smiling marine iguana wearing scuba gear. The others followed.

Tucker stopped beneath a tall tree with small green fruit. He tugged on a dark green leaf and it snapped free, a drop of white fluid beading from the stem.

The red dirt of the road dusted their boots, and their pants to the knees. Bushes and muyuyo trees lined the road on both sides. A mammoth *Opuntia* guarded the front of a hay hut, its prickly beavertail pads protruding in clusters.

Tucker suddenly cried out, dropping the leaf and rubbing his hand.

"What?" Cameron asked. "What is it?"

"I don't know," Tucker said. "Something stung me or something." He raised his hand to his mouth, but Rex grabbed him around the wrist.

"Don't do that," Rex barked. Tucker tried to yank his arm away, but Rex held it tightly. "Calm down and let me look at it." Turning Tucker's hand, he examined the small red patch of dermatitis. He crouched and picked up the leaf that Tucker had dropped, careful not to touch the white fluid leaking from the broken stem. "Manzanillo," he said. "Poison apple tree." He snapped his fingers at Derek. "Give me your canteen."

He poured water over Tucker's hand, smoothing it across the rash with his thumb. "It'll be fine," Rex said. He turned to the others. "Don't fondle the vegetation. You're not in a garden here."

The Station was a wide grouping of buildings arranged around a loop at the end of the road. They approached a plain, cream-colored building, a wooden sign hammered into the flower box out front. *Estación Científica Charles Darwin*.

Rex walked inside the administration building, calling out in Spanish. The soldiers waited impatiently in the hot sun. Tank set down the telemetry box and sat on it. It creaked under his weight. Juan gazed ahead at the crumbling Plantas y Invertebrados and Protección buildings, his face coloring with concern. Odd-shaped and fronted with large stones and concrete, the buildings were shaded by a large, swooping strip of roof that dipped in the middle, giving it the appearance of a ramp. Wires and extension cords threaded out the shattered windows of both buildings and across a collapsed deck.

Rex emerged from the administration building. "No one there," he said.

Juan pointed at the complex ahead. "We'll check here and you head down to Bio Mar. That is where, I believe, the seismology people were working."

Cameron and Rex jogged down to the Bio Mar building, passing a small dock with blue and white posts. Marine iguanas nibbled algae off the submerged planks. A 3.2-meter Zodiac was moored to the dock, a thirty-five-horsepower Evinrude secured to the wood transom. The Darwin Station decal was peeling off the rubber hull.

Inside the building, only a few overturned tables and a broken computer mouse remained. A rat was gnawing through the mouse cord. It looked up at them, its beady yellow eyes glowing. It did not scurry away.

Discouraged, they headed back. The others were circled up outside, and Juan leaned through the broken window of the Plantas y Invertebrados building.

"No one inside," Derek said. "Anywhere."

Juan pointed at a small laptop perched atop a makeshift desk. Flying marine iguanas drifted across the screen. "Someone's here," he said. "Somewhere."

There was a noise from up the path, then a boy approached on a bicycle. Ramoncito pedaled up to the soldiers and skidded to a halt in a cloud of dust. "¿Son estadounidenses?"

"Sí," Juan said, pointing at the others. "Ellos. Vamos a Sangre de Dios."

"Ah," Ramoncito said with a smile. "Mi isla." He switched to English and addressed them all. "You go there again on the drilling boat?"

"The drilling boat?" Rex said, confused. "No." He gestured to the buildings around them. "Is there anyone here?"

Ramoncito pointed up the path in the direction from which he'd come. "I would not see him now," he said.

"Why not?" Derek asked.

Ramoncito shrugged. "Catch you . . . later," he said. "Dude." He smiled, then pedaled off.

"There's no point in hauling this shit everywhere," Tucker said. "I'll wait here with Tank."

Derek tilted his head to his shoulder and spoke into his transmitter. "Szabla. Primary channel." He waited for her to sense the vibration and activate her unit.

Her voice emanated from his shoulder. "Szabla. Public."

Both Rex and Juan looked surprised, and Cameron realized they hadn't yet used the transmitters in their presence.

"Szabla, Mitchell," Derek said. "Everything clear?"

"Baccarat."

Derek looked puzzled.

"It's a brand of crystal," Rex explained with a smile.

"All right," Derek said. "We're nosing around. I'll check in in a few."

"I'll wait breathlessly," Szabla said before clicking out.

Cameron, Derek, Savage, and the two scientists followed the trail around until they reached the Tortoise Conservation Building, which was also empty. They walked silently out the back door, past the tortoise-rearing pens, in which short flat hutches of mesh and wood had been built over the soft dirt. The corrals were all empty, but the breeding groups' names were written on placards: G.e. Hoodensis—*Isla Española 2001*; G.e. Porter—*Isla Santa Cruz 2003*.

Beyond the corrals, a crude boardwalk curved up and to the right. They followed it in single file, Cameron leading the way. Giant tortoises lazed in enclosures below. In one stretch, the planks had given way on the right side, and they had to shuffle along the single intact board on the left, gripping the thin rail. The walk curved again and Cameron stopped suddenly, holding up a hand. Rex started to say something, but Derek grabbed him from behind, placing a hand over his mouth.

Up ahead, sitting on a crude bench built from log segments, sat a man. He stared down at the tortoise enclosure beyond the walkway, his hands dangling between his knees. His eyes were glazed and unfocused, his head cocked slightly to one side.

He was covered with dried blood.

Chapter 22   A man entered Samantha's room through the crash door, his movements slow and labored in his blue space suit. Samantha rose to her tiptoes and peered through his mask. "Who are you?" she asked suspiciously.

"Martin Foster. Infectious Disease." The doctor extended his hand. "I'm cross-covering from Hopkins."

Samantha shook the gloved hand, feeling slightly ridiculous. "Samantha Everett."

"Yes," he said. "I know."

"How are our patients?"

"Besides you?" Dr. Foster shook his head. "Going downhill. The pilot started with GI symptoms this morning."

"Goddamnit," Samantha said. "It's so frustrating having the antiserum right here in our hands and not being able to . . ." She grimaced. "Because of legal ramifications."

"Well," Dr. Foster said, removing a needle, "you *are* showing antibodies as well as antigens. If your body hasn't rejected them by tomorrow morning and the absolute viral count is decreasing, we'll get clearance to use the antiserum on the others." He smiled. "There was something of a public outcry."

Samantha's face lit up, almost comically. "Are you serious?" She held out her arm, clenching her fist to give him a good vein. He bent over, concentrating. Samantha couldn't wipe the smile from her face. "You know," she said, "they say a space suit puts ten pounds on you."

Dr. Foster looked up. "I thought that was a TV camera," he said dryly.

"That too." Samantha leaned over, glancing at his rear end. "Christ, no wonder I never get dates."

Dr. Foster finished drawing, pinching the needle off with a cotton ball. Samantha held the cotton ball in place, bending her arm and elevating it. "Is Tom in yet? He's been off cavorting—I haven't been able to get ahold of him."

"It was really irresponsible for him to take off Christmas Day," Dr. Foster said with a slight smile, speaking loudly so that Samantha could hear him through his mask. "Maybe you should speak to his superiors."

"I am his superiors. And when you're the world's leading viral electron microscopist, you shouldn't take Christmas off." She pounded her fist into her hand, imitating a drill sergeant. "There are responsibilities that come with this job. Sacrifices. That's why I haven't had a date in forty years."

"I thought it was the space suit and the ten pounds."

"That too."

"And your intimidating demeanor."

"All right—don't push your luck. I just need Tom to run a sample under the EM. I'd do it myself, but they won't let me out."

The tremendously exacting electron microscope, hypersensitive to minute vibrations and electromagnetic interference, had to be bolted into the concrete basement floor and surrounded with layer upon layer of copper mesh. There was no way they'd release Samantha to go down there herself, but she was anxious to get micrographs of the sample from Sangre de Dios.

"I'll have him paged," Dr. Foster said. "I'm sure he'll come in for you."

"Thanks. And get here early tomorrow to draw on me so we can get the antiserum into the patients."

"Assuming your blood work comes back fine."

Samantha waved him off. "Assume away. Just move your ass."

Dr. Foster paused on his way out, looking at her with concern. "Are you all right with all this?"

Samantha smiled. She pointed to the test tube that Donald had sent over, lying on its side on the counter. "Already on to the next thing," she said.

"Well," he said. "Maybe when you get out of here, we could go and get a cup of coffee. Or maybe see a movie."

"Don't you mean '*if* I get out of here?'" Samantha asked.

"I'm comfortable with 'when,'" Dr. Foster said. "And you're avoiding the question."

"Well, there's a lot going . . . I don't really . . ." Samantha was worrying her bangs with her hand. She stopped, looked at her hand, and lowered it. "Yes," she said. "I'd like that."

Chapter 23   Cameron inched forward on the walkway's rickety planking. She called out once, but the man did not reply. His face was streaked with blood, his clothes smeared and stiffened with dark patches of crimson. In places, even his hair was matted down with blood.

Derek and Cameron eased up to him, signaling Savage and the two scientists to hang back. Derek's hand rested lightly on his pistol. As they came up behind the man, he pointed down at a giant tortoise. It lazed under a crude shed roofed with corrugated metal. In the foreground stretched a small wall built of gray stones, and a tall *Opuntia*, its lower pads chewed off. "Solitario Jorge," the man said without turning around.

"I'm sorry," Derek said. "I don't . . . "

"No comprendemos," Cameron said.

The man switched to perfect English. "Lonesome George. Last of the *Geochelone elephantopus* of Pinta Island. His entire species was wiped out by feral goats in the 1960s. There's no one left for him to mate with. When he dies, the species dies. He grows older and older." He raised a blood-crusted hand to scratch his cheek. "Take a close look. We're witnessing extinction before our very eyes."

He turned to face them, and Cameron sensed immediately that he was not dangerous. With a dark band of a mustache, high cheekbones, and deep brown eyes, he exuded a digni-fied, almost princely air, even in his current state. He ex-tended a hand. "Diego Rodriguez," he said.

Cameron pointed at his hand, and he looked at it, as if noticing the blood for the first time. "Oh," Diego said, wip-ing his hand on his shirt, though the blood didn't come off. "Pig blood. Ran out of bullets."

Cameron grimaced.

Rex stepped forward. "Where's the seismology depart-ment?" he asked.

Diego laughed. "Got me."

"Is there anyone here?"

"Anyone here?" Diego leaned forward, still laughing. "I'm here."

"That's not particularly helpful, my friend," Juan said. "We are in need of the scientists here."

"I'm Acting Director of the Station," Diego said, with ex-aggerated gravity. "And the only remaining scientist. Oh wait, that's not quite true. Ramoncito is still here." His laughter quieted down and he wiped his eyes.

"Who is this Ramoncito?" Juan asked.

"He's the supplies boy. About fourteen. Very dedicated. You may have met him on his way to town."

"This is not a joke!" Juan barked.

"No," Diego said. "It isn't."

"We need to get to Sangre de Dios," Rex said.

"Best of luck. None of the local boats go near there anymore." He raised his hands, wiggling his fingers. "It's haunted."

"I'm outfitting the island with geodetic equipment," Rex said. "I was supposed to meet with the seismologists here to get the telemetry gear in place, and they were going to arrange a transport for us."

"They did have a boat arranged. They took it themselves to the mainland. Wisely, might I add." Diego sighed. "The last of my scientists."

"We need a boat," Rex said.

Diego glanced them over. "How many are you?"

"Nine," Derek said. "And supplies."

"Well, you're properly fucked, as the expression goes. Most boats have already struck out for the continent. The only one remaining that's big enough to get you all there in reasonable fashion is mine. And I retired."

"When?"

"About two minutes ago."

"What has happened to the Station?" Juan said, his voice growing angry. "Why are you in charge?"

"Why *was* I in charge?" Diego's knee was bouncing up and down, his foot resting on the planks. He stilled his knee with his hand. "Because I was the only one willing to stay. We haven't had grant money. No one was getting paid."

"Then how can you remain?" Juan asked.

"Because," Diego said, picking something from his hair and flicking it over the railing. "My family is filthy rich."

"He'll get along well with Szabla," Derek muttered.

Diego shook his head, still lost in his thoughts. "First the tortoises . . . then the turtles . . . then the iguanas and the birds and the trees."

"What the hell is he talking about?" Derek asked. Cameron shrugged. Savage lit a cigarette.

"It's all a loss. All my little projects here." Diego pointed to another tortoise enclosure, farther up the walk. "We moved that group of tortoises from Isabela before Wolf erupted. Would've been wiped out by the resultant flow."

"Well," Savage said, lowering his cigarette, "isn't that how evolution works?"

Rex looked at him, annoyed. "A philosopher."

"Survival of the fittest," Savage said. "All's fair, right? A volcano comes along, erupts, little fuckers can't get out of the way, tough shit is what I say. That's how evolution works."

"You seem to have a firm grasp of the concept," Rex said.

Diego took a deep breath. "Actually, now I'm inclined to agree. For as long as I can remember, I've put everything into it. Into this." He indicated the enclosures around him and the distant peaks of the island with a sweep of his arm. "And for what? What does it matter? As you say in America, I'm throwing in my towel. I've lost everything."

"You've lost everything," Juan repeated.

"Yes. Everything. My turtles, my workers, my title . . ." Diego lowered his head. "There's no point in taking you to Sangre. We're fighting a losing battle. Without ammo."

"We have work to do," Rex said.

"I just saw seven years of my work go down the gullet of a pig. I'm done. Find your own boat."

"You listen to me," Juan said angrily, stepping forward. "With your perfect English and your fake castellano accent. I may just be some mono from Guayaquil, but I can tell you this: There is more you could have lost." He jabbed a finger at Lonesome George. "There is more we all can lose. Things are wrong in the world, things do not go well? Tough luck amigo. My wife and daughter are gone because of bad timing and worse structural engineering. But I am not going to lose more to this . . . to this mierda. The ozone hole and these earthquakes and the foolish irresponsibility of others. I am *not*. These islands prove to me that life can still have meaning, that things can be logical and magical all at once.

And that is something worthwhile, a little glimmer of meaning in this mess before us."

Juan rested a hand on Rex's shoulder and Rex looked over at him, surprised. Juan continued to address the back of Diego's head angrily. "You might want to desert your responsibilities because things are bad, but don't make that choice for us. We are willing to stay, to do what we can, however small. Don't make these islands pay for your disillusionment."

Diego leaned over, lacing his fingers. His shoulders settled a bit, as if under great weight. Below him, a finch flew over and landed on Lonesome George's back. With painstakingly slow, deliberate motions and a resigned sigh, the tortoise pushed himself up on all fours and extended his long slender neck. The finch hopped around his shell, picking parasites off George's tough, leathery skin.

Diego watched. "Beautiful," he murmured. "So beautiful."

Juan stepped back, the redness fading from his face. He glanced around at the others, ashamed for losing his composure.

"We'll pay you well," Derek said.

Diego's laugh was tinged with lunacy. "Pay me in bullets."

"I'm sorry," Derek said. "I don't understand. How much do you want?"

Diego rose, slapping his hands together. "Two shots of bourbon. One neat, one on the rocks." He rose and glanced down at himself. "After I shower."

He walked past the others, pausing beside Juan for a moment. Juan looked down uncomfortably. Diego raised a hand to pat him on the side but lowered it again when he saw it was covered with blood. He headed down the walk back toward the Station.

"Come," he said.

DIEGO SAT contentedly at the bar before two shots, one poured over ice. He threw back the first, set it on the counter, and took a sip from the second. Tucker watched hungrily, working the thimble on his key chain. He was drinking passion-fruit juice. A feral kitten had sneaked into the bar. It was playing near the door, sharpening its claws on a wicker chair.

The Galapasón, a tropical theme bar at the eastern end of Avenida Charles Darwin, was open to the scorching sun, though a few pieces of plywood were laid across the high rafters, creating sporadic patches of shade. A pool table stood in the center of the bar, one leg propped up with a mound of old books. Hammocks swayed between 4x4s, and painted bas-reliefs of parrots stared out from the walls. A back alcove housed a junkyard tangle of broken furniture. A rat scurried across the dirt floor, disappearing between the yellow crates of Pilsener bottles, and the orange crates that held the smaller Club empties.

The soldiers were still finishing a *ceviche* of octopus, spiced with *ají*. It was served with soft, flattened potato patties mixed with *campo* cheese and onions and topped with *salsa de maní*, a peanut sauce. Savage signaled the bartender for another beer, which arrived quickly. He held up the bottle, regarding the upside-down Pilsener label.

Diego shrugged. "Ecuador," he said.

Cameron and Derek had grabbed a quick snack and left to stand guard over the gear, freeing up Szabla and Justin to eat. The soldiers and scientists sat in a row along the bar, ignoring the scurrying rats and the faint aroma of urine in the musty air. There were a few locals at the scattered tables, and two men played pool on the uneven table.

Having showered, loaded a bag with supplies, and changed into jeans and a long-sleeved nylon T-shirt, Diego was prepared to brave the sun and push out for Sangre de Dios. He drained the second whiskey.

The kitten rolled onto its back and swatted at the underside of the wicker chair. Diego glanced at it with enmity. After it put on a few pounds, it would be out like the other feral dogs and cats, scouring the landscape for tortoise eggs and land iguanas.

"You know," Rex said, "even if I set the GPS equipment on Sangre, we'll still need someone to receive the telemetric information here and relay it back to the States via computer."

"Well," Diego said, "you'll have to show me how the equipment works."

"I thought you retired," Juan said.

"That was the pig blood talking." Diego rose. "Let's get the gear set up at the Station. Then I'll pull the boat in and we'll load up."

They rose and headed for the door. Diego picked up the kitten by its tail on his way out. He stepped outside, twirled it once in the air, and smacked it against the wall. He tossed the limp body into a nearby trash can and started for the Station.

Chapter 24   They didn't have the luxury of waiting for dusk to avoid extreme UV exposure. Before they loaded the gear on *El Pescador Rico*, Diego made them wash their boots at the pier, in case they were caked with dirt hiding seeds, insect eggs, or other communicable material. Cameron was fascinated by the ritual—it was hard for her to believe that the ecology of each island was so fragile that it could be upset by the transport of a single seed. Though Sangre de Dios had already been compromised ecologically, Diego claimed that it could be further damaged by introduced species. Diego made Tucker throw out an apple he'd had in his kit bag since Guayaquil, and Savage had to hide his cigarettes in the top pocket of his shirt to save them from a similar fate.

The boat had been beautifully kept up—Cameron noticed Diego scrape some dried blood off the bow with his fingernail before boarding. Rex sat quietly on a cruise box, hold-

ing the padded nylon bags in his lap as they struck out for
Sangre de Dios. Diego kept them motoring west at about
eight knots. Derek threw the two Sigs back in the weapons
box and locked it.

They rounded Isabela's southern end, the foot of the
massive island's boot. Smoke, visible even through the
mist, curled ominously from the peaks of Cerro Azul and
Sierra Negra. Fernandina came into view only as they left
Isabela behind, settled back in the larger island's west bay.
The odor of fresh lava thickened the air, making the heat
even more oppressive. Finally, the sun began its drift to the
water, looming ahead until it extinguished itself in the Pacific.

Save the reflections of the stars and the occasional glimmer of dead fish floating on the surface, the ocean was suddenly black. The breeze smelled clean, full of salt and
distant vegetation. A full moon glowed overhead like a hole
through the sky. Nearly twenty hours after they left Puerto
Ayora, the moonlit, shadowy outline of Sangre de Dios cut
from the mist, the crown of a timid, pelagic animal come to
surface.

The squad members stirred and stretched. Justin laced his
fingers and turned his palms outward, cracking his knuckles.
Tank yawned. Savage flipped his Death Wind in his hand
and deftly jammed it into his sheath. He caught Szabla
watching him, but she quickly looked away. Cameron took
note of the curt movements and restless gestures with some
concern. After time off on the reserves, they'd all been
slowly finding their feet the past few days. Normally, when
transiting, the soldiers sat still and firm or prepared their
gear. On this mission, however, there was nothing to prepare
for. Just more waiting.

Concerned that the others' quiet unease would contami-
nate her, Cameron rose to stretch her legs. Juan was standing
by himself, watching the water splash against the bow. She
walked over and leaned on the railing beside him. The hull

cleaved a luminous white groove in the black pane of the ocean.

"We've always been wrong, you know," he said.

"No," Cameron said with a slight smile. "I didn't."

"That we are the royalty of the earth, that we should have dominion over the land and the seas because we are the most upright creatures that inhabit it."

Something about Juan's expression made Cameron refrain from commenting.

"All our importance has been robbed," he continued. "Before Copernicus, we thought we were the center of the universe; before Darwin, we thought we were created of the heavens." He chuckled, rubbing his chin. "Before Freud, we thought we were masters of our own minds." He gazed down at the waters below, tapping his ring on the railing. "And now this. Betrayed by the skies and the tides, by the earth's obligation to remain beneath our feet." He chuckled, but his eyes were pained.

"Not much of a point in faith anymore," Cameron said.

Juan looked over at her, surprised. "That's your conclusion?" he asked. He shook his head. "You must make your own faith. Your own little place in the midst of this chaos. Hold onto it like nothing else. That's what we all must do. Is that not why you joined the military?"

Cameron leaned forward, feeling the salty breeze across her cheeks. "Nothing quite so lofty," she said.

"Why then?"

She shrugged. "I never belonged anywhere. The teams gave me that. They gave me a place to belong."

Juan nodded, his mouth set in a firm line. "But they took something too, no?"

"Like what?"

He thumbed the edge of his ring but did not answer.

She felt herself growing defensive in the silence. "The military made an unquestioning commitment to me, and so I made one to it." She laughed, though she wasn't sure at what. "There are no complications for me here. Never." A small wave hit the bow and sent a splash onto her cammy shirt. She smoothed her thumb over the dark spot. "That's why I'm such a good goddamn soldier."

The boat banked and Cameron pushed off the railing and headed aft. She sat in silence for a few moments, watching Diego navigate the smooth waters as they closed on the island.

Cameron had glanced through the scant intel charts and maps during the tedious ride out. A roughly circular blob, Sangre de Dios had been formed by the Cerro Verde Volcano. It rose to an altitude of 515 meters at the apex of the dormant volcano. The peak sat off center, more than a kilometer in from the eastern coastline, a yolk floating to the right in a fried egg. From its peak to the eastern shore, the ground sloped sharply down to a cliff where, hundreds of years ago, an old fissure had fallen away, leaving only a vertical face. The stretch to the western coast followed a more gradual slope—eight degrees to the east side's twenty—and on this half of the island the vegetation zones were strikingly apparent: the coastal zone, the arid zone, the transition zone, and the *Scalesia* zone which capped the summit, forming a fertile apron of forest interrupted only by the caldera at the top. These zones ran in bands around the island, so distinct one could mark the actual line at the elevations where one zone ended and another began.

El Pescador Rico approached the southeast edge of Sangre de Dios. A sheltered cove, Bahía Avispa, came into view, lined with a white beach. Diego swung wide to avoid the rare coral reef that fringed the bay's eastern side. Sections of the reef had splintered in the quakes, leaving the bay full of jagged edges. He headed instead for Punta Berlanga, the western tip of the sheltered cove. A protruding horn, Punta Berlanga was named after the Bishop of Panama, Fray Tomás de Berlanga, who had accidentally discovered the islands in 1535. A mottled rise of salt-eroded columns and cliffs overlooking a stretch of flat, hardened *pahoehoe* lava,

Punta Berlanga received the brunt of the prevailing southeast winds and waves. On the far edge of the point, a series of blowholes erupted with a screech as the heavy surf forced geysers through the porous rock.

A decrepit wooden pier stretched out from the hard *pahoehoe* lava. There were no boats anchored. When they drew near, they saw that the pier was a splintered mess, destroyed in the last quake.

Diego cursed. "We'll have to drop anchor out here and Zodiac in to the point."

He slowed the boat, letting it crawl behind a string of tuff cones about a mile off the coast. Born of the violent interaction of water and molten rock, the tuff cones were composed of agglomerated ash. Sculpted by the tides and wind-worn on their southeast sides, they stuck ten to fifteen feet out of the water, the crooked fingers of a submerged giant. Several sea lions awakened on the tuff cones, barking at the approaching boat.

Diego's brow furrowed. "I've never seen them swim out here before. This colony usually congregates on the beach."

He set the bow and stern lines, then dragged the Zodiac overboard and cracked the bottle, holding the small boat steady as it unfolded. The sea was still, as before a storm, though the weather forecast was clear. "We'll have to take the Zodiac in in shifts," he said.

"From here on out, buddy pairs are in full effect," Derek said. "Same as in Guayaquil. Juan, you join Tank and Rex."

The boat rocked and Rex stumbled, leaning against the cabin wall and knocking Diego's speargun from its mount. The speargun bounced on the slippery deck and disappeared into the dark waters with a splash. Diego shook his head but said nothing. First into the Zodiac, Tank offered Rex a hand, which Rex ignored. Diego, Szabla, Juan, and Justin followed, hauling their kit bags and loading the majority of the boxes.

From his seat near the throttle, Diego pointed to a backpack still on *El Pescador Rico*. "We'll need that," he said. Derek handed the bag down to Justin, who opened it, revealing a PRC104 high-frequency radio.

"In case we need to contact the Flintstones?" Justin asked. He tapped his shoulder near the transmitter bump. "We got comms covered."

Diego shook his head. "Our satellite radio at the Station overloaded," he said. "The only way to reach anyone in Puerto Ayora is with this."

Justin nodded, looping the bag over his shoulders, and Diego cranked the throttle. The Zodiac sped off, the sound of the engine fading into that of the waves. The others sat in the rocking boat and waited. Savage unsnapped the button on his knife sheath, then snapped it again with a click. After a while, Cameron heard the drone of the approaching motor. Diego steered the empty Zodiac to the side of the boat, thumping against the wood.

Cameron tossed her kit bag into the Zodiac and hopped down. The others grabbed several more cruise boxes and the weapons box and followed her. They motored quietly to shore.

Waves seethed up the barren, rocky shore at Punta Berlanga, sending crabs scuttling across the moist, black lava and through the tide pools. Large blocks of rock rose in the foreground of the sculpted cliffs, stained white with guano. The wind lazed slow and steady, rousing an occasional swallow-tailed gull from its roost.

To the right, the beach stretched along the curve of Bahía Avispa, a white strip. Glancing west to east, Cameron saw the abrupt line where the upthrust blocks of Punta Berlanga ended, giving way to the low sand dunes protected by the reef and subject to the quiet erosion of the southeast tide.

The soldiers leapt overboard when they felt the lava skim the bottom of the Zodiac, pulling the small boat forward with splashing steps to keep momentum from sea to land. The water was different from the nighttime air only in consistency; the temperature seemed identical. The surface of the *pahoehoe* was rippled and intestinal; it had been formed during flows when fresh lava oozed forth in tongues from beneath the quick-hardening crust. Mats of *Sesuvium* herbs, dense patches of evergreen mangrove, and low tangles of saltbush with fat green leaves had somehow pioneered the barren lava.

The rest of the squad met them, hoisting the Zodiac to keep the scraping to a minimum. With their woodland cammies and jungle boots, the soldiers were blurs in the night. They jogged the boat back toward the cliffs, setting it down where Rex and Juan waited. Aside from the birds stirring in the cliffs and the hiss of the surf, the island was surprisingly quiet. A few *Opuntia* cactus trees broke the skyline at the edge of the cliffs.

Cameron gazed up at the stars, more than she'd ever seen in the night sky.

"Not a creature was stirring," Justin murmured.

Tucker and Szabla unloaded the comms boxes and kit bags from the Zodiac as Cameron deflated it. They dragged them a few feet and stacked them side by side by the gear from the previous trip. Rex watched them carefully when they got to the GPS equipment. Szabla pretended to drop the box filled with tripods, and Rex nearly fell over trying to catch it.

Tank grabbed the two heavy cruise boxes that housed the general purpose tents and tugged them along the lava, the muscles standing out on his thick arms.

"All right," Derek said. "Someone grab the weapons box off the Zodiac. We're gonna camp—"

A howling split the air above their heads. Savage ripped his knife from the sheath as they instinctually backed into formation. The howling died into a moan and then faded away. Savage slowly lowered his knife.

Justin and Tucker scanned the area, still trying to adjust to the darkness. Rex and Juan found Tank immediately, crowding him from each side. The wind kicked up again, blowing the blunt edge of Cameron's hair across her cheek, and she pulled it back and hooked it around an ear. The howl resumed. She backed down toward the water, gazing up at the cliffs.

"Cam," Derek hissed. "Get back here."

"It's the wind," she said, smiling. She pointed to a gaping black hole in the side of the dappled cliff walls. "A cave. The wind's sucking across the entrance." She was surprised at how quickly the wind had kicked up; a few moments prior, the air had been almost deathly still.

"The salt and wind have worked hollows into the cliffs all along here," Diego said, wiping his brow with a nylon sleeve. "And there are irregularities in the basalt where land fell away from the fissures." He smirked. "Nothing to be frightened of."

A blast of wind hit them so hard that Justin staggered a little under its force. Rex put one hand on his Panama hat to keep it from blowing off. The howl reached a scream.

"What the fuck!" Justin said, as Savage slid his knife back into its sheath. "That's a little embarrassing." The others joined his laughter.

Derek cleared his throat. "I think we can safely say—"

The ground rocked violently beneath their feet, a grinding noise filling the air. Szabla was knocked over, thrown against the base of the cliff.

"¡Mierda!" Diego yelled, his voice almost drowned out by the rumbling. "We've got a shaker. Head down to the water."

The sound of cracking rock filled the air above them, and a shower of dirt slid from the cliff, falling over their heads. Juan ducked the debris, banging into Szabla.

"Move away from the cliff!" Rex yelled. "It could slide."

A rock about the size of a skull struck Justin from behind, but fortunately, his backpack took the brunt of the blow. He went to a knee under the force of the rock but was quickly up and running again, hustling Rex and Diego along before him.

Szabla went down, almost taking Juan with her. She

struggled to find her feet, and Juan stepped toward her, arms spread wide to keep his balance on the rocking earth. He tried to pull her up but was having trouble maintaining his own footing.

Cameron grabbed Derek's arm and yanked him down toward the water, his shoulder popping with the force of her pull. He stumbled after her until the water was up around his thighs, fighting to keep his balance in the suddenly thrashing waves. Tucker, Justin, Rex, Diego, and Savage were already in the water, and Tank was running toward them on the slippery rock.

"Where's Szabla?!" Derek yelled. He looked around frantically. "Fuck, where's Juan? Where's Juan?"

Cameron saw them at the base of the cliff, trying to stand under the shower of rocks and silt. Juan slipped and landed on his back. He rolled to his hands and knees and Szabla hoisted him up under one arm.

Cameron backhanded Derek's chest. "There!" she yelled, pointing.

Derek turned to the others. "Stay here!" he yelled. "That's an order." He ran toward Szabla and Juan, smacking Tank on the shoulder as he passed him. "Tank, come!" Without hesitation, Tank turned and followed him.

Juan was finally on his feet, but the ground was loose because the freshly fallen rocks kept rolling and shifting. His canteen dangled from its strap, dancing around his stomach. Grabbing Szabla around one of her biceps, Juan stepped forward onto a mound of rocks. A creaking sound from above startled him, and he turned to see an *Opuntia* bending over the brink of the cliff. With a screech, it split, snapping in a fork up the line of its meter-wide trunk. The weighty cactus tree plummeted down at them.

With all his might, Juan flung Szabla away from the base of the cliff, lifting her off her feet. She hit the ground in a roll and didn't stop until she was up and sprinting for the water. The force of hurling Szabla threw Juan backward, his shoulders striking the base of the rocky wall. He slid down onto his ass, slumping into the ground, blinking hard as if to fight off a haze.

The cactus tree sliced the air a few yards in front of him, smashing into the lava. For a moment, it rested upside down, creaking and moaning, as though deciding which way to fall. Juan raised his arms to protect his face, his mouth open in a silent yell. With excruciating slowness, the cactus tree fell away from him, toppling toward the water.

The ground slowed its shaking and then, aside from the light pebbles drumming their way down the cliff face, it was still. Juan's breath left him in a gasp of relief.

Derek and Tank clawed their way over the fallen cactus tree, the thick, moisture-retaining spines digging into their palms and knees. "Juan!" Derek yelled. "You all right?"

"I'm fine." Juan tried to sit up but grimaced sharply and clutched his side. He collapsed again, fighting weakness and gravity. "Just need . . . a little . . . hand here."

Derek stepped forward, high on the cactus tree, and took Juan's hand, gripping it firmly around the thumb so that he could better bear his weight. Tank stood behind him, boots smashing down the cactus pads.

"All right," Derek said. "One . . . two . . ."

An aftershock rippled the ground and Derek's feet went out from under him. The cactus spines dug into his back even through his cammies, and he grunted with pain, but he didn't let go of Juan's hand. Juan moaned, jerked forward by his arm. Derek managed to sit up, his hand still tight around Juan's. They were only about two feet from each other, their eyes level.

"I got you, buddy," Derek said. "I still got you."

A large lava rock, the size of a sailor's chest, dislodged from the top of the cliff. It banged once against the face, letting loose a scattering of dirt and stone, and was free in the air, hurtling down.

They both looked up just as the rock struck Juan, glancing

off the side of his head and smashing into his lap. His hand was ripped from Derek's with such force that his fingernails left red lines down Derek's palm.

Juan grunted under the impact, a spray of blood leaving his lips, and then he was buried under the rock, only the top of his head visible. His legs stuck out awkwardly beneath it, twitching. His canteen was smashed to pieces through his thighs.

"Jesus God," Derek whispered. "Jesus God."

Tank stumbled forward, pulling his boots free from the cactus tree, and stood above the boulder and Juan's body. For a moment, it was deathly quiet.

Then they heard the rasping.

Juan's head tilted and pulled back from the rock. The entire right side of his face was awash in blood, a shard of cheekbone glinting somewhere in the mess. Breath rattled through him. His lips faded away into crushed teeth. The bloody maw opened. And screamed. A splattering of blood left the mouth with each cry.

"Get it off!" Derek yelled. "Get the fucking thing off."

Tank struggled forward, cactus pads stuck to the bottoms of his boots. Lines of sweat streaked from his hairline, curving down his ruddy cheeks.

Derek grabbed the rock and fought against it, but it didn't budge. He felt a jagged edge tear into his right hand, but he strained against the wound with all his might.

The screaming quickened.

Tank laid one massive hand on Derek's shoulder and hurled him aside. He spread his arms and seized the rock in a massive embrace. Dipping low on his haunches, he prepared himself as though for a power-lifting squat.

The screaming continued—harsh, rattling cries filled with liquid. Juan started to jerk back and forth, flailing against the rock. Blood was splattering all over the place now; Derek could see droplets filling the air even over Tank's shoulders.

"Jesus, kill him. We should just kill him," Derek yelled.

But he had no gun. He found himself looking around for a
rock to use as a makeshift weapon, his stomach cold and
pulsing at the thought.

Straining with all his might, Tank rose from his crouch.
He groaned through his clenched teeth, the sound rising to a
roar. His face filled with blood, swelling until it looked as if
it would explode if pricked with a pin. His shirt split straight
down the back.

The boulder shifted in Juan's lap and then rose, hovering
barely an inch above his smashed thighs. With another roar,
Tank leaned back, hugging the rock to his chest and getting
it about two feet off the ground. With the force of his entire
body, he tried to hurl the boulder to one side, but it dribbled
out of his arms, thunking into the lava.

Juan lay motionless, his jaw open with his dying scream.
His arms were twisted up to his chest, one hand bent out at a
grotesque angle, a nub of bone protruding from the wrist.

Tank swayed as he looked at the body, his arms moving
like pendulums. He tried to clench his hands into fists but
could not. They dangled open in defeat. Red scrapes ran all
the way from the insides of his wrists up across his chest.
His shirt hung from his shoulders in ribbons.

"Let's go," Derek said. He rested a hand on Tank's shoulder, but Tank shook it off. "He's done," Derek said sternly.
"Let's clear out before more aftershocks hit."

Tank nodded once, a slight movement of his head. Derek
rested a hand on his shoulder, turning him toward the water.
Tank grunted with his first step. Derek stabilized him as best
he could with an arm around his waist, but it didn't really
help.

They crested the cactus tree, and Tank stumbled roughly
down, taking a spray of spines across the back of his thighs.
His feet jarred against the lava, and he would have kept going down to his knees if Derek hadn't caught him, staggering under his weight. Tank righted himself, whimpering like
a puppy.

Szabla took an instinctive step forward, but Cameron

grabbed her shoulder. "Orders," she said. Breathing hard, Szabla pushed Cameron's hand from her shoulder, but stayed put. Tank leaned hard on Derek as they approached, his movements stiff and pained.

A section of the cliff gave way, burying Juan's corpse and the Zodiac in a surge of rocks. As the last few stones tumbled to the top of the mound, Derek locked his arms around Tank's waist, lacing his fingers and straining as they stumbled across the slippery black rock into the surf. They tried to duck a four-foot wave, but it hit them square in the chest. Tank came up gasping, facing the others. To the west, water shot through the blowholes, sending screeching blasts into the air.

Szabla's face was blank. "Juan?" she asked.

Derek shook his head.

Justin leaned into Cameron, and she pressed back reassuringly with her shoulder. Tucker looked out across the rough ocean, shifting uncomfortably from foot to foot.

Savage smiled. "Welcome to Sangre de Dios," he said in a low purring voice.

Tank's legs gave out, and he hit the surf with a splash. It took four of them to lift him out of the water.

Chapter 25   The tremors subsided and soon Derek didn't even have to brace against the waves. The mound of lava rocks at the cliff shifted, sending a trickle down one side that flowed gentle and steady like hourglass sand before stopping. The air stilled.

Trailing long, slender streamers, a few red-billed tropicbirds circled overhead, preparing to return to their nests in the cliff walls. Baby Sally Lightfoot crabs scrabbled across the lava, their bright orange shells seeming to glow against the dark rock.

The soldiers waited silently for another aftershock, standing thigh-deep in the water. After about fifteen minutes, Derek sloshed up onto the flat lava plain. He turned to help Tank pull himself up, and the others followed.

The stack of cruise boxes and kit bags remained before the cliff walls, barely beyond the reach of the fallen rocks. The cruise boxes' hard tops had been dinged up, but they hadn't collapsed. The weapons box, along with several cruise boxes, was buried in the rubble with the Zodiac. Derek gazed at the collapsed section of the cliff. There was no way they'd be able to get Juan's body, the Zodiac, or any of the buried gear out from under that much rock. Not without a bulldozer. The weapons had been useless anyway, though Derek was not looking forward to filling out a report detailing the missing ordnance.

The soldiers assessed the terrain in silence. Rex looked pale, almost sickly, and he repeatedly glanced over at the mound of rocks burying Juan's body. Finally, Szabla smacked him on the chest. "Relax. All that staring's not gonna make him any less dead."

About a hundred yards east, the lava and cliffs faded into the low-lying sand dunes. The beach was well clear of the cliff and other overhangs, safe from falling objects during earthquakes and tremors.

"We'll set an LUP down on the beach," Derek said. "To-morrow, we'll see about moving up somewhere stable and establishing permanent camp."

The soldiers dragged the cruise boxes across the lava to the beach and began to set the lay-up point, assembling the tents and stacking supplies. Derek and Cameron took inventory.

They'd stay one buddy pair to a tent. Diego was supposed to have shared the fifth tent with Juan; now he'd have it to himself.

Tank could barely fit on the standard-issue foam sleeping pad, so he sprawled out on the ground. Once he lay down, he couldn't get back up. Tank was drowsy with the pain, which was a bad sign, given his extremely high threshold. Once, in Copenhagen, he'd sustained a rifle butt blow to the head without passing out. Justin tried massaging out the spasms in his legs, but the muscles were too tightly knotted. Though Justin's trauma bag was on the boat, he always carried a few extra items in his kit bag, including Toradol. He gave Tank a 60 mg injection.

They mustered near the tents around a hurricane lamp, Derek facing them with his back to the night, rubbing the exhaustion from his eyes. They'd pinned Tank's tent flap open so that he could look out on the meeting.

Cameron thumbed an eyelid, thinking of Juan sitting on the edge of the mausoleum, his wedding band a thin, gold streak in the night. She tapped her ring, checking it was still safe around her neck.

Rex cleared his throat nervously. "Look," he said. "I don't mean to be mercenary, but we're still going to complete the survey, right?"

Savage made a sucking noise, clearing something from between his front teeth. "I didn't drag my shit all the way here to turn tail and run at the first sign of a falling rock or a dead spic." He winked at Diego. "No offense."

Diego shrugged, not recognizing the slur.

"We're fucked on the Zodiac," Derek said. "Justin, tomorrow, you're gonna take a swim out to the boat, figure out how to get the rest of our gear to land. How's the Prick one-oh-four?"

Justin swung the backpack off, plunking it on the sand. The material was torn where it had been struck by the falling rock. "It took a blow," he said, as he carefully removed the radio. Cameron was relieved to see that the radio proper and the S-folded whip antenna both appeared to be intact. The size of an old-style VCR, the radio was a confusion of buttons and dials. The handset usually worked like a telephone, but both the receiver and transmitter were smashed.

After tuning the radio, Justin keyed the handset to break squelch, pushing the button on the side so that a burst of static would go through. "There's no way," he said. "We can't speak or get anything back."

"And my phone's buried over there." Rex gestured to the fallen cliff. "So that's it? We have no contact with the outside world?"

"Just not with the other islands," Derek said. He tapped his shoulder, indicating his subcutaneous transmitter. "We can still reach base through these. They're satellite."

"We gonna call in?" Justin asked.

"I don't see what for," Derek said. "Our job was to get Rex here, help him get his trinkets in place, and split. Far as I can see, that objective has not been compromised."

"I'd like to get one of the GPS units set early tomorrow morning," Rex said. He pointed at a narrow trail that led up through a break in the cliff walls of Punta Berlanga. "I'm thinking right up there if I can find suitable rock. After that, we gotta survey the island for other locations."

Derek crouched, letting a handful of the fine, flourlike sand run through his fingers. "We have camping gear, food, and kit bags with clothes and personals. From the boat, we need to grab medical supplies, scuba gear, mosquito netting, backup white fuel for the hurricane lamps, extra MREs, and K-bars. All the GPS equipment intact?"

"Yes," Rex said. "One of the tripods is a little bit—"

"That's good," Szabla said. "Then we can focus on getting the shit up and running and getting the fuck out of here."

Tank moaned inside his tent, trying to straighten his legs.

Derek rose, brushing his hands off on his pants. "Anyone . . ." He stopped to clear his throat. "Anyone want to say anything? About Juan?"

A silence filled the air, broken only by the soft sounds of the ocean behind them. Justin toed the sand.

"A few words or anything?" Derek added.

Savage coughed. Tucker blinked.

"Guess not," Szabla said.

CAMERON HELPED pull several cruise boxes around the hurricane lamp to serve as makeshift benches. The others' eyes were heavy with exhaustion. She knew she looked equally spent, but sleep seemed unappealing with the memory of Juan's death so vivid.

Savage sat off by himself on the beach, legs crossed Indian-style, staring out at the dark water. Szabla watched him, the light from the hurricane lamp flickering across her face. Diego lay on his back across two of the cruise boxes, his arms dangling so his fingers brushed the sand. Szabla's face darkened when she glanced in the direction of Juan's buried body. "What a waste," she said.

Rex was leaning back against the cruise box, his face tilted up toward the heavens. "Have you heard of Enrico Caruso?" he finally asked.

Clearly annoyed, Szabla studied the hard surface of the cruise box between her legs as the other soldiers exchanged glances. "The tenor?"

"The tenor. On April eighteenth, 1906, after a riveting performance in *Carmen*, he retired to his suite in the Palace Hotel in San Francisco. The quake hit at five twelve in the morning, took the rear wall clean off the building. Well, Caruso was something of a superstitious guy." Rex lowered his eyes from the stars finally, looking at Szabla. "Italian," he said. Szabla bit back a smile, and Rex continued. "His conductor found him weeping in his room. To calm Caruso down and distract him from the aftershocks, he convinced him to look out on the devastation and sing. And Caruso did. Streets rent and broken, streetcars bent like toys, water mains shooting geysers, people sobbing and running and bleeding, and here's Caruso, singing at the top of his lungs, his voice ringing through the rubble, clear as a bell." Rex paused, shaking his head.

"This all looks like a mess to you," he continued. "A big fucking mess. The quakes and the sun, falling rocks and dead animals. But it all has rules. Nature always follows definable rules." He pointed at the crumbled cliff wall in the distance, the mound of rock that formed Juan's makeshift grave. "The principal shock must've been east-west, given the damage moved along a north-south vector. That means

this rumble was a little gift from the East Pacific Rise." He
scratched the stubble on his chin, his eyes on the dark sky.
"The earth's movements can be regulated, sometimes predicted. That can save lives."

He caught Szabla's eye again and stared her down. "Getting these GPS units in place is my way of singing through
the disasters, of trying to win something back for our side."
He laughed a short, dying laugh and ran his hand through his
lanky black hair. "I know you all think the military has better things to do right now. I know that I'm an arrogant, nar-
cissistic bastard, and that doesn't help much either. But we
have the opportunity to accomplish something here. So what
do you say you all just back off a few steps and give me a
hand?"

They sat in silence, listening to the sounds of the island.
Rex cuffed his sleeves, revealing a deep scar on the back of
his right forearm.

"What's that?" Cameron asked, indicating the scar with a
flick of her head.

Rex glanced down at it, as if noticing it for the first time.
"Candlestick, eighty-nine World Series. The Loma Prieta
quake. I caught a flying hot dog vendor's box on the arm."
He laughed. "Hardly heroic."

Szabla dug a piece of dirt out from under a blunt fingernail.
She sat up straight and pulled off her cammy shirt. Her skin
was dark and smooth, the blocks of her stomach standing out
like bricks beneath her jog bra. She turned around, revealing
a knot of scar tissue just below her left shoulder blade.

Diego glanced over from his sprawl on the cruise boxes.
He was tickling his face with a strand of beach morning
glory. Clearly uninterested in their story telling, Savage began doing push-ups on the sand outside their circle, slow
and methodical.

"Trying to help an old lady in Bosnia," Szabla said, patting her scar. "House caved in, she was stuck beneath some
stones. Picked her up, threw her over a shoulder to clear her
from the building. She pulled a knife on me."

"That's a stab wound?" Rex asked.

Cameron smiled, knowing the story. Szabla hooked Justin's neck with her hand and yanked it roughly and affectionately. "You think my buddy over here would let me meet my end from Mother-fucking Hubbard?"

Justin grinned. "I hit her with a board."

"And missed."

"Well, Szabla tripped and dumped the old bitch—"

"And the board hit me instead, right on the shoulder."

"A board left a scar like that?" Rex asked.

Szabla and Justin exchanged a glance, starting to laugh. Cameron smiled, looking down and shaking her head. "It had a nail in it," Justin said.

"So genius over here wallops me, I got a two-by-four stuck in my ass, and the cunt claws her way up and takes off down the street like Jesse fuckin' Owens."

"You think that's bad? You want to talk stupid?" Cameron stood up, pulling down her pants and turning around to display a four-inch scar beneath her right buttock.

"Cam, Jesus," Justin said.

She yanked her pants back up and zipped them, forgetting the top button. "We're lifting out to Alaska of all places, for a block of winter warfare training. I have my blade out to get through a canvas strap on one of the supply bags and I catch a glimpse out the window of the sun setting over the tundra—just beautiful. So I put down the blade and lean forward, watch for a few seconds until it dips below the horizon. I sat back down, right on my knife."

"She screamed so loud the pilot thought we were under attack," Derek said. "Thirteen stitches. Right on the helo, in fact." Derek laughed. "Cam bent over the corpsman's knee like a wayward schoolgirl."

"And boy did she holler," Tucker added.

"I did not. Not after I first sat down and the damn thing went up my ass."

Szabla grinned. "There was definitely some whimpering going on, girl."

Justin shook his head. "I should have married a teacher." He looked at his wife. "All right, baby. Button your pants."

"What? Oh." Cameron looked down and fixed her top button.

"Gotcha beat," Tucker said with a wry smile. He held up his left hand and spread it before the light. His entire palm was scarred with dark burn tissue.

"Jesus, Tucker, when did that happen?" Cameron asked.

"About a year back. I was fucking around with my thermite grenade, spinning it around, watching a little tube. Well, the spoon flew and I didn't notice. So I keep spinning it, Duke's up four in the third quarter, and all of a sudden I look over, the thing's glowing that hard white flame. So I yell, try to dump it, it's stuck to my hand for a second and I shake it loose. It burns through the sofa, the floorboards, and down into the apartment under mine. I had to run down the stairs, bang on the door to warn them." He ran the hardened flesh across his cheek. "Went straight through their kitchen table."

They all laughed, and Tucker lowered his eyes to the light of the hurricane lamp.

Diego pulled himself up from where he was lying and stood in the center. He faced the others, his features shadowed. "There's a tiny catfish, a parasite that resides in the warm waters of the Amazon," he said. "Lives on blood. It normally slithers into the gills of a larger fish and erects a sharp dorsal spine to lodge itself into place." He held up a finger, mock-teacherly. "The problem is, it can mistake a stream of urine underwater for the small water currents passing through the gills of a fish. It swims up the urethra of the unfortunate skinny dipper and . . ." he made a papping sound, splaying his fingers wide to indicate the dorsal spine erecting. Cameron bit her bottom lip. The others stared at him, wide-eyed. "Has to be removed surgically," he continued.

"The whole thing?" Szabla asked breathlessly.

"No," Diego said. "Just the fish." He pulled his belt free, unbuttoned his pants, and pulled them down, his underwear along with them. He cradled his uncircumcised penis in his palm. Szabla stared at the elongated scar with a mix of horror and reluctant interest. Justin reached up with his hand and pushed his own jaw closed.

Diego raised his arms and slapped them to his sides, letting himself hang free in the night air. He pulled up his pants, shot Szabla a wink, and headed for his tent.

AFTER WASHING his face in the cool, salty water, Savage returned to the ring of cruise boxes and the flickering hurricane lamp. The others had already retired to their tents. Justin had stopped to check on Tank, leaving Szabla alone in their tent. It was lit inside by a lamp, and Savage saw Szabla's shadow clearly defined against the green glow of the canvas. He froze outside the small circle of tents, transfixed by her silhouette.

Szabla pulled off her shirt and lifted her tags over her head, winding them around her hand. Probably hated sleeping with anything around her neck. Her undershirt was tight enough that Savage could make out the exact lines of her body. Szabla didn't have large breasts; hers were more like plates rising solidly off her chest. Cameron had the only real pair of knocks on the squad.

Voices murmured within Tank's tent. Cameron and Derek's lamp faded, then turned off. Savage watched Szabla bend to remove her shoes, then she took off her pants, wriggling as she pulled them over her hips. She tossed them in the corner where they landed silently on the sand. He adjusted himself in his pants, wondering if she knew he was watching her. He bet she did. He looked out across the ocean, trying to ignore the silhouette to his left. The waves rolled in, easing up the shore and fizzing as the foam smoothed over. When he looked back at Szabla's tent, the lamp was off.

He paced around the small ring of tents a few times, then

walked back to the camp and straddled a cruise box. He glanced over and someone was sitting right next to him. He jerked back, sliding off the cruise box, the Death Wind out of the sheath before he realized that it was Szabla. She laughed quietly, her teeth flashing in the darkness.

"You better be grateful you didn't swing that thing at me, boy, or you'd be wearing it right about now." She was wearing ripped camo shorts and a white undershirt. Her clavicle showed above the collar of her shirt, an elegant line beside the hard curve of her deltoid. Her skin was wet with the ocean mist, humidity, and sweat.

Savage couldn't help glancing down at her hard body, though he tried not to. He thought she might have noticed because she smiled. He scratched his head, lowering his eyes. "I should put a cowbell around your neck," he said.

"I'll try not to read too much into that," she said. He laughed. "Couldn't sleep," she added. "Just wanted to come out and say hey."

"Hey."

Her lips pressed together, betraying her amusement. "Hey."

He was trying to look everywhere except at her eyes, but it finally got too awkward, so he raised his head. She was looking straight at him. Szabla wasn't a flincher; she had no qualms about staring right through him. They stared at each other for a few moments, not touching, not knowing what to say.

Szabla started to speak, but then Justin stumbled sleepily from Tank's tent, massaging his neck with one hand and yawning. He froze when he saw them. Szabla looked at him with wide eyes, like a deer caught in headlights, and then he shook his head, just once, and walked to his and Szabla's tent.

When Szabla looked back at Savage, her eyes were different. He didn't drop his stare even as she turned, trailing a hand on the cruise box, and headed back to her tent.

Chapter 26   The morning came fast and glorious, breaking over the distant arc of the ocean and turning the water to a dappled sheet of orange and yellow. A scattering of cirrus clouds textured the sky. Derek sat on one of the cruise boxes, the toe of his boot stirring the sand. Again, he'd been unable to sleep. Finally, thoughts of Jacqueline had driven him from the tent into the open, where he could breathe better.

From beneath heavy lids, he watched the beach around him take shape with the light. Quickly, even the cliff walls of Punta Berlanga were visible. Sailors had painted or chiseled the names of their ships on the lava in a kind of antiquated graffiti—*1836 Gabbiano, St. George, Wanderlure.* Juan's grave sat sadly unadorned. It was like all the other recently formed mounds, except hidden in its rocky wash was a bloody corpse.

Twenty yards off, a bull sea lion wallowed ashore on muscular flippers. He barked, shuddered so his fat rolled heavily around his body, and bellied down into the sand to draw some warmth from the sun. His coarse whiskers sloped down, waving in the breeze and matching the wiggle of the small nubs of his ears. He pushed his flippers flat against his side where his blubber was thinnest and lazed over to one side, turning a deep brown eye in Derek's direction.

Closer to Derek, a female waddled ashore, her pup struggling to keep up with her. She stopped a few feet from Derek, keeping her distance from the male. A yellow warbler lit on her head, hopping and pecking at flies.

The tents rustled with the sounds of morning. The soldiers' internal clocks were nearly impeccable; they rose at first light, regardless of time zone.

Szabla stumbled over something and cursed.

Cameron stepped from her tent and stretched, scratching her hair. Behind her, she heard Rex emerge from his tent. He went down to the water's edge immediately, filled a jar from a reddish patch of water, and held it up to note its tint. In the distance, a wave slapped the lava shore, sending a row of spouts up through the blowholes.

The others emerged and gathered around Cameron, watching the sea lion and her pup. Tank was on his feet, but he grimaced as he lifted his foot to rest it on a cruise box.

"Shit, LT," Szabla said. "You get any sleep? You look like hell."

Derek looked up at the green humps of the highlands in the distance. "I slept fine."

A tiny wasp flew near Cameron, and she swatted it, ducking. It flew in a mad circle and came back at her head. "Bahía Avispa," she said with a grimace. "Wasp Bay."

The wasp buzzed near Szabla and she shot out her hand, catching it. She shook her fist, threw the dazed insect down, and ground it into the sand with her boot.

Justin walked down to the ocean and splashed water over his face. On his way back, he looked down at the loose laces of his boot. He turned to sit on a nearby rock to tie them when the rock erupted in a flurry of barks. He leapt up just as the male sea lion spun around, snapping jaws inches from his ass. Justin sprinted back to the group, losing his boot along the way. The sea lion waddled after him a few furious steps, his bumped head bouncing on his thick neck, barking his displeasure.

Justin pressed his hand to his chest, ignoring the others' laughter. The male sea lion slowed, turning a nasty glare in Justin's direction. He slid down onto his belly, emitting a few more barks for good measure. Szabla tried to imitate

Justin's startled expression but deteriorated into more laughter. Savage flipped a cigarette into his mouth and lit it with a quick flash of his lighter.

Justin pulled his boot back on, hopping on one leg. "Jesus, that got my clock going," he said, his face still red.

"Don't mind him," Diego said, his lips pressed together in a smile. "He's just more territorial because he's not part of a colony." He glanced up the empty beach. "I wonder where the rest of the colony is. There weren't very many sea lions out on the tuff cones."

"Do you keep track of that?" Szabla asked. "I thought you were a herpetologist."

"Galápagos inclines everyone to pursue avocational interest across the beams."

"Boards," Cameron corrected with a smile.

"Ah, yes. Across the boards. When my turtles were hatching at Punta Cormorant, there were at least four botanists trying to muscle in on the action." Diego smiled good-naturedly. "No one wanted to miss out on the fun."

The female sea lion rolled onto her back, nearly squashing Cameron's foot. She sidestepped and walked to the nearby sea lion pup, leaning over to pet it. Its head was slick against her palm.

Diego cursed at her sharply, and Cameron straightened up. "What?" she asked.

Rex looked away with irritation. "You can't touch them."

"I don't see why . . ."

The pup moved toward its mother, but the mother rolled away from it. She barked at it a few times, then waddled to the water, leaving her pup behind.

"The scent. You can't . . ." Diego stopped, exasperated and upset. "You left your scent on it. The mother won't care for it now."

Cameron's eyes widened. "I didn't know," she said.

"Then ask," Rex said. "Or keep your goddamn hands in your pockets."

"It was a mistake," Justin said. "Back the fuck off."

"A few rules," Diego said, trying to keep the anger from his voice. "Don't touch or feed any of the animals. When you go anywhere, walk single-file to reduce the chance of disrupting mating grounds or buried eggs. Do not, under any circumstances, go up to the active caldera. Don't take any souvenirs, and don't leave anything behind."

Savage sucked hard on the cigarette, dropped the butt, and heeled it into the sand. Diego walked over and picked up the cigarette butt, holding it up for the others to see. "Not anything," he said. "If just one tobacco plant springs up, there's nothing in the island's ecology to stop it from spreading everywhere. It's a risk we don't take."

The pup rolled onto its stomach, its head rotating back and forth as it searched for its mother. They all did their best to ignore it.

Derek rubbed sleep from one of his eyes. "Me and Cameron—" His head had been turned toward his shoulder, causing Cameron's transmitter to vibrate, but she whispered a command to still it. "Me and Cam'll head up and scout stable locations for a base camp."

"The edge of the *Scalesia* forest is probably the safest region of the island," Diego said. "The fields near the village."

"How many live in the village?" Derek asked.

Diego shrugged. "A few, maybe none. Last I heard, Ramoncito's parents were still here. The island has been less than hospitable, especially these past few months."

"I believe Frank set his camp near the village," Rex said. "I'll take a look through it. See what he left behind."

"I'll join you," Diego said. "I'd like to check if anyone's here, make sure the livestock are secure."

Derek glanced at his watch. "That's fine. When we get back, we'll set the first GPS unit and scout locations. The rest of you wait here. We'll muster at 0800." He gazed up at the white smudge of the sun. "And make sure you hydrate heavily," he added. "It's gonna be a hot fucker."

The sea lion pup waddled a few feet toward the surf. Tilting its head back, it brayed softly in the direction its mother had disappeared. It took all Cameron had to turn her back on it and follow Derek off the beach.

Chapter 27   Samantha practiced Tae Bo in the corner of the slammer, supplementing her roundhouses and side kicks with late-night-movie sound effects. In reality, she had no idea what she was doing, but on many a sleepless night, she'd watched the Tae Bo infomercial with a perverse interest. Given that she had no better options while she waited for Tom Straussman to return with the electron micrographs, she figured the least she could do was practice her grunting. Plus it helped her keep her mind off her test results, which would be in any moment. She'd spent the night fidgeting, praying the antiserum would be approved for the pilot and flight attendant, and that their viremia hadn't progressed extensively.

There was a knocking on the window, and Samantha glanced over, one foot extended awkwardly before her. Colonel Douglas Strickland, Fort Detrick Base Commander, stood rigid in the hallway, watching her with something like disdain. Samantha lowered her foot and snapped off a crisp salute. Her hair had fallen forward in her face, and Kiera's NVME T-shirt was damp with sweat.

She walked over to the window. "Sir," she said.

Strickland watched her for a moment before speaking, his jaw shifting slowly to one side, then back again. Samantha wondered how he could stand like that—shoulders back, chest forward, beret tucked neatly beneath one elbow and pressed to his side. She made a note to work on Iggy's posture.

"Dr. Everett," he said. His nose bunched like a rabbit's, then loosened.

"Yes, sir."

"I'd imagine you're quite impressed with yourself, having backed us into a corner with this media stunt."

"Well, it—" He raised a hand and Samantha stopped short. When Colonel Douglas Strickland raised his hand, people generally stopped short.

"Allow me to proffer a bit of advice. I am not in the mood to field even the slightest amount of horseshit from you. I am here to speak, not to listen, and you are here to listen, not to speak. Is that clear?"

Samantha opened her mouth. Closed it. Nodded.

"Your viral load has continued to decrease, and we've cleared the antiserum to be used on the pilot and stewardess."

Samantha began to smile but stopped when she read his expression.

He continued, his face betraying little emotion. "We've sent this case through for internal review. A JAG officer has already been assigned to the investigation. I am going to do everything I personally can to see that you're shitcanned. You may have the chops for science, darling, but an army major you're not. That said, I hope this ploy of yours is successful, that you might have something positive to remember during your early retirement."

He turned sharply on heel and began walking away. Samantha raised her fist to the glass and knocked once. He turned around.

"Sir," she said.

He raised his eyebrows, ever so slightly.

"I'm a Wellesley graduate with an M.D. from Hopkins, a Ph.D. in microbiology from the NIH, extensive clinical training at the EIS, and field experience on six of the seven continents. I ran the Viral Special Pathogens Branch at the CDC and, for the time being, I'm the Chief of the Disease Assessment Division here." She pushed an errant strand of hair off her cheek. "Don't call me darling. It just makes you look like an ass."

Colonel Douglas Strickland stared at her for a long, hard time. His mouth twitched once—Samantha wasn't sure if it was in anger, or the beginnings of a smile—and then smoothed back into his impenetrable face.

"Very well," he said. "Dr. Everett."

Chapter 28   Rex hiked up the small trail cut into the cliff walls at Punta Berlanga, Derek, Cameron, and Diego following quietly. Above the cliffs, the ground was all rock, covered with low, scrubby saltbushes resembling haystacks. Rex let Diego navigate through the masked booby mating grounds. They crested a small rise, and dozens of the birds spread before them, spaced evenly across the lava.

One booby took a few halting steps and sky-pointed, angling its neck straight so its beak shot upward toward the sun. A bright white bird—save jet-black markings at the wing tips; a stout, yellow-orange beak; and a dark ring circling its beak and narrow-set eyes—the booby was odd-looking. It lowered its beak, panting, vibrating its wattle to shed heat. Most of the other boobies sat with their heads turned backward, accessing oil from glands on their rumps and brushing it through their feathers. Somewhere, a male sang a hollow, rustling whistle of a mating call.

A chick stumbled awkwardly out onto the path, and Diego halted, letting it cross. A fluffy white creature that resembled a little snowman, the chick leaned forward into the breeze, spreading its wings to practice flapping. Its white downy coat was patchy, its neck thin and fragile. Diego crouched, patiently waiting for the booby to cross. Cameron started to step around, but Diego raised a hand, snapping his fingers sharply, and she froze.

"Do *not* walk through the nesting grounds," he said.

Another masked booby chick stumbled ahead of them, its feathers ripped from the right side of its head. Darkened blood had crusted down its neck, and it wobbled unsurely on its feet. "What happened?" Derek asked.

Diego pointed to a nearby nest. "The females lay two eggs, but they only care for one offspring. The runt is murdered by its sibling, cast out to die of starvation or exposure, or attacked by its parents and killed."

Derek shook his head. "Christ," he said.

Rex shrugged. "Limited resources."

The chick fell over and struggled to rise, its eyes flickering in the sockets. Its wings pulsed twice, then stilled. Diego stepped over it and signaled the others ahead. They passed a group of male frigate birds in a tree ballooning their bright red gular sacs to draw the attention of females flying overhead.

Once they passed the aeries, Rex was glad to reclaim the lead. The steepness of the island's east side allowed them to pass through the vegetation zones quickly. Palo santos dominated the arid zone, their forked, skeletal branches overgrown with wispy vines. From a burrow hidden beneath a flourish of saltwort, a land iguana watched them pass, not even bothering to lift its head. A distinct dusty yellow, the land iguana had a smaller crest than its marine counterparts, and its tail was shorter, not needed for swimming.

The underbrush thickened and grew more lush as they hiked up into the higher-altitude transition zone. Pega pegas—short-stemmed trees with spread branches and coarse, lichen-covered bark—sprouted virtually everywhere, set off by the occasional mango tree. The higher reaches were infiltrated by introduced species, plants that the farmers had imported from the continents—avocado and mango trees, *cedrelas*, and balsas. These plants had proved aggressive in their active dispersal, invading the fragile vegetation with a predatory ease. Citrus sprang up like weeds wherever their seedlings had blown.

Clearly the main coastal thoroughfare, the trail climbed patiently upward before widening into a brief dirt road graded by the farmers. Rex pulled to a stop at the base of the road, which was split with a wooden tower rising fifty feet into the air. A structure built of weathered planks and crisscrossing boards, the tower supported a splintery ladder up one side, leading to a crow's nest of sorts, a precarious shack perched like a belfry. A makeshift widow's walk, it usually afforded the inhabitants a clear view out to the horizon, so they could anticipate the arrival of supply ships and the return of local fishermen.

The wind made a loud rushing noise as it whisked through the top of the watchtower. Leaning an arm against the structure, Rex paused. The road continued on, stretching a little more than two hundred yards between and past the farmhouses before fading into the *Scalesia* forest. Slender groves of towering balsas crowded the road. On either side of the tree-lined road sat crop fields and expanses of cleared pasture.

Most of the village houses were nestled among the balsas, but a few sat farther back, situated in the middle of plantain or yuca fields and angled to face the shadowy mass of the *Scalesia* forest. At its maximum, the island's population was twenty-three, but it had been rapidly dropping since the first quakes. The houses had seemingly been abandoned, and the fields had become overgrown with shrubs and scattered domestic plants. Big grassy wastelands, the fields would take decades to be reclaimed by the native forest.

Well into the cleared field to the west of the road, a few cows congregated in a pen beside a small *bloque* house, just beyond a stretch of castor oil plants. "We must figure out how to kill them," Diego said, watching the livestock graze. He ran a sleeve across his dripping brow. "But I'm pleasantly surprised by the lack of goats and dogs."

"That must be Frank's," Rex said, pointing through a stand of citrus toward the remains of a camp. Two canvas tents, a rocky fire pit cradling ashes and scorched stones, a large aluminum specimen freezer—all arrayed in the pasture about a hundred yards beyond the house, farther upslope toward the forest. A piece of canvas on one tent flapped loudly in the wind, the noise carrying up the dusty road.

Until he saw it, Rex hadn't grasped how imposing the

specimen freezer was. A metal block large enough to pack a
big mammal, like a rhino, head-to-tail, it looked as if it had
fallen from space. He tried to picture a supply boat dropping
the thing off on the coast of this untamed island, but the image failed him. Built of aluminum, it wasn't as heavy as it
appeared, but getting it up the mountainside to the village
had certainly been an honest day's work for a few unsuspecting crewmen. He imagined Frank, hands set on his
sturdy hips, fishing cap shading his eyes, barking out commands and pointing the way. Maybe the expedited delivery
charge of $400 wasn't exorbitant.

"So," Rex said to Derek as he started for Frank's camp,
"you run a pretty lax ship. Not a lot of saluting and 'Sir, yes
sirs' going around." He wove through the patch of citrus
plants, passing alongside the small house. The others followed him, Diego still mumbling about the livestock left unattended.

"SEALs are like thoroughbreds," Derek said. "You don't
want to reign them in too much, especially during down time.
But we spin up at a heartbeat when the shit's about to hit."

Rex placed a hand against the wall as he rounded the corner, Cameron at his heels. "Well, let's hope that's the—"

A screaming face met him, an ax whistling through the air
at his head. Rex yelled and raised his arms protectively just
as Cameron hit him from behind, taking him down hard. The
ax sliced just above his head and stuck in the side of the
house, sending a spray of mortar back into Derek's face.
Derek shoved Diego clear, and Diego tumbled to the soft
grass. Cameron sprang up to a crouch, one hand protectively
pressing down on Rex's head, the other instinctively slapping her hip for a pistol, though there was none.

Ax still raised, the dark-skinned man looked at them with
confusion just as Derek struck him beneath the ribs with a
stun blow to the solar plexus. The air left him in a deep bark,
like that of a seal, and he tumbled to his knees, clutching his
gut. Cameron had him bent forward in a choke hold when a
pregnant woman stepped heavily from the doorway, crying,

waving her hands, and yelling in Spanish. Rex stood, feeling slightly queasy.

"It's okay!" Diego shouted, pulling himself to his feet. "He didn't mean it."

"*Okay*, my ass," Cameron yelled. "He came at Rex with a fucking ax." She bent the man's head forward even more sharply, and his face darkened a few shades. His mouth was working open and closed, trying to find air.

The pregnant woman continued to chatter in Spanish, and Diego talked over her, translating for the others as quickly as he could. "You scared them . . . they thought the island was abandoned . . . there's danger here, something that's been picking off the villagers . . . stalking their livestock . . ."

The woman stepped forward, pleading with Cameron, and Cameron shook her head, clearly not keeping up with the Spanish. Cameron released the man, who fell onto all fours, vainly trying to suck air in. Finally his lungs loosened, inhaling in a deep screeching rush, and he almost convulsed, his shoulders heaving. "Lo siento," he said between breaths. "Lo siento, lo siento."

Derek looked at Cameron, and she stepped back, her arms loose at her sides. "He says he's sorry," she said.

THEY ALL sat around the wooden table in the small house, Floreana bustling near the sink gracefully, despite her enormous belly. Diego was pleased to make the connection between Ramón and his son, and he conveyed that Ramoncito was doing well at Puerto Ayora. At the mention of her son's name, Floreana stopped pumping the spigot handle abruptly. She took a moment to gather herself before returning to washing the dishes.

She had served them *encebollado*, a native tuna soup laden with onion and yuca. Cameron watched the bulge beneath Floreana's apron, scratching her forehead at the hairline. "Are you nine months?" she asked in Spanish.

Floreana shook her head nervously and held up six fingers.

"Jesus," Cameron muttered. "She's huge for six months."

Ramón said something, and Diego nodded. "He said he wishes they'd left like the others, but he doesn't think he can move her safely now given how big she is. He thinks she'll deliver early."

Floreana reached over to clear Cameron's plate, and Cameron laid a hand on her arm. Their eyes met, Floreana a bit surprised.

"When we leave," Cameron said, "we'll take you with us. Get you to a hospital where you'll be taken care of." She spoke slowly so that Diego could translate.

Floreana smiled, her eyes filling with emotion. She placed her hand over Cameron's and squeezed it once tightly.

Derek tapped his spoon against the edge of his bowl. "I'm not sure you can make that promise, Cam," he said softly.

Floreana cleared several more of their bowls and stood washing them, hunching forward so that her stomach didn't press up against the basin. Cameron watched her for a moment, then lowered her eyes to the table. She ran a hand through her hair, troubled.

"You're right," she said. "I'm sorry."

"I'm having a bit of trouble with the accent," Rex said to Diego. "Ask them if they knew Frank."

Diego spoke with Ramón, and Ramón smiled at the mention of the man. "Sí," he said. "El huevo gordo." He pointed at his wife, and when Cameron looked puzzled, he held his arms out to indicate a big stomach.

"Yes," Rex said in Spanish. "He was a touch on the heavy side."

Ramón spoke slowly, so Cameron was able to keep up with his Spanish. "He came here a few times, trying to get me to come look at something he'd put in that big freezer of his. He always seemed upset, his face sweaty and red, and he stumbled through his Spanish, so it was difficult to understand him. Finally, I told him I was busy with my crops and animals and I had no time for his fancy toys and ideas. I told him nosing around like that was bad luck. And I was right."

Ramón sat back and folded his arms, a sad expression on his face. "At first I thought he'd just gone home and left his things behind because that's how Norteamericanos are."

"But now?" Rex asked. "Now what do you think happened to him?"

Ramón spoke rapidly for a few minutes, losing Cameron. She waited patiently, catching a phrase here and there. Ramón finally finished and Diego stared at the table, tracing a ridge with his index finger.

"What'd he say?" Cameron asked. "What's that last phrase mean?"

Diego raised his hand and let it fall to the table with a slap. "Tree monster," he grinned.

REX SLOWED as he approached Frank's deserted camp, letting Cameron and Derek catch up to him. Diego had stayed behind to discuss with Ramón the ecological considerations of the mostly deserted island.

Something in the emptiness of Frank's camp made it seem haunted. Maybe it was the incessant flapping of the loose tent canvas, the ominously large specimen freezer, or the canteen dangling from one of the tent posts, as though Frank had just hung it there and gone for a hike. Some trash was scattered near the entrance to the first tent—jars and books and tools. A black Gore-tex slicker lay on the grass, blown, Rex figured, from the post. It was eerie seeing these things, objects stripped from the dead.

The ground was extraordinarily soft underfoot. Though the sun had dried the dew quickly, a few beads of water still clung to the little spiderwebs threading the lush grass. Nearby, several giant tortoises lay retracted into their shells, their high-domed backs rising from the grass like boulders.

The loose canvas flap on the tent snapped in the breeze, its rope swaying as they approached. Cameron fisted the cord, pulling it tight. The noise ceased immediately, leaving a sudden silence. She looped the loose end through a hole in the canvas, knotting it. The wind kicked up again, filling the fresh silence with a low whistle as it carried through the shack atop the watchtower down the dirt road.

The sun bounced off the specimen freezer so strongly it made them squint. Derek raised an arm against the glare as Rex strode to it and examined the thick lock that jutted out from the door just beneath the handle. The size of a shoe box, the lock had a jagged mouth of a key slot. Around back, there was a vent for the humidor, which cleared the moisture from the freezer so as to preserve the specimens. The vent's grate caught on steel teeth if it was forced inward, locking it into place to prevent scavengers from getting in and devouring the specimens.

Rex tapped the lock with his fingers, swearing under his breath. "We'll search for the keys, but I'd bet Frank kept them on his person."

Derek checked the freezer door, testing it with his fingers. Pressing his ear to the door, he knocked twice with his fist, gauging its thickness.

"Tucker packing any C4?" Cameron asked. Derek backed up, shaking his head.

"Even if we did have some, there'd be no way to reseal the freezer," Rex said. "The heat would turn the specimens to Jell-O in about five minutes." He groaned, banging his forehead lightly against the aluminum. It sent a tinny echo through the interior. "And there's no way we can haul this whole thing back to civilization."

"What do you think's inside?" Cameron asked.

"I don't know," Rex said. "But it must be for multiple specimens—it's certainly larger than any land form on the islands. It's also locked, which means Frank collected something before he disappeared." He tapped the door with his fingernails, making a hollow ping. "Ain't curiosity a bitch?"

Rex returned Cameron's smile, then ducked into the

larger tent, surveying the dim interior. A rotting, fecund smell permeated the space. A mat and a single sleeping bag lay on the ground, along with a hurricane lamp that had broken in a recent tremor, a wooden chest, and a toiletries bag. He lifted the lid of the chest, and a swarm of tiny wasps rose up, clouding around his head. He cried out and stumbled backward, tripping over the chest. Swatting at the wasps, he shoved through the tent flap. The swarm lifted from around him in the breeze, flying in several tight swoops before disappearing.

Cameron and Derek looked at Rex, startled, then amused by his disheveled hair and red face. "Any stings?" Cameron asked.

"No. Podagrionids. Torymid family. Predators of mantid larvae." Rex dusted off his pants. "They use their sharp ovipositors to pierce the spongy egg cases before they've hardened, and lay eggs inside. Their offspring hatch and feed on the developing larvae." He clapped his hands together and sank them in his khaki pockets. "They don't sting."

Cameron's lips pressed together in a hint of a smile. "The expression on your face, you could've fooled me."

Rex ducked back inside and approached the chest, raising the lid more cautiously. Sure enough, inside lay a segment of an ootheca about the size of a playing card, dotted with holes. He shooed the few remaining wasps and held it out before Cameron and Derek. "Case in point," he said. He turned the segment over, his fingers sinking into it. "Looks like it sustained some UV damage," he said. "That would have made it easier for the wasps to penetrate it." He held it closer to his face. Frank had written the estimated hatching date on a piece of tape stuck to the ootheca—*11/25/07.* "So Frank *was* alive through the end of November," Rex said. "But this is odd. Mantids usually don't hatch until April. This is out of season."

He pulled one of Frank's T-shirts from the bed, wrapped

the ootheca segment, and stuck it in his bag before heading
into the other tent, which Frank had apparently used as a
biostation. Cameron followed him in, and Derek waited outside. A folding card table remained stubbornly on its legs in
one corner, though all the equipment it had held had slid to
the ground in a quake—a cassette-tape case filled with
glassine envelopes, a 160-watt mercury vapor lamp, a 10x
loupe, a UV lamp, a Nikon with seven rolls of film, a dissecting microscope. Three killing jars sat in a cluster on the
ground, the layers visible through the glass—crystalline
cyanide, sawdust, plaster of Paris on top.

A sketch pad caught Rex's eye. He picked it up and set it
on the card table, pulling an equipment chest over for a seat.
When he flipped to the first page, an overscale sketch of a
mantid stared back at him. Below it was taped a ripped segment of text that Rex recognized as belonging to an unpub-
lished insect listing, one of several sheaves of reference notes
about island fauna that Frank brought with him on surveys.

The paper was titled *MANTIDS*, and it read: *Galapagia
obstinatus: endemic species found on Baltra, Floreana, Isabela, San Cristóbal, Santa Cruz, Sangre de Dios. Conven-
tional collection methods—beating vegetation, malaise trap,
or at lights. Arid to humid zones, though heavily prefers humid. Closely related to Musonia and Brunneria.*

The "author," or discoverer of the species, was listed as
"Scudder, S.H." in an 1893 article titled, "Reports on the
dredging operations off the west coast of Central America to
the Galápagos to the West Coast of Mexico and in the Gulf
of California, incharge of Alexander Agassiz, carried on by
the U.S. Fish Commission Steamer Albatross during 1891,
Lieut. Commander Z. L. Tanner, U.S.N., Commanding."

Derek ducked into the tent, his hair damp with sweat. "Jesus, the sun," he said.

Rex waved a hand to silence him, focused on the next
page in the sketch pad—another sketch, this time of a praying mantis ootheca. It was ensconced along a branch on a

tree that had fallen over, making a clearing in the forest and leaving the ootheca exposed to the sun. Rex tapped the bulge of the ootheca segment in his bag. "Frank must have pulled this from the ootheca he drew," he said. "The picture explains the sun damage."

To caption the sketch, Frank had scrawled the mathematical symbol for "approximately" and then *250 offspring*. Beside that, he'd written *Ten viable*.

Cameron pointed at Frank's note. "What's that mean?"

"Mantids usually lay oothecas from which two hundred to two hundred fifty nymphs are spawned. I don't know what 'ten viable' means. 'Viable,' as an evolutionary term, means that a mutated organism can develop and survive given favorable circumstances, but I don't see how that would be relevant here." Rex shook his head. "That's Frank for you. Typically vague."

He flipped the page, but the next sheet in the sketchbook was blank, save nine tallies, ticked off like a billiards score on a chalkboard. Rex tapped the sheet, frustrated. "Frank usually took copious notes," he said.

Outside, the flap came loose on the other tent, snapping in the wind, and they all started at the sudden sound.

Derek shrugged. "That was before the tree monster got him."

Chapter 29   Samantha had finally drifted off when she heard Tom Straussman yelling at her through the glass. She swung her legs over the edge of the bed, rubbing her eyes and feeling like a zoo animal.

"Get over here!" Tom shouted. "Take a look at this!" He slammed a micrograph against the glass and Samantha hazily rose to her feet and shuffled across the slammer, muttering something about ticktacktoe.

When she saw the micrograph, her eyes widened. The virus that Dr. Denton had sent over, stored in the dinoflagellates of the water samples, had been blown up to enormous magnification. The micrograph showed several pairings of slender strands connected by horizontal bars, like tiny ladders. The pairings were all twisted and bore a remarkable resemblance to DNA, which was odd since the magnification was only high enough to capture gross viral particles.

Samantha stared at the print, her mind racing. It was unlike anything she'd ever seen.

"I've sent it to diagnostics to run genetic sequencing on it," Tom said. "Reverse transcriptase, polymerase chain reaction, nucleic acid probe test—the whole nine yards. I'd like to see if we can find a match in the gene bank."

Samantha tried to swallow, but her throat clicked dryly. She felt the movement of her heart in her chest. "You won't find a match in the gene bank."

"Well, we'll see after diagnostics—"

"You can run diagnostics all year, it's still not gonna show us how the virus acts." She blinked hard, trying to focus. "That shipment of rabbits for the Crimean Congo tests. Did it arrive?"

Tom nodded.

"I want them in here," Samantha said. "In the operating room." She pointed through the crash door. "And I want a pellet of the virus." Tom started to object, but Samantha closed her eyes, feeling her heartbeat pounding in her temples. "*Now!*"

Fifteen minutes later, she stood in the operating room, the rabbit cages at her feet. A syringe full of the virus poised in one hand, she bent over and opened the top of the cage, pulling up a rabbit by the scruff of its neck. Tom and several other colleagues watched her from the observation post. Samantha injected the first rabbit, setting it back in its cage, then followed with the remaining five. The other scientists looked on silently.

She finished and crossed to the window, looking at Tom. Behind her, the rabbits thumped softly in their cages.

"The first rule of virology," she said. "Let the disease be your teacher."

Chapter 30   Szabla pulled her shirt off and tossed Tucker a bottle of sunblock, pointing to her back and straddling the cruise box. Justin was working Tank's hamstring and from the expression on Tank's face doing a pretty good job.

A wave rolled in, hitting the lava plain to the west and sending up steam-whistle bursts through the blowholes. Just above the water's edge, a ruddy turnstone picked at sea lion afterbirth. Szabla turned and faced the island, admiring how the low shrubs of the beach gave way to dry, rocky terrain and tree-spotted slopes. Above the slopes the green-hazed mountaintops presided over the island, imperious and remote, lurking behind fingers of *garúa*. "What a fuckin' place," she said. "From desert to forest in a stone's throw."

Tucker smeared a handful of sunblock across her shoulders, rubbing it high on her neck and along the rims of her ears. Justin eyed the sunblock across Szabla's back. "I don't see what you need that shit for, given you're a native people."

Szabla turned to face him with a half-smile. "You'd better watch your mouth, boy, or I'll tell your wife to bitch-slap your shit in line like she normally does."

"Please don't," Justin said. "She's been doing a lot of curls lately."

"Where the hell did Savage go?" Szabla asked, looking around.

Tucker pointed down across the face of the cliffs. "He wandered off that way while you were pulling your shirt off."

"He makes no causal argument," Justin said.

Szabla rose and pulled her tank top on, adjusting her bra. "I'll go grab him."

She took off at a jog along the beach, kicking the sand behind her in white sprays. She slowed when she stepped up onto the lava plain that spread like an apron out from the base of the Punta Berlanga cliffs. The lava was slick with sea spray, and the tide pools were clogged with brown floating algae and dotted with black-shelled snails.

She put her foot down on something live and it twisted and squirmed out from under her. Leaping back, she stumbled and went down hard on her ass, breaking her fall with the heels of her hands. A shape moved on the rock, black against black, and she realized she'd almost crushed a marine iguana.

A fat lizard about two feet long with tough folds of black skin and a row of spikes running from its neck to the base of its substantial tail, it had a prehistoric appearance. Two beady black eyes peered out from the lumpy white scales encrusting its face.

Szabla stayed still for a moment, suddenly aware that all around her, the lava was covered with marine iguanas, some longer than two feet. Their gray-dusted black scales blended perfectly with the dark rock. Several were pushed up on their front legs in a position of elevated basking, allowing the breeze to cool them off. They all lazily rotated their heads toward her.

One of the marine iguanas made a sharp sneezing sound, spitting through its nose to clear the brine, and a few others followed suit. Though Szabla knew they were harmless herbivores, they looked fierce, almost ferocious, and she rose quickly to her feet.

A promontory abruptly interrupted the curve of the cliffs to the west, angling out into the sea with a spill of rocks. Szabla headed for the point, carefully avoiding tide pools and iguana colonies. She waded out around the cliff, navigating her way through patches of green sea urchins. The water surged in, forcing her toward the wall, but she held her ground, planting her boots underwater against a flat lava ledge as the undertow spent itself.

A large spray of white mangrove sprouted from the outermost point of the promontory like a strange tumor. A fallen beetle floated on its back below the leaves, paddling in little circles with the bicycling movements of its legs. Szabla pulled back the mangrove, revealing a small crescent of black sand nestled just beyond the promontory, cliffs towering protectively above and around it. She inhaled sharply.

Naked, Savage was standing on the dark beach, gazing out at the brilliant aquamarine bay. Szabla drew back slightly, hiding behind an outcropping.

Savage rested his clothes in a mound atop his boots. He stepped into the water, dipping his hips beneath with a slight grimace, and backstroked in circles as the birds swooped to their nests in the cliffs above him.

A penguin wiggled through the water and shot up onto a shady nook in the cliff, sticking out its belly to shade its feet. It was very small, standing little more than a foot tall, its white underbelly a dot against the dark lava. It opened its beak, panting to expel heat, and spread its wings to pick up the breeze. It shit on its feet to cool them off.

A manta ray lazed through the water to Savage's left, and he turned on his side, avoiding it. He leaned back, pulling his bandanna free, his hair soaking in the water. He ducked underwater, then slicked his locks back over his head.

Szabla watched in silence, the sun beating down on her. Sweat glistened across the top of her chest, and her forest-green tank top was ringed with moisture along the scoop neck. His back to her, Savage exited the water. He shook his hair from side to side, sending droplets of water flying. Szabla couldn't take her eyes off him.

She hadn't realized how long his hair was since the bandanna took up most of its length, but seeing it now unbound, she would have bet it reached his shoulders in the back. For a man over fifty, Savage was in remarkable shape. His back was grooved with muscle, his calves firm knots. When he turned,

Szabla was shocked by the definition of his chest and shoulders. A patch of hair spread across his pectorals. The hair was neatly contained; it didn't climb back over his shoulders.

Her eyes traced over his naked body as he stood, slapping the sand from his feet. A scar compassed his right arm at the peak of the biceps. Her transmitter vibrated silently beneath the skin of her shoulder, surprising her. She started and had to step to regain her balance, her foot plunking loudly in the water. She looked up anxiously, standing in full view of Savage.

He was still naked, holding his undershirt. He didn't look up, but he smiled as he bunched the shirt in his hands and pulled it over his head. "Tell 'em I'll be there in a minute," he said, not raising his eyes. He made no effort to cover himself.

He had known she was there all along. The thought filled her like a chill and she took a step back. He still didn't look up.

He leaned over to grab his pants, his dick visible beneath the hem of his shirt. Szabla moved quickly back across the boulders. When she was safely out of view, she leaned back, resting her head against the cliff wall, waiting for her heartbeat to slow.

She waded back to the flat lava, her wet cammies heavy around her thighs, and began to jog back to base.

CAMERON RECOGNIZED Szabla's distinctive run from a distance. Szabla arrived winded, her breath coming in gasps, and she doubled over before Derek's glare, leaning heavily on her knees. "Savage is . . . Savage is coming," she gasped.

"What were you two doing?" Justin asked.

"Jealous?" Rex interjected, raising an eyebrow.

"Yes," Justin said. "I've been desperately pursuing Savage, but he won't give me the time of day."

Savage approached the group, making no effort to speed up. Noting Derek's irritation, Cameron checked her watchface. 0759. Savage pulled up within the minute, calmly swept his hair back under his bandanna, and smiled at Derek innocently.

"All right," Derek said. "Diego, why don't you lead the others to the village so they can set base camp? I'm thinking we should set down in the eastern pasture, the one across the road from Frank's old camp. The village is deserted except for one family."

"A husband and wife," Diego said. "The woman is embarrassed."

The others looked at him, nonplused. He stared at the sky, checking his English. "*Pregnant*," he corrected. "She's pregnant."

"Frank Friedman disappeared without bothering to pack his belongings," Derek said. "And he'd ordered a huge freezer to store specimens of some sort. Something weird went down around there."

"You don't buy that superstitious nonsense, do you?" Rex asked. Cameron smirked—now that he'd put some distance between himself and Frank's camp, Rex was feeling tough and scientific again.

"You're the one with the missing colleague," Derek said.

"It's important that we not lose focus of our objectives," Rex said.

"Christ," Szabla muttered. "He's turned into Cameron."

"Frank probably got stuck in a lava tube somewhere or shot in Guayaquil," Rex continued. "I hardly think the tree monster got him."

"Tree monster?" Tucker asked.

Savage let his breath out in a quiet hiss of a laugh. "Tree monster," he said. "I've seen a few of them before."

"Tall tales have been trickling in from this island for years," Diego said. "But this tree monster is a new one."

"I want you to exercise caution," Derek said. He rubbed his temples, as if staving off a headache. "Stick near to camp, maybe scout the area a little bit. Me and Cam'll assist Rex with the first GPS unit, and we'll muster at the base in a few hours." When he looked over at her, Cameron was taken aback by the dark circles beneath his eyes.

Rex removed the equipment he needed to set one GPS unit, and he, Derek, and Cameron left the others grumbling around the gear. It would be a tedious hike for them, given that Tank could barely walk and would be unable to carry his share of the load. Diego gamely declined to join Rex, offering to help the others move upland.

After navigating the narrow trail up the cliffs, Rex headed west, occasionally consulting his Brunton compass and squatting to tap the ground with his rock hammer. Over his left shoulder, he'd looped one of the circular nylon bags. Derek bore a tripod base in similar fashion, using the leather strap attached to one leg as a sling. Cameron hauled a backpack full of additional gear. They waited patiently as Rex started and stopped, assessed and thought. He spent at least ten minutes at every fissure, jotting down measurements in a small notepad he kept wedged in his shirt pocket.

The sun hammered down on them. Rex felt his skin baking even through the thick layer of sunblock. They finally arrived at a flat wedge of *pahoehoe* onto which the surrounding saltbush had not yet encroached. Though it was an older flow, it had remained coherent, having survived the cooling with minimal cracking. It had already been instrumented, and Rex toed the weatherproof case of the old seismograph with disdain.

A pair of waved albatross clattered through their courtship dance, nuzzling beaks, sky-pointing, and exchanging squawks, but Rex hardly noticed. He focused instead on the basalt, taking into account its alignment with the slope, and the readings from the Brunton compass. It looked stable, the lava less vesicular and porous than that surrounding it. He banged on it with his rock hammer and got back a nice "ping." More fractured rock would have absorbed the sound, giving off a duller "thud," but this stretch of lava was, for the most part, unjointed. He finally rose, tapping the rock hammer in his palm. "This'll do."

Cameron swung the heavy backpack off her shoulders, setting it down on the ground with a thump. "What the hell's in this?" she asked. "Concrete?"

"Actually, yes." Rex removed a small bag of cement, then a gas-powered hand drill. He went to work on the ground, drilling out a circular, six-inch indentation.

"What does this do exactly?" Cameron asked, indicating the equipment with a sweep of her hand.

Rex leaned back, sitting on his heels. He removed a brass plate from the backpack, to which was attached a one-inch hollow rod that extended vertically downward. A U.S. Geological Survey seal was stamped in the metal, and the center was notched with a broad cross. He drilled the plate into the ground, burying the rod in the lava.

"This plate is what we refer to as a 'benchmark,'" he said. "The GPS units as a whole measure the rates of deformation of the earth's crust, using the benchmark sites as reference points."

Rex signaled for the tripod, and Derek handed it to him. Once snapped open, the tripod was about five feet tall. Rex screwed a tribrach mounting plate into the top of the tripod, then centered it above the benchmark. He poured water from his canteen into the Redi-Mix sacrete and began stirring.

"These units are capable of capturing the latitude, longitude, and vertical position of this point down to millimeter accuracy. Once we get five more GPS units in place, we'll have a whole network by which to judge any surface deformation. If the earth trembles, shifts, slides, cracks, or wiggles, we'll know it."

Derek leaned over and helped him cement the legs of the tripod in place. When they finished, Rex stood and carefully unzipped the padded nylon case, revealing a thin, discoid antenna. He mounted it atop the tribrach, snapping it into place with its built-in clamps, then connecting it with a cord to a computer he pulled from Cameron's bag. He placed the computer in a tough, yellow briefcase, took off his Panama, and wiped his brow with his shirt sleeve.

Derek clapped his hands once. "All right," he said. "Let's hit it."

Rex smiled. "Oh no," he said. "That was the easy part. The antenna has to be perfectly horizontal." He began to turn the knobs on the tribrach, delicately adjusting the tilt and glancing at the leveling bubbles.

Cameron took a gulp from her canteen and tossed it to Derek. When it became clear that Rex's meticulous adjustments would take a while, she sat down on the ground. Feeling a fleck of dirt beneath her right contact, she removed it, cleaned it in her mouth, and popped it back in. When she ran a sleeve across her forehead, it felt tender. The beginnings of a sunburn.

A mockingbird bounced out from the cover of a saltbush. Pausing, Rex raised his hand, forming a loose fist and kissing his curled index finger, making a shrill, squeaking call. The mockingbird bounced up to Derek, fluttering its dusty brown wings. It peered up at the shiny metal canteen, and he pulled it back out of sight.

"You won't find many shy animals here," Rex said, turning his attention back to the tripod. "They've grown up in a paradise of sorts. No native predators, abundant food, little exposure to man."

In a sudden burst, the mockingbird flew up and landed on Derek's head, its white underbelly brushing against his hair. It leaned over Derek's forehead and took a hesitant peck at one of his eyebrows, the jet of its tail feathers shooting straight up in the air.

Cameron laughed. Derek tossed the canteen on the ground, and the mockingbird flew over, balancing carefully on it and pecking it curiously.

Having established the baseline position, Rex engaged the antenna's self-leveling mechanism and stepped back. He glanced up at the sun, his squint resembling a scowl. "All set," he said.

A wave of fatigue struck Cameron when she stood, leaving her lightheaded. She resisted the urge to rest a hand on her stomach.

Derek grabbed her shoulder gently to steady her. She laughed, a high-pitched, unnatural stutter. "Just sitting down too long," she said.

Derek looked at her with concern, then bent over and picked up the canteen, causing the mockingbird to flutter off to a nearby saltbush. It called to him in a shrill burst of annoyance. Rex leaned over, beginning to pack up the installing equipment.

Derek offered the canteen back to Cameron, but she shook her head. His eyes dropped from her face to her stomach briefly, and she turned away self-consciously.

"We'd better get you out of this sun," he said.

Chapter 31   Breathing hard, Szabla and Diego swung a cruise box down onto the grass beside the others. Justin followed suit with an armful of canteens and two kit bags. It had been their third trip hauling gear up the slope from the beach, and they were ready for a break. Savage had been surprisingly quiet, working with the steady assurance of a mule.

They'd been stacking the supplies in the middle of a large field on the east side of the road, about a hundred yards from the *Scalesia* line up-slope. The balsas along the road cleft the two fields, blocking Ramón and Floreana Estrada's house from view.

"Introduced species," Diego said, pointing with a grimace at the twinning strips of trees along the road, taller and thicker than their endemic counterparts. "Balsas. Planted here by voyaging Norwegians close to seventy years ago. They cut down the *Scalesias* to clear pastures but left those aliens to spread." A lone quinine stuck out from the alley of balsas, its smooth, reddish bark striking a contrast with the gray balsa trunks. "I hate those goddamn trees." He went back to his bag, digging for his canteen.

Tank limped over to a giant tortoise and sat on it heavily. It settled on the leathery stumps of its legs, retracting its head sleepily into its shell and emitting a hiss. Tank glanced down the road, past the watchtower to the sea.

"Get off the tortoise," Diego snapped.

Tank struggled to rise but could not. He kneaded the muscles of his thighs, the sun catching his scalp through his flattop. Diego turned away in anger.

"You'd better heal your shit up," Szabla said to Tank. "You're supposed to be our workhorse. All this pulled muscle crap's getting old real fast." She crossed her arms, appraising the others. "Since I'm the bitch in the group, I'm gonna play housekeeper and get camp up." She pointed to Savage and Tucker. "Why don't you two run a quick surveillance, edge of the forest? Get the lay."

Savage looked up. Spit. "Why us?"

"Because I'm the ranking officer and I don't feel like doing it," Szabla said. She flashed a dead grin. "Move your shit."

Savage and Tucker walked side by side to the front rank of *Scalesias*. As they rose, the trees seemed to spread to bouquets, green, intertwining sprays that resembled broccoli tops. Vines twisted their way down the thin, scrubby trunks as if seeking out Amazonian waters. Small pepper plants waved in the breeze. Savage stopped.

Tucker rotated his Iron Man watch around his wrist to clear the sweat from beneath it. "What is it?"

Savage closed his eyes. Behind them, the wind hummed through the watchtower. Two dragonflies zoomed together in a crazed dance, and a cow mooed somewhere in the distance. The heat came off the ground in waves. Opening his eyes again, he stared into the forest, seeing how it grew dense and claustrophobic just a few paces in.

"Nothing," he said. He stepped forward, and Tucker fell in

behind him. Though they'd never called wind for each other, and though they were both years from their last mission, they fell into a recon step by force of habit, patrolling about fifteen meters apart—the distance of a frag grenade's casualty radius.

The trunks leaned and bent; one even swooped in a loop-de-loop before rising up and sprouting branches. In places, the bark was overrun by bright, red-orange lichen. Thick with yellow butterfly leaves, passion-fruit vines hung from the trees like scarves. Where they'd died, they were thin and brittle, holding the trunks in fragile embrace.

Savage made his way through the dense terrain, assessing the wilderness around him. Elsewhere on the island, the creatures were curious and unafraid, having evolved to lounge in safety. Marine iguanas could be picked up by their tails; hawks could be pushed from trees with shovel handles; turtles could be piggybacked to deeper waters. There was even something frank about the vegetation of the other zones; the solitary silhouette of the cactus against the sky, the vulnerable stands of mangrove, the exposed dots of the palo santos spaced like trees in an orchard.

The forest alone held secrets. Treetops dusted with mist. Strange calls from unseen birds. Large rocks that rumbled and walked away on tortoise legs.

A vermilion flycatcher swooped between the leaves, a bright red dart in the shady understory, and Tucker grinned, pointing and looking over at Savage. But Savage wasn't there. Tucker spun to his right, where he'd last seen him. Savage let out a high-pitched whistle and Tucker turned again. His reddish beard shaped in a smile, Savage stood five yards off behind him. A tiny star spider scurried across a leaf inches from his face.

Tucker ran his tongue along the inside of his lip. "Didn't see you walk over there."

"I didn't. I floated." Savage shot him a quick wink. "Why don't I take point for a while?" Tucker nodded his consent, but Savage had already turned and headed off into the foliage. Tucker followed him into the shadows.

Not a trace remained of their casual, off-duty attitudes. They moved like two legs of a single animal—always maintaining space and closeness, forging ahead with a consistency of pace and movement. Savage's shirt was soaked through with sweat, the sleeves clinging to his biceps when he swung his arms. He fell into a trance of sorts, letting his eyes blur so they took in the plants and birds and dappled shadows.

THE PARTS of the creature's mouth bristled eagerly in anticipation. She sensed the presence of something living with her antennae and from the subtle vibrations of the ground. She rotated her head so that she could view her surroundings directly through the center of her compound eye, where her vision was sharpest. Her binocular vision enabled her acute depth of field perception.

The approaching prey triggered special receptors in her head, and she sent out nerve impulses, expertly gauging the distance and angle of her impending strike.

UNDERFOOT, THE clay gave way to mud, Savage's boots making a wet sucking noise when he pulled them free. He slowed, the span of his shoulders a green stroke against the cooler green of the forest. His hand flickered out to his side. It moved just three inches in the dim light, but Tucker halted immediately. Lowering his foot, Tucker eased his weight down gradually, even after his boot struck the mud.

They stood in perfect stillness for a long time before even daring to turn their heads and look around. Savage gazed at the line of trees, his eyes fighting to adjust to the shadows and small patches of intense sunlight. He backed up to Tucker, his blade out and hanging loose at his side. He moved slowly, making no sound save the brush of his cammies. He halted next to Tucker. They waited, listening in the breeze.

"There's something there," Savage said softly. His face

was slick with the humidity, dark with sweat at the sides of his head along the edge of the bandanna.

He and Tucker stood side by side, breathing in unison. They stared ahead at the shadows, the trunks of the trees, the waving leaves. Something wasn't right up ahead, but Savage couldn't put his finger on it.

The sky cracked with lightning, followed quickly by thunder. They heard the rain before they saw it, pattering atop the leaves of the canopy. It filtered down to them slowly, trickling through the network of treetops and branches. The air around them split in several narrow falls of water. "What do you think?" Tucker whispered.

Savage looked ahead again, but the surroundings were losing focus. "The rain's gonna cut visibility and the ground'll go to shit. Even more."

"Any bears or anything like that?"

Savage shook his head. "No predators. Just a hawk or two, a harmless snake. Nothing dangerous in here."

Tucker shook off a chill. "Guess we just spooked."

Savage reached out a hand, letting a stream splash onto his palm. "Been known to happen," he said. He glanced back into the forest, the air gray and heavy with rain. "Let's see if those slippers made it back to base yet."

He kept the lead on the way back.

Chapter 32 Base camp was set by the time Cameron, Derek, and Rex returned, the five tents spotting the pasture. The sky over the forest was clear now; the rainfall had stopped as quickly as it had begun, never straying beyond the high altitude side of the transition zone. The grass around the base camp and the canvas tents were wet.

Since they were short on white fuel for the hurricane lamps, Tucker, Diego, and Justin cleared a fire pit. There was plenty of wood to burn, and in addition to providing light, a fire would make a good gathering site. Finding a few trees that had fallen in the recent earthquake, they'd rolled over the broken segments of trunk to serve as benches. Then, they'd torn up the grass within the ring of logs to ensure the fire wouldn't spread, leaving only a circle of dirt.

Tank had fallen asleep sitting on the tortoise, which was now walking slowly toward a mud wallow. His boots dragged along the ground, his head lolling with each of the tortoise's tedious steps. He'd accidentally left an empty cruise box open beside his tent during the rainfall; it had caught the water running off the tent roof in its waterproof liner, filling with water.

Szabla shadowboxed behind her tent. Savage whittled something into the bark of a nearby quinine tree. He didn't bother to look over as Cameron, Rex, and Derek approached. Though she'd been looking forward to seeing him, Cameron shot Justin a stern glance as he approached, to stop him from greeting her warmly.

The team circled up around the fire pit, pulling out their meals, ready to eat. Sealed in thick brown plastic bags, the MREs were high-energy, high-protein, and easy to prepare. Savage sliced the top of the tough plastic with his Death Wind and slid the contents out onto the ground—a plastic spoon, a vacuum-sealed cookie bar, a tiny Tabasco bottle, apple jelly in a tube, cocoa beverage powder, vacuum-sealed crackers and tube cheese, cardboard boxes holding pouches of potatoes au gratin and ham omelet, and a packet containing gum, coffee grounds, matches, sugar, salt, and a few pieces of toilet paper for when the need arose, as Justin often put it, to "take a squeeze."

A long, thin plastic heat bag warmed up when exposed to water. Savage filled it from his canteen, slid the omelet pouch inside, stuffed the whole thing back into the cardboard casing, and set it at a tilt against a nearby rock.

Tank lay flat to rest his intercostals, his hands laced across the back of his neck. Justin was already digging into his meal, spooning mushy barbecue pork into his mouth. Rex watched him with disgust until Szabla tossed him a heated MRE pouch.

Rex glanced at the carton. "Tuna with noodles? You expect me to eat this?"

"Sorry, princess," Szabla said, squeezing a tube of cheese onto a cracker. "We're outta lobster."

"What chemicals are used to heat this crap?" Rex asked angrily, reaching for Szabla's heater bag. Szabla slapped his hand, and he withdrew it, surprised.

"Doubt they're biodegradable, Doc, if that's your concern," Savage said through a mouthful of cookie bar.

"Heaters and processed food." Rex shook his head. "So much waste. Did you know geothermal energy sources could provide the world's energy twenty times over?"

"Fascinating," Szabla said.

"But what do we have instead? What legacy do we leave? Ozone depletion, acid rain, anthropogenic emissions, industrial pollution, nuclear waste, urban smog, high-altitude cooling, increasing global mean surface temperature, fossil fuel combustion, biomass burning, deforestation. We're like children. Stupid, vicious children." Rex paused, exasperated. "What's next?"

"The Red Sox'll win the World Series." Szabla leaned forward, forked a hunk of tuna noodles from Rex's pouch, and ate it. Tank grabbed the pouch from Rex and tilted it back over his open mouth, emptying it.

Derek stuck his spoon into his apple jelly tube and turned it upside down like a Popsicle before throwing it aside. Cameron eyed the tube in the grass. "Diet?" she asked.

Derek ran a hand over his stubble, and Cameron noticed how gaunt he looked. "Yeah," he said. "Need to slim down for swimsuit season."

Diego stood quietly and picked up the discarded tube, setting it in a trash bag. Cameron watched him, but the others didn't seem to notice. Rex picked up another MRE and turned it upside down, searching for the opening.

Pale yellow tinged faintly with green, a sulfur butterfly flew a lurching figure eight overhead. It lit on Rex's shoulder, but he did not notice it. Diego reached over, trapping the butterfly's wings between the lengths of two fingers. Ever so delicately, he grasped the butterfly's fragile body with his other hand, then blew gently on the wings so they parted, revealing their full span. With a graceful flick of his wrist, he released the butterfly to the air, and it fluttered off. He glanced over at Cameron and smiled.

"Justin," Derek said, "after lunch, I want you to swim out and retrieve your trauma bag and the other gear we discussed. See if you can figure some way to anchor closer to shore for when we take off in four days. Get back here by 1500. That give you enough time?" Justin snapped his head down in a nod. He was the best swimmer on the squad, and he prided himself on his specialty.

"The rest of us'll break into buddy pairs and sweep the island. Once we find the other five sites, then we can focus on setting those last GPS units, getting the water samples Rex needs, and clearing out."

Grabbing the thin cardboard box, Savage slid out the contents, then pulled the warm omelet pouch from the heater. He sliced the top open and dumped in the cocoa powder, then the Tabasco, stirring the whole concoction together. He raised a spoonful of the mush, white shot through with red and chocolate swirls, to his mouth. "We gonna make it back for New Year's?" he asked. "I got a stripper name of Mary Anne, said she'd get me firing both pistons if I can swing through Boseman."

Justin caught Cameron's eye and made a jacking-off gesture with his fist.

Rex stood, picking up another antenna. "You can consider that your incentive."

Rex took Savage and Tucker to sweep the northwest quadrant of the island. Between the dark lava beach, the 103-meter rift, and the wide lava plain, he hoped to locate at least two sites. The hike from the *Scalesia* zone down the western coast was a gradual one. The transition zone slowly faded into the parched browns and grays of the arid zone—the stout plugs of Candelabra cacti, the dry, chalky ground underfoot.

At one turn, a land iguana lay across the trail. Rex stepped carefully over it, but as Savage passed, he flipped it over with the toe of his boot. It landed on its back and squirmed over to find its feet before beating a sluggish retreat. Tucker laughed, and Rex turned and looked at Savage angrily.

Rex signaled Savage forward, and Savage came, tossing the Death Wind at a cactus. It stuck with a thunk, and he pried it out, twisting it and sending a chunk of spines flying.

"What the hell was that?"

Savage lifted the bandanna off his head and used it to mop his brow. "Survival of the fittest," he said. He flexed, curling an arm up Popeye-style.

Rex could feel anger flushing his face, and he fought to keep his voice steady. "That animal is the most magnificently adapted creature on this island."

Savage cleaned beneath his thumbnail with the end of the blade, tracing it gently along the darkened line. "Not anymore," he said.

Rex shifted the bag on his shoulder. "Maybe it took two, three hundred thousand years for a land iguana to be born with longer claws. A random mutation. The thing is, with longer claws, the land iguana can pull the spines out of cactus pads. That meant it could eat the pads, so it had access to a wider range of food. This mutation was passed along to its offspring, which also enjoyed the benefits of these claws. Soon, they outcompeted the normal iguanas for the limited food resources on the island. They thrived, the older iguanas died out, and land iguanas with more substantial claws became the norm for the species." His cheek quivered with anger. "That, my friend, is survival of the fittest. Kicking a defenseless animal to show how big your dick is, is not."

Savage kept his eyes on the tip of the knife beneath his fingernail. "Been thinking about how big my dick is, have you?"

"Yes. Of course. Since I'm a homosexual, I want to copulate with every male in the vicinity. I have nothing better to do on this survey but devote my thoughts exclusively to you and your penis."

Tucker took a step back, his foot sliding on the gravelly slope. "Whoa," he said. "You're a butt stabber?"

Rex raised his hands. "Where the hell have you been?"

"But you didn't . . . No one said anything." Tucker rubbed his hands together, squeezing his fingers.

Rex turned around, heading down the slope toward the steaming rift. "Don't ask, don't tell," he called over his shoulder.

The curved scar of the rift followed the island's contour, spewing sulfurous gases. The ground itself consisted of an ashy sand, which gave way here and there to sheets of newly hardened lava. The only vegetation that had taken hold were *Tiquilia* plants—small gray herbs growing in humps like tiny mounds of cobwebs.

Rex stopped a good distance from the rift, studying the ornate inlay of hardened lava. Some regions were ropy and fluid, indicating a more recent flow, but others had been smoothed by thousands of years of wind and erosion. He could feel the heat rising off the lava even through his shoes. Tapping the ground with the rock hammer, he assessed its consistency.

Savage shifted from foot to foot. Tucker squirted a dollop of sunblock into his palm and smoothed it across his face, then tied his T-shirt around his head to cut the sun.

"I'm getting mighty tired of this shit," Savage said.

Rex raised the Brunton compass and glanced at the reading. "That's not really my concern."

" 'Not my concern,' " Savage grumbled. "It should be your fucking concern. You got Navy SEALs here. If we wanted to lug gear and fold underwear, we would've been swabbies on *USS Fuckstain*. If someone's gonna pull my ass out of a nice comfortable jail cell, it could at least be for some goddamn action."

Rex tapped the rock with his hammer, gauging the vibration. "You think you're so forceful, all of you," he said. "With your guns and your combat training. As if that does any good in a time like this. The earth is rearranging itself in Biblical proportions, and you're standing by with a handful of bullets. Correction: with no bullets." He laughed, low in his throat, and looked up. "I'm a doctor, Savage. You're a fucking Band-Aid."

Savage stepped forward, but Tucker blocked him, laying an arm across his chest. Rex stood quickly, his arms raised defensively, glowering at Savage.

"Don't take the bait, buddy," Tucker whispered to Savage. He patted him on the chest, and Savage took a step back.

Savage's upper lip quivered, itching to curl up into a snarl. "Fuck this," he said. He turned, storming off down the slope past the rift.

"FREEZE!" Rex yelled.

Savage halted. He turned slowly, facing Rex. "What now?"

Rex crouched and picked up a baseball-sized lump of basalt. He tossed the rock once and caught it, then threw it in a high arc toward Savage. It struck the ground about five feet past Savage in the direction he'd been heading. Breaking the thin crust of the lava and leaving a black outline in the ground, it continued down into the earth, falling through the deep cavity left where the underlying rock had dissolved and retreated. Savage waited to hear a thud when the rock struck bottom. There wasn't one. He stared at the small black hole in the ground, a pinpoint opening to a massive underground cavern.

Rex began to walk off in the opposite direction. "This way," he said.

Chapter 33   Cameron gasped when they crested the hill and the lagoon came into view, a disk of water nestled within a craterous swoop on the southwest margin of the island. Inlaid a mere fifty yards from the ocean, the deep green waters struck a sharp contrast to the blue beyond the narrow barrier beach. She rested her hands on her head, taking in both the breadth of the lagoon and the endless sheet of the ocean in a single glance.

Diego paused beside her, amused, and Derek brought up the rear, lugging two canteens and wearing a kit bag like a backpack.

"I thought Navy SEALs were not supposed to gasp," Diego said.

The lagoon had been formed six and a half years ago, the result of a tsunami caused by the Initial Event. Its eighty-five-percent salinity was double that of the ocean, caused by the continuous evaporation of the trapped waters. Due to the high salt content, only algae and shrimp survived there.

Striped with layer upon layer of compressed volcanic ash and dark black lava, the walls of the lagoon had eroded in twists and divots, leaving them dappled with smooth, rippling formations. A few pink flamingos stood in the shallow reaches, heads dipped upside down in the bright green water, inverted jaws sifting for food as their tough, bristled tongues suctioned water.

The mud around the lagoon had hardened and cracked, giving it a shattered appearance—myriad pieces of a puzzle fitted but slightly spread. Between the venous cracks, the mud was smooth and white.

A flamingo lumbered over to its young, opened its mouth, and regurgitated milk from its stomach. Cameron opened her mouth, then closed it.

"It is difficult to get to Galápagos," Diego said. "But once you're here, it is easy to want to stay." Removing a sample jar from his pack, he hiked slowly down to the lagoon, leaving Derek and Cameron with the view.

Cameron watched him skillfully navigate the incline before turning back to Derek. From the mats of brush to their right, a *farolete* rose, a four-foot orange cone of prefabricated modular rings. A navigation aid that functioned like an unmanned lighthouse, it had the seal of the Instituto Oceanográfico painted on its side, along with the precise geographic bearings of the unit—Latitude: −0.397643, Longitude: −91.961411.

Derek rested a boot against the *farolete*, and stopped dead. He was ashen, his face frozen in an expression of disbelief, amazement, and fear. Cameron stepped back quickly, following his gaze to the edge of the brush near her feet.

Inching slowly toward her was a plump, segmented larva, its head eight inches long and rounded. Almost three feet in length, it elevated its torso off the ground, its head cocking slightly to one side. Its mandibles curved into the slit of its mouth. Gills quivered behind its head. Cameron could see her terrified expression in the glassy sheen of the larva's round eyes. She felt her heart double-beat in her chest, and her hands went slick with sweat. The larva emitted a soft, gentle coo, and Derek stumbled back, tripping over his feet and falling down.

His yell echoed back to them from the walls of the lagoon. Cameron pulled him to her side speechlessly as the larva lowered itself flat to the ground again. It inched forward and Cameron and Derek stepped back. Diego was scrambling up the slope of the lagoon, calling out, but they were transfixed by the strange creature before them and couldn't respond. Cameron wiped the sweat from her face with a sleeve, her cheeks raw, sunburnt, and trembling.

Panting, Diego reached Derek's side and leaned over, hands resting on his knees. When he saw the larva, he inhaled sharply. He stepped back, tears rising to his eyes. The larva inched forward again, prolegs squirming to find holds in the ground, and Diego stepped forward cautiously, leaning over it but ready to spring back at the slightest indication of danger.

Cameron grabbed him by the arm and yanked him back. "Let's just take this slow," she said through clenched teeth. Her chest was heaving beneath her top. "Let's just take this slow," she repeated, more for her benefit than for Diego and Derek's.

Diego stepped around the larva, pointing at the bushes. A thin path had been cleared; the larva had literally eaten its way through the dense underbrush. "Hay Maria Santísima," Diego said. "Its consumption is extraordinary."

"What the fuck *is* it?" Derek asked, his voice wavering. He rocked a little on his feet.

Diego leaned forward again, mumbling as if to himself. "An arthropod of some sort, probably an insect. Eruciform larva, a caterpillar, maybe. Distinct head, aristate antennae, three pairs of true legs off the thorax, multi-segmented abdomen." He reached out a hand but drew it back quickly when the larva's head turned to track its motion. "¡Coño la puta madre!"

Cameron could not tear her eyes from the thing's head. The wide saucers of the eyes connoted an innocence and gentleness she had seen before only in mammals. The cooing sound issued from the larva again, a soft click moving beneath the surface of the sound.

"Impossible," Diego said. "Insects have no lungs, no vocal cords. They only make stridulating noises, from rubbing their legs or wings together. It must be pushing air through its cuticle, or scraping its segments together. It must be . . ." He stared at the larva's open mouth, the sturdy stocks of the mandibles.

"It's soothing," Derek said. "The noise."

"It has holes in its sides," Cameron said, pointing to the oblong spiracle openings, one on each side of each abdominal segment. "Maybe the air's coming through those."

She yanked a thorn tree up by its roots, protecting her hand with her shirt. Holding the bottom toward the larva, she shook it before its face. The larva's head moved slightly side to side as it eyed the dangling roots. Its segments seemed to contract and then spring, launching its head toward the thorn tree. It got its mouth around the base of the thin trunk and began munching. Cameron watched in amazement, the larva pulling its front segments up off the ground as it ate its way up the stalk toward her hands. She released the tree before the larva got too close. It finished the trunk on the ground, then looked at her again.

"Is it dangerous?" Cameron asked. "It looks kind of . . . I don't know . . ."

"Personable?" Diego offered.

"Something like that."

Diego reached out a hand and touched its terminal segment. "I don't know. I've never seen anything like it. But it doesn't have stingers, claws, or spines, and there's no warning coloration. Its mandibles are strong, but that's common in larvae. It has glands posterior to its labial mouthparts, probably to expel silk for a pupation chamber. It appears to be herbivorous, but it might be an opportunistic carnivore. The size is alarming, but I'd guess it's not danger—"

The larva turned its head in response to his hand, and he pulled his arm quickly back out of reach.

"Convincing, Doc," Derek said. "Real convincing."

"Will it metamorphose?" Cameron asked.

"I would guess so," Diego replied. "It is distinctly larval. Maybe a large butterfly, or . . ."

"A tree monster?" Cameron finished. They all watched the larva for a few moments. "Do you think there are others?" she asked.

Diego shrugged, nodded, shook his head. "I have no idea. I've just never . . . I've never. I suppose there could be just this one, but I have to believe that it's a species of sorts, that it has a . . . that there are others. But we can't take a chance . . . if we never see it again, it could be . . . could be tragic . . . an opportunity like this . . ." He slid his lip to one side, chewing it.

"What are we going to do with it?" Cameron asked.

Diego rose from his crouch and scratched his head, his elbow pointing out like a flag. "I don't want to move it, but if we leave it, we could easily lose track of it. And even though we haven't seen any, there could still be feral dogs roaming the island. It could get killed. We need to make sure we at least have an opportunity to examine it. We could return it afterward, right where we found it." He looked at them sheepishly, as if waiting to be contradicted.

Finally, Cameron glanced over at Derek. "Do you think it'll fit in your bag?"

THE OTHERS' faces reflected Cameron's thoughts. Tank, Rex, Tucker, Savage, and Szabla sat on the logs near the fire pit, flabbergasted. The larva crawled on the soft grass to the side of Derek's tent, and Diego stood over it, guiding it back toward the circle of logs. Derek stood, ghost-white and gaunt, staring into the dark stretch of the forest to the north.

"You gotta be shittin' me," Savage said.

Tucker cleared his throat loudly, bringing up a mouthful of phlegm. "There's no way."

Tank stood up, then sat back down. "Fuck," he said.

"What the . . . I don't . . . What is . . . I'm a . . ." Szabla stopped, evidently realizing she wasn't making any headway. She was deeply flushed.

"Kinda cute, ain't it?" Cameron asked.

Placing his hands on the larva's back safely behind the head, Diego elevated it slightly. Its prolegs wiggled in the air, searching for a hold. Cameron laughed and Tank couldn't help smiling. He walked over to the cruise box that had filled with rain and splashed some water over his face.

"We found it at the fringe of the arid zone," Diego said. "It's partial to shade, so it's probably disposed to the forest. The cuticle seems more papery and fragile at the back of the thorax—probably UV damage. My guess would be it worked its way down from the forest under cover of the palo santos."

"If its straying so far from the forest is anomalous," Rex said. "What was it doing?"

Diego didn't have an answer. The larva stopped squirming momentarily, regarding Derek's boot with an almost human curiosity.

"Should we name it?" Cameron asked, only half joking.

"Why all this ha-ha-look-how-cute-shit?" Szabla said, regaining her composure. "That thing could be dangerous. It could be whatever all this shit is about—all these superstitions. Could be what took out that scientist friend of Rex's."

"He wasn't my friend," Rex said slowly, still spellbound by the larva. It rippled forward over the grass, using the stumps of its prolegs for traction. It gazed up with its oversize eyes, its mouth working as if it were chewing something.

"I hardly think this thing is capable of killing a human being," Derek said. "We don't even have evidence that anything's actually happened here. No proof. Only stories. Even that guy with the ax—"

"Ramón," Cameron said.

"Yeah, Ramón. Even he couldn't show us anything concrete."

"So it's just a coincidence that weird shit is going on here, people are disappearing, and we discover this Caterpillar-That-Ate-New-York-City motherfucker?" Szabla said.

Diego cleared his throat and started to speak. "I don't think—"

"Plus it'll metamorphose," Szabla continued. "Could hatch God-fuckin'-zilla all we know."

"And we have an obligation to see that it *does* metamorphose," Diego said.

"Maybe it's an alien," Tucker said. "Or from the inner earth or something. Up through the earthquake cracks."

"Or maybe there was a radioactive spill somewhere," Szabla said, raising her hands and wiggling her fingers. She snorted. "This isn't *Them*."

Rex pressed his lips together, suppressing a smile. "I'd guess it's a mutation or an entirely new species."

"Big fuckin' mutation," Savage said.

Rex shrugged. "With the state of the ozone layer, who knows? Life on this planet has evolved over hundreds of thousands of years to function successfully within specific parameters of solar radiation. When those parameters are drastically altered, it's a DNA free-for-all." He coughed once into a fist. "The larva's size indicates some kind of hydrostatic skeleton. Without one, it would collapse into a formless puddle."

"How can that be?" Diego asked. "An internal skeleton?"

"Look at the size of it," Rex said. "How can it *not* be? It also must have an advanced respiratory system, some kind of mutated breathing apparatus. It could never have grown to this size relying entirely on tracheae to attain oxygen. Maybe primitive membranous lungs?" He glanced nervously at the three gills quivering behind the head of the larva.

"How do you know this shit?" Tucker asked. "All of a sudden, you're the Professor from *Gilligan's Island.*"

"You forget, big boy, I'm an *eco*tectonicist. Though I happen to loathe the life sciences, I am extensively trained in them." Rex flashed a quick, insincere smile. "I know everything."

Savage rose, picking up a stick and stepping toward the larva. He leaned forward, jabbing at the larva's head. It backed away from him, shaking its head as if it had a bad taste in its mouth.

"What the fuck are you doing?" Diego said, yanking the stick away from Savage.

"Oh. Playing mommy, are you?"

Derek's face was flushed. "Cut the shit, Savage."

"What's with the Florence Nightingale routine? That thing could be dangerous."

"My point," Szabla said. "My point exactly."

Diego spoke to Szabla in an even, steady voice. "Larvae represent the feeding stage of an insect's development. The weight and size increase is usually confined to this part of the cycle. You know it can't hatch something inordinately larger than itself. You know there are rules."

When Szabla looked up, the intensity in her eyes was startling. "That's a three-foot-long insect." She pointed at the larva, which had curled up in a ball, burying its small head beneath the coils of its body. "Don't talk to me about rules."

"Loathe as I am to admit it," Rex said. "She does have a point. This phenomenon, scientifically speaking, breaks all the rules. Insects don't grow to this size. All assumptions have to shift, including those about its harmlessness or menace." The brim of his Panama was low, almost hiding his eyes. "This must've been what Frank got himself into before he disappeared. But why a sketch of a mantid? Mantids are hemimetabolous."

"Translation?" Tank said.

"They don't undergo a complete metamorphosis. They don't have a stage of development that looks like this."

"What are we gonna do with it?" Szabla asked. "I don't want it sleeping near me."

Savage flipped his Death Wind around his hand and caught it by the handle. "That thing comes near me, I'm skinning it," he said. "Science be fucked."

"That's my call to make," Derek said. "And our orders are to assist Rex."

"So?" Szabla looked at Derek. "This isn't part of his survey."

"It is now," Rex said softly.

Diego shook his head with disgust, glaring at Szabla. "Could you really be so shortsighted as to—"

"Shortsighted?! I am a soldier first and foremost, and I'll be goddamned if I'm gonna sit by while you bring a potentially dangerous creature into my base camp!"

"*Your* base camp?" Cameron asked. She glanced over at Derek, but his eyes were far away.

Tank stood up, spreading his arms wide to try to calm everyone.

"This is a wonder of nature," Diego said. He angrily readjusted the band that held his ponytail.

"Then don't mind me wondering," Szabla said. She charged forward, knocking Diego to the side. Placing her foot on the larva's back, she pinned it wriggling to the ground. It hissed as air leaked through its spiracles.

Rex came up off the log. "Don't you dare handle it!"

"Sit down, Szabla," Derek mumbled.

Szabla palmed the top of the larva's head, yanking it back until its mouth spread. Tucker and Tank looked at each other uncomfortably as Szabla peered inside, checking out its mandibles.

Derek stepped forward, yelling. "I told you to sit the fuck down!"

Szabla started to say something and Derek shot out a hand, grabbing her around the throat and yanking her off the larva. She grabbed his wrist with both hands, choking. The other soldiers stood up, and Rex took a fearful step back.

"Jesus, LT," Tucker said.

Szabla gurgled against Derek's grip as he walked her back over to the log, his arm corded with muscle. The other soldiers froze, unsure how to react. Derek sat her down, his hand still tight around her neck.

Cameron rested a hand gently on Derek's shoulder. "Derek," she said softly. He relaxed his grip, and Szabla gasped for air. Cameron reached out and pulled his hand slowly away from Szabla. His face was drawn and gaunt, fatigue shot through his features. "I am in goddamn command of this outfit, and no one here is to forget that," he growled. He walked a few paces off. The others watched him nervously as Szabla caught her breath. Diego reached to check her throat, but she slapped his hand away.

Derek crouched down and stroked the larva's cuticle. Its flesh was soft, cushioned with a thin scattering of pliant hairs.

"This animal has never before been seen," Rex said, breaking the silence. "We're not letting it go or killing it."

"And why do you make that call?" Szabla asked, her voice a rasp.

"Because it's my mission," Rex said. "You're just along to schlep my gear." Derek said nothing to disagree. Rex caught Diego's eye and Diego nodded at him reassuringly. "We'll keep it the next few days while we finish setting the units," Rex continued. "Then take it back with us to study."

"*If* we decide to remove it from its habitat," Diego said softly.

Something large crashed through the trees lining the road behind them. Everyone whirled, Savage grabbing for his knife as he turned. He lowered it when he saw Justin high-stepping through the tall grass toward them. Cameron's arm was shaking, and she grabbed it so that no one would notice.

Justin pulled his diving mask off from around his neck and flung it to the ground. He approached with angry steps, his eyes lowered. "Goddamnit. It's gone. The bow line must've frayed against the tuff cone in the earthquake. The boat swung into a shelf of submerged lava—the stern line sheered." He sighed, resting his hands on his hips. His cheeks were flushed, red near-circles that made him look half his age. "The fucking thing floated away."

Chapter 34   Cameron pressed the heels of her hands to her forehead. When she removed them, they left white imprints for a few seconds. Derek spoke into his transmitter, tilting his head to his shoulder. "That's the lay of the land," he concluded. "We have no way back to Baltra. We're gonna need an extraction."

The transmitter crackled, then Mako's disembodied voice came through. "How are you on food and water?"

Derek glanced at one of the cruise boxes, full of MREs and canteens. "About a week."

Justin ran a hand nervously through his dirty blond hair. "I don't like where this is going." Szabla laid a thin finger across her lips.

They sat on the logs around the ashy fire pit. Despite the fact that they'd been constantly applying sunblock, they all showed the early signs of sunburn. Derek stood in the middle, his back to the pit, and Cameron sat on the end of the log nearest the tents, keeping an eye on the larva. For the time being, it had stretched out against the base of the log, resting in the shade.

Diego had set up the PRC104 radio with the whip antenna and was trying to reach the Darwin Station. Though he couldn't speak through the handset, he was keying it so that it would break squelch in Morse, sending an SOS. The odds of someone's overhearing the radio in his office were low, especially since the Station was close to deserted, but he was playing long odds that one of the locals or Ramoncito would happen by.

"Why can't I just radio Puerto Ayora for you?" Mako asked. "Have 'em send a boat?"

"Because," Diego said. "Even if there was another appropriately sized boat, which there isn't, the satellite radio there is broken. There's only a PRC104 with a whip antenna, like this one. It can't pick up signals from the continent, let alone North America."

Mako was silent for a few moments after Derek relayed the information. When he finally spoke, his voice sounded tinny, distant. "We're chin-deep in shit with skirmishes at the Peruvian border. Don't know when we can get you a helo." His sigh came out angry, even through the transmitter. "You know how we are with air assets right now, Mitchell."

"Yes, sir." Derek grimaced, his pale lips dried and cracked.

"I'll see what I can do."

"Very well, sir."

"First time you called in, you lost your ammo. Now it's the boat and your weapons. Think you can manage not to lose anything else until we speak again?"

Derek cleared his throat, angling his mouth toward the transmitter. "Yes, sir," he said, but Mako had already clicked out.

"Well, that went swimmingly," Rex said. He stood, slapping his hands to his sides. "I need to check in with Donald. Update him."

"How're you gonna do that?" Savage said. "Ain't got no radio."

"I thought . . . I thought I could use one of your transmitters," Rex said.

Tucker stiffened. "Oh, for Christ's sake," Szabla said, glaring at Tucker. "Grow the fuck up." She yanked the arm of her tank top down off her shoulder, revealing the bump of her transmitter. She turned to Rex. "Come here," she said.

Rex sat beside her, and Szabla activated the transmitter, then had the military operator connect them to the New Center's telephone line. Rex leaned forward to speak into the transmitter, his lips close to Szabla's bare shoulder.

"Rex," Donald said. "I'm glad to hear from you. Got some strange results back from that dino pellet."

"We've had our share of oddities on this end as well," Rex said. He filled him in on Juan's death, losing the boat, and the larva that Cameron and Derek had discovered.

There was a long, breathless pause. "I'd do anything to see that larva," Donald finally said. "I'll ready the lab in case you bring it back."

"What were you saying about the dino pellet?" Rex asked.

"I was correct. About its containing a virus. Dr. Everett was unable to identify it—they have it in a nucleic acid probe test now, but I doubt strongly it'll correlate to any gene bank specimens. They just E-mailed me the micrograph—the virus looks like curved ladders, like segments of DNA."

"What are its effects?"

"They've yet to figure out its pathogenicity, but Everett's extremely concerned. Have you been taking water samples?"

Rex glanced over at Diego, who momentarily stopped keying the handset and reached into his bag. He pulled out the two jars they'd filled with water samples—one from the waters off Punta Berlanga and one from the lagoon. "Yes," Rex said.

"Well, take more. A smattering through the island—hit any standing water reservoirs—and around the coasts so we can pick up samples from each of the major currents. I want to source this thing, see how it entered the water supply. As far as we know, it's only near Sangre de Dios—there's nothing in the recent records from nearby waters to indicate the virus's presence elsewhere."

Rex's hair fell in straight, lanky wisps over his forehead. "Of course," he murmured. "The drilling boat." He turned to the others, excited. "Remember that kid on Santa Cruz asked us if we were heading here again on the drilling boat?"

Diego shot to his feet. "The deep-sea core drilling boat!"

"The who?" Tucker asked.

"They took several cores off the coast here," Diego said, pointing south to the sea. "Just beyond Punta Berlanga."

"What's going on?" Donald's voice squawked. "What's all the commotion?"

"There was an ODP boat through here," Rex said. "Pulling up cores. It could've unleashed this virus from where it was buried in the ocean basin. Virogenesis is usually localized like that. The core holes left behind in the ocean floor could be like . . . like that cave in Kenya, the one they think is the hiding place for the Marburg filovirus."

"Kitum Cave," Diego said. "On the slope of Mount Elgon." He stood and unscrewed the whip antenna, pulling the cylindrical segments apart and S-folding them.

Rex turned back to Szabla, looking somewhat ridiculous speaking into her shoulder. "The cores will be refrigerated and archived on one of the boats—get them thawed out, see if any thermophilic microbes have survived the refrigeration, and get them over to Dr. Everett to see if they're infected with the same thing. If they are, odds are they're what infected the dinoflagellates to begin with."

Donald agreed and clicked out.

The soldiers stared at Rex and Diego blankly. Szabla ran her fingers up along the front of her neck, testing the tender skin above her larynx. Derek averted his eyes from her, and she turned back to Rex.

"You want to tell us just what the fuck you're talking about?" she asked.

CAPTAIN BUCK Tadman shifted his damp cigar to the left side of his mouth, leaning over the prow of the 143-meter advanced drilling ship and watching the waves crash against the hull. The cook stood next to him, wearing a stained white apron.

"You want my marital advice?" Buck said. He smacked the back of one hand into the other. "Buy a belt with a thicker buckle." The cook threw his cigarette into the foaming waters and headed back to the kitchen.

A thin man in spectacles walked past Buck and waved, and Buck sneered at him, spitting the plug of his cigar on the damp deck. The man scurried away toward the laboratory. Buck was tired of scientists. And his ship, the SEDCO/BP 469 was overrun with them—paleontologists, sedimentologists, petrologists, magnetics specialists, geophysicists, geochemists, geodipshitologists. All the degrees tacked on behind their names made the ship roster look like alphabet soup. He supposed it made sense—the boat was a floating research station, after all.

They'd left port in San Francisco over two months ago, setting out on Ocean Drilling Program Leg Seventeen, a six-

month cruise that would take them down the west coast of
South America, around the Cape, and back up to Florida.
They'd stop at key sites along the way, pulling up plugs of
earth from the ocean basins and seeing what information
they encoded about the origin and evolution of oceanic
crust, marine sedimentary sequences, and the tectonic evolution of continental margins.

Funded and managed by the Joint Oceanographic Institu-
tions for Deep Earth Sampling and the U.S. National Science Foundation, the Ocean Drilling Program ran four
advanced drilling ships around the globe, each converted
from a petroleum drilling rig and engineered to collect core
samples of rock and sediment. Buck's boat, the SEDCO/BP
469, was the finest of these.

Buck gazed proudly up at the derrick rising over sixty
meters above the waterline. Two men attached the four-
coned tungsten-carbide roller bit to the drill pipe, along
with its stabilizing weights. Once the bit got rolling, it
would slice through the ocean floor like a razor coring an
apple. The taller man signaled another member of the drill
floor crew, and the assembly was lowered to the moon
pool, a hole seven meters wide in the bottom of the ship.
The assembly entered the water through a funneled guide
horn.

The machinery wound up, a clicking and humming of me-
chanical and hydraulic devices that extended the drill string
down to the ocean floor. The spot they hovered over was
5,500 meters deep; it would take the drill bit roughly twelve
hours to hit bottom.

Once it did, they'd rotate the drill string, pump surface seawater and drillers' mud down the drill pipe to remove the cut-
tings and keep the bit cool. The plugs of earth, safely
ensconced in an inner core barrel, would be pulled right up
out of the ocean floor and through the drill string to the ship,
where scientists would run it to the lab and pore over it for
days. They'd check the six-inch-wide, ten-foot-long plugs for
fossils, gas pockets, bubbles, patterns in the mafic and olivine

minerals, and tiny, heat-resistant organisms called hyperthermophilic microbes. Sometimes, they'd even run a Gamma Ray Attenuation and Porosity Evaluator to measure density.

Buck barked out a few commands just to feel important, enjoying how the workers grew uneasy under his eyes. He chomped the end off another cigar and twirled it beneath his thick gray mustache before lighting it. A deck hand jogged up. "Someone from the New Center on the radio," he said. "A Dr. Donald Denton."

"And?" Buck asked.

"He wants to talk to you. Says it's urgent."

Buck walked in slowly to the radio in the control deck, enjoying his cigar. When he spoke into the receiver, his voice was gruff. "Yeah? Help ya?"

"Mr. Tadman, Donald Denton here, New Center of Ecotectonics in Sacramento. I understand you did some core drilling off the coast of Sangre de Dios?"

"Always good to be understood," Buck said.

"I need to get my hands on samples from those cores. We have reason to believe that the drilling unleashed a new virus from the oceanic crust. In fact, the virus might be present in the thermophilic microbes living in the archived cores. It's quite urgent; I've spent the better part of the past few hours figuring out how to get ahold of you."

"Then you've been wasting your morning," Buck said. "We skipped the goddamned Galápagos this time down. Too much shakin' and bakin'. Drilled Sangre last leg. The cores are archived up in your neck of the woods."

"Where?" Donald's voice conveyed his exasperation.

"Scripps Institute. Right in La Jolla, California." Buck pronounced the "J" hard in "La Jolla" and gave the end of "California" a western spin—Californ-i-ae.

"Excellent. Thanks very much."

"No shit off my back. Oh, and Doc?" Buck shot a puffy jet of cigar smoke across the radio. "It's *Captain* Tadman."

Chapter 35   "Tell Iggy that peanut butter will get it out, but he shouldn't go to bed chewing it to begin with." Samantha shifted on the small bed, cradling the phone to her ear with a shoulder. "No, you can't go to the NVME concert, Kiera. Because you're . . . how old are you again? Well, there. See—that's much too young to be going to a concert."

She gazed at the ceiling, having memorized each line, crack, and bump over the past two and a half days. She should have made sketches of the ceiling the last time she was in the slammer; she could have wiled away her hours now analyzing the changes in the plaster.

Donald had called to let her know he was sending her thermoproteaceae pulled from a deep sea core, of all things. Evidently, they'd survived being archived and refrigerated at Scripps, which she supposed made sense—they could endure temperature extremes, sometimes thriving in environments of up to 113 degrees Celsius. Donald suspected that the thermoproteaceae were infected with the same virus as the dinos. Once the sample arrived, she'd hand it off to Tom so that he could get it under the lens for comparison.

She was wearing scrubs now, finally having changed out of her children's clothes.

"Are you remembering to take your meds?" she continued into the phone. "Uh-huh. And aren't you getting report cards or something soon? After the break?" Her face softened with empathy. "I know, I know, honey. English does suck."

Someone banged on the window. Samantha sat up, nervously straightening her hair once she realized it was Dr. Foster. It was a losing battle—her hair stood up in tangles where she'd been resting her head on the pillow. He made her simultaneously buoyant and insecure, a mixture of emotions to which she was unaccustomed. She was unsure if she needed buoyancy and insecurity in her life. She pulled on a surgical cap to hide her crazy hair and scurried to the window, speaking rapidly into the phone.

"There are plenty of fourteen-year-olds in day care. Oh. Well, just pretend you're the teacher's assistant or something. Maricarmen will get you over to the college to pick up your microbiology assignment. Good. If there are any problems, make sure she calls me. All right, sweetie. Tell your European brothers I love them." She snapped the phone shut and faced Dr. Foster with a smile.

"Kids?" he asked.

She nodded.

"I have two myself." Samantha nervously adjusted the surgical cap, and Dr. Foster looked at her with amusement. "Getting ready to scrub in?"

She worked her lower lip between her teeth for a minute, gathering her thoughts. "Look, Martin, I wanted to say . . . well, I don't really date. It's not that I don't want to. It's more that I don't know how. And, well, I could save you the time of finding out how badly I'm gonna botch—"

He held up his hand and she stopped, mouth open. "There's a space suit through the crash door," he said. "Suit up—I need to show you something."

She was into the space suit in ten minutes, and then she was free from the slammer, shuffling down the long, white hallway by Dr. Foster's side. She knocked over a tray of folders with a puffy hip, and Dr. Foster stopped to pick them up for her. For the rest of the way, he guided her, a hand resting softly on the small of her back.

She turned to him, awkward and mushy in the space suit. "Romantic, isn't this?" she said sarcastically.

"Yes," he replied. "It is."

They reached another slammer unit, and he pointed through the large plate glass barrier. A woman whom Samantha recognized as the flight attendant lay on a bed near the window, weak, pale, and dotted with fading bruises, but very much alive. Samantha could tell, even from her present state, that she was an attractive woman. Gorgeous blue eyes paired with flowing blond hair gave her a sexy, if somewhat unsophisticated, look.

The woman tried to pull herself up to a sitting position, but couldn't. She turned slightly, her swollen face looking through the glass at Samantha. She reached out a hand, touching the window, and Samantha raised a glove and rested it on the glass near hers, feeling her eyes tear up.

"She's not out of the woods yet, but I think she's going to pull through, she and the pilot," Dr. Foster said softly. "The titers have decreased substantially. She wanted to see you."

The insides of the flight attendant's lips were stained with dried blood.

"Tough little blond, huh?" Samantha murmured. She blinked back the growing moistness in her eyes, staring at the woman's thin arm extending to the glass. "Maybe I should've been a stewardess. More job security." She leaned forward until her mask bumped against the window. "Are there any openings on your airline?" she asked.

The woman shook her head, confused. "What?" she mouthed.

Samantha smiled. "Nothing." She turned to go, but Dr. Foster gently grasped her elbow, turning her back to the window.

The woman was breathing hard, her chest rising and falling beneath a thin hospital gown. A tear spilled from her eye and ran sideways down her cheek to the pillow. She opened her mouth, her lips forming soundless words.

Thank you.

Chapter 36   His boots hooked up on one of the logs and his hands resting in the grass, Savage began a series of decline push-ups. Tucker watched him, his thumb working away on his thimble like a small piston. Justin paced loose, meandering circles around the fire.

Diego and Rex had set out several hours ago to circle the coast and collect water samples. Despite Justin's advice, Tank had escorted them to try to walk the remaining stiffness from his back. The scientists had planned to concentrate on the southern coast, where the cold Peruvian Oceanic Current would have carried the infected dinoflagellates to the island from the deep-sea core holes.

At the base of the log, the larva curled around Derek's ankles. "What if it gets hungry?" Derek asked.

"If it starts crying," Savage grunted between push-ups, "you can always breast-feed."

Accordioning its segments, the larva squirmed up onto the log. It raised its thorax, its true legs spread in the air, and angled its head toward Derek. He looked back. They gazed at each other for a few moments, exchanging information in some wordless tongue. The larva made the cooing noise, just once, then lowered its thorax. Its prolegs pulsed and tensed, moving its body forward into Derek's lap. He raised his hands, allowing the larva to ease across his thighs.

Szabla stood up brusquely. "I don't like this. I don't like it at all."

Derek rested a hand on the back of the larva's head. "It's fine, Szabla. Sit down. Sit *down*."

Szabla sat.

Cameron watched the larva in Derek's lap, noting just how much they were juxtaposed like mother and child. She looked away, scratching her nose. "Requesting permission to check on the Estradas," she said.

"Who the fuck are the Estradas?" Szabla asked.

"Ramón and Floreana."

"Who the fuck are Ramón and Floreana?"

Cameron turned to Szabla, unamused. "I'm not requesting permission from you." She turned back to Derek, but he was lost again, gazing down at the larva. "Well? Derek?"

Derek looked up. "Huh?"

"Can I go?"

"Where?"

"To check on the Estradas?"

"Why do they need checking?"

"I don't know, I just thought I'd . . ." Her voice trailed off, leaving an awkward silence. Justin tried to catch her eye, but she refused to look over at him.

"The woman *is* pregnant," Justin said, turning to Derek. "It might be wise for someone to look in on her." He bit an edge of nail off his thumb, spitting it aside.

Derek shrugged. "Fine," he said. He nodded without looking at Cameron. "Go."

AGAIN, CAMERON found she had some trouble with Ramón and Floreana's Spanish. She asked Ramón to repeat his question and listened extra carefully.

"Why did I come?" Cameron repeated to make sure she'd gotten the question correct. Her Spanish wasn't great, but since she didn't have Diego to translate like last time, she had to forge ahead with it. She shrugged. "I suppose to check up on you." She turned to Floreana. "To make sure you were okay." She pointed to Floreana's stomach, and Floreana smiled. "Are you all right?"

Ramón smiled and walked over to his wife, leaning over to embrace her from behind. She set down the small blue quilt she was stitching and smiled. "I'm happy," she said.

"Are you still worried about getting off the island?"

Ramón reached around his wife, laying his hands on her stomach. "Once she gives birth to our son, then we will worry about getting off the island." His eyes saddened. "Our island."

"What are you going to do for work? When you leave here?"

"I don't know. I'll find something." Ramón took a deep breath and sat down at the table, sliding his hands along the rough, wooden surface. "There are things that matter and

things that don't." His eyes traced over his wife lovingly—
her crow's feet, the dark wave of her hair, her full stomach.
"It's simple."

Cameron started to sit down, then decided not to. "Well,
I'm going to do everything I can to make sure you're taken
care of," she said.

Floreana's smile was beautiful. She noticed Cameron's
eyes drop to the baby quilt. "Do you have children?"

"No," Cameron said. She smiled curtly, backing up to the
door. "No," she said again.

"Perhaps you could stay for some—"

"That's all right," Cameron said. "I really should get
back." She nodded once and left before Floreana could
protest.

Chapter 37   Derek walked down the two-hundred-yard
stretch of dirt road toward the watchtower, the sturdy balsas
rising overhead, the forest looming behind him like a broad,
slumbering beast. He climbed the makeshift ladder and
reached the top of the wobbly structure, a decrepit open
shack with an overhang about fifty feet up.

He faced south toward the darkening blue of the ocean,
leaning heavily against one of the shack walls, which
groaned under his weight. A big wave rolled in, disappearing from view beneath the cliffs of Punta Berlanga, and then
he saw the five distinct sprays of the blowholes shooting up
in the air. They misted, dissolved. He wondered if the slight
moisture he felt against his cheeks was the water from the
blowholes reaching him up here, kilometers away.

His eyelids felt heavy, almost leaden. He fought them
open, and his vision blurred. He let it, taking in the island
like an Impressionist landscape. Since the mission's start,
he'd hardly slept at all. He nodded off and almost toppled

from the tower, awakening at the last moment and grabbing the wall. Adrenaline pounded through him.

He needed to sleep. Climbing slowly down the ladder, he headed back to base and ducked into his tent early.

The humble fire fought the dusk. The larva rustled in the grass, no longer needing to seek shade. Rex and Diego had been analyzing its movements, seeing how it responded to light and touch. They'd already grown accustomed to its gentle, lethargic movements—there was something almost hypnotic about them.

Savage dumped an armful of firewood near the pit. He noticed Szabla way off down the dirt road, staring at something against the base of a tree at the forest's edge. He ducked through the alley of balsas onto the road and walked up to her.

"Look," she whispered, pointing. "A praying mantis." The mantid was about eight inches tall, standing in a patch of weeds by a thick gnarled root. "She's a big one, huh? I almost didn't see her there. I was just watching these finches."

A few finch chicks hopped among the rocks, searching for grubs and beetles. The mantid regarded them with interest.

"Growing up, we called praying mantises 'soothsayers,' " Szabla said. "My mother said they point the way home for lost children."

One of the finch chicks hopped close to the patch of weeds. With a movement too quick to see, the mantid lunged forward, crushing the chick in its front legs.

Szabla's smile faded.

The mantid's head lowered beneath the squawking beak and the chick was still. The mantid continued working on the chick, turning it with its legs. It pulled back into the weeds on its spindly legs.

"Back home," Savage said, letting his hand come to rest on Szabla's shoulder, "we called them 'Devil Horses.' "

THE DIRT around the fire pit was growing scorched, dark sediment settling over it like snow. Cameron toyed with the ring around her neck, rubbing the top of the sapphire with a fingernail. Tank tried to stretch his lower back, then sat on the log next to her and rested a heavy forearm across her shoulders.

The larva munched the back of the log on which Diego sat. The harsh, steady sounds of its mandibles grating the wood filled the air. Szabla, Savage, and Tucker sat across the fire from it, clearly uncomfortable. The base of the log between Diego's feet splintered, then gave way, and the larva's head poked through, its jaws working around a mouthful of wood. Diego reached down and gently stroked its head.

Its appetite seemed nearly insatiable—Diego and Rex had been experimenting with it for the past hour, feeding it everything from cactus pads to palo santo branches. They still had not determined whether it was carnivorous, but it had shied away from a full-grown land iguana, which Rex had attempted to feed it despite Diego's protestations. Now, swollen with food, the larva sprawled along the edge of the rainwater-filled cruise box near Tank's tent.

Derek emerged from his tent into the dark tropical night, rubbing his jaw. His eyes were bloodshot, the rims red.

"Thought you were trying to get some sleep, LT," Cameron said.

Derek took a swig from a canteen. He rubbed his eyes, then massaged his temples with the heels of his hands. "How do you know I didn't?" he asked.

"I don't know," Szabla said. "Your charming disposition."

A sudden splash caused Cameron to turn to the cruise box, and she realized the larva had scaled one of the sides and fallen in. Diego was up in a flash, leaning over the open cruise box. The others crowded around him as he reached into the murky waters.

"Is it all right?" Cameron asked, surprised by the concern in her voice.

Rex pushed through the others to Diego's side, staring down into the cruise box. The larva squirmed along the bottom, wriggling like an eel as Diego tried to grab it.

"Wait," Tank said, pointing. "Look."

Rex grabbed Diego's arm, pulling it back. Derek signaled Tank to step back to let the firelight through. The larva's thrashing slowed. "Pull it out," Derek said. He looked worried, almost upset. "Pull it out."

"No, wait," Diego said. "It's breathing. Look." He pointed to the larva's gills, which fluttered underwater. "Holy shit. The gills must feed an air bladder, or versatile lungs of some sort."

"Holy shit is right," Tucker said. "This thing gonna fly too?"

"Maybe that's what it was doing when we discovered it," Diego said. "Heading for the ocean." He grasped the larva firmly around the base of the head and pulled it from the water. It dangled before him, squirming in the air, its abdomen curling. Its obsidian eyes glowed in the firelight, its spiracles emitting the cooing sound.

Diego set the larva on the ground. It sputtered, expelling water from its gills, its body humping and straightening against the dirt.

"I think we should kill it," Szabla said. "Take it apart, see what it is."

Derek, Diego, and Cameron glared at her with outrage. "Exterminating species went out with rail barons and the Third Reich," Rex snapped.

"I agree with Szabla," Savage said. He flashed a dramatic thumbs-down, Roman-emperor style.

Justin stood up, knocking his hands together angrily. "Now that's a big fuckin' surprise."

"Nobody's gonna kill this thing," Derek said.

Szabla ran her fingers along the raised line of bruises on her neck. "Or what, LT?"

They broke up, heading for their respective tents. Though the larva had shown no sign of straying, Diego emptied the cruise box and placed it inside. "I'll keep an eye on it tonight," he announced. Closing the lid, he began to drag the cruise box toward his tent.

Diego heard the larva's fluttering coo as he pulled the box through the flap and lit the hurricane lamp. He set it in the corner, then sat on his bed, staring at the closed container. A simple rectangular box, containing perhaps the most startling aberration of nature to be discovered in his lifetime. And he was the discoverer. Maybe his surname would even find its way into the animal's taxonomic nomenclature.

The canvas flap whispered and he glanced over and saw Derek hulking just inside his tent. He started, almost falling off the bed. "You startled me," Diego said.

Derek did not reply. The light from the lamp played across his face, the flame reflecting in his bloodshot eyes. He'd let his beard go several days, and it rasped beneath his fingers when he ran his hand up across a cheek. "I want to take a look at it," he said, jerking his head toward the cruise box. "Alone."

Diego placed his hands on his knees, feeling himself start to sweat. "I thought we agreed we weren't going to hurt it."

Derek looked at him, his eyes finding sudden focus. They were sharp, offended, but the look quickly faded. "If you want to keep this thing in *my* base camp with *my* men, I need to take a closer look at it."

Diego crossed his arms. "Why do you have to be alone?"

"Maybe you'd prefer to leave the larva outside and take your chances that it'll still be there in the morning?"

Diego stood and headed hesitantly for the flap. Derek did not move out of his way, and he had to squeeze past him to get out of the tent. He halted outside, tilting back his head and taking a deep breath, then turned and peered through a gap in the flap.

Derek waited a moment before crossing to the cruise box, slowly lifting the lid. The interior was bathed in darkness. He raised the lamp, leaning over to peer inside.

The larva's head rose slowly from the darkness, tilting. For a few moments, Derek stood quietly, the larva regarding him and cooing from its spiracles. Finally, he leaned forward

and lifted the larva out of the cruise box as he would a baby
from a crib, gripping it around the thorax. Its abdomen
curled and loosened, dangling beneath it. It may have just
been the light, but its head looked remarkably anthropomor-
phic—the large, round eyes, the mouth closed into a clean
line, mandibles retracted.

Derek pressed the larva against his chest. Spreading his
large hand awkwardly on the back of its thorax, he walked
with it, its bottom abdomen segments tapping against his
stomach. Then he cupped its head, rocking his hand gently
so the antennae swayed.

Unable to contain himself any longer, Diego ducked
through the flap, clearing his throat angrily. Derek quickly
held the larva out away from him. He placed the larva
brusquely back in the cruise box, handling it now with an
objective expediency.

The larva rustled in the darkness, then squirmed up the
side of the cruise box, its thin antennae bobbing ever so
slightly as its head broke into the light.

Derek watched it for a moment, as if resisting the impulse
to rest his hand on its head. He snapped Diego a quick nod
on his way out of the tent.

Chapter 38   Something about the humidity made
Szabla come alive. The air was a blend of moisture and
warmth. Sex, heat, and danger were indistinguishable from
one another in the tropics, separate movements of the same
dance. The rain started, slow, warm, and building, pasting a
few wayward strands of hair to her cheeks.

Alone, she sat on the log, keeping an eye on the night. The
larva and Derek's violent behavior had thrown her for a
loop; she'd found it difficult to settle into sleep. She wasn't
the only one with insomnia—Tucker lay on his sleeping pad
behind the tents, charting the constellations in a spare log

book, and she could see Derek's silhouette shifting around in his and Cameron's tent.

Having sat on her shoulder in the hot sun all day, the solar cell was fully charged. Szabla removed it from her shoulder, the Velcro giving with a tear, and snapped it into a clunky, olive-drab elbow light. They'd brought only non-tactical lights; despite its interchangeable lenses, the unit gave a broad, bright signature.

Tilting back her head, she let the rain fall into her mouth. Her cammies and tank top were molded against the curves of her body. She was as wet as if she'd just stepped out of a shower, the rainwater pouring over her face, drenching her hair, even pooling in her jungle boots.

She flipped the light and caught it by the end. The sound of the rain was soothing and ineffably exciting. She was oddly aware of each muscle in her body—the ripples of her stomach, the solid curve of her thighs, the divot that split her deltoid when she raised her arm. She jerked her neck to one side, and it cracked all the way from the base. The wet tank top clung to her chest, forced out by the points of her nipples.

She thought about Savage's body, hard and untan. The thin patch of hair across his chest. She'd caught him looking at her a few times, staring at her mouth until she could almost feel it growing hot under his eyes. She bent her head to the top of her biceps, licking the beads of water. They were salty with the ocean mist, even up here in the highlands. She lowered a hand, pressing it down the slope of her stomach.

She rose suddenly and walked to Savage's tent, ducking inside. He was sleeping peacefully on his Therm-a-Rest. Szabla pulled her shirt over her head, quietly removed her boots, and then stepped out of her pants, one leg, then the other.

Savage's eyes remained closed, his breathing constant.

She crossed naked to the sleeping pad and sealed his mouth, pressing her palm firmly over it. He struggled awake, one hand shooting to his knife like a reflex, but she was already working at his pants and had him out. He was hard from sleep.

His eyes widened as he recognized her, and he froze, blade pushing against the soft flesh of her bruised neck. She sat on him with a shudder, arching her back. She saw herself from far away, her knees pushing into the pad on either side of him, her hand clamped down over his lips, her teeth biting the inside of her cheek. She worked on him quickly, violently, the blade against her throat, her hand pressed over his mouth the entire time.

He was pinned down so tight he couldn't even react to her movements, but she felt him building as she came, biting even harder on her cheek as her hips rotated with a mind all their own.

She pulled herself up off him, her throat leaving the blade, and he gasped for air when she removed her hand. His pants loose at his hips, hand still stretched upward holding the blade, he looked around as if trying to figure out where he was, what had happened. She got dressed with her back to him, then turned calmly, amused by his shocked expression. A thin scratch, beaded with two tiny drops of blood, stretched across her throat where the knife had been.

"Thanks, soldier," she said, not untenderly. She ducked through the flap and disappeared into the rain.

**28 DEC 07
MISSION DAY 4**

Chapter 39   Cameron shot from sleep, her body drenched with sweat. She ran from her tent, awash in nausea. Derek called after her, but she didn't stop until she was clear of base camp, falling, her knees pressing in the dewy grass, and then she was heaving, hard and heavy, bringing nothing up.

Derek was two steps out of the tent when Justin passed him, running for his wife. Szabla poked her head through the flap behind Justin. "What the fuck's going on?" she shouted.

Justin caught up to Cameron, crouching before her. He rested a hand on her shoulder, but she shook it off.

"I'm fine," she said. Between gasps, she wiped her mouth, leaving a smear of dirt across her chin. Sweat darkened her blond hair along the temples.

The others were out of their tents now a good distance behind them, mulling around and glancing over at them. Diego had set up the radio again and was clicking his way through an SOS.

"Morning sickness?" Justin asked.

The grass felt slick and cool beneath her hands. "Where am I without this?"

"Without what?"

She gestured blindly behind her at the base camp. "I never realized how much I need it," she said. "Orders, mission objectives, chain of command. Heat-'n-Serve priorities. They keep things simple. You do your job, and that's all you have to focus on. No mess." She pushed herself back into a sitting position and spit out a gob of saliva. Justin waited for her to catch her breath.

"The teams have always kept things neat for me. Kept them in control. Locked away behind a starched uniform." She laughed, a short stutter that died quickly away. Off behind them, she could hear Tank taking a leak against a tree. "I'm an adult, and I hardly know how to think for myself."

Justin rested a hand on her cheek and she let him.

When she spoke again, her voice was soft with fear. "How can I have a baby if I don't even know how to think for myself?" She shook her head. "I can't. I can't have this baby."

Justin brushed a wisp of hair off her forehead. He leaned forward to kiss her, but she pulled away.

"Doesn't this upset you?" she asked, her eyes fierce and daring.

Justin swallowed hard. "Only one thing upsets me."

"What's that?" Cameron said.

He rose, letting his hands slap to his thighs. "That you never asked what I wanted."

Chapter 40   The larva made its way through the thick vegetation, pulsing along with ripples of its abdominal segments. Its remarkable head pivoted slowly from side to side, its large, round eyes taking in the surroundings.

The larva had fared well in its brief time in the forest, surrounded by an inexhaustible supply of vegetation. The previous day, it had accidentally felled a large *Scalesia* after eating its way through the base, but it had escaped unharmed. Remaining close to the ootheca had proved advantageous, as its fellow broodmates had spread out rather than remaining nearby and competing for food.

Overlying the epidermis and basement membrane beneath, the larva's cuticle was beginning to flake where it scraped the ground. Its cuticle was loose all around so that it shifted within it when it moved.

The larva was growing. It would soon molt.

The cuticle split behind its head, and it began to wriggle forward. The small hooks on its prolegs anchored to the substrate to keep the cuticle from moving with it. The larva continued to struggle forward, stretching against its own skin and gulping air, broadening itself. The split in the cuticle widened, and the larva pulled itself through the top of its old body, its tiny true legs scrabbling on the ground. Its new exoskeleton was an even more vibrant green.

The new skin was wet and tender. It had not yet hardened, nor had the muscles firmly attached to it. It needed to remain immobile until its new cuticle hardened.

The larva tensed at the quiet scrape nearby. Limbs stiff with age, the feral dog broke from his hiding place in a patch of ferns, lunging at the larva. The larva curled into a protective ball, but not before the dog's mouth closed over its head, its teeth piercing the top of its thorax. The dog swung his head once and the small green body flapped in his mouth like a doll, rotating under the captive head with a sickly crunch.

Drawing his kill up in a bunch between his legs, the dog slid to his belly and began gnawing on the larva's rich tissue. As he worked his way through the head, the dog bit into the larva's mandible. The pointed end pierced the dog's gums, coming free from the head, and he let out a series of yelps.

Backing up and shaking his head, the dog thrashed until the mandible fell to the forest floor. He mouthed the larva, pulling it away through the underbrush. The larva's abdominal segments dragged on the ground behind it, kicking up a trail of rocks and dirt.

"WHAT IN the Jesus Fuck was that?" Justin whispered to Szabla, the dog's yelps vibrating in his ears.

Szabla held up a hand to quiet him. Aside from the usual sounds, the forest was silent. "Dog," she said. "Sounded like."

Justin raised the canteen and shook it, allowing the last few drops to fall into his waiting mouth. They'd been surveying the forest for the better part of the morning. Since Rex had headed off with Derek and Cameron to set the third GPS unit near the lagoon, he'd charged Justin and Szabla with locating suitable bedrock within the forest.

The forest had a freshness from yesterday's rain. In the cups of leaves, nooks of logs, and footprints in the mud, the rainwater pooled in twinkling disks. The air was hot and humid, scented so sharply Szabla could taste it in the back of her throat.

Justin moved in the direction of the yelps, thin branches bowing out of his way. Szabla hooked his shoulder with a hand, pulling him to a stop. "I'll take point," she said.

She passed him and started ahead. She couldn't help looking around in wonder at the varied flora—mint with purple flowers, vines with leathery leaves, the occasional white orchid flowering from a *Scalesia* trunk. A brown finch wove through the tree trunks, making a soft shushing call. Justin imitated it, turning to watch it disappear.

Szabla stopped when they reached an area where the forest floor was disturbed, leaves and dirt kicked up in a recent struggle of some sort. She sniffed the air. "Something smell funny to you?"

"Well, I wasn't gonna say anything, but—"

She cut him off quickly. "Kates. For once in your life be serious."

Justin looked at her sheepishly. "It was such a good setup, though."

Tilting back her head, Szabla inhaled, flaring her nostrils. Justin wrinkled his nose at the odor. "Something is rotten in the state of Sangre de Dios," he said.

Szabla noticed the shiny stock of the mandible hidden among a mat of decomposing leaves. She picked it up, holding it out in a shaft of light that broke through the canopy. "Looks like a mandible," she said. "From another larva."

Justin stepped forward into a patch of ferns, and one of his legs shot out from under him. There was a whispering sound and then he was gone. Into thin air.

Szabla stood dumbfounded, staring at the ferns and fallen leaves woven together on the forest floor. She approached them slowly, reaching out a boot to test the ground.

Justin's laugh scared her half to death; it was deep, resonant. "I gave the Lion his courage, the Tin Man a heart, but what would you like, dearie?" his voice bellowed, echoing within the ground. "A new set of dumbbells?"

Szabla yanked back her leg, almost falling over. "Justin,

knock it off." Her voice was less stable than she would have liked. "Where the fuck are you?"

"I don't know," his voice boomed. "In some kind of cave. I would get up and look around, but I kind of landed on my head."

Szabla swept back the ferns, revealing the gaping entrance to the lava tube, which sloped gently down into a horizontal shaft. Justin blinked against the light. He had only rolled in a few feet. He glanced up, then shot to his feet, scrambling toward the entrance.

The ootheca pulsed on the roof of the lava tube, strung along the thick *Scalesia* root just above where Justin's head had been. The remaining closed chamber was writhing, wiggling the rest of the mighty egg sac. The cords that had lowered the other larvae were shriveled up; it looked as if the ootheca had sprouted curled wood shavings.

"What the fuck is that thing?" Szabla asked.

"A quiche. Why don't you try it?"

"You scrambled out of there pretty fast for a goddamn quiche."

"Well, you know. The whole 'real men' bit." Justin grimaced. "Looks like we found our larva's happy home."

Szabla started for the ootheca, then thought better of it. "Jesus," she said. "Each of these chambers is bigger than a human womb." She took one last look before ducking back out through the ferns, swearing softly to herself.

WITH ANNOYANCE, Savage watched Tucker pace around the fire pit.

"So why aren't they back?" Tucker checked his clunky Iron Man watch again. "Over twenty minutes past muster, and Justin and Szabla are never late."

Suntan lotion smeared thickly across their burnt faces and necks, the other soldiers stood, even as they dug into their MREs. A few dark clouds had begun to gather. Though they cut some of the glare, they did nothing to stifle the heat. Tank did a deep knee bend and grimaced. Straightening up, he bit his lip, wincing through obvious pain.

Diego had set the larva loose on the mound of firewood. It was contentedly working its way through a fresh *Scalesia* branch that was still weeping from the severed end. It stopped its mastications from time to time to track the movement around it. Rex refilled the hurricane lamps from the sole white-fuel bottle, holding the cap in his mouth.

Tucker stood up and paced abbreviated circles. "Relax," Cameron said through a mouthful of cookie bar. She bent back her front pants pocket and glanced at the digital clock face sewn into the cloth. "It's fine. They probably stumbled across something."

"Like a complete set of Russell Wright dinnerware?" Rex asked.

"Why aren't *you* more worried about it?" Tucker said. "You are his wife."

Cameron's eyes were flat when she looked at him. "Not here," she said.

Savage rolled his eyes, stabbing his fork into a pouch of scalloped potatoes. "This fuckin' crew," he muttered. "Faggots and couples."

Derek clamped his teeth, raising the corners of his jaw. He crossed the circle of the fire pit and crouched, bringing his face inches from Savage's. Savage took his time looking up at him, finishing the pattern he'd been tracing in the dirt with his heel before meeting Derek's eyes apathetically.

Derek raised a hand to rest on Savage's shoulder but evidently thought the better of it. Wise choice. He spoke calmly. "I will not have this mission compromised because you want to play bad new kid on the block. You push me about one more inch and I will have no reservation about skulling you and leaving you out here to rot."

A pulse was beating in Derek's temple. Savage watched it work as Derek fought to maintain composure. He met Derek's eyes, refusing to blink until Derek stepped back.

He'd known Derek would step back. He tilted his head, sniffing the air. "I can smell it on you," he said. "Weakness. You've lost your killing nerve."

"Try me," Derek said. "Just you fuckin' try me."

As Derek walked away, Savage pulled his knife from the ankle sheath, flipped it once in the air, and tossed it at Derek. Derek stumbled back to get out of the way, and it stuck in the log. "Sure thing, LT," Savage said.

Cameron reached over, pried the knife from the log, and lofted it over her shoulder at Savage. He stepped back out of the way and plucked it from the air.

"Believe it or not," Cameron said, still not turning to face him, "we're really not all that impressed with knife tricks here."

Savage stood foolishly holding his knife.

Szabla's voice broke through Derek's transmitter after he activated it. "Mitchell. Szabla. We found something. You'd better grab the pencil necks and head uphill."

Diego carried the larva into his tent to secure it in its cruise box. Rex stood excitedly, screwing the cap onto the small fuel bottle as he headed for the forest.

Savage stuffed two more forkfuls of potato into his mouth and stuck the gum and matches into a pocket on his cammies. By the time he turned to go, the others had already disappeared into the trees.

THE OOTHECA vibrated on its root, sending a spill of dirt trickling from the roof of the lava tube. Cameron stepped back toward the sunlight, glad that Derek had cut the ferns that covered the entrance. Savage had yet to arrive.

Justin peered down the dark hole of the shaft and shivered. "How long is this tunnel?"

"It's a lava tube," Diego said softly. "We're standing at the southern entrance. It runs about three hundred and fifty meters before finding its way back up through the forest floor."

The paperlike covering of the ootheca's last closed chamber split down the center.

"Jesus," Cameron said. "It's hatching."

"Have you ever seen anything like this?" Derek asked.

"It's an ootheca of some sort," Diego said hesitantly. "It resembles that of a mantid, but it's much larger, and with fewer chambers."

"It's like an oversize variation on the ootheca we found in Frank's camp. The one he sketched." Rex raised his fingers, running them along the hard line of his jaw. "Why only eight chambers? Why not two hundred fifty-something?"

"I don't know." Diego shook his head. "It looks like this animal, whatever it is, has fewer offspring, but places more resources in them. Better equips them to survive."

A slick green head emerged from the chamber, wiggling and pulling a tadpole-like body out behind it. It was weakened and stunted. Writhing in its membranous sac, it lowered slowly on its thread. Spellbound, they watched it descend. The larva managed to break its head and thorax free from its sac, but its prolegs were still pasted to its abdominal segments. One of its true legs was misshapen; the others looked shriveled and useless.

It was sure to die.

"That's it. That's our thing we have back at the camp," Justin said, as if the thought hadn't occurred to anyone else. Shaking off a shiver, Tucker took a step back, his hand instinctively digging for the hard metal cylinder of the thermite grenade buried deep in the cargo pocket of his cammy pants.

"It's hatching like a mantid," Rex said, rolling the fuel bottle between his hands. "But mantid nymphs don't look like this. They're usually just smaller versions of adults."

"I found this, too," Szabla said, holding out the mandible from the forest floor.

Diego examined it. "It's one of the larvae's sawing mouthparts. A mandible." Even the meager light left a sheen on his forehead. He glanced back up at the ootheca. "There *are* more of them," he said, his voice colored with both excitement and concern.

"If there's one larva for each chamber, that means there are eight of them," Rex said, stepping forward and touching a finger to the side of the egg sac. "At least from this ootheca. We have one locked safely in the cruise box at camp, the one whose mandible Szabla found, this one hatching, and there's presumably another that didn't make it." He pointed to the corner of the cave where several mouthparts lay.

Cameron crouched above the half-buried pieces, raising a mandible to the light. It was already covered with ants. "They must not be edible, these parts," she said. "There are two mandibles here—probably from the same animal."

The larva squirmed on its thread, emitting a pained, high-pitched squeal as the air rushed through its spiracles.

Tank held up four fingers, raising his eyebrows. "He's right," Szabla said. "Assuming this is the only ootheca, we got four more of these things out there."

Savage burst into the lava tube just as the larva squirmed free of its thread, dropping to the ground. Diego touched a finger to his lips, and Savage joined the circle wordlessly, watching the larva attempt to crawl. Its squealing was high-pitched and sharp, like air leaking slowly from a balloon. The larva managed to squirm forward a few inches, leaving a trail in the dirt behind it. Its skin was still moist and tender.

Rex absentmindedly handed Savage the white-fuel bottle as he stepped forward to get a closer view of the larva.

"Jesus, we should . . . help it or something," Derek said. He looked around frantically.

Savage unscrewed the cap of the fuel bottle, stepped forward, and poured a trickle of white fuel up the length of the larva's body. It squirmed at the touch of the liquid.

"Goddamnit," Diego said. "What the hell are you . . . ?" He crouched over the larva, running a hand gently along the soft, pliant hairs. "Thank God. It seems to be all right."

Pulling the matches from the pouch on his cammies, Savage flicked a match across the striker with his thumb, shooting it at the larva. It landed on its back, igniting the white

fuel. The larva's spiracles emitted a screech as the small
flames spread, burning down into the still-unhardened cuticle. It struggled forward as the fire attacked its body.

"What the fuck did you do that for?" Rex yelled.

Derek turned and seized Savage by the shirt, but Savage
was watching the larva die and didn't react. The shrieks
brought Derek's attention back to the larva, and he released
Savage and crouched over the dying animal. Diego was on his
knees, his hands opening and closing impotently. Cameron
stared at the ground. She could feel the sweat hammering
through her pores, her heart pounding in her fingertips.

The larva writhed in place, unable to scrape itself forward
any farther, the flames eating away small holes in its body.
The screeching was weaker, and the clicking noise became
audible beneath it. A pasty material foamed from its mouth.

With a last squeal, the larva shuddered and died, curling
up. The fire dwindled, leaving behind only a blackened
husk. Thin, fragile bones protruded from holes in the cuticle—a slender snake of a vertebrate and what looked like a
parallel series of large, curved wishbones. Diego and Rex
had been right about the internal skeleton.

"What the fuck was that about?" Derek screamed, his
voice echoing down the shaft.

"You said we should help it," Savage said. "I did."

Diego rose. "You've just destroyed what could be a one-
of-a-kind specimen," he barked. His hand sliced through the
air, fingers splayed. "¡Coño tu madre!" he cursed.

Her breath hitching in her chest, Cameron stared at the far
wall of the cave, where a line of ants were streaming up and
carrying away tiny pieces of the ootheca.

"That thing was gonna die anyways," Szabla said.

Rex turned on her angrily. "That's your logic? Brilliant.
Fucking brilliant. You're like eight-year-old boys lighting ants
on fire with magnifying glasses, pulling wings off butterflies."

"He might have just done us a favor," Szabla said, smacking Savage on the chest with the back of her hand.

"We don't know that these larvae are dangerous."

"I'd rather not find out."

Rex turned to Derek, his eyes hard and angry. "They're *your* troops, under *your* command. It's your job to keep them in line."

Derek looked at the burnt little corpse, his eyes loose and unfocused. "We do not just kill whatever we want to. It isn't natural."

"Bullshit!" Savage yelled, the veins in his neck bulging. His fingers were white-knuckled around the shaft of his knife. "Natural," he growled. "What the fuck is natural anyway? Anything we want. Anything we are. Everything we make is from the earth and our own primitive brains. Nuclear missiles, Agent Orange . . . " He flipped his knife in the air and caught the blade end expertly between his thumb and index finger. ". . . knives. They're all natural. Don't be so arrogant to think otherwise. So don't you give me this natural shit when you only kill things that are ugly, all right? Because I've killed 'em all. Women, children, babies. I could tell stories that would make your heart jump out of your fuckin' body. And you know what? It's all the same. There is no natural. There are no rules."

Derek started to speak, but Savage raised the blade and pointed it at him, inches from his eye. "That's a blood lesson, LT. Learn that."

THEY GATHERED in the clearing outside the lava tube except Savage, who stood staring out into the forest, one foot resting on a gnarled tree root that rose out of the ground like an arm from a grave. He raised a wedge of plantain to his mouth, thumbing it against the side of his Death Wind.

He was a good distance off from the others as they circled, speaking in lowered voices so that he wouldn't hear them. Cameron watched Derek with concern, her mind reeling with all she'd just witnessed. She wondered why Derek didn't order Savage over.

The forest blurred before Cameron's eyes then focused, pinpoint sharp. "I hate to sound like a broken record here," she said. "But we have one objective, and that's to fulfill the mission. No more, no less. Anything that doesn't help us meet that goal is irrelevant."

"I'm the AOIC here," Szabla said.

Cameron looked at her a long time before speaking. "Yes, Szabla," she said. "We know."

Diego had wrapped the remains of the larva in his shirt to carry back to base. He stood with his feet a little too far apart, gazing blankly through the trees. "Smooth-billed ani," he said. The others looked and saw nothing, but then a black bird burst from a branch, shooting through the understory.

"How the hell do you notice that stuff?" Tucker asked.

Diego smoothed his mustache with his thumb and index finger. "No puedo ver las hojas," he said. "I don't see the leaves." His voice was smooth and sorrowful, like a slow-rushing river. He looked at the opening to the lava tube, shaking his head sadly.

Rex walked over to a puddle trapped on the concave slope of the basalt at the base of the lava tube, his hand digging in his bag for a sample jar. He filled it, tilting the jar to take in the water, then held it up to the light. When viewed through glass, rather than against the black stone, the water was tinted red. Cameron watched him put the jar in his backpack with the others and return slowly to the circle, a thoughtful expression on his face. When he saw her looking at him, he shook his head, puzzled. "Dinoflagellates in the water."

Diego's brow furrowed. "How did phytoplankton get all the way up here?"

Cameron turned her attention back to Derek, who was a sickly white.

"You all right, LT?" Justin asked.

"Yes," Derek said sharply. "I'm fine. Everything's fine. We're gonna finish forest recon, find a slab of bedrock, and muster back at base at 2000. I want the fourth GPS site picked before we turn in."

"I want assurances that there won't be any more predatory behavior like that," Rex said.

"Fine," Derek said. "You have my assurance. Anyone who acts other than under direct orders will answer to me." He raised his eyes—tired, flat points of green.

"What about him?" Diego said, indicating Savage with a jerk of his head.

"I'll handle him."

"This is my survey," Rex said. "You know."

Szabla's eyes were intense with dislike. "You've made that clear," she said.

Derek glared at the small group. "Let's roll out."

They shuffled into movement, paired off, and headed into the forest. Tucker passed Savage without slowing, and Savage followed him into the underbrush.

Szabla paused by Derek, studying his face as if trying to get a read on it. Her whisper was barely audible to Cameron, certainly not to the scientists. "Look, LT, I think those things might—"

"Roll out, Szabla," he snarled. He did not look over at her.

She lingered for a moment by Derek, clearly wanting to say something else, but he didn't acknowledge her, not even when she jerked her neck to the side to crack it. Justin waited patiently at the brink of the foliage. When she finally came, he let her take point.

Derek and Cameron stood alone in the clearing, dusk spreading the shadows around them into planes of black. The ground rumbled slightly, but the movement didn't escalate into a full-blown earthquake. Derek didn't even seem to notice.

"You all right, Derek?" she asked.

"Fine," he said sharply, still averting his eyes. "I'm gonna bust Savage's ass if he touches another baby."

Cameron drew her lips together and out, concerned. She had shared Derek's visceral reaction watching the thing die on the ground, but Derek seemed to be slipping down the slope of his emotions.

She cleared her throat uncomfortably. "It's not a baby, Derek."

His laugh was empty. "No shit. I didn't call it a baby."

They stood there dumbly with the whistle of the wind through the trees and the calls of strange animals all around them. Cameron watched a star spider make its way up a mossy log. She cleared her throat uncomfortably. "Look, Derek, I know this must be hard, in light of—"

"You don't know anything, all right?" Derek said gruffly. He turned away from her, clenching his jaw. "Let's go."

Cameron took note of the pulse beating in his temple before turning and starting the trek back to camp, her canteen bouncing against her hip like a trophy kill.

Chapter 41   Tucker and Savage stopped for a moment to rehydrate in the darkness, the smell of dampness lingering in the air. Tucker broke the long-standing silence by clearing his throat. Savage watched him expectantly. "Everything has a name back home," Tucker said. "Streets, house numbers. You can always say where you're going, where you been. Not here. Just trees and dirt and hills. You could lose track of yourself here."

Savage scratched his beard, fingers losing themselves in tangles of hair. "Or find yourself." He worked his cheek between his teeth, shifting his jaw and feeling the flesh roll between his molars. "Your LT—he's not standing firm right now."

Tucker did not respond.

"What's all that shit you guys were talking about at the briefing back in Sac? About something he went through?"

"Derek's been a soldier for a long time," Tucker said.

"Doesn't matter. I seen veterans suddenly lose their killing nerve one day and . . ." Savage drew a finger across his neck and made a slicing sound. "Can happen to anyone, anywhere. Saw it all the time in Nam. Good buddy of mine went into a village, bayoneted some old bitch. Kept him up nights, thought she looked like his grandma back home. Next day he got the shakes, starting in his hands, spreading up his arms. His fire team takes a walk through a village, stumbles in on six Charlies in a hut, my buddy freezes up, couldn't pull the trigger. Lost the whole team, except one man."

"Sounds like a bit of a war story," Tucker said derisively.

"Don't it, though?" Savage replied quietly. He pursed his lips. "But it happened."

"How do you know?"

Savage looked away. "I was the one man."

He walked off into the woods, and after a moment, Tucker followed. The quiet encroached on them. Every sound magnified—the crunch of leaves underfoot, the sighing of the wind through the branches, the strange cackling calls of the petrels.

They reached a stretch of forest where a fault had rent the ground, engendering a constellation of smaller cracks. Trees protruded from the earth at strange angles, struggling to keep hold of the crooked rock beneath them, the last few feet of their tops turning straight up. Clumps of browning Spanish moss dangled over the branches like dead rats.

Savage glided across the fallen trees, the upthrust blocks of stone, the cracks in the earth that seemed to stretch down all the way to hell. Tucker's steps were unsteady in the gloom. At one point, he nearly lost his footing at the edge of a rift, but Savage was there instantly, a firm hand on his arm to pull him back. As abruptly as the disrupted section of land began, it ended, fading into vines and leafy domes.

THE NIGHT was jet black, as though the moon had simply vanished. It was raining again, not hard rain like last night, but a soft misting through the air. Szabla and Justin had been walking for hours. It seemed that all the large masses of rock they'd located were either cracked, or dangerously near a

cliff or fissure. Having stripped off her cammy shirt, Szabla
cut through the foliage in her tank top. It clung wetly to her
breasts and stomach, and when she ran a hand across the
ridge of her clavicle, it came away slick with moisture.

A length of snake draped across a fallen tree limb, brown
with yellow flecks. She pointed at it to alert Justin and kept
moving. Mating dragonflies zoomed dangerously, coupling
briefly and separating to dodge tree trunks. She remembered
hearing about birds that mate in a midair dive, sometimes
rocketing to their death because they can't break off the act.
She glanced behind her, checking Justin's position. Turning
her mouth to her shoulder, she muttered into the transmitter,
"Murphy. Primary channel."

TUCKER ACTIVATED his transmitter, grinning when he heard
Szabla. "We're secure."

Her voice came through with exceptional clarity, as if she
were standing right beside him. "This shit's making me nervous," she said in a hoarse whisper. "Have you noticed the
look in Derek's eyes? Like he's a few bulbs short of a full
string."

Some dirt had collected under Tucker's Iron Man watch,
and he dug it out with his pinkie. He snapped a stick off a
tree and used it to lop a frond off a plant. Savage was a good
twenty-five feet behind him, out of earshot. "I don't know,"
Tucker replied. "He is the LT."

"He sure as hell's not acting like one. He's acting like the
scientists' fuckboy. I spoke with Mako earlier. Private con-
versation. He was concerned but political. I'm thinking the
rest of us should round up. Have a chat."

"What'd Cam say?"

"What the fuck does it matter what Cam says?"

"Well, maybe we could—"

"Don't move," Savage growled.

Though Savage had startled the hell out of him, Tucker
froze. Savage stood about five feet to his left in the shadow

beneath the dipping bough of a tree. Tucker hadn't seen him come up on him; he'd just heard a voice issuing from a patch of darkness.

Tucker was vulnerable from three sides, shadows all around him. He sensed a presence right beside him, the darkness shaping itself into something rudimentary and life-like. Panic flickered through his eyes as he slowly turned his head to get his bearings. He tightened his grip on the stick.

"Tucker?" Szabla's voice crackled through the transmitter. "You there?"

The connection was breaking up with the rain, and Tucker prayed it would go dead. He'd have to speak to deactivate the transmitter, but he knew not to make a sound. Lips trembling, he tried to shush Szabla, but the air seemed to stick in his throat.

He hadn't moved an inch, not since Savage had spoken. His foot was raised mid-step, poised about four inches above the ground. A roll of thunder filled the air. Sweat beaded across his forehead.

"Not an inch," Savage hissed. "Don't even exhale."

Because it was supporting all his weight, Tucker's left leg started to quiver, ever so slightly, in the thigh. He flexed it and it stilled. More rain swept to his face and he blinked against it, fighting the water out of his eyes. His hand was white-knuckled around the branch. Some mud slid from the bottom of his raised boot and slopped to the ground.

A flash of lightning lit the air, and he saw dangling beside and above him the enormous creature, not more than an arm's length to his right. She swayed upside down from the branch of a tree, blending in almost perfectly with the fluctuating foliage all around her. Her forelegs were folded, as if in prayer, her wide wings pulled in tight across her back. If she weren't right next to him, he wouldn't have even seen her among the branches, twigs, and leaves.

Normally a greenish-tan, the creature's eyes had turned

black for the night. Set in a triangle between them were the ocelli, three smaller eyes used only to distinguish the degree of light. They glimmered like pearls beneath the arc of her antennae. The hooks on the ends of her legs were clamped shut around a wide *Scalesia* branch about fifteen feet above the ground; it creaked when she swayed.

Tucker turned his head with excruciating slowness and looked into her face. Her front antennae vibrated in the breeze, her mouthparts quivering, and for an instant, Tucker caught his own frightened reflection in her black eyes.

Szabla's voice cut back in sharply. "—next in command. I'm thinking we could use a little leadership—" Tucker jerked ever so slightly, and the creature's antennae snapped erect at the movement. His nostrils flared, his chest jerked with a quick intake of air.

The strike was so quick Savage couldn't even see it. The raptorial legs flashed out, folding over themselves and crushing Tucker within them. Tucker screamed as the spikes dug through his flesh, almost scissoring him in two. His arm was pinned to his side. The strike took three hundredths of a second.

Tucker's stick tumbled to the ground.

The creature dropped from the branch, landing expertly on her legs while not relinquishing her hold on Tucker. Her frightful head lowered to the back of Tucker's neck, the mouth spreading wide, a collection of living tools.

Savage charged the creature, swinging his knife at the prothorax. The blade glanced off the hard waxy exoskeleton, unable to dig into the smooth surface. Though the blow didn't puncture her cuticle, the creature swayed back with its force. Tucker's free arm flailed, his hand fisting the air as he screamed. Savage grabbed his arm and pulled, though he knew the thing had him wrapped up too tight. Blood spurted from Tucker's mouth, spilling over his chin.

The creature would have struck Savage were her raptorial legs not wrapped around Tucker's body. She flung Tucker to the ground and lowered herself swiftly, standing territorially over his body.

Savage staggered back. Beneath the creature's abdomen, Tucker squirmed in the leaves. The creature spread her mouth, though no sound issued forth. Then air hissed from her spiracles, forcing Savage back another step.

A stream of blood ran down one of Tucker's arms, stark red against his white flesh. Savage could hear him rasping through a punctured lung. He was lost. There was no way he was going to pull through.

But it was in Savage's blood to stand ground when there was a comrade down. He stepped back farther out of the creature's range and reverse-gripped the knife with the blade running down along his forearm, sharp edge out, ready to punch. The creature tilted her head, watching him curiously. It was night all around them, but in the lightning he could see the rain running off her sides. Her mouth opened in another silent roar, a maw of mandibles, maxillae, and labrum, and she drew herself up to her full nine feet. Behind her, her abdomen and wings stretched back, thick and firm, like a horse's body. Though Savage was across the clearing from her, she seemed to tower over him.

She gave a startle display, spreading her wings and rearing up on her hind legs, filling the entire space between the trees and revealing two eyelike markings on the insides of her front legs. The upper part of her abdomen scraped against her underwings, producing a harsh hissing. She lowered herself, then stepped deliberately back behind Tucker's body and struck him with her front legs, knocking him a few feet across the ground. He howled, more in fear than pain, and tried to struggle away. His intestines were spilled on the ground beside him, and one of his hands was trying to scoop them back inside his body as the other clawed him forward.

Savage was frozen with indecision, unable to venture within range of the thing without being killed but desperately wanting to get his hands on it. He hoped for Tucker to pass out. But Tucker had never passed out, not from pain or panic. He kept moving, clawing and scooping like a wind-up toy running out of steam.

The creature's raptorial legs flashed out again, snatching Tucker off the ground and curling his body in toward her face. He screamed as the mouth approached him. The mandibles cut into the back of his neck and then he went limp in her front legs, twitching.

Savage and the creature watched each other as she ate.

She chewed with her mandibles, holding and manipulating chunks of flesh with her maxillae. Tucker's head rolled off and struck the ground with a thud. The creature made no effort to pick it up.

Savage watched one of Tucker's arms go down, the elbow sticking out of the preoral cavity. Despite her strong cutting jaws, the creature was a messy eater. It was not a pleasant meal to see consumed in any event, but the image of Tucker's various parts protruding from the creature's mouth was sickening.

Savage crouched and glared at the creature, wiping the rain from his eyes with a swipe of his arm. "I'm gonna fuckin' kill you," he whispered, almost lovingly.

The creature paused, as if she had heard him. She lowered her head, tearing a thick band of meat from Tucker's flank, and when she looked up, Savage was gone.

Chapter 42   Cameron jerked to her feet when she heard something crash through the brush at the edge of the forest. They all squared defensively until Savage's figure cut from the dark, charging toward them.

"Where the fuck were you?" Derek yelled. "You're over an hour late and we couldn't transmit to Tucker. Szabla said his transmitter just cut out."

Savage didn't answer as he neared the circle of logs, his eyes steeled on Szabla.

"Where's Tucker?" Cameron asked, concern coloring her voice.

Without slowing, Savage passed the fire pit and seized Szabla's undershirt around the thin arm straps. He tore the straps forcefully to the sides, ripping the shirt down the middle and exposing her breasts. He towered over her, his knee pushed tight between her legs on the log as she leaned back. Before anyone could reach him, his knife was out of the sheath and pointing at the small raised circle of her transmitter. Cameron and Derek were tense on their feet, ready to pounce on Savage if the opportunity arose.

"This is not a fucking toy!" Savage yelled. "Fuck!" He stepped back and threw the blade hard at the log. It stuck deep. Tank was between him and Szabla in a flash, but Savage didn't make another move toward her. He yanked the bandanna off and ran his fingers through his hair, grabbing the back in a ponytail before throwing his hand off to the side. "He's gone. He's fucking dead."

Mouth ajar, eyes glassy, Szabla sat dumbfounded on the log, making no effort to cover herself. In the silence that ensued, Cameron walked over and pulled Szabla's shirt back up. She stood in front of Savage and raised her face to his. "What happened?"

"He got eaten. By this huge fucking thing. With snapping front legs. Like . . . almost like a praying mantis."

Derek snorted. A strange expression worked its way across Rex's face, then vanished. He turned to Diego and something passed between them. Cameron's stomach turned over once, as it sometimes did just before she vomited.

"What are you talking about, Savage?" Justin said. "Where the fuck is Tucker?"

"It was swinging upside down like a fucking bat and it grabbed him in those legs, clamped down on him like a bear trap." He shook his head. "You shoulda heard him screaming."

Cameron sat down heavily. "Is this a fucking joke?" Derek asked.

Justin's breathing was so shallow it sounded like panting. Szabla dipped her head, running a hand across the back of her neck, her nails leaving red streaks. She murmured something in a low whisper. They stood for a few moments in silence, breathing together. Savage glared at them expectantly.

"Fuck this," Justin finally said. "*Fuck this.*"

"Calm down, Justin," Derek said. "We don't really know what's going on here."

"What the fuck do you mean we don't know what's going on?" Savage yelled. "I just told you there's a mammoth fucking creature on the loose. Nine feet tall and just as long. We have to kill that motherfucker."

He stripped off his shirt and flung it to the side. His body gleamed with sweat. "We gotta kill the larvae. They're its offspring. We got one in the tent and four more in the forest." Savage held up three fingers at first but got the fourth one up quickly. "We gotta get to them before they transform."

"I am not standing by while you attempt to exterminate a species," Diego said. "So don't even think about it."

"Nothing's transforming," Derek said wearily. "And we don't know that these larvae or the egg sac have anything to do with what you saw. We don't even know what you saw. The worst thing we can do is jump to conclusions."

"We don't have time *not* to jump to conclusions."

Cameron spoke in an uncharacteristically low voice. "He may be right, Derek."

Derek shot her a glare reserved for liars and traitors. She recoiled from it.

Savage threw his arms out to his sides in frustration. "They teach you this in leadership school, champ? You've been a whole lot of indecision since we landed here."

For a moment, Cameron thought Derek might charge Savage. He was clenching his jaw, the corners of his cheeks flexed out in points. His voice was calm, but there was an element of lunacy hidden in it. "You weren't getting along so good with Tucker, were you, Savage?" Derek asked.

Savage froze. He glowered across the fire at Derek, his beard bristling as his mouth worked noiselessly on words. When he finally spoke, his voice was so close to a growl the words all rushed together. "I would love nothing more than to slit your throat and paint my face with your blood."

"Having some problems with him, you're a little loose around the pegs to begin with, maybe you slipped and your knife got stuck in him. Seems a bit more likely than a nine-foot mantis, doesn't it?" Derek jabbed a finger in Savage's direction, his upper lip curled into a snarl. "You'd better fucking pray you didn't touch him."

Szabla still had not spoken. A spot on her right cheek was quivering like crazy even though she wasn't close to crying. She was never close to crying. Tank sat quietly, digging a stick in the dirt.

"Let's go," Cameron said. "Let's run a recon, see if we can find Tucker." She caught Savage's eye. "Or recover his body."

"Nobody is going anywhere unless I tell them to," Derek snapped. "What, are we gonna search in the dark with flares and elbow lights? We don't have any tactical lights. We'll wait till morning."

Savage backed up on his heels, laughing. He raised a finger and pointed at each of them in turn. "You're a bunch of fucking cowards. Tucker's been your comrade for years. Let me tell you something." His eyes gathered emotion. "Whether I liked him or not, I just saw a man go down before my eyes and I'm gonna do something about it."

He stormed over to Szabla and she flinched away, but he was just retrieving his knife. Resting a boot on the log next to his Death Wind, he yanked it out, running it back and forth across his thigh. It sliced the fabric of his pants, opening a slit as thin as a paper cut. He pointed the tip of the blade at Derek. "You want proof?! I'll bring you proof."

Cameron ran after him a few steps as he headed for the

forest, but Derek yelled at her, "Cameron, get back here. Let him go."

Cameron halted and Savage disappeared, fading into the blackness between the trees.

DEREK ISSUED combat orders, taking the first patrol. Marching along like a dazed distance runner, he circled the fire, then headed all the way out around the perimeter of the open field, keeping a safe distance from the forest on the north side.

Diego removed the larva from the cruise box and placed it outside. He tested its responses to a number of stimuli—different touches, movements, and sounds—until the larva inched away, curled up and ceased responding at all. Tank was reclining on the grass, a safe distance from where the larva lay. Cameron stared at the larva blankly, trying to quell the storm rising inside her.

His boots shushing through the grass, Derek walked past them. The fire flickered over his face. He'd completed the route five times, passing right in front of them, and not once had he spoken. Aside from the large black crescents under his eyes, his face was pale. His lips, moving as he mumbled to himself, looked blue.

Savage had left his shirt on the ground, and Szabla leaned over and picked it up. Removing her ripped undershirt, she slid his shirt over her bare skin.

Derek moved past them and around the fire like a ghost, and Szabla raised her head to watch him walking away. She tried to laugh, but it came out angry. She lowered her voice so that Diego and Rex, sitting on the far log across the fire, couldn't hear her. "He's not being level and he's not making good assessments."

Cameron ran her fingers through her hair, scratching her scalp near the back.

"He's not taking charge," Szabla hissed. "He hasn't been on top of things since he's been back. It must feel too similar to—"

Cameron interrupted, her voice slow, weighed down. "He'll get it under control. He always does." She leaned over and gently touched the larva's back before she realized what she'd done and pulled her hand away.

"I called in to Mako today. Just before I paged Tucker."

Tank propped himself up on his elbows. Cameron turned slowly. "You did *what?*" she asked.

"You heard me. I am the AOIC and I have grave concerns about Derek's ability to lead this mission. Now that a legitimate threat has been introduced into the equation, I'm even more concerned. We need to bump him and reestablish the chain of command."

"With you taking over."

"That *is* how it works," Szabla answered coldly.

Cameron found a stick and pushed it into the ground, her lips pressed together. "Glad we're being supportive. His comrades in arms. I mean, if he can't count on his platoon—"

"Cameron. Fuck you and wake up. This isn't Aunty Jane going into rehab. This has turned into a serious military op. Loyalty is not the most useful attribute right now."

Cameron cleared her throat sharply. "What'd Mako say?"

Szabla looked away. "My complaint has been registered, but he doesn't want to contradict an officer downrange. If he shuts Derek down, it looks bad all the way around. It would take a substantial amount of pressure to get him to do that— we're not gonna have the time to tap dance around."

"So what are you saying?"

"At some point, it might be worth being more . . . active, even if it means we get brought before the commander when we get back," Szabla said. Cameron shook her head, cursing softly. "You're gonna be key here, Cam." Szabla leaned back, studying the sky. "You're the one everyone trusts, though why exactly that is beats the shit out of me."

Cameron looked over at Justin, but he was watching the fire, the flames playing across his face. Tank angled his arm back, cracking his shoulder.

"Regardless of how swell and interesting our scientists and Derek might think this thing is," Szabla said, jerking her head toward the larva, "we have no idea what it's gonna metamorphose into. Savage's story may be true."

Tank regarded the larva suspiciously. Justin laughed, a dry, hollow laugh. "Or we could be wrong and this thing could be harmless."

Cameron's face contracted as though she were going to cry, though she felt no tears moving through her. "I hope so," she said quietly. She rose, brushing the dirt from the log off her behind. "In any event, I'm gonna go warn Ramón and Floreana."

"Who?" Szabla asked, but Cameron was already heading for the road.

Szabla pried a piece of bark off the log between her legs. "Maybe the world *is* coming undone," she said. "Cam didn't request permission."

THE WIND was drawing through the watchtower again, howling like a banshee. Somewhere, moving beneath the surface of the sound, Derek thought he heard his baby daughter's laugh. It twirled like a wind chime and vanished back into the howling.

He trudged along the field, reflecting about responsibility. It was something he spent a lot of time thinking about, particularly Before. He had a responsibility to complete the mission, to assist in all aspects of Rex's survey, but there was also something more than that. A responsibility to life, a responsibility to protect things that could not protect themselves.

He had failed once already.

Chapter 43   Cameron called out once as she neared the small house so as not to surprise the couple or find herself on the wrong end of a swinging ax. She gazed at the dark stretch of the forest in the distance, the ribbons of *garúa* hanging in the air like bands of fabric.

Ramón met her at the door, his dark hands and dirty fingernails pronounced against the light *bloque* on which they rested. "Hello, gringa," he said. Cameron noticed for the first time the space between his front teeth, a gap from which he drew attention away with the sharp line of his mustache.

"Hola," Cameron said. She started to speak, but he stepped forward and embraced her. Awkwardly, she allowed herself to be hugged.

"You are good to have come and checked on us," he said.

"How is she?" Cameron asked.

Ramón stepped back, gesturing for Cameron to come inside.

Floreana was sitting in a wide wooden chair at the kitchen table, her legs spread and her stomach bulging out before her. She was dozing off, her head rolling forward before snapping back up. Cameron and Ramón watched her for a few moments, and Cameron felt her first smile in a long time rise to her lips. Floreana's eyes finally flashed open, catching a glimpse of the visitor, and then she was wide awake, scolding her husband.

"It's all right," Cameron said. "I'm just glad to see that everything's okay. How are you feeling?"

Floreana groaned, lacing her hands dramatically around her belly, as if carrying a load of laundry. She stood, arching forward to stretch her back. When she saw the expression on Cameron's face, her smile vanished. "What's wrong?" she asked.

Cameron shook her head. "I'm sorry to alarm you." She looked down at her boots, her men's size-ten feet. "As if you don't have enough on your mind right now."

"What?" Ramón asked. His thumb twitched against the scar of his index finger.

"Well, that thing you talked about, whatever it was, it may have killed one of our men. I'm just concerned . . . I'm concerned if it comes near here that you . . . the baby . . . I don't know." Cameron's face was flushed, though she had no idea why. She fought to keep the softness of her emotions from seeping into her voice. "I would stay here myself to stand guard, but I can't. It would be breaking orders."

Ramón smiled at her affectionately, and Cameron realized how foolish she must sound to this kind, simple man—a woman offering to protect his house.

"We'll be all right," Ramón said. "Though I thank you."

"For what?" Cameron asked.

Floreana stepped forward, resting her hands on Cameron's shoulders. "For your thoughts," she said. "For your kind eyes."

Cameron looked down. She twisted her boot on the dirt ground, leaving the imprint of a fan.

"You are not like most of the others, you know," Floreana said, tilting her head in the direction of the soldiers' base camp. "We have watched them, joking and planning and quarreling." She shook her head. "You are not like them."

The urge to respond defensively rose in Cameron's throat—just as quickly, it quelled. "Why?" She surprised herself. Her cheeks were burning and her eyes felt loose, as if they were slipping in their sockets.

Floreana raised a hand, laying it gently on Cameron's cheek. Cameron had not been touched like that by anyone except Justin since childhood. She felt suddenly young and naive, powerless. "You have so much to give," Floreana said.

Cameron raised a hand, gripping Floreana around the wrist and pulling her arm away. She smiled once, curtly. "I'm sorry," she said. "I'm . . . not used to . . ." She studied the small fireplace, feeling Ramón's and Floreana's eyes on her.

She turned to leave, then stopped herself. Slowly, she raised her head, again meeting Floreana's eyes. She saw her own trembling hand pointing at Floreana's stomach. "May I?" she asked.

Floreana nodded. "Of course."

Cameron reached out and laid her hand across Floreana's full belly. Her knees felt weak, on the verge of buckling, so she sank down, planting them on the dirt floor. Floreana pulled the blunted edge of Cameron's hair off her cheek and drew her softly toward her stomach. Cameron turned her head, resting her ear flat against the globe of Floreana's belly.

She closed her eyes and listened.

Chapter 44   Savage was back in the forest. Sometimes he felt he belonged there—that was his curse and his blessing. A kid from the bad side of Pittsburgh, a city of smokestacks, drab concrete, and cigarette butts in gutters, and yet he'd spent more time than he'd care to remember surrounded by nothing but fronds and trees and things that went hiss in the night.

Slung low in the fork of a tree as if awaiting prey, body streaked with dried mud and grime, eyes beading white behind a mask of filth and the dusty tinge of a wild man's beard, Savage cocked his head and listened for the faintest sound. Camouflaged with mud, he blended into the branch, coiled along its length like an anaconda. He dropped from the tree and stepped into the hunt.

Stalking through the wilderness, hunting and being hunted,

it made his balls tighten with the thrill. He could still remember the way it felt when he belly-crawled up behind a cluster of gooks on a stakeout, stood with his M-60 hammering in his arms like a living thing before they could even turn around. Like he'd shattered the third plate with as many baseballs and won the fuckin' Kewpie doll.

He was shirtless, streaked with mud and rain and sweat. He moved effortlessly, picking through the terrain like a native thing, whistling behind tree trunks, easing through underbrush, flowing through showers of vines so precisely that he blended with their movement.

Using no compass, he navigated through the darkness, feeling the plants wet against his face. He paused about a half mile from the spot where the creature had struck, pulling the Death Wind from his ankle sheath. He flexed his arm, curling his fist to his chin, and made an incision along the backside of his forearm. It was not deep; it would let blood, but not too much blood, and it would heal quickly.

Turning his face up so the rain fell across his cheeks, he exhaled deeply, the noise whisked away in the wind, then continued through the mud and the leaves.

Blood curled down his arm, wrapping itself in thick bands around his wrist, moistening his palm and fingers until they were hot and sticky. He left blood on the fronds and leaves, in droplets on the mud, on tree trunks against which he leaned.

He left his blood on the forest.

THE CREATURE cleaned herself fastidiously, rubbing her forelegs over her face like a cat. She pulled her antennae down, sucking the blood off them, then wiped her eyes. It was essential that she remove all food from her eyes and antennae so that it wouldn't interfere with her sensory perception.

Bending her enormous head down, she nibbled free the chunks of flesh stuck in the tines of her legs.

She fluttered her translucent underwings once, folding

them neatly beneath their protective outer wings, and headed back toward the thicket of bushes nestled between the trees in front of her. She stopped and retched twice, long shudders originating in her abdomen, and brought up Tucker's thermite grenade. It flew from her mouth as if she'd spit it, plopping in the mud beside Tucker's head.

She eyed it curiously.

A distant vibration reached her antennae and they snapped upright. She froze, holding one foreleg off the ground like a bird dog pointing, and waited for further vibrations. There were none.

But then it reached her antennae, the pungent reek of alarm pheromones.

Slowed by the considerable weight in her belly, she plodded in the direction of the scent, swiveling her head to glance around for the wounded prey. Her movements were conspicuous, brazen.

There was an almost arachnid jerkiness to her walk, but also an odd grace. Despite the formidable length of her body, she never scraped against trees or broke branches, not even with her rounded back or hind legs.

The rain washed over her and the forest, confusing her slightly since it made the leaves and twigs vibrate with small, lifelike motions. It appeared agitated, the forest.

The first drop of blood she came across was nestled in the palm of a large fern frond, protected from the rain by a broader frond that stretched over it like an umbrella. She paused, sensing the blood. Then she sped up, crashing through the underbrush, her antennae quivering, her eyes focusing to take in mosaic after mosaic of the forest. Her feet pressed hooflike imprints in the mud.

The blood trail was clearly marked, smudged through the mud and the plants. She crossed a hunk of tree bark liberally doused with blood and her head pivoted a near half turn on her thin neck, her mouth working like a pulsing heart.

Then the trail ended.

She stopped, a vine draped scarflike over her shoulder. Her raptorial legs were raised, snapping back on themselves, hungry mouths. There was no more blood, just rain and leaves and air so hot it steamed beneath the canopy. She leaned forward, her head inches off the ground, and examined the mud, then the tree trunks and the plants surrounding her. Craning her neck, she ran her head over the ground like a vacuum cleaner.

Ten feet behind her, one of her footprints vibrated, then the mud bubbled upward beneath it as though the earth were belching. A dome pulled itself from the sticky earth, mud thick with filth draining off its sides in gooey sheets.

As the mud fell away around it, two arms became visible, ridged at the shoulders, then the back haunches of some jungle thing. The haunches rose like a sprinter's in the blocks, then Savage pulled himself erect. His eyes blinked open, flashes of white amidst brown.

In a single clean movement, the mud slid from the Death Wind knife clutched in his hand, plopping to the earth. The blade gleamed cold and steel.

He saw the creature's antennae snap to attention. She started to turn her head.

Savage's heart pounded in his ears. He heard nothing, though he knew he was yelling at the top of his lungs as he charged; it was just him and his heart thundering through his body as he leapt up on the thing's back, his boot almost slipping off the slick waxy exoskeleton before taking hold in a crunch of wing and body. He propelled himself forward across the length of the abdomen toward the torsolike thorax, arms outstretched to hug the big boulder of a head that was swiveling to look directly at him over its own body. His shoulder struck her cheek just before the razor-sharp mandibles could turn into him like tusks, and the thing reared like a stallion, her wings kicking open beneath his legs, her spiked front legs flailing and crushing closed. He would've slid off had he not locked an arm around the long thin neck, the crook of his forearm and biceps cinched against the thing's throat, and his yell fell into a growl though he still couldn't hear it. He was snarling through clenched teeth like a dog, his face heavy with mud and his bare chest flat against her body as she reared and shook and reared again, her cutting jaws snapping shut on air and air and air. The edge of his knife was inches from his cheek.

The creature pivoted, striking the base of a tree roughly and bringing down a scattering of leaves over Savage. He held his arm tight around her neck, locking up the wrist with his other hand, and nuzzled his face into the union of his fists under the knife, smelling mud and the scent of his own warm flesh.

Something crunched, a seam bursting in the cuticle, and the creature paused, only for a moment, but that was enough. Yanking the head to the side with all his force, Savage ripped the knife through her neck, digging so deep he could feel the ooze against his knuckles. The creature's hissing went silent in a whistle of air that bubbled wetly from the severed trachea in the gash. Shaking and twitching, she fell, her front legs folding so she looked as though she were kneeling. Her back legs gave out and she collapsed, Savage riding her down into the mud like a cowboy, his legs forked over the spot where her thorax met her lengthy abdomen.

He flung the head aside, and it flapped limply from the sheet of flesh hinged on the intact cuticle at the back of the neck. His boots sank in mud almost to the ankles when he slid off the abdomen.

The rain had cleared some of the mud from his body, but he was still filthy. His hair was heavy, tangled with grime. He sheathed his blade, patting it once affectionately.

He recognized the sour taste in his mouth. Combat juice, they used to call it, the saliva that flooded one's tongue along the sides. Some water had collected on a frond, and he poured it over his mouth and chin, drinking. Crouching to rest by a tree, he plucked a granadilla from the mud and split the shell with his thumbs, scraping his bottom teeth along the lining of the skin to get at the meat.

Once he no longer felt his heart moving in his chest, he rose and faced the dead creature. He grabbed her back legs and tugged, and the large body slid easily in the mud. She was surprisingly light given her size. She'd had a good fighting build—large body surface in proportion to bulk, low weight to leverage her strength.

It had taken him nearly an hour to get out there; it would be at least three more pulling the thing back to base camp. He began the trek, clenching the back legs between his biceps and sides and dragging the corpse behind him. The wings crumpled up under the body, their slickness helping him move it through the mud.

Time passed in a crawl. He heard rats rustling around him, and when he glanced back he saw them there, feeding on the head and the tender flesh of the neck in droves. At first he paused and shooed them off, but eventually he grew too tired. As long as they didn't take the head off altogether, he no longer cared.

At one point, he noticed the red top of Tucker's thermite grenade, half-buried in the mud. He picked it up, stuffing it into a pocket, before returning to the body.

The body caught in bushes and branches and more than once between tree trunks. He'd have to back up and reroute, his breath coming like fire from his lungs, his face pounding with the heat.

The creature's legs wore blisters under his armpits and along his biceps and the ridges of his palms, but he dragged his kill onward with the dull, plodding determination of a machine, afraid to rest in case the pain set in.

When he reached the edge of the forest, a vicious fatigue overcame him. The creature's head was still there, lolling behind the body, but one of the eyes had been eaten out, an antenna chewed down to a nub. His knees almost buckled when the body caught the friction of a band of rocks, but he had come too far to drop now, so he pulled on toward the flickering light of the fire.

They watched him approach with large horrified eyes. Derek rose from the log, but the rest couldn't move. Cameron took a halting step back. Szabla's mouth was wide-open, and Justin looked as though he'd just swallowed something live. Diego slid from the log onto his knees.

They didn't even dare to blink as Savage pulled the mangled body into the ring of logs around the fire and released it, his arms going to knots and his legs cramping the instant he stopped. Rather than thumping to the ground, the creature's legs stayed right where he'd let go of them, sticking out like the arms of a wheelbarrow. The body stretched before them on the grass like a dropped buffalo, the fire reflecting off its shiny cuticle.

Savage moved slowly to face Derek. "There's your fuckin' proof," he said.

Turning his back, he staggered to his tent.

Chapter 45 John Mako's voice betrayed his annoyance, sounding sharp and tinny as it echoed through Derek's transmitter. "This better be something goddamn important, Mitchell, to pull my tired ass out of bed *again*," he barked. "You're a fully functional half-platoon of Navy SEALs. I send you on a mission that involves mostly equipment hauling and ass-wiping, and you've all been calling in every five minutes with your panties in a knot."

Surprise flickered across Derek's face. "Who else has been—?"

"Though it's probably a big surprise to you and that pain-in-the-ass scientist—" Mako continued.

From his crouch by the creature's body, Rex gave a big,

smiling, beauty-pageant wave. The others were arrayed around the fire, the larva snuggled along the base of one of the logs. Cameron stared at the body, drowning in something like disbelief.

"—there are more important things on my desk and in the world than you and your cataclysmic troubles getting a couple of satellite dishes nailed down to some shit-stripped island in the middle of the goddamn Pacific."

Derek's face was pale, his voice wavering. "We lost Tucker, sir," he said.

There was a long pause. "You lost Tucker? How the fuck did you lose Tucker?"

"There's something here on this island, sir. A . . . a creature of sorts. We're concerned there are more."

A longer pause. "Mitchell, let me talk to Kates. Cameron, that is."

Cameron rose to her feet and clicked on. "Yes, sir."

"Is this aboveboard, Kates?"

Cameron cleared her throat. "Yes, sir. It is. We seem to have run into some kind of a . . . what appears to be a large insect, sir, and I—"

"A large *insect?*"

"About nine feet tall. Sir, I know it doesn't sound . . . " Cameron sat back down on the log. She looked at Diego and he raised one eyebrow until it disappeared beneath the shaggy line of his bangs.

"And this large *insect* ate Tucker? Is that what happened?"

Derek blinked hard a few times. "Yes. Sir. We really need . . . we really need that extraction. Sir."

"Or the large insects might eat you."

"Well . . . " Derek looked at the enormous body slumped beside the fire. "Actually, there's no longer . . . we don't know . . . it's quite complicated. Sir."

"Indeed," Mako replied. "Perhaps you can comprehend some complications with which I'm contending on this end of the wire, soldier. The army's deploying two more battalions this week to deal with outbreaks along the Peruvian border. Colombia's a mess from the southern border through Bogotá, we're down to our last task force, and I have NATO, the UN, the OAS, and my own lovable superiors leaning on me to provide more manpower from Mexico to Chile. That's not even bringing domestic problems into the equation. To say that our air assets are one hundred percent committed is something of an understatement. In light of this, you'd like me now, at three thirty-seven in the fuckdamn morning, to call the Commander of Naval Special Warfare Group One and ask him to redirect a helo from the mainland to the Galápagos Islands so that a half-platoon of reserves don't get devoured by giant bugs. Is that about the gist of your request?"

Derek's lip twitched. Szabla stood with one foot on the corpse like an old-style game hunter while Diego and Rex examined it. She turned and headed for the tents.

"Yes. Sir."

"Mitchell, I have two words for you, and they're not especially pleasant. Would you like to hear them?"

"No, sir."

"I didn't think so. I don't know what kind of peyote you've been smoking down there, but I don't like having my chain yanked unless it involves soft lighting and Vaseline. Don't be surprised to find yourself waylaid with a Page Thirteen when you limp your sorry ass back to base. Do I make myself clear?"

Derek opened his mouth, but nothing came out. The others exchanged frustrated glances. Cameron stood. "Sir," she said. "This is not a joke."

"Listen, Kates—"

"*No*," Cameron said. "You need to listen." Tank drew back his head, eyebrows raised. "This is a real threat," Cameron continued. "There is a large organism here that appears to be predatory. We have no weapons, and we're stranded on the island. You need to take steps to assure our safety, and we need orders in the meantime."

Her transmitter hummed with silence. "First of all," Mako finally replied, "you watch your *goddamn* tone when speaking to a superior. Is that clear?"

"Yes, sir."

"Now, I don't know what the fuck is going on down there, but I will arrange for an extraction. We'll untangle this mess when you get back. In the meantime, Dr. Rex Williams is still running the show—I can't overturn a direct order from Secretary Benneton. Do I make myself clear? Mitchell?"

"Yes," Derek said. "Sir." Mako clicked out.

Four flares protruding from her back pockets, Szabla reemerged from Rex's tent, holding two tripods. She threw one tripod on the grass and turned the other upside down, spreading its legs. About an inch thick, each leg was a hollow aluminum cylinder tapering to a strong steel-alloy point. She began to unscrew a leg from the tribrach.

"What are you doing?" Rex said. "Those are my tripods."

The tripod leg came free and Szabla tossed it to Tank. He caught it in front of his face. "Not anymore," Szabla said.

Once detached, the legs were good weapons—metal spikes that could be used as blunt or stabbing instruments. Szabla disassembled tripods until each soldier was armed with a spike. Rex glanced at the large body near the fire pit and elected not to protest.

"LT?" Cameron said. One foot resting on a log, Derek stared at the forest from the depths of a stupor. Cameron snapped her fingers sharply. Derek turned slowly, his eyes finding focus. "Weren't you about to send a buddy pair to search through the farmhouses for weapons?" Despite her efforts, irritation found its way into her voice.

"What? Yeah. Yes." Derek jerked his head at Szabla and Justin. "Go search through the farmhouses for weapons."

Szabla tossed the flares on the ground and rose slowly, studying Derek. Another log gave way in the fire, sending a sprinkling of embers into the air. "Is that order coming from you, or from Cameron? Because last I checked—"

"It's coming from me," he snapped. "Get moving. And steer clear of the forest."

Swinging the spike at her side, Szabla headed toward the road. Justin removed a fresh solar cell from his shoulder and snapped it into his elbow light, but did not turn the light on. Cameron tossed him a spike, and he followed Szabla into the darkness.

Using Cameron's transmitter, Rex updated Donald on the day's events. After a lengthy discussion, the two scientists decided to speak the following day when Donald heard back from Samantha. In the meantime, he promised to contact Secretary Benneton and continue to pressure the navy for an early extraction for the soldiers, and appropriate support for the scientists, should they choose to remain on the island to study the animals.

Diego had busied himself with the radio again, keying Morse on the handset in hope of someone's picking up the signal. He looked up when Cameron stood over him. She pointed to the radio. "Hope you're asking Santa for guns in addition to a boat."

"Plenty of guns in Puerto Ayora, just no bullets," Diego said. He keyed the handset, alternating long and short breaks. "But there's plenty of TNT from the ejército." He looked up sternly. "*Only* if we need it to protect ourselves."

Backpack slung over one shoulder, Rex walked over, exhaling heavily as he sat on the wet grass beside Diego. The others were talking over by the fire, but only the murmur of their voices was audible. "What do you think?" he asked, jerking his head toward the creature's corpse. Green hemolymph oozed from a crack in its cuticle.

Still fiddling with one of the knobs on the radio, Diego turned to him, his eyes glazed. "I don't know what to think. The brownish-green cuticle clearly serves the purpose of camouflage, so my guess is it doesn't stray far from the forest. Even with its exoskeleton, direct sun exposure would dehydrate it rapidly. It resembles a mantid, and appears to hunt like a mantid, but the proportions are off."

Rex smiled. "Yes, they are."

"No, I mean the thorax is more slender and upright. The raptorial legs are overly developed, as are the grasping hooks and leg musculature. Do you see the strength through the claws and legs?" Diego shook his head. "Like a gorilla."

"That's how it climbs—its size rules out its relying on surface adhesion like an insect."

"This isn't an insect," Diego said, setting down the radio handset.

"You mean we can't just burn palo santo branches for repellent and call the exterminator?"

Diego laid his hands on the exoskeleton. "The cuticle's tough, almost impossibly hard, even over the abdomen. My guess is it's female, as the wings don't extend past the tip of the body."

Crouching, Cameron glanced at the wings. "So that's how you tell, huh?"

Diego leaned over and, lifting one leathery forewing, tugged at the delicate transparent underwing beneath it. It slid out smoothly, the firelight playing through it and casting a yellow glow. Diego had to stand up and walk backward as it continued to unfurl. "The surface area of the wings has increased exponentially in relation to the body."

"Can it fly?" Cameron asked.

Diego released the underwing and it slid slowly back beneath the protective tegmina of its own accord. "Even given the exponential increase in wing size, I doubt it could bear this much weight aloft." He sat back down, rubbing the ends of his fingers with his thumbs. "It's a different organism, almost as though something took a mantid's basic features and reshuffled them." He looked at Rex. "What do *you* think?"

Rex paced around the body. "Three-segmented ectothermic quadropod, filiform antennae, mandibulate mouthparts, tegmina and hindwings, seemingly asocial. Physically, it's distinctly terrestrial as an adult, even though the larvae are aquatic. I assume those *are* its larvae."

Diego smoothed his mustache with his thumb and index finger. "I would agree. Even if it can breathe underwater like the larvae, it's not at all suited to aquatic movement."

Coos issuing from its body, the larva inched over to Derek. Absentmindedly, he ran a hand over its abdomen segments. "Listen to that," Rex said. "And now to this." Placing his hands on the adult creature's back, he pressed down. A hissing filled the camp as air escaped the hockey puck–sized holes along the abdomen segments. "The sounds from both the larva and adult come from the spiracles. They must feed an internal respiratory organ, as we discussed."

"How the fuck?" Diego shook his head. "How the fucking fuck?"

Rex pulled seven water-sample jars from his backpack and set them on the ground in a line before Diego. They were each neatly labeled, with the time, date, and source location. Rex reached for an elbow light and turned it on, running the lens behind the row of jars so they each lit up in turn with a blood-red glow. The others glanced over, intrigued by his theatrical presentation. Sensing Rex was about to convey something useful, Cameron signaled them over. Derek sat on the nearest log, while Tank and Savage stood.

"What appears to be different about these samples?" Rex asked.

Diego studied them, puzzled, as Rex ran the light back across them. "Nothing."

"Exactly. However, the three on the end aren't taken from the ocean. One is your lagoon sample, I took one from a clear puddle in the road, and this is the one from the natural basin near the lava tube."

"I saw you," Diego said. "But that's impossible. They're all tinted red from dinoflagellates. But dinos are generally pelagic. How did they get from the ocean to the highlands?"

"Well," Rex said, pleased with himself, "dinos can go into a dormant, sporelike state, which allows them to survive extreme conditions, like dehydration and low temperatures. They're most highly concentrated in the waters off the southeastern point of the island—the water that gets shot through the blowholes. My guess is that the spores get blown around in the wind streams and settle all over the island through the garúa mist. The little landlocked pools have a decent amount of salinity from the blowholes and the mists, which permits the spores to bloom again. This means the virus, contained in those dinoflagellate spores, could reach animals from the highlands to the coast. I think it found a susceptible species. *Galapagia obstinatus*."

Diego shook his head, his face drained of color. "How?" he asked.

Rex reached into his bag and pulled out the segment of the sun-damaged mantid ootheca that Frank had kept in his tent. It was peppered with parasite wasp holes. Holding it up, Rex closed one eye and peered through one of the holes, telescope-style. "UV damage kept the ootheca from hardening enough to prevent parasitic wasps from drilling through the shell. The virus probably invaded the ootheca later through the wasp holes, acting on the developing mantid nymphs that weren't eaten by wasp offspring, and altering their genetic composition before they hatched."

Diego picked up a jar, turning it in his hand. "How do you know *these* dinos are infected?"

Rex pursed his lips. "We don't. They look normal under a standard lens, but we can't definitively determine whether they're infected without running a gel, and we don't have the equipment here. But we do know that they were infected two months ago when Frank pulled the samples and had them shipped to us."

Diego handed him back the jar. "But we don't even know what the virus does to begin with. It could merely be a plant virus. You're completely hypothesizing."

"A new virus appears on the same island we discover a massive living aberration ... I just can't help thinking they've got to be linked, either through direct or shared causation."

Diego shook his head. "This animal could be an ordinary mutation."

Cameron looked at the jagged moons of the mantid's mandibles, flickering darkly in the firelight.

"I don't know about that," Rex said.

"Why not?" Diego looked up, his eyes alight. "Evolution doesn't progress slowly and evenly—it progresses in sudden and giant leaps. The Cambrian Explosion, the Permian and Cretaceous Extinctions—all blinks of the eye." He paused, pulling his hair back to band his ponytail more tightly. "Think of the reptiles dying out during the Mesozoic Period, the graptolite's rapid decline after the Ordovician Period, the sudden evolution of complex Metazoa. The fossil record has always shown punctuated equilibrium—mass extinction and abrupt origination." He pointed to the mantid corpse. "Speciation like this can take place in a geological instant."

Cameron looked over at Rex, unsure of what to make of Diego's sudden tirade. Rex cleared his throat before speaking. "A geological instant is hundreds of thousands of years."

Diego looked down at his pants, stained with mud and torn at one knee. "Well, it just got shorter."

A piece of charred wood collapsed in the fire, startling them both. Diego crouched over the dead, slumped mantid. He reached out and stroked the waxy cuticle covering the abdomen. "Beautiful, isn't it?"

Rex nodded. "Beautiful, yes. And fearful."

A whistle from the darkness indicated Szabla and Justin's return. A few seconds later, Justin stepped into the light, carrying a shovel. A length of rope looped over one shoulder, Szabla appeared next. A hammer protruded from her back pocket.

"That's it?" Tank asked.

"The farmers took most of their shit with them when they

left, especially their tools," Szabla said. "There's no gasoline anywhere, or oil, and the machines seem to be on empty."

"The supply ship," Diego said. "It stopped coming months ago."

"Well, what do we have?" Cameron asked.

Justin cleared his throat ceremoniously. "Four chainsaws, one with a snapped guide bar, a tiller with a burned-out motor, what looks like a broken-down ribbing plow from 1902—"

"Equipment the Norwegians left years ago," Diego said. "Useless."

"—six empty gasoline cans, plenty of rope, one enormous purse seine with a three-foot tear, loose concrete blocks from the houses, four wheelbarrows, a hammer, two Phillips-head screwdrivers, a burnt frying pan, a case of fishing hooks, a flat-edged hoe snapped in half, a length of hose, a trowel, and Ramón has an ax that he wisely elected to keep." He shook his head. "The generator is out—appears to be totally useless."

"Is there gas in the tiller we could siphon for the chainsaws?" Cameron asked.

"Not a drop."

"Insecticides?" Tank asked.

Szabla snickered. "Yeah, there was an eight-foot bottle of Raid, but we left that behind." She looked down at the jars, still arrayed in a line. "What's up with that?"

"Rex thinks there's some kind of virus on the island," Cameron said. "Maybe affected the animal life."

"Well, I'd say we're not in great shape," Szabla said. "Mostly useless shit left behind. Right now, the GPS spikes are our best bet for weapons. Can't see troweling one of these motherfuckers to death." She tilted her head, cracking her neck. "I say we take cautionary steps."

They all slowly turned their eyes to the larva. Its abdominal segments contracted, pushing it upward in the middle. It squirmed forward, fleshy prolegs pulsing, true legs rasping against the grass. It stopped when it touched Derek, wedging itself against his leg and the ground, and stilling.

Szabla stood up and walked over, twirling the spike around her hand. She threw it at the soft ground a few feet from the larva and it stuck like a javelin. She looked from the larva to Derek, her implication clear.

Derek's face was wan in the firelight. "You heard our orders."

"We're gonna take those orders to the grave," Szabla said.

"That's one of the responsibilities of being a soldier, Szabla," Cameron said. "If you don't like it, you can go home and bake cookies."

"Soldiers have no obligation to die pointlessly. They have an obligation to follow mission-relevant orders."

"You have an obligation to follow *all* orders," Derek said.

Szabla tilted her head back, her nostrils flaring as she tried to calm herself.

Rex stood up, the usual expression of arrogance missing from his face. "I just wish we could get into Frank's specimen freezer. It might give us some answers."

Savage stood from his seat on the log and stepped over the edge of the fire toward the scientists, the flames licking at the back of his pants. He rocked the Death Wind back and forth along his palm with his thumb. Rex rose defensively.

Savage reached into one of his pockets and pulled out Tucker's thermite grenade, the one the mantid had regurgitated.

"Well, gents," he said, "today might be your lucky day."

Chapter 46   They were at the aluminum specimen freezer in minutes. The breeze was moist against their faces, mixing with their sweat. The freezer stood before them, unchanged and unyielding against the wind-fanned grass. They circled it as if it were a shrine, Derek pressing the larva to his side.

Savage tossed the thermite grenade to Cameron, who pulled the pin and rested it atop the thick shoe box–sized lock that protruded just beneath the handle. She was angry with herself for not remembering Tucker's grenade earlier— he always brought it with him on missions, nestled in the cargo pocket of his pants. His good-luck charm.

It took a while for the chemicals to mix, then the grenade emitted an intense white flame, like a welder's arc. They looked away as it melted down into the lock. There was no need to guide it through the metal, and the entire lock fell to the ground with the still-burning thermite.

The heavy door creaked open a crack, then sucked shut again.

The grenade kept melting right through the grass, and Derek kicked aside what was left of the lock and covered the grenade with dirt. Diego shook his head but said nothing. Derek reached for the thin metal handle and the door swung open to meet his hand. He turned and looked at the others for a moment before pulling it open.

"Lantern," he said.

Szabla stepped forward, the hurricane lamp dangling from her hand. As it swayed, it threw Derek's shadow across the door, oversize and distorted against the silver surface.

He pulled the door open, and they were greeted with the familiar smell of unliving flesh. Eight gnarled little bodies swung on specimen hooks, underlit by the hurricane lamp so they threw sinister patterns through the freezer. They were all close to three feet long, green, and contorted as if they'd been in great pain when they were slaughtered. Aside from that, none of them looked anything like the others.

A button on the compressor in the back cast a wan glow, pale like moonlight. The breeze shook and twirled the bodies like wind chimes.

The soldiers and scientists moved among them, looking

up in revulsion. One creature had a massive jaw shaped like a shovel and a scattering of eyes across its forehead; another had the vulgar hunch and primitive brow of a chimpanzee. The body farthest away had eight furry legs protruding from its midsection, and its shadow was framed perfectly on the back wall of the freezer. Its body was that of an enormous spider, its head something between a canine and primate.

"Jesus H," Rex whispered. "It's like a Lariam nightmare."

The larva cooed, squirming in Derek's arms. In the far corner, a tangle of hooks lay on the floor.

The wind pivoted one of the bodies and its leg struck Szabla in the back of the head. She grabbed it without flinching and turned the body to examine its front side. It had the smooth slender belly of a lizard, curling back into a tail that, due to rigor mortis, ran parallel up its scaled back. The face had the broad snout and yellow teeth of a crocodile, and an iguana's pouchlike cheeks.

Behind Szabla, Justin shuddered.

The inside of the door had a heavy bolt that allowed collectors to lock themselves in in case predators were drawn to the scent while they loaded specimens. With slight maneuvering, the bolt could be disengaged and removed.

Tank pulled the bolt free from the door and held it by his side. It was thicker and heavier than the spikes; it would make a better weapon.

The hurricane lamp continued to cast lunatic shadows all across the constrictive walls and ceiling—dangling limbs, paws split in fingers, heads enlarged and misshapen. The soldiers' faces were drawn and bloodless among the beasts, which dangled among them like repulsive mobiles.

"If these manifestations are due to a virus, it's unlike anything I've . . ." Rex's voice trailed off. Diego's jaw had literally dropped; he gazed at the new creatures around him with a wonder bordering on disbelief.

Of the hung hooks, one was empty. Thick and barbed like a meat hook, it scraped against the far side of the freezer, metal on metal. The sound resonated within the bare freezer walls until Cameron grabbed it, holding it above her head like a subway strap.

She turned to face the others beneath the small dangling bodies, her neck flushed all the way down to the line of her breasts. She could only remember being this stunned once before—when she'd opened her rifle case and found the engagement ring Justin had hidden there for her.

"There were close to two hundred fifty chambers in the ootheca Frank found," Rex said, his voice hushed from fear or reverence. "Every one filled with a mutant—a new prototype. Of those two hundred fifty, only ten stood a legitimate shot at hatching." His breath caught in his throat. " 'Ten viable.' That's what Frank wrote. Here are eight of them."

Diego laughed, a choke deep in his throat. "Look at the variation—it's incredible. Something caused the parents to breed all different offspring. Adaptive radiation in a single generation, of a single brood. It's like a genetic brainstorm."

"Or a genetic nervous breakdown," Szabla added.

"What's that accomplish?" Justin asked. "Aside from scaring the shit out of me?"

"If they all mutated the same way, it would be a case of the genes putting all their chips on one number," Diego said. "Having different offspring raises the odds considerably that one of them will take to the environment, or find a way to survive."

"Or two," Szabla said, counting the eight bodies again.

"Or two of the offspring. Exactly."

"How could they mate if they were so different?" Derek asked skeptically, looking at the bodies in the air all around him.

"I'd guess that those with the capacity to metamorphose do so into adult mantids like the one Savage killed," Rex said. "They only look different in the early stages."

"I still don't get it," Cameron said, noticing that Derek was cradling the larva to his chest protectively. "The larvae are so much smaller than that thing that killed Tucker."

"Insects do have the capacity to increase over a hundred-fold in size from birth."

Diego shot Rex a sideways look. "It's not an insect," he said. "Even if we are referring to it as a mantid."

"So given that you people are all such tree huggers," Szabla said, "why do you think Frank hunted these eight down and killed them?"

"I can't imagine," Rex said.

"He must have realized they were a threat to him, a threat to the people on this island," Justin said.

Something dripped from one of the corpse's legs. Cameron ran a hand lightly over her head to make sure nothing had landed in her hair.

Rex snapped his fingers. "In Frank's notebook, he tallied a nine count, meaning, I think, that he'd located nine of the ten offspring that had hatched and made it into the wilderness." His eyes clouded. "He must have kept one alive to observe, and it mated with the tenth one that he didn't find."

"So, the million-dollar question is: What did the one he kept look like?" Szabla asked, eyeing the empty hook over by Cameron. "Why did he keep it alive?"

The freezer door banged loudly behind them with the wind and they all jumped, the air thick with bodies. The larva cooed and squirmed in Derek's arms. When the door swung open again, they could see Savage's silhouette crouching just outside on the grass. They watched him through the corpses. Steam rose off his body in the mist.

"Why did God make puppies cute?" his outline grumbled.

They watched him expectantly.

He spit once to the side and wiped his mouth. "So we don't kill 'em."

Chapter 47   Wordlessly, Derek handed the larva off to Diego and split off from the others. "I'm gonna check out the purse seine," he called over his shoulder. "Which farmhouse?"

"It's got a healthy tear," Justin said. "Plus the rope is old and cracking."

Derek stopped but did not turn around. "Which farmhouse?" he repeated.

Justin was silent for a moment before answering. "Last one down on the west side of the road."

Derek started walking again. Cameron followed him a few steps toward the road, but when Derek still didn't turn around, she realized he wanted to be alone and fell back.

Rex walked by her side, several feet behind the others. "Something is going on with your squad," he said softly. "And things on this island are going to get more complicated."

Cameron looked dead ahead, her face blank.

"I'd like to know I can count on you," Rex continued.

"You can count on me to uphold my orders, and to act in the best interests of my—"

Rex waved her off, his arm painting a short, angry stroke in the night air. He pulled ahead, leaving her to walk alone.

They reached base exhausted. Justin collected an armful of wood, sticking close to the tents, then dumped it next to the fire and tried to wipe the grime off the front of his shirt. Tank stoked the flame with the freezer bolt. He raised a branch in front of him, gripping it tightly at the ends, and snapped it in half with a grunt. He added the two pieces to the fire.

They all tried to ignore the enormous corpse to the side of the logs. Somewhere inside it were the mangled remains of Tucker.

The larva cooed in Diego's arms as he set it down near the fire. "It's getting heavier," he said quietly.

When he straightened up, Szabla was standing right beside him, tapping the spike in her hands, her eyes gleaming. Aside from Cameron, the others didn't yet notice; they clustered around the far log, talking in hushed voices.

Diego eyed the spike, taking a step back. Szabla stepped toward the larva and Diego snatched it quickly away. He tried to sidestep Szabla, but suddenly Savage was there in his way.

Cameron looked at Savage's eyes, gone dull in the night, and was alarmed by what was lacking in them. She walked over, the others following.

"I'm not dealing with another one of those." Szabla pivoted and pointed the spike at the large body.

Diego stood quietly for a long time, holding the larva and staring off into space. It pulsed in his arms, squirming through the crook of his elbow. Its true legs pinwheeled in the air, searching for footing, and he turned it to his chest, the soft prolegs clinging to his shirt.

"Even your boy Frank judged the offspring to be dangerous," Szabla continued, more calmly. "He was picking them off one by one. But he didn't kill one because it was cute, because it appealed to him and amused him. That's a benefit of its appearance. You coddle it until it metamorphoses. Why do you think it was so easy to spot? It doesn't hold us to be a threat."

Diego set the larva behind him on the grass and stood before it protectively. His face had the hard, grim cast of a statue's. Rex shifted on his feet, intense discomfort clouding his features. Diego made a noise of disgust from deep down in his throat.

"A lot of animals exist in symbiotic and parasitic relationships in nature," Rex said. "Flying in under the radar, taking advantage of other species' needs and weaknesses."

"Like those feeder fish that hang out on sharks?" Justin asked.

"Or like cuckoo birds," Rex added softly. "Cuckoo birds lay their eggs in other birds' nests. The parasite egg usually requires less incubation and hatches first. Then the chick throws the other eggs out of the nest so it can get the foster parents' full attention."

"And the mom takes care of that motherfucker since she doesn't know it's not hers," Szabla said. "I was bio queen undergrad, so don't be pullin' no wool on my ass."

"You don't understand the full workings . . ." Diego's throat was dry, so he paused to lick his lips. He looked down at the larva, lying peacefully in the grass, its prolegs wide and momentarily unflexed.

"A lot of animals persist because they inspire a foolish protectiveness in others," Rex said.

Diego glared at Rex, his eyes flickering with the light from the fire. "Don't you *dare* side with her," he growled.

"I'm not siding with anyone," Rex said. "I'm merely attempting to analyze the situation from all sides. We need to be able to discuss this reasonably. Let's start by demystifying the phenomena. The larvae are appealing because of specific, definable attributes—large heads, large eyes, a capacity for attention. They're fascinating. These characteristics conventionally enhance parental investment; here, they serve to increase other species'—most notably humans'—tolerance, favoritism or identification . . . take your pick. Let's be aware of this and act accordingly. We can't be victim to our softer instincts when dealing with these creatures."

"This isn't about 'softer instincts,' " Diego barked. "Goddamnit, don't you see?! This has nothing to do with sentimentality. The larvae shouldn't be protected because of affinity or compassion, but they also shouldn't be killed because of fear. Who knows what benefits we can derive from studying them?" His eyes moist, he pounded a fist into his open palm. "We need to know more. We need to discover more. We can't stop this amazing process now. We have no idea where this is headed."

"That's exactly my fucking point," Szabla said.

The larva squirmed in the grass. A seam had opened up in its cuticle, just behind the head.

Diego snapped the band from his ponytail, ran his hand through his hair, pulling hard, then banded it again. When he spoke, his voice was shaking. "Do you really want to turn this incredible thing into a dead end?"

"It might be incredible if we had guns and boats and the luxury of a little fucking distance," Szabla said. "But we don't. We're stuck on an island, weaponless, with no extraction set, and people are dying." She raised a hand to scratch her cheek, her arm crossing her chest so her biceps stood out like a tennis ball. "This ain't no science project. It's us versus it. And guess whose side I'm on."

A ripping sound drew their attention back to the larva. It had pulled itself free of its old cuticle, squirming out of the shell of its former self. It rippled forward, its new skin moist and an even more vibrant green.

Taking a deep, sorrowful breath, Tank pulled himself to his feet. He walked slowly over and stood behind Szabla and Savage. Justin looked from them to Diego and Rex.

They all glanced over at Cameron.

"What!?" she said sharply. "Why are you looking at me? Szabla's the AOIC."

Szabla clicked her teeth together, keeping her mouth closed. She squinted, drawing the skin tight across her high, hard cheekbones.

"What would we do to it?" Justin asked, though he didn't really want an answer.

The larva wormed up against Diego's leg and froze. Tank averted his eyes. "Cam?" Tank asked softly. He ran a shaking hand over his head, taking a deep breath.

Cameron felt all their eyes on her, felt the presence of the larva by the fire even though she couldn't bear to look at it. Even Savage was waiting on her response.

With the slightest movement, Cameron shook her head. "We're under orders," she said. "To assist Rex on his mission."

Szabla raised a hand, quivering with rage, and pointed to

the large mantid body by the fire. "We *are* the fucking mission now."

Cameron looked to Rex. "What'll it be?"

Rex took a moment, gathering himself.

"Don't you dare," Diego whispered. "You could be single-handedly forcing a species into extinction."

Rex crouched, pinching the papery shell of the larva's old cuticle between his fingers. "Let's quarantine it," he said. "Keep a close eye on it until we get word back about the virus tomorrow."

"Well, I'm afraid you don't have the luxury," Szabla said. She advanced toward the larva. Diego stepped forward to block her, but she shoved him roughly aside. He stumbled and went down. He looked to Cameron, appealing to her with his eyes. Rex looked furious but held his tongue.

"Szabla," Cameron said. "If you're altering orders, I think we should wait for Derek to—"

"Zip it, Cam," Szabla barked.

Justin stepped forward and helped Diego to his feet.

Cameron pointed to the larva. "That's an entirely new creation," she said. "Something that's never lived before. Ever. I don't think you can just decide unilaterally to kill it."

"I'm the senior officer right now," Szabla said. "I can decide whatever the fuck I want."

"Look, Szabla, I'm only saying—"

"Why are you having such a reaction to this, Cam? To this thing?"

"Back off, Szabla," Justin said. "She's just arguing chain of command."

"Not with that face, she isn't. This ain't her normal stain-in-her-school-dress-following-orders crap. This is different."

"You don't have a right—the authority *or* the right—to do this," Cameron said.

Szabla turned sharply and faced Cameron. "Step back, girl," she said. "That's a direct order from your superior officer. Need I be more explicit?"

Cameron felt her face growing flushed with the heat from the fire and her blossoming anger.

"Step back," Szabla repeated.

Cameron stepped back.

"Goddamnit," Rex said, glaring at Cameron. "Why can't you think for yourself?"

"It's not my job to think for myself," Cameron said, her voice sounding distant and foreign. "We're a military squad, not a think tank."

The larva raised itself up, its thorax nearly perpendicular to the ground, its head tilted and attentive. Cameron felt a wave of nausea wash through her and her knees buckled, just slightly. Justin steadied her with an arm around her waist, which he dropped once she got her legs under her again.

"Mammy! Bring Miss Scarlet her smelling salts," Szabla said derisively.

Rex glared up at the stars, his hands on his hips. Tank ran a hand over his sunburnt scalp.

"Who's gonna . . ." Justin's words were choked with phlegm. He cleared his throat and started over. "Who's gonna do it?"

Savage studied the fire, knowing the answer before he even raised his head. He closed his eyes in a long blink, bouncing his head once in a nod, then rose.

When he seized the larva around the base of its head, air escaped it in a screech, and Cameron felt herself sucking shallow breaths to keep from breaking. Savage walked right in front of her, the larva squirming and squealing in his grip, and seized the spike leaning against the log beside her.

A figure cut from the shadows and a hand fell across his wrist, pale in the darkness. Savage jerked away and dropped the larva, drawing back the spike until he saw it was Derek.

"What are you doing?" Derek asked, stepping over the log. His eyes were cold and glassy, the skin on his face stretched tight with stress and fatigue.

His eyes narrowed on Szabla's until she looked away. He crouched above the larva and ran his hand along its side, over the bumps of its abdominal segments.

Derek looked at Diego, and Diego shook his head.

Rex said, "I didn't want them to . . . They wouldn't listen."

The pulse in Derek's temple worked like a spasm. His fingers, thin and pale in the moonlight, continued to stroke the larva's back.

"Derek," Szabla said, attempting to soften her voice. "We can't afford to follow scientists' orders anymore. We're playing in a different game here."

Derek stood and walked to Szabla, leaning forward until his face was inches away. Cameron did not recognize his eyes at all. Savage took a step over so that he was standing behind Szabla.

Cameron rose uneasily to her feet. "Easy, LT," she said.

The scientists watched quietly. It was as if a spell had been woven around the camp, and everyone hesitated to speak for fear of shattering it.

Szabla finally took a small step back, not giving up much ground. She turned and faced Cameron, and then Cameron noticed Derek's eyes on her as well, and she realized that everyone was looking to her, waiting for her move.

She inhaled the sharp island air, gazing at the perfect black beyond the edges of the fire. Something small fluttered overhead. The seconds stretched themselves out into what seemed like hours.

Cameron stepped over and stood behind Derek, her shoulders squared, her elbow brushing his. Justin followed suit, and then Tank, and then Szabla took another step back and sat on the log. Savage twirled the spike around his hand like a bandleader's baton and turned his back. Szabla's mouth contracted in a straight line and she scowled at Cameron, her eyes lit with disappointment and anger.

Derek exhaled deeply, his shoulders settling. "Rex?"

Rex turned to him, his face ashen.

"The first order of business is putting the larva in a safe place," Derek said. He glared at Szabla. "For us and for it. Then, we secure the island and determine if there are any more adult creatures here. Are we agreed?"

Rex started to speak but had to clear his throat and start over. He spoke in a brisk, scientific voice; that seemed to help him regain control. "Yes. Whatever occurred here in the formation of these animals was anomalous enough that I believe we can proceed cautiously with the assumption that there is only one lineage. Of the ten surviving offspring that Frank noted, he captured eight, and Savage killed one. That means there could be another out there somewhere, if it survived."

"Don't female mantises eat the males after they mate?" Cameron asked.

"Some," Diego said. "Not all. Female *Galapagia obstinati* have been known to."

"Well, let's hope we got a Gloria Steinem motherfucker," Szabla said.

"Would it have metamorphosed?" Cameron asked. "The surviving larva?"

Rex said, "I would think so. Especially since they evidently mated."

"Gentlemen," Cameron said, looking at the two scientists. "You're gonna have to help us out here. What are we up against? If there's another one out there, we need to know its habits, strategies, any weaknesses we can exploit."

Diego and Rex exchanged a long look. "Neither of us are entomologists," Diego said. "Do you have any way of contacting one?"

"Yes," Rex said. "I can ask Donald to."

"We don't have time to wait," Cameron said. "In the meantime, what do you know?"

"Well," Diego began slowly, "we'll have to continue to assume these animals have behavioral traits in common with the mantid the virus infected and altered."

"And?" Cameron urged. Derek stood silently beside her.

"They don't hear as humans do. They can only detect ultrasound, which filters to them through a slit on the mesothorax, so they generally need movement or vibration to sense prey. They tend to be stationary hunters. They await their prey, taking advantage of camouflage and their lightning strike."

"So if we move to pursue it, we'd be the ones at a disadvantage?" Cameron asked.

Diego nodded.

"We might have to risk that," Justin said.

Cameron waved him off. "We'll argue later. What else?"

"They need the shade," Rex said. "They're hesitant to leave the forest understory during the day. Especially to hunt—they have a hard time in the hot sunlight. I'd imagine that's truer now than ever before, given the UV. But at night, they'll roam anywhere. They'll also be attracted to light at night, like most insects."

"How about the eyes?" Cameron asked. "Will blinding it help?"

"I'm not going to help you figure out how to maim this animal," Diego said.

"You bet your ass you are," Szabla said.

"We need this knowledge," Cameron said. "We'll decide later if and how we're going to deploy it."

"Yes," Rex said. "Blinding it will help. And taking out a single eye will compromise its depth-of-field perception. Their antennae are also strategically essential."

Szabla took a breath and exhaled deeply. "Couldn't we poison it? Use some venom from indigenous snakes or something?"

They looked at Diego. "There is one poisonous snake here," he said reluctantly. "But it's a sea snake and quite rare."

"Anything else that could harm it? Or that it'd be afraid of?"

"Well, aposematically colored insects—red and black ones—often sequester unpalatable substances from their host plants, so animals seek to avoid them. But I don't know. If we're basing this assessment on the physiology of mantids, we have to remember mantids have iron digestive systems. They can eat anything—paint, rubber, lighter fluid. In lab, I even saw one eat an insect straight from a cyanide jar."

Rex nodded. "I'd guess we'd need something stronger than snake venom."

"So how would we kill it?" Szabla asked. She glanced down at the spike at her side. "I mean, how'd you take it, Savage?"

Savage told them.

"What's so funny, Szabla?" Cameron asked.

"Nothing. It just figures," she said. "It just figures."

"If there is another," Rex said, "let's hope it's a male. They're smaller, and they tend to be less aggressive. It's too bad they're such a solitary order. If it was a bull seal, we could just round up a bunch of females and it'd come running."

"Could we lure it with bait?" Cameron asked.

Rex grimaced. "Well, we've just figured out why we haven't run across any feral dogs or goats since we arrived. And even though mantids are known for eating prey larger than themselves, I'd guess a cow would be too large. It could kill one, probably, but would have a hard time eating it."

"Sea lions?" Tank asked.

"They've wisely retreated off the island to the tuff cones," Rex said. "Plus we'd have a bitch of a time dragging one up near the forest. I'd say the only reasonably sized prey is us." He smiled. "I volunteer Savage."

"Anything else you can think of?" Cameron asked. "Anything at all?"

"They'll only eat live bait," Savage said. They all looked at him, surprised. "I've seen one eat a deer mouse. Started with the whiskers. Ate its whole face off before it got through to the brain and killed it."

"Imagine that," Justin murmured. "An insect eating a fucking mammal."

Cameron looked to Rex, hoping to gauge the accuracy of Savage's story. He nodded. "I once saw one devour a gecko from the tail up. Hard, tireless mastication—combing the flesh, grinding the bones. Took over an hour. The gecko was alive for at least half of it."

Justin was pale. "Let's hope there aren't any more adults."

"Let's keep busy while we're hoping," Cameron said.

"We'll sweep the forest at first light." Derek swayed on his feet, then caught himself.

"Why not now?" Cameron asked.

"You want to go trekking through a predator's natural environment in the dark with bright lights to attract its attention? Use your goddamn head, Cam. We'll wait for first light, then see if there's another adult kicking around."

"If we locate it, are we cleared to kill it?" Szabla asked.

"Yes." Diego started to protest but stopped as soon as Derek held up a hand.

"But none of you are to lay a finger on any of these," Derek continued, walking over to the larva and picking it up. "I'll be keeping him with me tonight. Safely locked in a cruise box. Szabla, since you have so much excess testosterone to burn, you can stand first guard." He disappeared through the flap of his and Cameron's tent.

"We're assuming that there's only one lineage of mantids, but remember that's only an assumption," Rex said. "We have to be observant of the wildlife, see if we notice anything else that appears abnormal." He pressed his fingertips to his closed eyes. "We'll need to keep our eyes peeled for the four remaining larvae as well. Bring them back and keep them under observation."

"How do you know they haven't metamorphosed already?" Justin asked.

Savage raised the spike and pointed to the enormous slumped corpse beside the fire pit. "We'll know soon enough," he said.

Chapter 48   Floreana woke up screaming.

Ramón was on his feet instantly, as if he'd levitated out of bed. Floreana's screams had a different timbre to them, high-pitched and lined with panic. Her thighs were wet and sticky; her water had broken.

She was gasping for breath, the large sphere of her belly heaving with her respiration. Crying her husband's name over and over, she tore at the sheets, balling them in her fists. Ramón knelt beside her, resting his forehead on her sweaty temple, trying to soothe her with his voice.

"Already, cariñito?" he asked, his voice shaking. "How close? How close?" He took her hand and her nails left red lines down his palm.

The sheets around her had darkened with sweat. He spread her legs and looked, but he couldn't see the baby's head. He wanted to be prepared when it first showed so that he could support its neck and squeeze below his wife's vagina to make sure her flesh didn't tear.

"The blanket," Floreana gasped. "Do you have the blanket?"

Ramón held up the soft blue quilt she had finished the day before. "Right here, cariñito. Right here."

Floreana arched her back and shrieked. Her elbows were shoved back hard into the mattress, her hands gnarled, dangling from her limp wrists like claws. "It's not right," she groaned. "This is *not* right."

"It's okay," he said. "Everything's okay." He hoped she wouldn't notice the panic lurking beneath his eyes, the rush of blood in his cheeks.

Her eyes rolled back until he saw just moon slivers of brown beneath her upper lids. She began to seize.

Ramón fell on her, careful to keep his weight off her belly. She bucked and jerked, thrashing violently. One of her knees

popped up and caught him on the side of the head, and his
vision went momentarily blurry. He rose and took a step
back. Her face was a mask stretched tight across her skull.
Her arms rattled beside her like snakes.

He'd need to get help.

He backed up, knocking over a bucket with a clang. Grabbing the ax, he stumbled outside. Even with the sound of his
wife's thrashing urging him on, he was afraid to venture into
the dark. The sky was pricked through with pinholes, stars
colored yellow like the soft licks of a flame. His wife's
moaning followed him out into the night.

He'd need to find the woman soldier. She would help.
His wife's cries propelled him, but he stopped about fifty
meters from the row of balsas. The soldiers' base camp
was far away—across the road and well into the grassy
fields to the northeast. He might not have time to reach
them.

He paused, trying to fight away fear and frustration, his
eyes moistening. He peered in the direction of the soldiers'
camp, then headed back to the rectangular block of light that
filled the window of his house. Turning again, he stared at
the road, spilling tears.

He did not know what to do and did not have any time to
make up his mind.

Floreana's scream rent the night, startling him into action.
He ran off into his field, toward his supply shed at the edge
of the plantains. A rope could tie Floreana to the bed, then
he'd do his best to deliver the baby alone. As soon as the
baby was safely wrapped in the quilt, he'd go find the blonde
soldier and she'd know what to do.

His hands shook so badly it took him three tries to get the
little key in the shed's lock. Floreana's screams crashed
down on him like waves, and he cursed the southeast winds,
sweeping the screams west across the uninhabited *pahoehoe*
plains instead of east to the soldiers' camp. He swung the
door open and staggered inside, knocking over supplies on
the thin wooden shelves.

He groped in the dark for a length of rope, his cheeks damp as he tried to block out the sound of his wife's cries. Finally, he felt the coarse fibers against his palm. He yanked the rope from under a bag of fertilizer and draped it around his neck. The door had swung shut behind him, and he kicked it open, leaving it crooked on its hinges.

Another scream, this one impossibly high and protracted. I'm coming, mi vida, he thought. I'm coming.

He stepped through the narrow door frame into the night. The cry stopped, cut off mid-scream. He froze, breathing hard, lips trembling. Even from across the field, he could make out a stillness in the block of light from the window. The wind blew hot and lazy across his face, carrying with it the smells of moss and decomposing wood from the forest. He tried desperately to slow his breathing but could not.

He called his wife's name, just once. His voice sounded hollow and weak in the night.

The air reverberated with silence. He was filled with a sudden and undeniable dread. The ax slid from his hand, disappearing into the tall grass.

His eyes fixed on the window, he trudged toward his house, his boots dragging reluctantly across the furrowed soil and damp grass. The rope was slick in his hands, a rough-skinned eel.

After an eternity, he reached the side of the house. He headed for the door, leaning weakly against the wall. *Bloque* scraped against his bare shoulder, drawing blood.

He tried to call Floreana's name again, but his throat was too raspy and the sound came out a hoarse whisper. He paused just beside the doorway, gathering the threads of his fear. The silence unrolled around him like a black sea, endless and unremitting.

His teeth chattering, he stepped into the single room of his house. The rope slid from his hand to the floor.

His wife lay on the mattress, her lower body a muddle of flesh and blood. She'd been torn open from the inside. A splatter of blood ran up the wall beside the mattress, nearly four feet away. Her body was stiff and twisted, her back still arched.

On the floor lay a tangle of limbs and claws and half-shaped organs laid open to the outside air. The fetus. His child. A gnarled, cursed creature that looked as though it had been forged in some hell's oven—a collection of viscera and tissue, only some of it human.

It had expired before ever drawing air, and it lay, dead, beside its dead mother. Ramón's wife.

His skin felt intensely hot, as if it were burning off his bones. With slow, drugged movements, he walked to the mattress and straightened his wife's limbs, trying his best to lay her arms by her sides so that she looked relaxed. He pulled the thin, stained blanket across her lower body, thumbed her eyes closed, kissed her still-moist forehead.

He dragged a chair from the table over to the fireplace, above which some *bloque* had fallen away to reveal a brief stretch of rafter.

He fetched the rope from the doorway.

**29 DEC 07
MISSION DAY 5**

Chapter 49   Derek lay on his back in the dark of early morning, watching the rain patter on the roof of the tent. It slid to the sides and formed puddles, moving patterns of darkness. The tent looked alive, as if he were lying in the belly of some great beast and watching its stomach digest him.

The rain slowed, then stopped, leaving the canvas above bowed. Though morning was only a few minutes away, the sky was still gray. Cameron slept soundly on her sleeping pad to Derek's right, and the cruise box containing the larva was still safely latched.

Again, he had not slept. Frustration had honed its edge on his sleeplessness, but he resisted it. He rose and walked outside, where Justin was standing watch.

Justin turned his fingers in a reverse temple and cracked them sharply across his forehead as he yawned. He shifted on the log, groaning. "My ass feels like I just spent the night with the Marquis de Sade."

Derek stood with his hands on his hips, surveying the waving tops of the *Scalesias*. His face was swollen, puffy around the eyes and through the cheeks. He blinked long and hard and looked back at Justin, forcing his eyes to adjust. The spikes from the GPS tripods were lined up on the ground by Justin's feet. Beside them were four flares and the bolt Tank had taken from the specimen freezer.

He walked a few paces off and urinated into the higher grass. "Get the others mustered for recon," he mumbled over his shoulder.

THE SOFTNESS of the forest floor was surprising. Cameron felt it was yielding to her, giving way beneath her heavy boots. The spike swung at her side.

Moving stealthily through the trees in their cammies, their skin tender from the sun and greasy with sunblock, Cameron and Derek blurred from spot to spot like shadows. If they needed to, they could just disappear, stepping back against the trunk of a tree, lying flat on the forest floor, fading into bushes.

Once, in Iraq, she and Derek had been caught by surprise by a truckful of enemy soldiers. They'd been wearing their desert cammies, and they'd leaned back on the steep dune behind them, kicking sand over their black boots and letting more sand crumble down over their faces. The truck had rattled past them so close she'd been worried it would run over her feet.

Cameron led, forging through the branches with her shoulders and chest. When they didn't give way, she could usually snap them with a shove. Her legs were firm beneath her, solid through the thighs and ass. If she ever stopped working out, her figure would soften into voluptuousness. She didn't plan to ever stop working out.

Derek followed in her wake. Trapped beneath the canopy, the air was thick with humidity, stirring with clouds of gnats and particles of leaves and bark. About every ten yards, they'd pause, surveying the area around them and listening for movement. At all times, they had 360-degree security coverage. Cameron scanned the area to the front and the sides, and Derek covered the rear, turning in circles to check behind them. Their patrolling formation was tighter than usual because of the limited visibility; the canopy made it seem like it was dusk.

They fell into a rhythm, Cameron and Derek, when they worked like this, sharing each other's senses, movements, and instincts. Years of functioning as a buddy pair had welded them into one entity. They traversed the forest, two beating hearts moving through the thickets and tree trunks. They did not speak. They never even had to gesture when they switched point.

Cameron always knew where Derek was, not because she could hear him or see him, but because she sensed him, sensed the life moving behind her among the trees, the life for which she was responsible. If something happened to Derek, she sometimes thought, it would be almost as upsetting as if something happened to her own husband. That made his recent behavior all the more alarming.

Since they weren't humping gear, they didn't stop to rehydrate every hour as they normally would. Cameron's movements became almost hypnotic—the rise of her feet, the sink of her boots into the thick mud, the pattern of her steps. One, two, three, and a crossing side step to dodge a tree trunk. Her breathing was slow and even, her face damp with the heat. She felt sweat stinging her eyes.

About halfway to the forest's peak, a small clearing opened among the trunks of the trees, a break of a few square yards matted with decaying leaves and dead ferns.

Vines twisted their way along the ground, winding themselves through the low brush and darting up the trees around the clearing. The *Scalesias* stretched overhead, growing together in a living tapestry. Some of the larger trees faded away, their trunks reaching up and up until they were lost in the canopy.

The forest felt suddenly alive to Cameron. Like it was watching her.

She held up a hand, stopping Derek in his tracks. Her grip on the spike tightened. Derek sidestepped quickly behind a trunk, leaning against the white spotted bark.

The forest was moving all around her, leaves, fronds, and branches swaying in the wind. The slow, hypnotic motions reminded her of a mating dance. The air was musky with the scents of mud, hidden creatures, fresh and rotting fruit.

She scanned the area but saw only green and brown, vines dripping from branches like stalactites, foliage vibrating in the breeze. For a moment, she closed her eyes and listened. The buzz of insects, the flapping of a bird, the creek of bending trees. She opened her eyes again and saw nothing, though she still felt the eyes of the forest on her.

A length of vine by her foot hissed and slid away, rustling in the darkness. Between the trunks, the forest stretched on forever, a dim underworld.

Moving slowly to her right, stepping sideways foot over foot so that she could remain facing forward, Cameron headed out of the clearing. She counted off fifteen paces before Derek followed her. They disappeared into the shadows ahead.

A spiderweb broke across Cameron's face, but she didn't flinch. She wiped it away using the back of her hand that held the spike. The spider fell to the ground, scurrying clumsily for cover, and she crushed it underfoot. A triad of birds left a tree in a burst of noise, darting through the branches and calling to one another.

Cameron raised her hand and snapped her fingers. Derek froze and they stood perfectly still, Cameron resisting the urge to swipe away the last strands of the spiderweb stubbornly clinging to the bridge of her nose. Finally, she signaled him forward with two fingers and pointed to the ground, where a gnawed head lay, about the size of a medicine ball—the male's head that the female had chewed off during mating.

Cameron stepped forward and picked up the head carefully, as if concerned it would spring to life. The shell of the head was intact, but much of the insides had been eaten by ants. She tilted it in a shaft of light filtering through the treetops, admiring the hard, jagged line of the mandibles.

"Looks like it's just us and the larvae now," she said.

Chapter 50   Samantha nearly fell out of bed when she heard the loud banging at the slammer window. She jolted upright, eyes swollen with sleep, her hands immediately dancing along the countertop beside her bed in search of her glasses. She found them and pushed them onto her head at an angle. Her scrubs were twisted around her hips and she loosened them and pulled them straight.

Tom was at the window, his face animated with excitement. "It's the same virus!"

"What?" Samantha said. "Who?"

"In the thermoproteaceae living in the deep sea cores they pulled off the coast of Sangre de Dios. They must've been released from the crust by the drilling and entered the ocean, where they infected the species of dinoflagellates. Since the dinos were pushed toward the ocean's surface by quakes, they were made susceptible by UV exposure, and the virus must have bridged that structural gap. And get this—just like Dr. Denton noticed that the dinos were altered, somehow, genetically, the thermoproteaceae are all fucked up. Each one has a different genetic profile than the next."

"How is that . . ."

Tom shrugged. "Rajit's been playing with it in lab, trying to nail its etiology and pathogenicity, and make sense of the PCR test. The virus seems to contain a massive range of DNA code—blueprints for proteins from all kinds of species. The guys have already nicknamed it: the Darwin virus."

Samantha scratched her head. "Just don't name it after a location—the last thing we need right now is an outraged Chamber of Commerce somewhere."

"What's been happening with the rabbits?" Tom asked.

"Not a thing as of last night," Samantha said. "Cytopathic effect is what I'm thinking. We might have to bleed them, get the serum under a scope."

"Have you checked on them this morning?" he asked. She shook her head. "Well, you'd better hurry and take a peek before they shitcan you and ship you home in a bubble."

Still rubbing her eyes, Samantha trudged over to the crash door and pushed through into the next room. Tom waited for her at the window rather than walking around to the observation post. When she reappeared, she was ghost white.

"You'd better suit up and get in here," she said, her voice trembling. "You need to see this."

SEVERAL TABLES were set up outside the slammer window, a team of virologists and high-ranking officers gathered around them. Phones, faxes, and computers were running simultaneously, blinking, beeping, and ringing. Still clad only in medical scrubs, Samantha pulled a chair up to the glass and sat watching the others. Though her viral count was continuing to decrease, it was not yet zero; she would not be cleared from quarantine until she'd been held the requisite seven days. A stack of micrographs sat in her lap.

Colonel Douglas Strickland strode up the hallway behind

the makeshift workstation, his polished shoes clicking on the tile. The workers froze.

He pulled to a halt, facing Samantha through the window. "Dr. Everett," he said.

She smiled and nodded. "Yes, darling?"

He grimaced. "I've been informed we have something of a crisis on our hands."

"You could say that."

Strickland removed his beret and shuttled it through his hands. "If you continue to lend us your professional expertise in contending with this problem, I'm quite certain that such efforts will counterbalance the charges that have been leveled against you for your prior indiscretions. Assuming, of course, that you express remorse to the JAG officer."

Samantha stood up. "The only thing I'm remorseful about is that I placed myself in a position where my medical judgment was subject to military review."

"I would hardly—"

"Don't panic, Doug. I'll help you, but not for that reason. I'll help you because I'm actually still foolish enough to give a shit. So here's question number one for you: Is this something you've been working on behind the fence?"

Strickland's face drained of color. "You're implying that we developed this killer virus here on the premises for the sake of biological warfare?"

"We don't have time for implying—I'm asking outright. Is this virus out of the BW facility or not?"

Strickland stepped forward until his nose was almost touching the glass. His face was almost comically red, his jaw clenched. "Look at my face, Dr. Everett. Do you think I'd be exhibiting this level of concern if I had any idea with what we are contending?"

Samantha looked at him. Believed him.

"I saw the . . . offspring of that rabbit." Strickland shuddered. Samantha did not imagine he shuddered often. "Creatures unlike anything . . . abortions, all of them."

"Unviable mutations," Samantha said.

"Did the virus actually impregnate the rabbit?"

"No. We checked the records from the Crimean Congo virus study—the one the rabbits were shipped in for. One was pregnant, a few days, maybe. The virus drastically accelerated the pregnancy, but it didn't cause it to begin with."

"Is this thing going to spread?"

Samantha shrugged. "As it stands, we don't know if it will infect humans. But technically, a virus's sole mission is to replicate. To survive, it's got to hop continually from host to host, usually mutating, adapting and evolving as it goes. Viruses are mindless—just as short-sighted as humans, in fact. They have no long-term strategy. This virus could run virulent through its population and extinguish itself by killing off all available hosts. Dr. Denton and I are crunching the numbers right now to estimate the odds of another mutated mantid lineage on Sangre de Dios."

"How does it function? This . . . Darwin virus?"

Samantha nodded at the bustling work station behind Strickland. "That's what we're working on now."

"What is your informed opinion—or your hunch—at this stage?" he asked.

She sighed, winding a fist in the bottom of her scrub top. "My preliminary analysis of the genetic sequencing has shown that the virus itself contains genetic sequences from myriad other life forms. Like all viruses, it invades the host cells, using their machinery to replicate itself. In higher organisms, it seems to splice into the site between a promoter gene and a gene expressed only during embryonic development—in the case of the rabbits, the HOX series. Because of that, the viral DNA is promoted only during embryonic development. During this time, it attacks the DNA sequencing of its host, inserting its own segments of functional DNA code into the equation, and using these materials like primordial building blocks to create new life forms in the next generation."

"Segments of functional DNA code?"

"Yes. They carry the marching orders for cells, causing

them to form complex structures, like wings, legs, skeletal configuration, lungs, and other structures with or without utility."

Strickland shook his head in disbelief. "So if this thing spreads, we could have dogs with gills? Humans running around with wings?"

"It's highly unlikely, but not impossible. We forget how closely linked we are genetically to other animals. Only about a thousand genes out of a hundred thousand differentiate us from chimps. Even organisms as distant from us as roundworms have DNA sequences similar to ours, like variant spellings of the same word. If something gets into the code of any animal and tampers with it, even a little bit, the phenotypic alterations can be extraordinary." She tried to straighten her glasses, but they still tilted to the left.

"How can it create . . ." His eyes glazed as he took in his reflection in the window.

"You have to understand how viruses function. They can't live outside their hosts, so it's to a virus's advantage for its host animal to survive and reproduce, passing the virus along. The Darwin virus alters the host plant or animal's offspring so it exists in a wide variety of organisms. Natural selection then acts as the executioner of the unfit, killing off those less viable mutations." She gestured to the crash door. "Like the rabbit's offspring. But if this virus is indeed playing with segments of functional DNA code, sooner or later, it's bound to come up with *viable* mutations—offspring that'll survive and reproduce in turn. The virus introduces wild cards to the genetic deck, and shuffles over and over—maybe thousands of times. On Sangre de Dios, it finally dealt itself a winning hand.

"It's like that famous example where you have a million monkeys on a million typewriters typing for eternity. Eventually, the argument goes, one of them would randomly type *Hamlet*. Evolution works in similar fashion. It's unthinking; all that's necessary is variation and sheer numbers. But think how much more quickly one of the monkeys would arrive at *Hamlet* were they already using words, or complete sentences, instead of merely letters. That's what's occurring here. This virus shuffles entire blocks of genetic code, drastically boosting the odds that viable off-spring will be produced. Those offspring that survive . . . they'd have massive fitness potential. It's as if they've evolved instantaneously. What usually takes millions of years has been hit upon in a single generation. That's what's occurred on Sangre de Dios. Bear in mind that vari-ation is not predirected in favorable ways, so when it's this massive, random, *and* viable . . ." She threw her arms wide and let them clap to her sides. "Those animals . . . it's amazing."

"Amazing?" Strickland took a deep breath. "The ramifica-tions if this thing spreads are horrific. Dangerous biological agents are an issue of international security. Do you know, Dr. Everett, that a plane carrying a hundred kilograms of an-thrax spores and equipped with a run-of-the-mill crop sprayer could fly over Washington, D.C., and deliver a fatal dose to about three million people? That a taxi could pump enough out its tailpipe on a sunny afternoon in Manhattan to kill five or six million people?"

"Yes, sir, I do." Samantha smiled curtly and turned back to the stack of micrographs in her lap. "I wrote that study."

Chapter 51 Donald's nasal voice clicked through Derek's shoulder. "Gentlemen," he said. "And women. I'm calling in from Fort Detrick, conferenced with Dr. Samantha Everett."

"You're in Maryland?" Rex asked. "You flew out?"

"Yes," Donald said. "And after I explain our preliminary findings about this virus, you'll understand why."

Donald introduced Samantha, and the squad circled tightly as she proceeded to explain what they'd gleaned about the virus so far. Diego and Rex interrupted occasionally to explain the scientific terms to the soldiers, and to update Donald and Samantha about what they'd discovered in the specimen freezer and the water samples. When Samantha finished describing her hypotheses about the virus, there was a long pause.

Cameron felt the blood leave her face. If she contracted the virus, it would go to work on the embryo inside her. She had stood in the freezer with the others, the infected bodies swinging and dripping all around her. She'd already had morning sickness once—she was hardly at the top of her game, and if things went south, there was nothing anyone could do for her. Tank was watching her, maybe with concern, but he averted his eyes quickly when she looked over.

"But if this is how the virus works," Diego was saying, "then why do all the larvae look identical? Why are they not all different like the last generation we saw captured in the specimen freezer?"

"The virus must go dormant after the first generation," Samantha answered.

"So the first generation is all different," Szabla said, "but the second wave of offspring resemble their parents."

Savage lit a cigarette and Diego didn't even bother to comment.

"Of course," Rex said. "From a fitness perspective, if one of the mutated organisms survives to reproduce, it would be advantageous for it to replicate its own phenotype in its offspring. Continued mutation would compromise stability."

"It's like the virus found a working model, so it's sticking with it," Szabla added.

There was a rush of air as Samantha sighed into her telephone in the slammer. "It's amazing," she said. "The virus has evolved such that it provides a one-time opportunity for massive mutation. An unthinking yet solution-oriented process to create new animals capable of filling environmental niches."

Savage exhaled a long, thick ribbon of smoke. "Evolution in overdrive," he said.

Diego stood up, sweat glistening on his forehead. "This could be an age-old process—the virus locked in the earth's core, living in thermophilic microbes, springing up at intervals of hundreds of thousands of years to revolutionize life forms. It could explain instances of rapid origination, anomalies in the fossil records. The jump from cold- to warm-blooded vertebrates. The archaeopteryx. The Cambrian explosion. The Burgess shale. We may be on the precipice of such a period." His hands were shaking. He put them in his pockets.

Cameron held up her hand. "Stop," she said. "First things first. How does the virus spread? Could we get it from one of these creatures?"

"It seems to spread in similar fashion as a blood-borne pathogen," Samantha said.

"What's that mean?" Justin asked.

"If you fuck one," Savage growled, "wear a condom."

"Don't have open contact with the larvae's secretions," Samantha said.

"Well, don't viruses mutate all the time?" Justin asked, his voice lined with panic. "I mean, what if this thing goes airborne?"

"Let's not get dramatic," Samantha answered calmly. "It's not aerosol-infectious now, and generally, viruses tend to retain similar properties as they evolve. Besides, you guys don't have mission-oriented protective posture suits, and even if you did, you wouldn't be able to bend over and touch your toes if you put 'em on."

"What steps should we take to ensure we don't get infected?" Cameron asked.

"Well, we don't even know if it *can* infect humans, though, clearly, we don't want to resolve that issue the hard way. So, for one, I'd steer clear of that specimen freezer. Those bodies are packed with the virus, and from what you said, they're discharging secretions copiously. The large body you have at the camp is probably still shedding. Burn it—for your safety, and so it doesn't work its way through the food chain as it decomposes. Do you have any antibacterial gel?"

"Yes," Justin said. "One bottle."

"If you come into contact with any secretions, rinse off and apply the gel. Handle the larva with care, but there's no need to be paranoid. Touching it won't spread the virus." Her sneeze echoed through the transmitters. " 'Xcuse me. I do have some good news for you. As Rex pointed out, the confluence of conditions that allowed the Darwin virus to find its way into a single viable animal host is quite extraordinary. If it operates like viruses that are similarly transmitted, the rate of infection we would anticipate in the type of contact between a virus-bearing microorganism and an insect embryo is only one in eight. Taking into account the wasp and mantid populations of the island, and the odds of infected dinos going to spore state, UV weakening an ootheca so it could be compromised by parasitic wasps, and the virus hitting the unhatched nymphs at precisely the right timing—we're looking at an estimated one in one hundred twenty-one shot that another mantid ootheca was infected. The odds that the infected ootheca would produce offspring that pulled the right combination of organs and structures from the resultant DNA soup to be viable are even lower, probably infinitesimal. It looks like the assumption you've been operating on—that there's only one mantid lineage—stands an extremely good chance of being accurate."

"So the larvae are infected," Diego said despondently. "All of them."

There was a pause before Samantha answered. "Yes, I would imagine so."

"If this virus does indeed increase mutation and speed generational turnover," Donald said, "that would explain a number of the things you've described about the animals."

"Like what?" Cameron asked.

"Well, the switch from incomplete to complete metamorphosis, for one."

"A two-stage metamorphosis allows an organism to take advantage of variant food sources," Rex murmured. "It opens up the range of food available to it through its life cycle. The larvae seem primarily herbivorous—"

"While the adults seem to prefer people food," Szabla said. No one laughed.

"It would also explain the mantids' accelerated rate of development," Donald said. "Early reproduction is one of the keys to rapid increase. A ten percent decrease in age at first reproduction is roughly equivalent to a one hundred percent increase in fecundity. The rapid cycling of generations entails, of course, extremely short intergenerational gaps. Think of the *Aphis fabae*."

"I often do," Szabla said.

"It's an aphid. Embryonic development for the next three generations actually begins in the mother's body before her own birth. If all her offspring survived, a single female could produce five hundred twenty-four billion progeny in a year. Not to mention cecidomyian gall midges, who eat their mother alive from the inside, only to crawl from her shell and be devoured by their own offspring two days later." There was a silence as Donald paused. "If this virus indeed hastens the infected species' radiation, don't expect your larvae to hold in instar stages too long. After another molting or two, you're due for a metamorphosis."

Derek gazed at the larva in his lap, clearly upset. "But how does the virus know to do all this?" he asked.

"It doesn't *know* anything," Donald answered. "It has adapted to act certain ways because it's been shaped over thousands, maybe millions, of generations by random mutation and natural selection. Its actions merely give the appearance of motive."

"Do you think the adults will *actively* hunt us?" Justin asked.

"As Rex pointed out, aside from the occasional dog, no other sizable and appropriate food source on the island comes to mind," Donald said slowly. "Livestock would be too large, iguanas too small, and they'd be unable to crack a tortoise."

"I know we're all in a bit of a creature feature mindset," Rex said. "But let's bear in mind that the mantids are not malevolent. They're animals that act on need and instinct— no more, no less."

Savage covered one nostril with a thumb and blew snot on the ground. He wiped his hand off on his cammies.

"None of the other wildlife seems to be affected," Diego said. "Why would the virus merely affect one species of animal like this?"

"Viruses tend to be most prevalent in one species," Samantha said. "The 'virus reservoir.' Like deer mice to hantavirus, monkeys to simian hemorrhagic fever, *Calomys callosus* to Machupo. But the Darwin virus has been present in a fairly wide range—microbes, dinos, mantids, and rabbits. The fact that it affects animals in the embryonic stage is troublesome, because that's the time when cells from different species most resemble one another. If it could infect a rabbit embryo, it's not unreasonable that it could infect a canine embryo, for instance. The long shot is that any of these infected embryos would actually be viable. As it stands, we only have one accountable virus reservoir—the mantid lineage."

"And what do you usually do with this 'virus reservoir?'" Diego asked. He closed his eyes, clearly not wanting to hear the answer.

"If we can, we exterminate it." Samantha's voice was soft through the transmitter.

Rex stood up, removed his dirty Panama hat, and poured

water from a canteen over his head. It dripped down the jagged wisps of his bangs, running across his stubbled face. "We had hoped to observe them for longer," he said. "It's quite an . . . quite an amazing thing happening out here." The wind sucked through the watchtower in the distance.

"Let's not be hasty," Donald said. "There still might be some way around killing them all. I'd like to confer with Samantha and the other virologists here and check back in a few hours. In the meantime, we're still doing our best to get you pulled off that island."

Donald and Samantha clicked out. The group sat around the dead fire, staring at one another across the ashes. Rex raised his hands, then let them fall into his lap.

"I don't want to exterminate this species," Diego said.

"It's not a new species," Rex said. He stood, running his fingers through his wet hair. "They're just manifestations of the virus." The others looked puzzled. "You've heard the expression that a chicken is merely the egg's way of making another egg?" No one looked like they had, so Rex continued. "Well, the mantid is just the virus's way of making more virus. These are sick animals. Infected and altered."

"This is how evolution works," Diego snapped. "Through sickness. Through mutation. It's a natural virus. These are all natural processes."

Savage leaned close to Diego, almost singeing him with the end of his cigarette. "I don't give a shit about natural," he growled. "Murder is natural. Eating one's young is natural. Don't pull that shit on me again. You're so worried about killing the right animals in the right places. Pigs are bad, but lizards are good. This tree belongs here, this bush should be pulled up. It's all bullshit. Who cares whether these things are natural or not? We're assessing risk here. Us or them."

A flight of birds erupted from the *Scalesia* canopy, fly-catchers and petrels, rising in crazed, looping circles. "But we could be . . . we could be terminating a species here," Diego said. "Many species."

"This island isn't ready for them," Rex said. Diego was shaking his head, so he stepped forward, addressing him softly. "You actively eliminate other feral animals—puppies, kittens, goats. These mantids are the ultimate introduced species—they could devour all the other animals, become just as damaging as pigs. Worse. We have no idea how they'll impact the ecology here. We might want to think about—"

Derek rose abruptly. "Nobody's making a move without my approval," he said. When he unclenched his hands, Cameron noticed the marks his fingernails had pressed into his palms. "Nothing is to happen unless I give the order. Is that clear?"

Suddenly, the ground bucked underfoot and Derek went down. A thin crevice opened up, snaking its way through the field parallel to the road. A few of the *Scalesias* at the forest's edge snapped, their branch-heavy tops smashing into the ground. Szabla and Justin's tent flapped up in the air, pinned down only by two strainers staked deep in the grass.

Szabla fell, landing on her back so hard her breath left her in a grunt. A hurricane lamp was smashed by a rolling cruise box. One of the logs by the fireplace dislodged from its muddy base and spun toward Szabla. She was sucking air, trying to pull herself up, but Cameron reached her first, grabbing one boot and yanking her clear just in time.

A large balsa by the road snapped at its base, plummeting down with a fierce whistling. It smashed into a lava boulder, splitting it with cracks. It lay on its side, palmate leaves riffling in the wind, gray bark standing out against the green of the pasture.

Rex watched the waving trees in the forest through the L of his thumb and index finger. A massive shudder shook the ground as a shelf of rock and silt sheered off the steep eastern coast nearly a kilometer away, then there was silence. Dust and dirt swirled in the air, refusing to settle. Derek pulled himself up and trotted to his tent, Diego scurrying after him. The others rose, dusting themselves off.

Derek stumbled from his tent, holding the larva along the

length of his arms. "Set it down!" Rex barked. "Don't handle it."

Derek placed the larva hastily on the grass, and Diego examined its soft underside. "It appears to be unharmed," Diego finally said.

An aftershock caused them to brace themselves, but it quickly passed. Savage reached over, wiping a smudge of mud roughly from Szabla's cheek.

"Well, that's a fucking relief," he said.

Chapter 52   Derek sat silently on a log, holding the larva in his lap and gazing at its glassy eyes as the others reassembled the camp, doing their best to ignore him. The scorching sun had finally begun to work its way to the water.

Justin helped Szabla get the tent straightened out and they ran a supplies check. Tank and Savage strained to get the log back in line with the others around the fire, and Cameron helped Rex and Diego test their equipment.

The mantid body sprawled in the grass, attracting insects and birds. After Rex and Diego examined it, taking copious notes, Tank and Savage dragged the body a few hundred yards east of the camp and built a small pyre around it, using firewood and leaves. It took a few tries to get the body ignited, but once it got going, it burned quickly, crackling like a fly in a bug zapper. The fire rose like a teepee, a cone of light fighting off the dusk. They came back, rinsed with water from the canteen, and rubbed gel into their hands.

Derek's transmitter vibrated four times before he took note. Lethargically, he tilted his head to his shoulder. "Mitchell. Public." The others gathered around quickly.

"Mitchell, it's Mako here." If Mako was waiting for a response, he didn't get one. "I just got a call from a colonel at Fort Detrick. Strickland. Do you know the name?"

Derek shook his head.

"No," Cameron said into her transmitter. "We don't."

"They're getting heavy into the science over there. Some
kind of virus you guys are exposed to. Said it had to do with
the mutated animal you were describing. That Denton fellow from the New Center's been leaning on Strickland and
our old friend the Secretary of the Navy to get you guys ex-
tracted. Said you're in grave danger."

"Déjà fuckin' vu," Savage growled.

"Problem is, that little rumble you kids just felt originated
off the coast of Colombia. A significant number of our air
assets were on the ground in Bogotá. We sustained heavy
damages; they're still sorting through the wreckage. I've
been on the phone this last hour trying to find anything to
pull you guys off that rock, but looks like we're snake eyes
for the time being. The good news is, I managed to block out
a Blackhawk and a C-130 for 2200 on the thirty-first. We'll
have you out in fifty-two hours."

"We might be insect shit in fifty-two hours," Justin
grumbled.

Derek and Mako stood off in silence, each waiting for the
other to speak next.

"I'm sorry, soldier," Mako finally said. "It's the best we
can do." He clicked out.

The others sat quietly for a few moments. Szabla rose and
went to her tent.

Cameron walked over to Derek, stopping with one boot
on the log beside him. "I'm gonna go check on the Estradas
again, make sure they're all right," she said.

"Are you asking or telling me?" Derek said, his eyes not
leaving the larva.

"Derek," Cameron said. "She's six months pregnant. I'm
gonna go check on them."

Derek studied her for a few moments. "I'm not going with
you. Grab a buddy."

Cameron signaled Justin with a flick of her head, and he
followed her across the field to the road. They walked side
by side, the watchtower looming ahead. In a few places, the

ground had buckled up in scarps, four- to five-inch lips in the road.

"Derek is not Derek," Justin said after a few moments. "We might need to think about doing something."

Cameron did not respond.

They reached the *bloque* house and Cameron called out, anxious to see the couple. There was no answer. The air around them took on another shade of gray as the sun dipped out of sight behind a row of plantain trees.

Cameron called out again, noticing the strain in her voice.

They passed beneath the window and turned the corner. Cameron stepped through the doorway into the house. She stopped dead in her tracks, momentarily blocking Justin's view. He stepped around her, then also froze.

Ramón's body dangled from the ceiling near the fireplace, his face a deep blue above the noose. The chair lay on its side beneath his feet. The wall near the bed was splattered with crimson. Floreana lay on the mattress, draped in a bloody sheet. On the floor near the foot of the mattress was a gnarled little creature. Cameron looked at its still-moist head, the small broken claw curled up at the end of a stumpy limb.

She felt her stomach rising in her gullet. Justin leaned over, hands on his knees, sucking air until he regained control. He and Cameron stood beside each other for what must have been fifteen minutes, staring at the three bodies, stilling their emotions, sweating in the thick air.

Finally, Cameron crossed to the mattress. Justin reached after her and said her name once, but she did not slow. She reached down and grabbed a clean part of the sheet. Slowly, she pulled it off Floreana, revealing her lower body.

Cameron emitted a small, almost animal sound, a cry deep in her throat that rose sharp and faded quickly. She raised a hand to her face where it hovered, unsure of what to do. She looked down and saw that her other hand was clutching her belly.

She backed slowly away from the bed, refusing to lower
her eyes to the baby-corpse on the floor. Justin watched her
as she walked to the fireplace. She righted the chair, stood on
it, and freed Ramón. His body flopped over her broad shoulders, bloodless arms dangling over her back. Justin stayed
where he was. She was grateful to him for not offering to
help. She carried Ramón to the bed and laid him beside his
wife. Noticing the newly healed cut on his index finger, she
wondered if that was the route by which the Darwin virus
had entered his body. Or maybe it had reached Floreana directly. Cameron's feet felt numb beneath her legs, insensate
blocks.

Her face felt hot, burning beneath the skin. She rarely became emotional, but when she did, she carried the signs
clearly on her face. Bloodshot eyes, flushed cheeks, a redness along the bridge of her nose. Her mother had always
said that it was her one tender trait.

Without a word, she turned and passed Justin, heading out
into the twilight. After a moment, Justin followed her. He
walked a few paces behind her back to the camp. Tank had
started the fire up again; Cameron could see it from the road.
She approached it slowly, the logs coming into view, then
the soldiers.

Cameron reached the camp first. "We're killing them,"
she said.

Derek's head snapped up. "Excuse me?"

"Whatever's carrying this virus."

"What are you . . . what are you talking about?"

"It can spread to humans. Floreana gave birth to a . . .
thing. It killed her. Ramón hanged himself. If you'd seen it."
Cameron inhaled sharply, her nostrils flaring. Her mind
raced with more thoughts than she could grab hold of.

Diego took a step back and sat down heavily. Derek's fingers fluttered once, then formed themselves into fists.
Cameron felt Szabla's eyes on her, steady and hard.

"We need to shift our objectives," Cameron continued.

"We need to contain the virus. I'm not leaving this island until we exterminate all carriers."

"That's not the mission," Derek said. "Those aren't your orders."

"Fuck the mission," Cameron said. "Fuck my orders."

Derek set the larva aside and stood, glowering. He came at her in a charge, but Tank and Justin stepped in his way, and then Savage and Szabla were up, both of them flanking Cameron protectively. Savage swung the heavy freezer bolt casually, whistling a couple bars of a melody.

Derek squared himself, pulling back his shoulders. He seemed stretched taut under the weight of it all, ready to snap. But if he made a second charge, there would be a fight, and there were four of them and Tank, and there was no way he'd dare.

Eyes wild, Derek looked from one face to the next. His mouth hung slightly open, but no words came out.

Cameron stepped out in front of the others. "I think we got it from here, LT," she said. She sounded miserable, even to herself.

Derek rubbed the bridge of his nose with his thumb and index finger, blinking tight around them. He started to speak, but still nothing came, and he closed his mouth dumbly. He turned to the larva, which squirmed along the top of the log. It arched upward, its true legs extending like antennae.

With trembling fingers, Derek reached down and smoothed his hands on his worn cammy shirt. One of his cheeks was twitching, just beneath the eye. He glared at Cameron for a long time. She met his gaze, unblinking.

Lowering his head, he stepped around the others and walked into his tent.

The silence seemed to fill them up, separately and together. Diego started to walk toward the larva, but Szabla took his arm at the elbow, very gently, and held him back. She shook her head.

Cameron looked at Tank, and then at Derek's tent. Tank nodded and walked over, standing guard by Derek's flap. She caught Savage's eye and something passed between them.

Savage picked up the larva roughly, swinging it by its posterior end. It squealed, a rush of air creaking through its cuticle, and tried to curl itself upward. Its wiggling shadow fell across their faces as Savage passed them, taking the spike that Cameron silently offered and heading into the dark night behind the tents.

Rex did not look over. Diego closed his eyes, lowering his head. He sat down heavily.

The air swarmed around Cameron and she felt her head go light. She refused to look behind the tents, afraid she'd see Savage with the spike cocked back over his head. Diego's eyes remained closed, his breathing heavy and irregular. Cameron thought he might be crying.

They waited, each alone with their thoughts. No one made eye contact.

Finally, Savage's figure cut from the blackness. The larva dangled beside him like a rag doll, the back of its head caved in. He looked at Cameron. Cameron thought of the virus running through the larva's body and nodded at the fire. He swung the body once, up and into the fire, where it crackled in the flames.

Savage handed Cameron the spike and sat down beside Szabla on the log.

Diego cupped his hand over his forehead, rubbing it hard. "Jesus Christ," he whispered. "You didn't even hesitate."

A log shifted in the fire, sending up a spray of sparks. The air smelled of burning wood, fresh like pine. Thin bones became visible in the glowing husk of the larva's body.

Savage leaned forward, his elbows resting on his knees, his hands dangling between his thighs. His bandanna was moist with sweat.

Szabla started to talk, but her voice was gravelly; she cleared her throat and started again. "Earlier, when you said you'd killed women and children. Was that true?"

Savage ran his tongue slowly across his teeth. "The jungle around Khe Sanh was riddled with tunnels," he said over the crackling fire. "If we came across spider holes, we'd drop grenades first and ask questions later." His hand made a loose gesture. "Never knew what you were gonna find when you looked in after." He laughed darkly, remembering. "A surprise every time, like a Cracker Jack prize."

Szabla watched him, leaning heavily on her hands until her ass rose up off the log. The others shifted uncomfortably but did not speak. Cameron's hand tightened around the spike until it grew numb and tingling, as though it were no longer part of her.

"Some surprises were worse than others. Sometimes they'd be moving families through the tunnels." Savage's face went slack. "Sometimes you'd be almost afraid to look down after, see what prize you won."

He stood abruptly. Cameron watched his bare back until it disappeared through the flap of his tent.

Chapter 53 Samantha hadn't called to check in on her children in sixteen hours. Every time she picked up the phone, she got hit with something new—a chart, a micrograph, PCR results, Szabla calling in with news of the mutiny and the human infection on Sangre de Dios. Though Samantha had spoken to Donald on a few occasions, this was the first time she'd worked with him in person. He was an amusing, pleasant-looking man, his wrinkled linen shirt spotted with sweat. They'd quickly formed a partnership of sorts; he sat right beside the slammer window so that they could confer. Their opinion of how to rectify the situation on the island would be key— Cameron and the other troops now in control were in firm opposition to Diego and Derek, with Rex leaning heavily toward the dominant party.

Samantha sighed. "Jesus, if something like this hit the mainland . . ."

"How do we know it's isolated to Sangre de Dios?" Donald cleaned the lenses of his spectacles on his shirt.

"We don't. But don't underestimate how difficult it is for a virus to spread. Viruses are fragile, subject to the harsh laws of natural selection like everything else. We only hear about the ones that make it—Machupo, Sin Nombre, Ebola. For every virus we've heard of, there are untold millions that die away, disappear."

Donald raised a silver eyebrow, amused. "Viruses are people, too?"

Samantha did not return his smile. "The Darwin virus is not going to be able to infect everything it comes in contact with. It's never shown up in water samples from any of the other islands in the archipelago, and only once in a sample from Sangre de Dios. But now we have a problem. We have a virus present in a stable life form without any natural predators. It needs the host organisms to survive, and it will spread further when the hosts reproduce."

"The animals are effectively quarantined on the island." Donald shook his head. "I just don't know that killing them off is the right choice."

"The larvae appear to be amphibious, Donald. And the adults are winged. All we need is for one to get taken by a pregnant shark, or fly—unlikely as that seems—from one island to the next in search of food."

"What are you saying?"

"I'm saying, we can never account for when, where, and how a virus will come out of hiding and threaten us. But if there was an island somewhere teeming with rats carrying the bubonic plague, what would you do? Wait and observe?"

"If the rats were evolutionarily unique, maybe." He sighed, removing his glasses and rubbing his eyes. "Are you suggesting we support Szabla and Cameron's decision?"

"The accountable virus reservoir needs to be exterminated. We're extraordinarily fortunate here; the ootheca chambers indicate the exact number of disease carriers to be found and killed, at least for this line of descent." She sighed, leaning against the glass. "For all we know, the drill hole off Sangre de Dios only shed the virus for a limited time. Rex claims that the dinos now present on the island appear normal, at least under a standard lens."

She looked at Donald, the sadness etching itself into the lines of his face. "The longer we sit on this thing, the greater chance it will spin out of control," she continued. "The spring months are coming on, and a whole new wave of reproductive activity from the island animals. Diatom bloom, red tides, increased seaborne pathogens as the ocean surface temp rises, El Niño breaking up the inversion layer and drawing rain down on the island. There'll be an explosion of life. With all the heat and reproductive activity, the virus could flourish. And if it gets into mosquitoes or maggots, forget it. Think about when eastern-equine-encephalitis-infected Asian tiger mosquitoes turned up in Florida." She grimaced. "You want to talk about a problematic introduced species."

Donald lowered his shiny forehead into a hand. Samantha softened her voice. "If this thing hits the mainland . . . it would spread like an STD. The results would be . . ." She shuddered, imagining a new generation of grotesquely altered babies. "The effects on humans could be horrid—and now we know it could be a reality."

Donald mumbled something and raised his hands in exasperation.

"We have this virus pinned down," Samantha said. "For this brief opportunity, on this island. Imagine if we ever had this for AIDS, how many lives would have been saved." Samantha's eyes seemed to glow with fearful intensity. "I don't want this virus crawling around that island."

Colonel Douglas Strickland walked down the hallway toward the slammer, and the group around the desks to Donald's right quieted. He approached the glass, addressing

Samantha only, as if the others did not exist. "We've had a breakdown in chain-of-command which, apparently, can't be rectified long distance."

"We know," Samantha said. "We heard."

"That's not even the biggest concern," he continued. "We can straighten that out back here. However, the latest developments regarding the Darwin virus . . ." He grimaced his stern grimace. "We're debating what degree of force the crisis necessitates."

Samantha frowned. "Degree of force?" she repeated.

"All the life on that island is potentially dangerous. We have to assume a worst-case scenario."

"But the rest of the fauna appear to be normal," Donald broke in. "We're even questioning if the dinoflagellates are still infected."

"But we don't know for sure."

"We never know for sure," Samantha said. "That's why we should do this in a limited way to preserve the island life. Euthanize the animals we know are infected, and then run tests on the plants, animals, and water to make sure they're clean."

Strickland laughed, a loud, hearty laugh. Samantha realized she had never even seen him smile before. His laughter had no element of spontaneity. "Oh yes," he said, once his laughter died down. "I'll just commit another squad of men to this endeavor from our copious resources. Perhaps pull them from Quito where they're de facto running the nation." Strickland's smile dropped from his face. "I want those drill holes closed over and the island sterilized."

Donald stood up. "That doesn't make any—"

Strickland stared at him, pushing him back down into his seat with his eyes.

Samantha rose, pressing her hands against the window. "What if we could guarantee that the virus reservoir was exterminated? Would you spare the island?"

"Top brass are flying in tomorrow afternoon. We'll decide our plan of action then."

"What about my request to get that crew off the island?" Donald asked.

"If memory serves, Dr. Denton," Strickland said, "you were the one so anxious to get those men *on* the island." He turned on his heel. "We're having air asset complications, but we'll be able to get a helo to your men by 2200 on the thirty-first."

"That may not be soon enough."

"Well, Dr. Denton," Strickland said. "In light of the amount of shit in which we would appear to have landed, it'll have to be."

DEREK HAD temporarily deactivated his transmitter, so the page from Samantha defaulted to Cameron, as his buddy. She'd been gathering firewood at the forest's edge, alone. The others were around the base. Cameron could see from their posture they were all uncomfortably aware of Cameron and Derek's tent. She didn't blame them. The flap was zipped, and Derek hadn't made a sound since retiring; she'd been tempted to peek inside to make sure he was still there.

When she clicked on, she heard Samantha's loud voice ring through the crackle. "Samantha here. Dr. Everett. Who's this?"

"Cameron Kates."

"You the one asking all the sensible questions earlier?"

"Yes," Cameron said. "I suppose so." I've got higher stakes, she thought.

"I have some tough news," Samantha said. Something in her voice was immensely comforting without being condescending. Cameron listened carefully as Samantha filled her in on her conversations with Strickland and Donald.

Cameron took a deep breath. "As you already know, we sort of reached that conclusion on our end as well."

"Donald took it heavy," Samantha said. "It won't be easy with the scientists. And you're going to need their help. If need be, I can bottom-line them on the decisions of my ever-astute superiors."

"I don't think that'll be necessary. I can handle it."

"Page me if you need anything."

"Thank you. But I won't."

There was a long pause. And then, "Cameron?"

"Yes?"

"Good luck." Samantha clicked off, and Cameron took a moment to collect herself before returning to the others. They'd noticed her talking but had given her space. She walked back with an armful of branches, and the others watched her expectantly. The fire was almost out, a glowing heap of embers. She caught Diego's eye. "Samantha and Donald back our decision to take out the remaining larvae."

Diego took the news calmly, with an air of mournfulness. "Why?" he asked.

She dropped the wood. "Because they're pretty sure that if we can't exterminate the virus reservoir and provide damn good evidence that the water samples are virus-clear by 2200 on Monday, there's not gonna be an island left to argue over."

Rex exhaled in a sharp sigh. Diego eased himself down onto a log.

When Savage looked up, his eyes were flat and dark like water-smooth stones. "Sometimes you have to destroy a village to save it," he said.

Chapter 54   It felt odd to Cameron, reconning with Justin. But since Derek was obviously out of the picture for the time being, and Szabla and Savage were standing guard over his tent, it made the most sense for her and Justin to pair up. Tank and the scientists took the western rim of the transition zone, hooking north around the *Scalesia* zone.

Cameron followed her husband through the dark forest,

covering the terrain with slow sweeps of her elbow light. The Estradas' violent deaths and the mutiny had drained her, so she tried to keep her mind on the task at hand. It occurred to her just how odd it was that they were out here to dispose of gentle creatures that crawled in the night. Such a task seemed discordant at a time when her whole body was yearning for softness.

When he'd realized that the entire island was at stake, Diego had yielded to their objectives, finally agreeing to help dispose of the larvae. His advice was simple—the larvae would be attracted to light and humans, and want to keep to the shade. The first larva they'd captured had never made an effort to flee, and it had all but sought Cameron out by the lagoon. It was part of the larvae's strategy to locate other organisms to look over them, a strategy that had worked out nicely on an island with few predators.

Diego and Rex had also urged that they all keep an eye out for any other irregularities in the flora or fauna.

Cameron and Justin marched through the foliage, the branches arched like gothic gables, the trunks rising like spires to the vast spread of leaves floating overhead. They were enclosed, the two of them, in a world of vegetation, and it seemed that the canopy above was the floor of another world just out of reach. It was cavernous, the forest, a living stomach dripping with vines and life.

Cameron had the sudden peculiar sensation that she was going to her wedding. Aside from the fact that she was alone with the man she loved and the night hovered ahead of them intimidating and yet unrealized, she did not know why.

She passed the entrance of a cave, more like a deep niche carved into the side of a hill, and noticed movement just inside. She called Justin back and he came quietly. They stepped inside, the light casting shadows broad and fearful.

The cave's wide entrance afforded a view of a cluster of avocado trees just outside—smooth trunks and wide, dark leaves. Rocks and boulders lined the interior. Cameron felt her stomach roiling as they stepped inside. Something flickered in the darkness, and she drew back her spike as Justin fell out to her right. She tried not to imagine what it would be like to batter one of the larvae. She pictured the smooth green head, the sentimental eyes, the soft prolegs that grasped and released, and she felt her mouth go dry.

There was a flash of movement behind a rock. Justin reached the rock first and shoved it over with his boot. Cameron held the spike cocked back over her shoulder like a golf club. A rice rat scurried for the cave entrance.

Cameron lowered the spike, relieved, her arm weak under its weight. She dropped her elbow light, and it dangled from its sling around her neck.

Justin turned to her, concerned. "You all right?" he asked.

She nodded, then shook her head, then nodded. "It's just that . . . I don't know if I could . . . they're so much larger than . . . their faces look so . . ." She stopped, lowering her head. "I don't know what the fuck is happening to me," she said. "I don't know why I care about this, Floreana, any of it." Anger colored her voice; it was proud, almost defiant. "I never used to care."

Justin waited patiently for her breathing to slow.

"I used to be locked on," she said. "All the time, you know?"

"I know," Justin said. "I know."

"But now I feel soft. Emotional." She was trembling. "I broke orders. I led a fucking mutiny. Because of my own . . ." She made a fist and tapped it against her stomach.

"You stepped into yourself," Justin said. "You made a decision." There were better words for what he wanted to say, but she understood him.

Cameron tilted her head back so that she wouldn't spill tears. "It's so messy though. I feel so fucking *messy*." Her mouth tightened as she looked at her husband. "Why didn't you?" she asked. "Make the call?"

"First of all, the squad wouldn't follow me."

Cameron digested this for a moment. "And second?"

Justin lowered his hands, his light crossing Cameron's, illuminating the back of the small cave.

"Second?" she asked again.

He raised his eyes, meeting hers. "I don't have your strength, Cam." He shook his head, looking away.

She reached out and laid a finger on his cheek, turning his face to hers. "There are better things than strength," she said.

"Okay, but look at Derek."

Cameron's voice dropped to a whisper. "Look at Savage."

They stared at each other in the darkness of the cave, their lights dangling and throwing shadows all about them. Justin moved forward and hugged her tightly, a combat hug, wrapping his arms around her and raising her off the ground as he leaned back. He seemed to slow when he set her down. For a moment, she felt the warmth of his cheek against hers, and her hands were on his shoulders and she pulled back a little and looked at him, looked at him hard. He kissed her gently on the cheek. She turned to face him fully, surprised, and they kissed again, softly, wetly. When the kiss ended, they regarded each other, slightly bewildered.

They set down their lights and spikes. The wind whistled outside, reminding them of the peacefulness of the still air all around them. Somewhere, deep in the cave, water dripped.

Justin reached over and ran his finger along the length of her necklace, picking up the clasp and moving it to the back as he often did. Then he reached for her cheek, but she grasped his wrist, stopping him.

He splayed his fingers as he pulled back his hand.

She was just about to say something when she heard the noise, a soft cooing with clicks moving underneath it.

"What? What is it?" Justin asked.

At the edge of the cave near the entrance, its head protruding from behind a boulder, a larva watched them inquisitively. Drawn by their sounds and the light, it had crawled into the cave to find them.

It arched upward, its thorax and head curving up from the abdomen.

Cameron leaned over, grabbing for the spike before she lost her nerve.

The larva crawled from behind the boulder, inching for the cave entrance.

"It's moving," Justin said. He stepped forward, knocking the elbow light with his foot. It rocked on the hard floor, its beam rolling across the cave.

Cameron ran over and seized the larva by the terminal segment as it was about to reach the entrance. She dragged it back inside toward the light, its tender cuticle scraping on the rocky floor. Air screeched through its spiracles, and it balled up like a fetus, half-lit in the dark.

Choking on her own breath, Cameron drew back the spike and struck it at the base of the skull. It was knocked into a lengthwise roll, squealing louder than Cameron could have imagined, and something squirted from the hole in its head. Its abdomen loosened and contracted, its mouth hanging silently open and she swung again, hearing something in its thorax give way. It screeched, trying desperately to drag itself away and her vision went blurry, and she was screaming "Die, why won't you die!" and swinging and hacking and pounding, but it still kept struggling even as its head came apart at the top. Its prolegs kept pulsing and air kept screeching through the spiracles, its mouth bent wide with the thrust of the mandibles. Beside herself with revulsion at it and herself, she raised the spike behind her like a spear and thrust it right through the center of it. It shrieked again, flailing, but at last its true legs slowed and then it was quiet, its mouth hanging open.

Her face in her hands, she gasped, fighting down a sob. Swaying in the dancing yellow light of the cave, her shoulders rising and falling in great heaves, the thing impaled before her, she leaned over and vomited so hard she felt her whole chest rising with the effort. Her stomach felt as though it were turning itself inside-out within her throat, a thick cord of drool and regurgitated food spinning from her bottom lip.

She retched until she couldn't bring anything up and then retched a few times more, Justin pressing his palm to her forehead to keep her head up.

HER SHOULDERS slumped with exhaustion, Cameron trudged into camp ahead of Justin, the larva draped across her arms. Sitting by the languishing fire, the others looked up with eyes dark and dreadful.

She dumped the body on the fire and watched the flames eat into it. Her expression had hardened, her face steeling itself with resolve. She stoked the fire with a forked stick.

Savage was crouching just like her on the far side of the fire, and she could barely see the outline of his shoulders and his thickening beard through the flames. For a moment, Cameron imagined she was looking into a mirror and seeing herself lit in fire, but the sensation passed like a warm spell of water in the sea.

"Three more," she said.

They sat silently around the fire until exhaustion finally caught up with them, and they drifted off to their respective tents, one by one, to steal a few hours' rest before the morning recons.

Having cleaned her hands with antibacterial gel, Cameron settled in for first watch, resting the spike across her knees. Diego sat, exhausted, leaning against the base of a log, the radio between his legs. He clicked tediously through his SOS. By now, Cameron knew the pattern by heart.

"Would it help if you told them I'd be willing to run future expeditions here, monitor the island life?" Diego asked, his eyes on the radio.

"I don't know," Cameron said.

His keying the handset was the only noise in the darkness. After a few moments, Diego raised his head. "They would really do it?"

Cameron looked at him blankly.

"Bomb the island," he clarified.

"If they deem it necessary, yes."

"Necessary." Diego laughed a short, sad laugh. "It'll leave this place nothing but barren volcanic rock. A dead hump of stone protruding from the sea, just like it was three million years ago." He clicked the handset. Long short long. "*Three million years*. Three million years of life taking hold here in minute, painstaking increments." His ponytail swayed as he shook his head. "One third of the plants here are found nowhere else. Half of the birds and insects. Ninety percent of the reptiles. These tortoises could be the same ones Darwin himself saw on his expedition. The very same ones."

Cameron did not respond.

"When you look around here," he asked "what do you see?"

Cameron shrugged. "Rocks. Trees."

Diego laughed his sad laugh again. He pointed to a small fern that rose from the matted grass past the fire. "Spores of ferns can resist low temperatures. They were sucked up in the air, probably blown out here all the way from the mainland, and they dropped to the earth with the condensation." He gestured to the *Scalesia* forest. "The first *Scalesia* seeds, probably carried over in birds' stomachs, or stuck to the mud on their feet." He spread his arms wide. "Legumes are plentiful here because the empty space between the embryo and external shell makes their seeds like little rafts. Cotton—resilient to long stays in salt water." He raised a hand from the radio, watching an ant work its way along his forearm. "Ants carried here on palm tree logs. Turtles using the pockets of air between their upper backs and shells to float out here, spiders surviving windstorms, dropping to the islands from three thousand meters."

He dropped his hands heavily to the ground between his legs. "You see rocks and trees. I see order and reason and design and beauty." He lowered his head. "Don't let them bomb this island."

"It got to this from bare lava," Cameron said. "It can do it again."

Diego studied her, and she grew uncomfortable under his

eyes. Finally, he looked away. His voice was hoarse when he spoke. "Some people never realize how valuable something is until they destroy it."

Chapter 55 For the first time in nearly 120 hours, Derek slept. He dreamed of Jacqueline's eyes, enigmatic swirling pools as dark as blood. He could have sworn they were lighter once, that they flickered with some hidden illumination, but maybe that had been his imagination.

The Night Of, he'd gone alone to midnight mass. The drive home afterward was peaceful, but the air had choked out of him when his house first loomed in view. It had looked different, imperceptibly yet terrifyingly altered. Branches had curled into the sky, skeletal fingers straining toward the moon. Shadows had fallen in chunks and blocks about the yard at all the wrong angles; the yellow paint had grown wan; the front door had gleamed as if afire. He'd known at once that something was dreadfully wrong within.

He stirred from his sleep, the inside of the tent lit green from the canvas. His dreams had been painfully vivid. He raised the flap of the tent and peered out, feeling like a captive, which he supposed he was. Tank sat on the log facing the forest. A spike leaned against the log beside him.

Derek almost stopped breathing when he saw the larva across the fire pit from Tank, its thorax elevated, its head tilted. It must have come from the west, inching into camp under cover of the tall grass while Tank watched the forest. Was it the same one? Maybe they hadn't killed it after all. With quiet, stealthy movements, he crept from his tent to the larva, his eyes trained on Tank's back. Though it was early, the sun had already begun its daily assault on the island; Derek felt it tingling across his cheeks and forehead.

When he got closer, he could tell that it was a different larva. It was significantly fatter and its eyes were lopsided, the left one a good half inch higher. This larva was over three feet long. It swung its head over, taking in Derek. He saw the gills along its neck flutter slightly, its thin antennae bobbing. Its eyes caught the first ray of the rising sun and reflected it back in twinning prisms.

Derek closed his eyes and an image flashed out at him from the darkness—Jacqueline's head raised high and proud, eyes ablaze like a prophetess's, a smudge of blood across her cheek. Behind her, curtains fluttering in the nighttime breeze.

When Derek looked at the larva again, he couldn't help thinking of the small, helpless face of his daughter. He inched forward, careful not to alert Tank, and raised the larva to his chest, supporting its weight with an arm along its underbelly. He held it, feeling the smooth cuticle of the head against his cheek. Its prolegs clung to him. Its cool head brushing his chin, he backtracked around the dead fire.

He almost dropped the larva when he saw Tank looking at him across the ashes of the fire pit. Derek instinctively turned the larva away from Tank, as if to shield it from his glare. He noticed Tank's hand tighten in a fist around the spike at his side, and before he knew what he was doing, he was off and running, clutching the larva to his chest, one hand hooked around its abdomen and one supporting its head.

He heard Tank shout behind him, but he kept running across the grassy field and into the forest, the branches snapping across his face until it was streaked with blood.

CAMERON AND the others were out of their tents by the time Tank returned from the pursuit. "Derek," Tank said, pointing and breathing hard. They stood watching the edge of the forest, as if Derek were going to reappear. Savage cursed under his breath.

"He has one," Tank said. "A larva."

"You'd better come clean with me!" Savage snapped, turning to the others. "What the fuck is going on here?"

The other soldiers looked at one another, deciding who would speak.

"Derek had an accident with his baby," Cameron finally said. "With his baby girl."

"What the fuck does that mean? An *accident*."

"Look," Cameron said. "It's not important. Let's deal with the problems at hand."

"This *is* a problem at hand."

"There's no need to waste time getting into details. His wife had postpartum psychosis. There was an accident. Derek's fucked up. He has a larva. Let's move on."

"What else did he take?" Rex asked. "A spike, a flare? What?"

"Well, I think he had a flare in his cargo pocket," Justin said. "That leaves us three." He looked around, double-checking. "The spikes are all here."

"All right," Cameron said. She stared at the ascending sun, trying not to squint. Morning already. She turned to Rex. "What's our time frame for metamorphosis?"

"I don't know, but I'd imagine soon. As Donald said, these things are turning over generations as quickly as possible. We saw that one molt already—they're on wildly accelerated development curves. Could be days. Could be less."

Justin checked his watch. "We may or may not be here."

"We could spend all our time today building traps for when the larvae transform, but I still think it's better to strike preemptively instead of waiting around and dealing with a bigger problem," Szabla said. "Let's see if we can round up any larvae this morning. We'll muster at 1300, at which time we can discuss Plan B."

"So the top order of business is still hunting down the larvae. We've got . . ." Cameron paused, counting in her head. "Two unaccounted for and a third with Derek."

"What about Derek?" Justin asked.

"I'll deal with Derek," Savage said.

"Don't even *think* about hurting him," Cameron snapped.

"You're not his mother," Szabla said. "Not anymore."

"What's your plan for dealing with him?" Rex asked Cameron.

"I'm hoping if he has some time, he'll come around. I'll try to contact him by transmitter in a bit. Hopefully, he'll re-activate it so I can reach him."

Savage smirked. "Think you can take care of business, do you?"

"Yes," Cameron said, feeling oddly unnerved by his patronizing grin. "I do."

Szabla tapped the spike twice in the palm of her hand, where it left a streak of dirt. "We can't fuck around with those things metamorphosing. If you see Mitchell and he won't cooperate, you're cleared to use reasonable force." She caught Cameron's eye across the fire pit. "I'm sorry."

"It won't come to that," Cameron said. "If anything, he'll hide. Protect the larva. Even though he's gone off the deep end, he won't want to start fighting us. He'll just disappear."

Savage played with his knife, digging something out of the sole of his boot with the tip. "It's a small island," he said.

"If Derek decided to hide in an elevator, it would take you weeks to find him," Cameron said. "He's a world-class soldier."

Savage squinted in the sunlight. "Doesn't seem to be playing the part on this little cruise."

Rex turned to Diego. "We should collect a few more water samples from the coast, hope they're all normal under the microscope." He looked at Cameron with concern. "A microscope analysis is probably not going to be sufficient for the final reckoning, but for now, it'll have to do."

"The rest of us'll go into the forest," Cameron said. "Szabla, Savage and I'll carry the flares. We only have three, so don't burn 'em unless you mean it. Justin, you and Szabla are the only intact team at this point, so you should recon together and I'll go with Tank and Savage."

"I'd rather you, Justin, and Tank teamed off," Szabla said.

"I don't think—"

"Didn't realize you were the OIC here," Szabla said.

Cameron bit her lip, debating whether it was worth getting into right now. "You're right," she finally said. "I'm not."

"Okay," Szabla said. "I pair with Savage."

"I'm sure you do," Justin muttered.

"What the fuck does that mean?"

"What the fuck do you think it means, Szabla? Keep your dick holstered."

Szabla lunged for Justin, but Cameron caught her around the waist and threw her back. Savage seized Cameron's arm, and she grabbed his wrist, stepping back with his momentum and yanking him off balance. As he stumbled forward, she locked his arm by snapping the heel of her other hand to the back of his elbow. She drove him down onto his knees, then his chest, pressuring the elbow so it was almost hyperextended.

Savage grunted, his cheek against the ground, a swirl of dirt kicking up with his breath. Cameron kept the pressure on to prevent him from reaching for his knife.

Cameron stepped across Savage's arm, twisting it and holding it firmly between her legs as she faced the others. Though her hair was hooked behind her ear, it curved forward, forming a point just under the side of her mouth. Szabla started forward but froze when Cameron tightened her hold on Savage's arm.

"We are not pulling this *Lord of the Flies* bullshit," Cameron said. "Because it's stupid, because it doesn't make sense, but most of all because we don't have the fuckin' time." She twisted Savage's arm with each phrase, and he strained even harder not to yell, the veins on his neck standing out like fingers. "Are we all clear?"

The wind sucked across the shed atop the watchtower and it moaned softly in the distance. Tank was up on his toes, arms tensed.

"We ousted Derek, but that does not mean there are no rules now," she continued. "As former AOIC, Szabla is acting senior officer and we will fall into line under her." They all nodded. Cameron looked down at Savage, as if just remembering him, and released his arm. She pulled him up to his feet. Rotating his arm painfully, he grimaced.

"Nice move," he said, not insincerely.

Chapter 56   Derek carried the larva pressed to his chest, and when he got tired, he bore it on his shoulders, looping it across so he could piggyback it. At first, it seemed uncomfortable being carried—he could feel its segments squirming and readjusting around his neck—but soon it calmed, adjusting to the rough ride.

He stopped once so that the larva could feed, and it did so energetically, working its way through a newly fallen branch in minutes. Sitting on the hot forest ground, he watched it, amazed by the unrelenting action of its mandibles. When it had finished, he leaned over to kiss its forehead but changed his mind. Pulling himself to his feet, he dusted his hands on his cammies, picked up the larva, and continued up the forested slope.

There was no plan, at least none he could think of. Keeping the larva safe was his only intention. He'd figure something out before the scheduled extraction tomorrow night; he just had to keep the larva secure until then. They'd want to take it back, study it—that much he knew.

All the ambiguities of his life took shape in a single goal: preserving the life of this creature. If he did that, maybe he could take back the rest of it. Maybe he could take back what he'd discovered that night. The Night Of.

The forest was even more dim than he had remembered. When he looked up at the sky, the rain started, as if on cue. And then it was hammering down, the leaves and twigs dancing with its descent. He took his bearings, gauging how far he had moved into the forest and up the volcano's wooded slope. He was close to the middle of the *Scalesia* zone. He could rest here and regain his energy.

A fat *cedrela* had snapped in the earthquake, the sharp shaft of the stump sticking up in the air. The trunk had fallen to the side, where it lay in a smashed heap of branches. The fallen tree was still attached to the stump by a hinge of bark and pulp, creating a small triangular area of shelter.

Derek left the larva beside the tree and gathered branches and broad leaves, which he wove loosely together to shield the shelter from both sides. He finished building the little hut and worked a splinter out of his palm. Pinching it until it stuck out from the bead of blood, he removed it with his front teeth, then spit it out. He turned to the larva and stepped back in surprise.

It lay beside the shell of its old cuticle, its sides barely expanding and contracting as it drew breath. It appeared to be exhausted.

He turned his mind away from the darkness he felt encroaching, from the dangerous reality he sensed but refused to admit. Picking up the larva, he moved it into the small shelter, curling up behind it. The heat made the larva uncomfortable, so it squirmed away from him but rested its head near his. He pulled the sheet of branches and leaves down across the front of the shelter and lay back, losing himself in the sticky webbing of his thoughts.

Voices pulled him from his delirium. He recognized Szabla's, coming from no more than fifteen feet, and he peered through a gap in the leaves and saw Savage's face, his eyes sunk in shadows. Even though they were close, he could not make out what they were saying.

As always, Savage was carrying his blade. He said something to Szabla, his voice a murmuring hum, then headed directly for the shelter. Derek froze, one hand hovering protectively above the larva's head. He prayed it wouldn't stir.

Savage thunked his boot down on the stump, inches from Derek, and assessed the terrain. Rainwater ran down the rubber surface of his boot, dripping onto Derek's cheek. Derek could practically feel the heat coming off Savage's body. He moved not a muscle.

Savage sheathed his knife, patting it on the side for good measure, and walked back to Szabla. They disappeared into the underbrush, their crackling footsteps fading away.

Derek exhaled. Though he hadn't realized it, he'd been holding his breath for nearly a minute. The larva shifted with the sound, seeking his body, as if for reassurance. It nuzzled into the hollow of his neck, and a flash of fear ran through him, but its mandibles remained retracted.

The ground rumbled suddenly, fiercely, and the tree rocked overhead. For a moment, Derek was worried that the tree would slide from the stump and crush them, but it held strong. He laid a hand protectively over the larva as the earth shook around them, then stilled. Aside from its abdominal segments bunching slightly, the larva did not move.

Lying on his back, Derek looked at the brief wisps of sky he could make out through the network of branches around him, the rain-heavy air, and the dark columns of the trees.

The forest suddenly seemed quite peaceful.

DEXTEROUSLY, SAVAGE moved ahead of Szabla in the rain. From time to time, she could make out the flash of his skin between the tree trunks. He rarely wore a shirt in the forest, but for some reason, the mosquitoes left him alone.

He called out to the larvae, "Hey little guys, you want some candy?" and then he'd laugh his forty-grit laugh.

All of a sudden, he was gone. Szabla scanned the area in front of her but could make nothing out in the dim light. She called his name once, her voice trembling ever so slightly, then reached across and fondled the ball of her biceps and felt her courage steel.

She stepped off the small trail they had been moving along and was immediately swallowed by the foliage. She circled around the area she had last seen Savage, holding the spike up above her head so that it wouldn't rustle through the branches.

"Quiet," she heard him grumble before he wrapped an arm around her and pulled her into the foliage, slapping a hand across her mouth. They sank to the forest floor until they were lying side by side, hidden beneath ferns. Savage eyed her for a moment, then removed his hand. He snapped his fingers and pointed to the right. "Something there," he whispered.

He kept his hand near Szabla's mouth, ready to cover it again if she spoke. She was silent, though, and they lay staring into the darkness. After a few minutes, a branch nearby exploded with motion. Szabla tensed until she realized it was only a bird; the large-billed flycatcher shot through the canopy, its sulfur-yellow belly the single spot of color in the gray air.

Szabla let out her breath in a rush and looked at Savage. The mud he had smeared across his cheeks and chest for camouflage had hardened, cracking like a pie crust. It was darker around his mouth; he looked like a predator after feasting on a kill.

He kept the grin on his face, a white floating crescent that reminded her of the Cheshire cat's, and she suddenly became aware of how close they were. One of her arms was pinned beneath his shoulder, her hand resting in the dirty tangle of his hair. He smelled of sweat and mud, and his body pressed against hers was the hardest she had ever felt, though he was over fifty years old. His muscles weren't inordinately large, but they were tight, hard like stones.

She turned her head slightly to face him full on, her cheek brushing against his beard. She held his eyes for a moment, her heart still pounding from the scare. Staring into his eyes was like looking into a black hole; they were bottomless, empty, tinged with gray. Szabla felt she was peering through the surface ice of a frozen lake, peering into death itself.

Her unease was clear as they separated and stood.

Savage cleared his throat, bringing up a plug of phlegm he spit out on a jet of air. It splatted against a frond and dripped to the ground. He stared at her, seeming to read her mind.

"You go places sometimes," he said, his voice soft, gravelly, and, if she wasn't mistaken, gentle, "you can't get back from." He looked up at the living ceiling above them. "I went into the jungle when I was eighteen, and I stepped out of life. I don't . . . I don't have a choice anymore."

Leaning back against the slimy bark of the tree, he watched a cluster of insects flutter around a branch overhead. Szabla looked everywhere but his eyes, then started back along the trail.

After a moment, he followed.

IT WAS one of the longest days Cameron could recall.

Since the larvae needed shade of some sort, she, Tank, and Justin skipped the sparse coastal zone. They swept the rim of the arid zone near the lagoon where Cameron had located the first larva, before heading north and making their way through the transition zone above the volcanic rift. Finally, they cut into the forest proper, cresting Cerro Verde around noon, steering clear of the caldera itself by circumventing it from the safety of the surrounding trees. At one point, a vantage opened, and Cameron caught a clear glimpse of the active caldera through the tree trunks—a long, flat plain of lava set off with the occasional jumble of rocks and dipping out of sight in the middle. Myriad fissures split the dark rock, through which the glow of hot magma emanated. Steam rose in wisps, curling into elongated apparitions before dissipating.

They paused reverently before continuing down the steep eastern side of the *Scalesia* zone. They combed the terrain in huge swaths, beating the underbrush and waiting for the small creatures to crawl forth so they could beat them to death.

Tank carried the bolt from the specimen freezer, and Cameron and Justin each held a spike. If they didn't start picking the larvae off soon, their situation would get worse. They still had thirty-four hours to extraction, and thirty-four hours could be a long time stuck on a tiny island with master predators on the loose.

They walked on in silence, taking in the trees and the short, darting movements of birds. Cameron's arms were whipped and raw from plant stalks and twigs. Her left shoulder had a large abrasion she might have gotten scraping against the rough bark of a tree, but she couldn't remember for sure. In fact, she couldn't recall the source of most of the aches and pains that shot through her body with each step.

At one point, she could have sworn she sensed Derek close to them in the forest, but when she listened, she heard nothing except the whisper of leaves against one another. She tried reaching him on his transmitter a few times, but it was still deactivated.

They circled up to take a rest, snacking from their MREs. No one stood guard. Cameron rested in a crouch, eating vegetarian tortellini out of the pouch. The rain had stopped, though the air was still gray and heavy. After ten minutes of sitting, Tank was still breathing heavily. Justin said something softly to him that Cameron could not quite make out, but she guessed he asked about Tank's injuries, because Tank shook his head and stood up quickly, pretending not to wince.

They started to leave, but Cameron stopped herself, went back to their rest spot, and cleaned up the plastic wrappers from the MREs, shoving them into her bag.

For four more hours, they painstakingly canvassed the forest, peering into bushes and caves, through the gnarled hollows of trees, and within clusters of boulders. At one point, Tank stopped, snapping his fingers sharply, and they all froze.

There was a slight scraping, like nails against bark, and they peered around nervously. Tank raised the freezer bolt behind his head, the knob dwarfed by his large fingers. Cameron and Justin moved slowly for cover behind a tree trunk, and Tank was left alone in the clearing. He took a hesitant first step back but stopped when the scraping came again. A cluster of ferns to his right split open, and a shadow charged out at him. As he stumbled back, swinging the bolt and missing, Cameron realized it was a feral dog, its spotted coat stretched tightly across its ribs. She felt the breeze from the dog's movement as it flashed off into the foliage. In an instant, even the sound of its running had vanished.

Tank swayed a bit on his feet, still clutching the bolt. Justin started laughing with relief, but no one joined him. He stopped.

They arrived back at base camp, defeated and exhausted, praying that Szabla and Savage had had more success. They ducked into Tank's tent to get out of the glaring sun, and Tank collapsed on his back on the ground. Cameron could tell he was really hurting, though she was probably the last person in the world he'd admit that to. "You sure you're all right?" she asked.

"Fine."

"Well, you know what usually makes me feel better after a long day of unsuccessful larva hunting?" Justin asked, glancing over to see if he'd made Cameron smile. "A good hot shower and a back massage. But since I can't have either of those, I think I'll go take a dump."

Even Tank laughed a little as Justin disappeared through the flap.

"Good kid," Tank said. He shook his head, leaving sweat stains on his pad. He ran his fingers across his tender forehead, drawing away peels of skin. He looked at Cameron sheepishly. "Forgot sunblock," he said.

Cameron cringed. She unscrewed the cap from her canteen and took a healthy gulp of water. She'd need to get to the ocean soon to rinse off the grime. It clung to her like another layer of clothing.

Above the barrel of Tank's chest, the strong curve of his chin was bristled with whiskers. Cameron had always liked being in Tank's large, serene presence—maybe it was the constant current of unspoken affection he sent her way. She felt the need to say something to him, something personal, but she didn't know what, so she was quiet.

Justin's voice from outside broke the silence. "Hey you guys! Check this out. Quick!"

They scrambled out of the tent and found Justin furiously buttoning up his pants. He started for the forest, gesturing them to follow. They passed through some recently cleared pasture, and soon the *Scalesias* were all around them. About fifteen yards in, he slowed, bending aside a leafy bush so that Cameron and Tank could see.

A larva, smaller than the others, with a light, almost yellow-green cuticle, had slid itself up a tree trunk, its prolegs grasping the moist bark. It worked its head back and forth, expelling a white sticky substance that looked like silk onto the trunk. It attached itself to the silk bedding and bent its head down to its bottom segment. It was weaving a cocoon around itself.

Cameron stepped forward, moving around Justin. "Incredible," she murmured.

They watched its graceful, repetitive movements with fascination. It had ensconced its lower half in silk when they heard approaching footsteps behind them. Cameron turned as Szabla appeared in the foliage, Savage trailing her by a few steps.

"I was wondering where you—" Szabla froze, staring at the larva. Without hesitation, she crossed to it and kicked it from the tree, sending a scattering of moisture through the air. It squirmed on the ground awkwardly, its lower body still encased in silk. Savage stepped forward and raised a foot to the tree trunk, resting an arm across his knee.

Reaching over without even looking, Szabla grabbed Savage's knife from his ankle sheath. She reached the larva in

four strides and drove the blade into the top of its head. A
gurgling noise issued from its gills. It flipped and twisted,
arching like a Halloween cat, its true legs splayed out in
front of it like wooden pegs. Green hemolymph bubbled
from the slit. It shuddered twice through its entire body, contracted slowly into a ball, and stilled.

Szabla glared at Tank, Justin, and Cameron, running the
knife across her thigh and back again. Cameron almost
retched at the smudge it left on her cammies, full of virus.
She felt Savage's eyes on her, reading her. "That's my tough
little soldier," he said, his voice amused and disdainful all at
once.

Szabla tossed the knife back to Savage, who caught it expertly by the handle. She picked up the larva, careful to keep
her hands clear of the hemolymph. "What's wrong, Cam?"
she snarled. "Forgot Floreana's little Sigourney Weaver trick
already?"

She headed back in the direction of camp, knocking
Cameron's shoulder hard as she passed her.

Chapter 57   Moths floated on the outskirts of blos-
somed plants, fortuitously brushing against stamens and
flower cups with their pollen-dusted proboscises. They scattered from Derek's footsteps as if in flight from a predator,
zooming in paired figure eights. The larva felt leaden in
Derek's arms, and it had grown more sluggish. It lazed
across his straining forearms, head and posterior end dangling.

Eyes alert, back hunched, treading rotting fronds and beetle shells underfoot, Derek paused only to lap tears of rain
from moist orchid blossoms. He found a brilliant white bud
brimming with water and gently plucked it from the bush.
Raising the larva's head with a guiding touch beneath its
chin, he placed the half-opened flower into its mouth. Its

mouth pulsed, sawing into the flower and moving it quickly
down its throat. When it was done, it squirmed over itself,
segments rotating, to look into his face.

Derek felt himself fill with something larger than himself,
stirrings in the empty spaces of his heart. The vibration of
his transmitter broke him from his thoughts. He'd reacti-
vated his transmitter about twenty minutes ago, though he
wasn't certain he wanted to speak to anyone yet. He thought
for a few moments, then set the larva down, cleared his
throat, and tilted his head to his shoulder. "Mitchell. Private.
Obviously."

The line hummed with silence.

"What?" he asked.

He realized he was surrounded by a tight ring of trees, and
he began clearing the space within them of rocks and leaves,
preparing a lay-up point. The exhaustion of the past week
had overtaken him all at once, it seemed. Though he'd dozed
a little last night, his head was still light with fatigue. He'd
need to get some real sleep soon.

Cameron's voice filled the air around him, and he found
its familiarity among the dirt and stones and trees soothing.
"Derek," she said. "Cameron."

He took a moment to center himself, then spoke, impressed with the evenness of his voice. "Let me guess.
You're huddled in *my* tent, probably sitting on *my* Therm-a-
Rest with the rest of *my* squad around you trying to see what
you can squeeze out of me."

The grass was heavy with dew at the edge of the forest.
Cameron stood in a tall patch that reached nearly to her
knees, looking out at the ball of the sun. About fifty yards
behind her, the others mustered in the shade of their tents,
eating MREs. The fire had consumed most of the larva's
body, leaving behind only a darkened husk.

"I'm sorry you think it's like that," she said, sounding
more upset than she'd wanted to let on.

"Well, you'll have to excuse me. When your soldiers
mutiny, it tends to make one a bit of a cynic."

She bit her lip to punish herself with the pain. "We're beyond that now." She almost called him "LT" but caught herself. "That thing is dangerous, and it's gonna metamorphose. We caught one weaving a cocoon earlier."

"What did you do to it?"

Cameron did not answer. His eyes closed and it felt so good that he almost dozed off right there on his feet. He swayed a touch, then forced his eyes open. The larva had inched its way around a tree trunk, its prolegs clinging to the bark. "It's beautiful, Cam," he said. "We need to get it to safety."

"It's packing a deadly virus," she said, the words coming in a rush. "It needs to die." They both reeled a bit with the bluntness of her statement.

"I never would have guessed you'd betray me," he said slowly. "That you'd violate orders, violate my trust."

"It's about more than that," she said.

"Sounds like Savage got to you through osmosis," he said. "There are no rules anymore, huh?"

"New rules."

"Well, while you're enjoying your new rules, remember that you're all in violation of direct orders from a superior—orders that still stand. Whether you like them or not, my orders are my orders. I haven't cleared any of you to kill these animals. They need to be protected."

Cameron took a moment, trying to place her thoughts in words. "This isn't going to solve anything, you know. About what happened to you . . . your family."

His laugh was tight and nasty. "What the fuck do you know about my family?"

Cameron let out an agonized sigh, clenching her teeth. "There's more going on with you than you're admitting."

"With me? You're light-headed, distracted, and barfing in the mornings. It doesn't take Dr. Spock to figure out—"

"You're at the end of the line," Cameron said. "Get your ass back to base, or there's nothing I can do."

"Is that a threat? That you're planning to use force against me?"

"If we have to, yes." She was quiet as the grass waved across her pants. "I've been responsible for your life more times than I can count," she said softly.

Derek froze.

When she spoke again, her voice had little emotion. "When you die, I'm gonna feel like I failed you," she said. "But I'm also gonna be wrong."

The others took note of her expression as she headed back into camp. "I think we're gonna have another mantid on our hands," she said.

It took a few moments for her meaning to settle over them. Justin tapped his forehead with his curled knuckles.

"We should probably rinse off," Rex said. "More thoroughly."

"But there are two more out there," Cameron said. "We need a Plan B."

"I'm with Doc for once." Savage ran a finger across the back of his neck, pulling away grime and a strip of sunburnt skin. "My Plan B is to wash the fuck off."

Chapter 58   The water in Bahía Avispa was as clear as glass, showing off the exotic fish and curls of coral beneath. It slid up onto shore, hissing across the sand. The ocean was a brilliant aqua, magnificently bright.

The body of the sea lion pup that Cameron had touched lay near a cluster of rocks, collecting swirls of flies. They filed past it toward the water, Cameron pausing for a moment to look at its creamy brown fur. No one commented.

Justin waded out into the water, shattering the smooth surface with a dive and moving like a black dart through the waves.

The others waded into the ocean, rinsing off their faces. Tank's mouth stretched tight when the cool water hit his sunburnt cheeks. Even Rex's neck sported a red stripe, visible when he removed his Panama hat. Diego sat on the sand, poking his finger into the ghost crab holes.

To the west, the waves rolled in, hitting the blowholes off Punta Berlanga and spraying up in the air. Cameron watched the water spread and dissipate, and thought about the virus she might be taking into her lungs this very minute. Her thoughts moved to her pregnancy, and she quickly redirected them.

Watching her husband's shadow fade into the waves, she absentmindedly walked along the wet sand. She was barefoot; one of the lessons she had learned in her first weeks of training was to get out of her boots at any opportunity—the longer she could avoid the combination of heat and humidity, the better her feet would fare through the course of a mission. She walked along the ocean's edge, then stepped into the water. It was cool at first touch but quickly felt neutral, even warm.

The water rose above her calves, dropping to her ankles when the swell ebbed. Her line of sight was undistorted when she looked through the water. She saw the bottom with astonishing clarity—the schools of little fish with yellow streaks turning in perfect unison, sleek rocks half submerged in the sand, the lines of her own broad feet and toes.

As she waded out, the water moved in minute ripples, hairline fissures in the glass surface. The waves had again ceased suddenly, as if stilled by a magic hand. The water darkened her pants to the thighs, and then she dipped her hips under, unbuttoning her worn shirt and pulling it off. She dragged it through the water on the end of her fist like a mop.

She felt a hand on her shoulder and she turned, expecting Justin. It was Szabla.

"Hey, girl," Szabla said.

"Hey." Cameron lowered herself beneath the surface up to her neck, feeling her nipples harden beneath her bra.

Szabla's black tank top was tight across her chest, as all her shirts were. "I've been a bit much here, I know." She sniffed hard, wrinkling her nose. "It's just, with Derek being a little loose around the edges . . . "

"No need to explain," Cameron said. "You've actually been right about things all along."

Szabla traced her fingertips along the surface of the water. "I know, but that doesn't sound as gracious."

Cameron laughed, dipping her head back and feeling the water in her hair.

"Your husband was worried about you, but he was afraid to bother you, so I came out to check."

"What's he worried about?"

Szabla shrugged. "He didn't say anything actually. I could just tell. You guys have always had a closeness that's not too hard to sense." She splashed some water over her face, rubbing her eyes, then squared and faced Cameron, studying her. "I thought you might be pregnant," she said. "But Justin said you weren't."

Cameron slicked back her wet hair. "He did, huh?"

She didn't meet Szabla's eyes, and Szabla didn't press the point. The water caressed their waists. They let it calm them.

Szabla skimmed the water with her hand. "You know something? All these years, I still don't know how you met."

"It's not so romantic."

"I figured."

"We overlapped for observation point training. A lot of deprivation crap to teach us to sit tight for long periods of time on lookouts. They starved us, dehydrated us, kept us up—you know the game. The final drill was we had to sit still in this room for thirty-six straight hours. No food, no standing up, no using the bathroom. If you had to go, you shit yourself right there. Anyone loses it, you start over. So we had to look out for everyone on the squad. You know, the teamwork bullshit. Around hour twenty, Justin starts to get edgy. Now, I knew him a little bit from around, thought he was decently good-looking and stuff. He is good-looking," she added, as if Szabla had disagreed with her.

"We were sitting there wet with shit and piss and he started shaking and I thought he was gonna stand up and start pounding on the door and fuck it up for all of us. So I leaned over and I said, 'Kates, look at me. When you think you're gonna lose it, just look over here into my eyes.' And he did.

"We sat there like that for the last sixteen hours, staring into each other's eyes. That's when I first fell in love with him. You can tell a lot about a person from looking into their eyes for sixteen hours. Not much you can hide." She smiled at the memory. "I don't think we even blinked."

"Wow. I'm speechless."

"Let me savor that," Cameron said.

Szabla shoved her and she stumbled, laughing and splashing.

"I apologized, you bitch. Besides, I'm your senior officer."

"Yes, 'cause we're known for our formality on the teams." Cameron bent her legs, drifting with the water up around her neck. "Sir."

"Navy SEALs. Golden bad boys. That's what my highly cerebral brother calls us. He's a Marine."

"A Marine. Jesus, I'm sorry."

"Yeah, so am I." Szabla raised some water in her cupped hands and moistened her face. "Marines. Fuckin' bullet sponges."

Cameron leaned back into the water again. The world went quiet and the setting sun was on her face and she wanted to stay like this, out here, half-dipped in water so pure she could watch the fish swimming around her ankles.

Cameron stood back up and faced Szabla. With the sun behind her, her face was shadowed, and Szabla couldn't see her mouth move when she talked. "I was so sure I was ready to walk away when Justin and I went reserves," she said.

"But the teams always filled a big place in me. Bigger than I knew. It's weird, but I never thought how much I'd miss it. Humping gear. Plugging wounds. Spaghetti and meatballs from a pouch. Blisters. Wearing pantyhose to keep the leeches out." She worked her bottom lip between her teeth. "I wasn't ready, though. I was relieved to get called back for this mission. Only it's not fitting right now, being a soldier. Not like it used to." She shoveled her hands in the water and brought them up over her head, feeling it wash down across her face.

Szabla stared out across the shimmering water. "Maybe it's time to move on for real. Hang up your M-4. Make your own schedule. Choose your own responsibilities."

Cameron turned to the side and the glare of the sun broke across her silhouette. Szabla squinted into the light as Cameron spoke. "I've parachuted from thirty thousand feet with oxygen and a forty-three-pound, one-kiloton-yield special atomic demolition munition strapped to my body." When she spoke again, her voice was flat. "But I'm not sure I'm up to that challenge."

JUSTIN WATCHED his wife bathing, Szabla at her side. Someone moved behind him, and cigarette smoke wafted over his shoulder.

"Must be nice," Savage said. "Having a wife like that."

"Yeah," Justin said cautiously. "It is."

They watched the women in the water for a few moments, Justin shifting his weight uncomfortably. "Looks like you lent Szabla your touch, huh?" Justin said, his eyes still on Cameron.

"You liked that?" Savage laughed. "How she took that little thing? She kills with the mercilessness of the rich."

"How'd you know she's from money? She tell you?"

Savage shook his head, though Justin still hadn't turned to face him. "In all my years of combat, I've only seen two types of people kill that well, with that much ease—the rich and the poor."

"Of course, you're the latter."

A chuckle came over Justin's shoulder, thick with smoke. "Of course."

The women started in toward shore, Cameron pulling her shirt back on. When Justin turned around, Savage was gone.

WHEN CAMERON stepped from the water, the sun felt like a lightbulb pressed to the back of her neck. The men were sitting atop a sand dune, their faces taking on a deep red hue. The long swishing tracks of a marine iguana textured the sand at their feet—the deep groove of the tail, the parallel brush marks of the feet on either side. Behind them, sea porcelain colored the white sand, a patchwork of red stems and purple flowers.

They all stood, their skin tingling from saltwater meeting sunburn. Szabla nodded and they fell out, heading for the small trail cut into the cliffs of Punta Berlanga. Diego froze, Tank knocking into him from behind. Diego touched a hand to his ear, tilting his head.

"What?" Szabla said to Diego. "Speak, boy."

A Zodiac burst from around one of the tuff cones in the distance, rocketing toward shore. Diego ran to the beach, jumping and waving his arms, but the speedboat was already heading toward them. As it drew nearer, Cameron recognized the small figure in the boat. Ramoncito. His large head seemed loose on his neck, bouncing with the impact from the waves. His shoulders were slumped, his hands loose on the throttle handle. He looked drugged.

The boat hit shore hard and skidded up onto the beach. Diego ran toward it. Ramoncito tried to step over the side but collapsed, falling face first onto the sand. Diego turned him over just as the others arrived. A deep maroon had taken hold beneath the smooth dark surface of his face. He was sun-scorched—lips cracked and bleeding, eyes swollen, hands blistered. He mouthed Diego's name, but no sound issued from his lips.

Cameron tipped her canteen to his face, spilling fresh water through his mouth. His tongue worked slowly in the water, lapping it.

Justin leaned against the Zodiac's bow, his shoulder brushing the Darwin Station decal. He gazed into the boat. It was stocked with twenty-four six-gallon fuel cans, many of them empty. Squeezed in the back near the rudder were two wooden crates, *TNT* written on their sides in red.

"Holy shit," he said. "Kid motored this thing all the way from Santa Cruz."

Chapter 59 They headed back for base camp, Cameron taking a long detour through the field where they'd burned the mantid. She returned to the others, who had assembled in Derek's old tent. It felt divine to be out of the sun in the soothing shade of the tent. Ramoncito was lying on his back on a sleeping pad. Diego and he spoke softly as the others looked on.

"I got the SOS," Ramoncito said. "And I understood it." He tried to smile, but the movement cracked his lips even more, and he winced from the pain.

Justin leaned over, examining the blistering on Ramoncito's back. He winked at Cameron. The burns weren't too bad.

"Single thirty-five-horsepower engine bringing you one seventy-some nautical miles at ten knots." Diego pushed Ramoncito's hair off his forehead and rubbed more lotion onto his sunburnt face. "You must've been on the open water for seventeen hours."

Ramoncito tried to smile. "Sixteen."

"Glass sea state," Cameron murmured.

Diego said, "You never should have come."

"You asked me to."

"Not you. If you received the message, I thought you'd get help."

"From who? I know my way home better than anyone. Besides, who would have listened to me?"

"The Captain of the Port."

"Yeah right. I had to steal the TNT from him. Fresh in from the army."

"You stole the—" Diego cut himself off, shaking his head. "Puta madre."

Szabla was on her knees in the corner, looking through one of the TNT boxes Ramoncito had brought along. Row after row of two-pound blocks lined the bottom beneath coils of wire and a scattering of blasting caps. Szabla picked up an olive-drab Clacker detonator and examined it with a smile. The two sides of the Clacker could be pushed together like a stapler to detonate a charge.

"Why'd you bring so much?" Diego asked. "There must be two, three hundred pounds here."

"I thought there might have been a slide, and we'd have to blast something out from under tons of rock. Like we did with that generator up by Media Luna. That was fun." He propped himself on an elbow and drank some more from the canteen.

"Not too much too quickly," Diego cautioned.

"You sound like papá." Ramoncito lowered the canteen. "Where are my parents?"

Diego turned to the soldiers. "You'd better give us a moment alone," he said to the others in English. Cameron nodded and led the other soldiers out. It was clear from Ramoncito's face that he was anticipating bad news.

Savage stopped at the flap. "Kid," he said. "You're one brave little motherfucker."

They all walked a few paces from the tent, leaving Diego to tell Ramoncito that his parents had died. Rex shook his head. "What a thing," he said.

"What're we gonna do?" Szabla said. "Our extraction's not till tomorrow night, but there's no way that boat can pull the weight of all of us, not on limited gas like that."

"Plus there's a space issue," Justin said. "Even once we

toss the empties, there's at least thirteen full fuel cans, and it'll take all of them to get back to Santa Cruz." He glanced at the others. "I don't know who the hell's gonna want to wait behind, though."

Cameron was watching a hawk hover above a knotted patch of shrubs just beyond the watchtower. It folded its wings, accelerating toward the ground. It dipped and then rose, and Cameron made out the silhouette of a rat struggling in its talons as it flew toward the sun. "We're the only thing that'll hold them on the island," Cameron said.

Szabla looked at her, head cocked. "Excuse me?"

"The creatures. You heard what Donald said—we're the only 'sizable and appropriate food source.' If those larvae metamorphose into adults, they're gonna be hungry. If there's no food here, they could very well fly elsewhere in search of it." Her face hardened. "I don't want that virus leaving the island."

"You want to stay here?" Justin asked. "As bait?"

"Yes," Cameron said. "I do."

"It's not likely that the adults can fly," Rex said. "Even though they have wings."

"But we know that the larvae are amphibious. Diego even said that the first one we found could very well have been heading down to the ocean. They could drift with the currents, wind up God knows where. If we're not here to track them down . . ."

Diego stepped out of the tent, his face heavy, and approached the others. "He wanted to see the bodies, but I told him . . ." He scratched his cheek, letting the sentence trail off. "He's too upset to even argue with me about staying."

Cameron nodded. "I'm sorry," she said.

"Yes," Diego replied. "So am I."

"You and Rex collected lots of water samples yesterday, didn't you?" she asked.

Diego scratched his forehead at the hairline. "Yes. From various points on the island and all along the coast, especially from the dino-rich waters flowing in from the deep-sea core holes."

"If you don't want this island bombed, I'd suggest you get back to the Darwin Station, run virus tests, and pray to God none of the samples are infected," Cameron said. "Contact Donald and Dr. Everett at Fort Detrick, where the decision's being made." She pulled her hand from her pocket and opened it to reveal a small silver disk, Tucker's transmitter that she'd pulled from the ashes of the mantid's belly. "Heat-resistant to two thousand degrees," she said. "Picked it from the bones. I already tested it. Just activate it and ask the operator to patch you through. Medical Division Wing, Slammer Two."

"We can't leave you all here," Rex said. "With . . . with the possibility of—"

"We have TNT," Cameron said. "We're soldiers. You're scientists. And you'd better get that kid out of here in case all hell does break loose." She looked at the other soldiers. "We came here a squad, I say we stay here a squad. We still have some business to take care of."

Tank nodded first, then Justin murmured his assent.

"What the fuck," Savage said. "Got nothin' better to do."

Szabla stared at Cameron long and hard, the line of her cheekbones glistening with sweat.

"You'll be in charge," Cameron said.

"Girl, that gets harder and harder with you around." Szabla shook her head. "Fuck it. We can't all fit in that boat, and it's our responsibility to clear the civilians." She nodded at Cameron. "I'm in."

"We shouldn't leave you here," Rex said.

Szabla smirked. "No need to be valiant for the sake of the ladies when we can both kick your ass."

Rex nodded seriously. "True," he said. "True."

Szabla stretched her arms with a groan. "We're minute to minute here. What's our defense if we can't get to those last two larvae in time? The adults are pretty antsy, pun be fucked. I can't see one just staggering into a pile of explosives and det cord. Look at the Rambo shit Savage had to pull just to get near it." She let out her breath, puffing her cheeks. "I mean, we can't exactly lob around blocks of TNT."

"Why not?" Rex asked.

Szabla bit back a smile. "This ain't a Road Runner cartoon. If we throw it, we can't time the explosion. Timing sucks in general with TNT, since it's not meant as a killing explosive. It's too unreliable to light a fuse set for less than thirty seconds anyways. It's always better to detonate it."

"The fuses aren't made for that," Cameron concurred. "Plus TNT has no frag—there's no shrapnel to expand the killing radius. We need to lock the creature's location before we detonate, hold it close to the explosives. Hopefully within an enclosed space so it'll blow like an internal charge. Walls won't allow the explosion to dissipate as easily."

Rex nodded. "Greater overpressure."

Tank formed a gun with his hand and tilted it at Rex with a clicking noise. "Freezer?" he asked.

"I don't know." Rex shook his head. "It would be tough to lure one in there without live bait, and we've already noted the island's lack of dogs and goats. Plus, I don't see her ducking into a metal box without great provocation."

"I agree," Szabla said. She turned her fist, making her biceps slide up and down.

"So what the fuck are we gonna do?" Justin asked. "Dig a pit?"

"Yeah," Savage said. "We are." They turned to him, surprised. "Once you get someone in a pit, you own 'em," he said. "You got elevation, you got 'em trapped—you can do anything you want to them. We lost guys in pits sometimes in Nam, steep pits. They'd try to scramble up the sides, but the mud would give way under their hands. Right in the middle of combat, with us retreating. They were fucked. I had an LT that'd shoot 'em before leavin' 'em there for the gooks to play with."

The silence that followed was broken by Cameron's laugh.

"What's so funny?" Justin asked.

"Nothing," she said. "I was just debating whether I should mention that I find the term 'gook' offensive. I guess the civility of my response seemed oddly out of place." She looked at Savage, amusement lingering on her lips. "I forgot who I'm dealing with."

A smile flashed somewhere in Savage's beard.

"But I do think it's a good idea," Cameron continued. "The pit. We'll camo the top of it, rig the bottom with explosives. All we need is to slow the fucker up for a split second to blast it." She glanced over at Diego. He looked upset but said nothing. "Let's get to digging."

"You don't have to," Rex said. "There are natural cavities all around this island. Gases within the lava that didn't rise and escape to the air. Sort of like trapped bubbles. Some of them barely break the surface, and then the tops erode." He turned east, raising a hand to shade his eyes. "I noticed a number of them just past the base camp," he said. "You should be able to find one of suitable size."

Ramoncito stepped through the flap, his face red from the sun and his tears. Rex walked over to him, removed his Panama hat, and set it on his head. "Ready to head back?" he asked.

Ramoncito nodded, still sniffling.

Rex signaled Diego and they headed to Diego's tent to gather the water samples.

The soldiers stood dumbly in a half-ring around the boy, waiting for the scientists' return. Ramoncito's face broke, and he started crying. Szabla and Savage turned away uncomfortably, and Tank chewed his lip. Ramoncito swayed, still light-headed from his sun exposure.

Justin stepped forward to steady the boy. After a moment, Cameron joined him.

* * *

LOADED DOWN with bags full of water samples, Diego and Rex stood at the edge of the road near the rows of balsa trees that Diego so loathed. Tank flipped Rex an extra tube of sunblock and Rex nodded his thanks.

Cameron checked the watch face sewn into the inside of her pants pocket. "It's 1500 now," she said. "That should put you back at Santa Cruz at 0700. You'll have about fourteen hours to set up your gear, run tests, and reach Fort Detrick with your results."

Justin removed his long-sleeved shirt and gave it to Ramoncito to protect him from further sun damage on the ride back. The sun was still strong, but it had softened, already beginning its arc to the horizon.

Ramoncito took it from him, gratefulness in his eyes. He probably wanted to decline the offer like a man, but the pain of his sunburn made him swallow his pride.

Justin smiled. "You'd better wait to smell the thing before you thank me. It's a touch ripe, but it'll keep the sun off you."

Cameron stood beside the two scientists, even after the other soldiers nodded their good-byes and began to convene near the tents. Rex shifted his canteen strap on his shoulder, squinting into the sun in Cameron's direction. "Guess you guys aren't so useless after all," he said. His cheeks had taken on color, just beginning to redden. He waited for Diego and Ramoncito to look away. "Thank you," he mouthed.

Cameron shrugged. "What were we gonna do? Draw straws and leave some of our squad behind?" She shook her head. "I don't think so."

"So that's it?" Diego asked. "Strictly a military decision?"

A sulfur butterfly danced a clumsy circle around Diego's head. It fluttered down, landing on his backpack, a pale yellow spot. Cameron reached over, plucking it gently off the fabric by clasping its wings between her fingers as she had

seen Diego do earlier. She took the butterfly's thin body between her thumb and finger and turned it over, blowing gently on the closed wings. They splayed under the soft
pressure of her breath, spreading open beautifully across her
hand. She swept her hand upward, releasing the butterfly,
and they watched it navigate the gentle southeast winds.
"Yes," she said. "It is."

"We'll do our best to get back and convince the government that we know more about science than they do," Rex
said. He glanced at the sweep of the dark forest. "Just two
more larvae constitute the accountable virus reservoir." He
nodded once, slowly, and they both understood the unspoken implication. Taking a small step back, he checked his
watch. "You have about nineteen hours to pickup. Are you
sure you'll be okay?"

Cameron shook her head. "No." She ruffled Ramoncito's
hair roughly and pointed down the road. "Get out of here,"
she said.

They turned and began walking down the road toward the
watchtower and the thin trail beyond. After a few paces, Ramoncito stopped and turned. Cameron was still standing
there, watching them leave.

Chapter 60   "We're gonna split duty," Szabla said,
standing before the fire pit. She jerked her chin, indicating
Cameron. "You, Justin, and Tank recon, try to beat the clock.
Make sure you sweep up along the cliff faces to the east—
no one's checked there too thoroughly yet. If you find
Derek . . ." Szabla turned her eyes from Cameron and continued. "Kill the larva he's protecting, and him if you have
to." She raised a finger at Cameron, though Cameron had not
reacted. "Don't you go all woman on me again now."

"Can you handle that?" Savage asked, eyeballing Cameron.

Cameron stood up and slapped her muscular thighs with her hands. "Of course."

After Cameron left, leading Tank and Justin into the forest, Szabla hydrated, then poured water from her canteen down her sweaty neck and back. When she turned to survey the expanse of the pasture to the east, Savage was already about fifty yards off, poking through the high grass and looking for holes.

It was fortunate there were air vesicles in the open field; searching the forest was a greater risk, since the foliage provided cover in which a mantid could hide. Plus, if one of the larvae did metamorphose, it would be better to lure it somewhere out in the open where they could keep an eye on it—after dusk, of course, so the sun wouldn't drive it away.

The heat was unforgiving, so Szabla pulled off her cammy shirt. Tossing it to the side, she headed out toward Savage in her black tank top. Savage was shirtless, his bandanna dripping—he must have doused it with water from his canteen. He was crouched, shaking his head. As she drew nearer, she realized he was laughing.

"I think I just solved the mystery of Dr. Frank Friedman," he said, pointing through the waving grass into a hole in the ground.

Szabla bent over, drawing aside the grass. The odor hit her hard and she drew back, waving an arm in front of her face. Savage laughed, a low grumble in his throat. Pulling her tank top up over her nose *bandido*-style, Szabla leaned over the hole again, looking down.

A bloated corpse lay at the bottom of the narrow twelve-foot drop, the sharply angled head indicating a broken neck. Having worked on the body for over a month, maggots, ants, and other critters had reduced the face and hands to grotesque appendages—clothes remained over the rest of the body, seemingly holding it together. A fisherman's hat lay on the ground a few feet from the head.

"All the shit going down on this island," Savage said, "and

the fucker died taking a header into a goddamn hole." He shook his head again.

It took them the better part of an hour in the baking sun to find an air vesicle appropriately sized for the trap. About ten feet deep, six wide, and twelve long, it was originally a spherical gap in the lava. Decades of erosion had worn away the top, creating sheer walls. Since the vesicle collected shade and moisture, and slowed evaporation, it contained an entirely different ecosystem: ferns flourished in shafts of light; stubby miniature trees sprouted up between the mounds of rubble.

Szabla and Savage stood facing each other across the length of the hole. Szabla's undershirt was pasted to her body and drenched through all around. She tried to spit, but it dangled from her bottom lip, a thick pasty cord. She spit again and it spun to the ground.

Base camp was about a hundred yards west, and the forest several hundred yards upslope. "This is good," Szabla said. "Nice and open. Nothing can sneak up on us here, and it's close enough to the forest that the motherfucker could see it and come if it had cover of night."

Savage nodded, his fingers rasping in his beard.

"Let's get some of that rock cleared from the base of the walls," Szabla said. "Make sure nothing can crawl out."

They headed back to base camp to retrieve shovels and some rope, steering clear of the hole in which Frank Friedman's body lay rotting.

THEY TRUDGED through the forest, Cameron hacking with the spike as if it were a machete when the foliage grew thick. Tank and Justin followed her silently.

When she heard the cooing, her legs went slack with the memory of the thing she'd beaten along the floor of the cave. She slowed down, Tank and Justin immediately halting to see what was wrong.

The sound was coming from behind a plant with thin

elongated leaves cascading to the sides. The leaves' serrated edges cut her hand as she pulled them aside, expecting to be greeted with the engaging face of another larva.

When she saw the dark-rumpled petrel's white face and black bill, her eyes welled with relief. The petrel had scraped a burrow in the soft soil and was guarding over her full nest of eggs. She squawked at Cameron indignantly, her wedge-shaped tail fluttering, and Cameron withdrew.

She stood up right into Justin, who had moved close behind her with the spike, ready to take care of the kill to spare her having to go through it again. A perversely sweet gesture. She leaned back into him just to feel his body against hers for a moment. His hands around the circle of her waist calmed her, and she winked at him before turning and cutting back into the trees.

The fact that she'd been certain of her obligation—that she had to kill the larva last night—had not made the task easier for her. She'd had to fight every instinct in her to swing the spike, to batter the thing to death.

She had not been trained to kill animals. Only other men, men with weapons and harsh accents. Combatants. Maybe she found killing the larva difficult because they were not political or malevolent, because they did not wish her harm or know how to wish at all. Or maybe it was because she was participating in the elimination of a life form—a task so vast, momentous, and irrevocable that she seemed to lose herself in the scope of its ramifications. At the very least, she found it simultaneously ironic and natural that it should give her greater pause than ending a human life.

The larvae were extraordinary, and literally unique. But the price they would exact were they to continue to exist was immense. The distorted thing Floreana had birthed refused to leave Cameron's mind even for a second; she carried it in every moment, a second, vicarious pregnancy on top of her unsettled own.

To the east, Cameron saw where a sheet of land had fallen away in the most recent earthquake, the forest ending suddenly in a cliff. She sat down on the edge, letting the spike clatter on the rocks beside her. Banging her heels against the precipice like a little girl, she kicked loose some pebbles, which spiraled down several hundred yards. She lost sight of them before she could see them splash in the water. The blood rushed into her legs in pins and needles. They'd been walking since sunrise, and the nonstop activity of the past few days was taking its toll.

The thought of the squad's rebellion filled her with shame and self-revulsion. Though she knew she'd been right in opposing Derek, she hadn't yet forgiven herself for it. The emotions playing through his face as he'd looked at them. Loss, confusion, fear tinged red with anger.

Justin sat behind her, his stomach against her back, his legs outside hers. Tank plopped down next to her and rested one of his paws on her shoulder.

"I'm gonna kick both your asses if you keep babying me like this," she said. "I'm fine, you know. Quit touching me."

Tank withdrew his hand, and Justin made to strangle her from behind, but she caught a pressure point under his elbow, and he released his grip quickly.

"Ouch!"

"Yeah, ouch. There's more where that came from, too." A breeze brought them the scents of the forest. "I'm feeling a little hopeless looking for these things," she conceded. "Needles in haystacks."

"We should head back," Justin said. "Help them with the hole."

Despite her earlier complaints, Cameron leaned back slightly into her husband.

Before them, the water stretched clear and endless to the horizon. It whispered against the base of the cliff beneath Cameron's feet, stirring in swirls of white, frothy bubbles. Fronds dipped in the breeze next to them, bowing politely.

"You're pregnant," Tank said. "Aren't you?"

Cameron sucked her bottom lip. It was salty from the air. "When did you know?"

He shrugged. "When I picked you up at your house."

They sat quietly for a few moments.

"I won't let anything happen to you," Tank said.

His voice was low and steady as ever, but something in it made Cameron bite her lip to keep back the emotion. After a moment, she reached for his hand, but Tank hesitated and looked at Justin, as though he'd been caught doing something wrong.

Justin nodded at him, as if to say, go ahead.

Tank's hand was large and warm—it enveloped hers easily. Cameron leaned between the two men, letting herself feel calm and safe, if only for a moment.

Tank pulled his hand back and the three sat again in silence. The blue-footed boobies plunge-dived to the waters and popped to the surface. American oystercatchers hopped along the rocky coast, their bright-red bills and yellow eyes standing out against the dark lava.

"In another life," Tank said, "this would be a beautiful place." He leaned back on his hands, the red skin of his scalp visible through his thin, bristling hair.

Cameron looked from the stunning view to the spike lying beside her, the end still stained with the larva's fluids.

"Yeah," she said. "It would."

Chapter 61   The sky drained quickly of color. Derek murmured and dozed in fits, the leaves soft against the side of his head. He was back outside his house The Night Of, his legs weak and fluid beneath him, knowing something was dreadfully wrong. The house had looked like a church, a demonic church.

Panic had seized his guts, gripping him like a cramp, but he'd fought it off, refusing to run, refusing to lose his head.

The front door hadn't been hot to his touch, not hot as he'd imagined it would be. It had swung open slowly, uncreaking, a coffin standing on end. He'd managed to choke out his wife's name once, and then again. When she'd answered, her voice had been light and airy, like silk afloat on wind. "In here," she'd called. Her voice had seemed to issue from the dining room.

He'd staggered through the kitchen, knocking over a chair, leaning on the countertop to gain his balance. The knife block had been on its side, a black slit where the largest blade should have been.

He'd paused just short of the doorway to the dining room before shuffling weakly forward, sucking air, his chest heaving, his face blotched crimson.

He'd seen Jacqueline standing at the head of the table like a high priestess over an altar, a ghost in the blurry movement of her nightgown. He'd seen the curtains fluffed behind her with the night breeze. He'd seen the smudge of blood across Jacqueline's cheek. He'd seen the small flaccid limb, the arch of the tiny dough-soft fingers on the lacquered rosewood, four slivers of crescent moon. He'd felt his heart beating in his temples, his hands, his eyes. He'd looked at her, transfixed, unperceiving. He'd known what she was going to say before her mouth moved, before he'd heard the words.

"No bugs," she'd murmured.

Suddenly he was yelling and shuffling backward on the forest floor on all fours, slapping at his face, swiping at the cobwebs of the memory. He slammed into a tree before realizing where he was, within a small ring of *Scalesias* in the highlands of Sangre de Dios.

His breath caught in his chest when he saw the thing woven between the two trees across from him. A pupation chamber. About five feet tall, cylindrical, and horizontally striated, the cocoon was a dull beige. A sticky substance ran up along the trunk on each side, securing the cocoon to the tree. It bulged near the center, like a body bag.

It was pulsing.

Derek tried to crawl backward, again hitting the tree trunk behind him. He stood, gazing at the cocoon in horror and amazement. His lips trembled, trying to form sounds.

The cocoon seemed to float in the shadows, framed by the dark trees stretching up around it. It looked almost holy, the circle of moss, like the apse of a cathedral. Derek felt as he had as a boy when he'd stepped forth from his confirmation, surrounded by a group of relatives. Their eyes had all been on him, and for a fleeting moment, he'd felt he must have been something holy for so many adults to be staring at him in his too-tight suit.

Derek's knees jarred the ground when he fell, bringing him back to the forest. He felt wetness on his cheeks and realized he was crying, though he wasn't sure why.

A grumbling creak came from within the cocoon.

Though the sun had already slipped beyond the horizon, the sky was still lit with its distant glow—a light shade of purple. A heap of cumulus clouds drifted, barely visible through the treetops. Derek was crying so hard the world seemed to streak before his eyes—the trees, the purple sky, the light sheen of the cocoon.

He turned to his shoulder and it took him three tries to say the name so his transmitter could read it. "Cameron," he finally sputtered. "Primary channel."

Cameron was in the vesicle when Derek's voice clicked through. Tank had been shoveling like a back-hoe, clearing out the excess rock at the bottom. They were all working now, using the light of the hastily made torches that Justin had stuck in the ground at the edges of the hole. "Yeah?" she said. "Derek? Derek?"

"Are you private? Get private."

Cameron threw her shovel aside and scrambled out of the hole, using a knotted rope they had tied to a spike up top. She was careful not to bring more rock tumbling down beneath her feet. She felt Szabla's angry eyes on her as she ran toward the camp, and she knew her secrecy probably upset Justin as well, but she owed Derek at least that. She ran until she was clear of the others, leaning over with her hands on her knees. For a moment, she thought the transmitter had cut out, but then she realized that the wavering noise was Derek sobbing. "Derek," she said. "What's up?"

Derek wiped his eyes and stared at the cocoon. It was wiggling now, and he could see something moving beneath the surface. It was creaking as it stretched.

Cameron tried to be patient, but her voice wouldn't allow it. She heard a noise in the background, like the supports of a bridge groaning. "Derek, what's going on there?"

An image moved through him—four tiny, lifeless fingers curved on lacquered rosewood. "It was my fault, Cam," he said. "I should've known it was going to happen."

"What's there, Derek? What's going on?"

"I don't know. I think . . . I think she's changing."

"Is there a cocoon?" He didn't respond, so she forged ahead. "Derek, listen to me very carefully. Find a branch, a rock, anything. You have to protect yourself. You saw that thing Savage dragged back here."

Weighted with grief and exhaustion, Derek searched the area for a suitable branch. He finally found one. It was a bit thicker than he had hoped for, but he could still get his hands around it well enough to swing it with some force.

Shoving himself up to his feet, he clutched the branch tightly, searching for rage. He stepped forward, raising the tree limb above his head, but became nauseously weak. He crouched, his head bowed as if in supplication, his shoulders heaving with sobs.

"She's just a baby, Cam," he said. "She's just a baby."

Cameron looked frantically at the forest. Somewhere in the dark patch of trees this was all taking place, and she was unable to do anything about it. "Derek, listen to me. If you don't pull your head out of your ass ASAP, we're all gonna be in a fuckload of trouble. Now toughen up! Do it!"

Derek stumbled to his feet, moving toward the cocoon. It swayed and convulsed, something pumping beneath its surface. He drew back the branch like a baseball bat, flexing his

arms and his shoulders and throwing his full force into the
swing. He struck the side of the cocoon, rocking it between
the trees. It was hard, and much denser than he'd expected.
He was just drawing back the branch again when a massive
splitting sound filled the air. A seam had opened straight
down the pupation chamber.

"It's hatching," he said. He stepped back in horror. "Jesus
God."

"Run, Derek! It's too late—we're gonna have to deal with
it later. Get the fuck out of there. Come back to base. Just
run!"

Derek fought through the weakness. Closing his eyes, he
felt anger return slowly to him, felt his soldier's instincts
quickening his heart. When he opened his eyes again, the
world was back in focus. "And leave everyone else to pay?"
he said, his voice thick with mucus and tears. He shook his
head. "Not again."

He clicked out as Cameron screamed into her transmitter.

The others ran toward her from the hole, Justin leading
the way. She was still yelling when they got there, and then
she fell silent. They stood around her expectantly. It was impossibly silent.

Derek saw a head rear through the slit and burst the shell
of the cocoon like a melon. Pieces of hardened silk clung to
the mantid's face in slimy strips as it slowly emerged. The
new head was an open maw—sawing mandibles, yawning
labrum, quivering maxillae. The face was alive with motion.

He snapped the head to one side with a swing of the
branch.

The mantid's body slowly followed the fearsome head.
First, a pair of snapping legs, then the thorax, then the orb of
the abdomen. The mantid unfolded from the white pupation
chamber like a phoenix rising. Her head lifted on a high,
towering neck, a ring of crusted silk clinging to her throat
like a gory necklace. She rose unsurely on her legs, then
shook herself like a wet dog, freeing her limbs from the
slime and drawing out her mass.

It seemed inconceivable that the larva could have metamorphosed into such a large and terrible thing. The mantid was expanding still, like a chick fluffing itself out after hatching. Derek darted forward and struck its back with a solid blow, but the wing didn't crumple. He aimed for the thin neck and swung, but the mantid reared up and he hit only her armored thorax. He ran quickly out of range before she could focus on him.

Her raptorial legs practiced a few quick snatches at the air, jackknifing shut like a steel trap. She approached him, leaving the husk of her cocoon clinging to the trees.

When her front legs lowered, Derek lunged forward, hammering her head with a flurry of blows. The attack seemed to confuse her, and it kept her from striking. Sometimes hitting the head, sometimes the thorax, he continued his assault as the mantid adjusted to her new body and the onslaught. Finally, she raised a front leg, blocking a blow, and the branch snapped. Derek hurled the remaining piece at her, his arms aching.

She reared up, towering over him, rank and fetid. He stared up into the black pools of her eyes. Her mandibles spread slightly as her raptorial legs drew back. In the brief stillness before the strike, Derek drove himself up at the mantid, a whirlwind of fists and elbows.

The soldiers stood around Cameron on the dark grass, the distant torches at the hole flicking above the shadowy outlines of their faces like infernal halos. Cameron was shuddering all over, though it wasn't more than cool, and she crossed her arms against her chest to keep them from trembling. She opened her mouth to speak, but her jaw was shaking, so she closed it.

They stood in silent rank, waiting for something, though no one knew what.

Echoing from the darkest folds of the forest came a petrifying scream. It circled them once, twice, then departed, leaving only the wind whispering against the grass.

Chapter 62   Samantha couldn't remember the last time she'd slept. Despite the continuing activity at the makeshift work station outside the slammer, she dozed off, forehead pressed to the window. Donald came over, amused, and tapped lightly on the glass. She awoke with a start. "I didn't do it," she said.

He smiled, cuffing his sleeves. "I feel we conveyed the environmental and medical complications quite admirably to your superiors."

"First time I've offered expert testimony through a window."

"I'm relieved Rex and Diego made it off the island." Donald crumpled his shirt in a fist and released it, admiring the new folds and wrinkles. "I hope the others will be all right." He brought his lips together, his white beard bristling. "A courageous bunch."

"I like that Cameron," Samantha said. "Smart and tough. That's how I want to be when I grow up." She heard the clicking footsteps that announced Colonel Douglas Strickland's approach, and when she looked, she was shocked to see Secretary of the Navy Andrew Benneton at his side. On his way from a Senate subcommittee meeting, Benneton wore a sharp, well-tailored suit. Donald stood nervously, fingering the back of his chair.

The men shook hands, and Benneton nodded to Samantha through the glass.

"I'm glad to hear Rex is safe," Benneton said. "We're going to be able to get the rest of the squad off the island in a little more than twenty-four hours."

"How about the air strike?" Donald asked. "Is it called off?"

Benneton shook his head sadly. "I'm sorry, Donald, but

the team here feels that the risk of the Darwin virus's spreading is unacceptable."

Samantha banged her head gently against the glass. " 'The team here.' I trained half the goddamn 'team here.' "

"As soon as the squad extraction is complete, we're going to send in a B1 from Baltra. Neutron bomb," Strickland said. His tone was smug, almost proud. He removed his beret, pressing it to his side with his left elbow. "We received UN approval this morning."

"That's a surprise," Samantha muttered.

His legs shaking, Donald eased himself down into his chair. "A neutron bomb. That'll kill all the terrestrial island life. Boil the surrounding waters and send out a shock wave. Everything within miles . . . dead."

Strickland ran his tongue neatly across his lips. "That is the point, Doctor."

Benneton looked away, annoyed with Strickland's tone. Samantha sensed that there was no love lost between the two.

"Andrew," Donald said. "If I could inform you that the known virus reservoir was exterminated, and the island's water system was no longer infected, would you be willing to hold back the air strike?"

"Can you inform me of that?"

"No," Donald said. "Not yet. But Rex and the Acting Director of the Darwin Station, Dr. Diego Rodriguez, are heading to the Station to test water samples as we speak, and it is my understanding that the soldiers are hunting down the remaining carriers."

Strickland shook his head. "I don't think that's sufficient grounds to—"

"Dr. Everett," Benneton said, cutting Strickland off. "Do you think we will have reached a plane of reasonable security if these criteria are met?"

"Yes," Samantha said. "Of course, we never know when this virus could resurface, but if Sangre de Dios's water system is uncontaminated and the accountable virus reservoir exterminated, that provides us with as much guarantee as we're ever going to get." She glared at Strickland. "Certainly as much as a bombing will give you."

Benneton mulled this over. "Given our current lack of manpower, how can we monitor the island for a future reemergence?"

"A lot easier than if it's been irradiated," Samantha said.

Donald made a calming gesture. "Dr. Rodriguez has offered to monitor the ecological activity there on a regular basis, as well as keep an eye on the unicellular phytoplankton in surrounding waters. We can also take steps to quarantine the island."

Benneton pursed his lips, as though lost in an internal debate. "If you can give me those assurances," he finally announced, "then I will call off the strike."

Strickland inhaled sharply, his nostrils flaring. "I'm not sure—"

"*If* and only *if* those conditions are met," Benneton said. He ticked them off on his fingers. "The water system clean, the accountable virus reservoir exterminated, and continued supervision of the island. I'm sorry, Donald, but that's the most slack I can free up."

"Can't you delay the bombing?" Donald asked.

Strickland snickered. "Oh sure. I'll just ask the Air Force to permit the Chairman of the Joint Chiefs of Staff to proceed to the Caracas summit without flight escort. Maybe pull air support from the three battalions we're shifting down the coast to Guayaquil." His usual grimace returned. "Given our limited resources, we need to find the most efficient means of neutralizing the situation."

"I don't think you comprehend the gravity of what's happening on that island."

"Oh, I certainly do, Doctor. Make no mistake about it—I'm aware we have a big-league problem on our hands. That's why we're going to deal with it in big-league fashion. We're juggling a constellation of logistics to get those planes to Baltra on the thirty-first for the 2200 extraction and 2300 bombing."

Strickland glanced at his watch. The digits blinked red and steady: 1903, 30 DEC 07. "You have twenty-six hours and fifty-seven minutes. I suggest you urge your colleagues to use them well." He placed his beret atop his head and adjusted it with a sweep of his index finger. "Good day."

He snapped a crisp salute to Benneton and headed up the hall.

Chapter 63   Szabla pushed an electric blasting cap into a block of TNT, then taped the block to two others, creating one large brick. Since the Clacker detonator was generally used for Claymores, manufactured C4 charges with molded-in shrapnel, Szabla had to jerry-rig it. She spooled off a good length of wire running from the Clacker, spliced it, stripped the insulation, then performed a western union splice with the two wires of the blasting cap to ensure a good connection.

She held the Clacker in her hand, turning it over. It was about the size of a fist. Once she "clacked" it by clicking the ends together, the charge would run down the wire to the blasting cap, which would initiate the block in which it was ensconced, sympathetically detonating the remaining two blocks.

"Good to go, baby," she said. "We'll just veil it like a trap, and when that thing falls through, we'll green haze the motherfucker. Walls should collapse right in." She glanced down the length of the hole, assessing its span. "We're gonna need to veg up the top—we should use dead branches because they'll give easier. Savage estimated the last fucker at two, three hundred pounds." She turned to the others. "Go get some branches and leaves and shit. At least six branches."

She crouched, lowering the torch to afford Tank more

light. He was removing the last of the rock from the far corner. Grunting, he heaved another shovelful up onto the grass.

"Um, maybe I'm a little slow here, but don't we have to go into the forest to get 'branches and leaves and shit'?" Justin asked.

"Uh huh. At least dead, brittle ones," Szabla said. "Over there, Tank," she added, turning back to the hole and pointing to a mound of rock in the far corner.

"And isn't there an enormous people-devouring creature in the forest?"

"Uh-huh."

Justin looked from Szabla to Savage and Cameron, then back to Szabla again. "If *a* equals *b*, and *b* equals *c* . . ."

"If we don't get this covered before it starts raining," Szabla said, "we can forget it." As if to punctuate her point, thunder rumbled across the sky. She could've sworn she felt the ground vibrate beneath her feet.

"But visibility's for dick right now," Justin said. "Maybe we should wait."

"We're trying to kill the thing, Kates, not build it a fucking swimming pool," Savage growled. He glanced over at Cameron. "Let's go."

Justin picked up an elbow light, and Cameron looked over at him, hands on her hips. "It'll be drawn to artificial light," she said. "Leave it."

She and Savage headed for the road, and Justin reluctantly set down the light and followed. The balsas towered in lines on either side. Cameron searched the bases of the balsas for dead branches, but Szabla was right—to find the longer branches and foliage they needed, they'd have to press into the forest itself. There hadn't been many fallen branches in the transition zone to begin with, and they'd used what they had found earlier for the fire.

The sky opened with a gentle rain. Cameron's sleeves began chafing around her arms with the moisture. Justin pulled off his shirt and tied it around his waist. The rain made its way down through the ridges of his stomach, and the muscles of his arm shifted as he swung the spike by his side. Cameron paused for a moment to admire him before ducking through the foliage.

The rain pattering atop the canopy made it sound as if they were inside a drum. They gathered wide fronds and long branches, moving quickly, their eyes darting nervously about. Each time Cameron reached out to snap a frond off a plant, she half expected to see the creature's face hiding behind it, jaws spread and thrusting. Sick as it sounded, she hoped the creature had gorged itself on Derek and was now resting.

The air smelled of decomposing leaves in the mud, dust trapped beneath the canopy overhead, and the swirls of insects buzzing around the trunks. The ferns whispered against one another. A large rat scurried unseen along the forest floor.

The moonlight was surprisingly strong, even through the trees and rain. Though Cameron had to squint as she searched the ground, she could make out the twisted outlines of fallen branches from a distance.

She stealthily approached a branch lying between two trees. She circled it, checking the area for any sign of the creature, then grabbed it, backing up and pulling it behind her until she felt the dirt of the road beneath her boots. Justin was waiting, a mound of foliage at his feet. Savage emerged a moment later, arms laden with leaves and branches. The rain had momentarily ceased.

"You two look like trees in a school play," Justin smirked. He shoved his spike through his belt, then picked up an armful of fern fronds, pressing them to his chest so that he could use his other hand to drag the branches.

Cameron eyed the length of the road. Aside from the trees along the sides, there wasn't much cover in which the creature could be lurking. They walked slowly, dragging the branches behind them in the dirt. To their right, they could see Frank's specimen freezer standing out in the field, a silver block. When they were about halfway to the watchtower, they cut left through the line of trees into the field and trudged past camp toward the others.

Cameron adjusted the branches in her arms as they arrived at the hole. Szabla took one look at the collection of branches and shook her head. "That one's not gonna be long enough," she said, pointing. "We'll need one more."

"Not long enough my ass," Justin said. "It's long enough."

Szabla walked over and hoisted the thick branch. She stared at Justin, holding the branch horizontally over the hole, her muscles flexed. "Grab the other end, Kates."

From the opposite side, Justin took the branch and lowered it to the lip of the hole. With painstaking care, Szabla set her end of the branch down, where it just missed the last inch of ground. She threw the branch aside.

"Fuck it," she said. "Maybe we'll only need five."

She jumped down into the hole and laid the block of TNT on the ground, dead center. The wire ran up and out of the hole to the Clacker, which lay in the grass about five feet from the edge of the hole. Using the knotted rope, she climbed out.

Savage notched the remaining five branches deeply in the middle to ensure their breaking under the mantid's weight, then they laid them across the hole and smoothed wide fronds on top of them. One end of the hole remained exposed, showing the blackness beneath.

"We're gonna need one more branch," Savage said.

Tank patted Cameron on the shoulder, angling his head toward the forest.

"All right," Cameron said. "We'll be right back."

"I'll go instead," Justin said.

"No, it's fine. We got it."

Justin started to protest, but she raised an eyebrow to silence him. Tank leaned over and plucked the freezer bolt off the ground. It was at least a thirty-pound bar, but he carried it like a Wiffle-ball bat, tapping one end casually against his palm.

They walked in silence to the edge of the field. Cameron

scanned the forest, hoping to see the end of a fallen branch peeking out from beneath the leaves, but there was nothing. Except for mounds of leaves, scattered twigs, and the husks of a few rotting oranges, the ground was bare. The forest receded into blackness between the tree trunks. The noises of living things echoed from the void.

There was never silence in the forest, Cameron had learned. Birds cackling, rain pattering, rats scampering, but never silence. Even the air seemed to be alive, seemed to move and feel and whisper all around them.

"We're gonna have to go farther in," she said. "I don't see any here."

Tank raised the bolt from his shoulder, gripping it by the knob like a nightstick. The spike Cameron held against her thigh seemed delicate in comparison.

She started into the darkness, Tank following closely behind.

The mist turned slowly to rain again; they heard it first in the treetops. Drops danced along the leaves, bending them under their weight until they dipped at the stems, spilling. The rivulets darted through openings, drizzling down in streams around them.

"Gimme a six-pace lead," Cameron whispered loudly. She had to raise her voice; the sound of the rain was amplified beneath the canopy.

The strength of the downpour increased until it sounded as if they were under fire. Despite his size, Tank was incredibly graceful, moving through the undergrowth with the agility of a deer. Cameron had to turn and make sure he was following. Were he Derek, she would have known exactly where he was at all times. She wouldn't have had to check his location, wouldn't have had to point to direct him. Tank was excellent, but Derek had been the best. Derek had been like a part of her.

Floreana's deformed baby clawed its way back into her thoughts and she drew her head back slightly at the image. She noticed her fingers trembling and she balled her hand into a fist, clenching it until her fingernails dug painfully into her palm. When she opened her hand, her fingers were still trembling, so she slapped herself once across the face, hard. Tank saw her halt, heard the ring of the slap, and waited unquestioningly for her to move again.

She inched forward, fighting desperately to clear her mind. There would be time to mourn, she hoped, for Derek and for other things lost. Now was not the time to go limp with grief or weak with horror. Cameron was trained precisely not to mourn or pity, not to cower at times when she most should. She had already let it in, the softness of her emotions. And now, as she stalked through the forest, bending aside fronds with her arms, chest, and face, she swore it would not happen again.

As she moved, she overturned heaps of leaves with her boot to see if they hid any lengthy branches from sight. They needed just one branch: one more branch and the trap would be ready.

A flash of lightning illuminated a small clearing ahead, and she saw a bough sprawled across the fecund ground like a knotted snake. Thickly gnarled, bowed up toward the middle, and seared by lightning at one end, it lay amongst a scattering of bark peels.

Cameron raised her hand, snapped her fingers once, and pointed. Tank swung wide, holding back to keep surveillance behind them. Out of habit, she winced as she stepped into the clearing. Years of ops had made her accustomed to sniper fire; she hated moving from cover, no matter the circumstance.

She leaned back to survey the treetops, envisioning the creature swaying upside down from the branches overhead. The trunks rose up into darkness, shadowy and dripping with ants, but free of danger.

She felt her shoulders relax as she moved farther into the clearing. She circled the branch once, her eyes picking through the trees around her, then backed up until she felt it against her heel. She stepped back so the branch was between her feet and glanced down at it quickly. With relief, she noted that it was long enough to stretch across the hole. Keeping her eyes on the forest, she crouched to grab the branch.

As if on cue, the rain stopped the instant her hand touched the bark. It didn't taper off; it ceased at once and completely. Cameron could suddenly hear how hard she'd been breathing. She started when water splashed on her shoulder.

Her fingertips rested on the bark of the branch. With the cessation of rain, the forest seemed unnaturally quiet. She felt that the silence should have enabled some clarity of thought, but it did not. Something chirped near her, in the leaves.

She was paralyzed in her crouch. The trees surrounded her in their various sizes, some towering up through the canopy, some just beginning to spread their branches, others thin and bare like telephone poles.

With increasing conviction, she sensed that something was wrong, though what it was she could not figure out. Her breath coming in short quiet gasps, she stared at the trees around her, the dense foliage curling from the soil, even the branch beneath her fingertips, but everything seemed in order. When she rose to stand, both her knees cracked loudly at the same time.

She looked for Tank and he flashed her a dour thumbs-up when he read her expression. Things were clear behind them.

She stepped toward the far end of the clearing, wielding the spike like a saber. She stopped at the edge, resting an arm against the nearest tree trunk. The bark felt smooth against her sleeve. Her eyes tried to pierce the darkness beyond, but she couldn't make anything out. Her knees tensed as she waited for something to fly out at her.

Nervous about leaving the darkness unattended, she risked another quick glance back at Tank. He was holding firm, scanning the terrain behind them. The glint of the steel bolt in his hand calmed her a bit, but her confidence wavered when she turned back to the forest. It was breathing, the forest. It was alive—near her, on top of her, all around her. It was watching her.

She choked down the fear rising in her throat, setting her bottom jaw forward and clamping down on her upper lip. The pain brought her back from the edge. She sucked air deeply, drawing it into the far corners of her chest, and exhaled through her nose. She was fine. There was nothing out there.

Leaning back on her heels, she shoved off from the tree. Above her, the tree moved. A head swiveled around on an impossibly elongated neck. It looked at her, eyes as wide as globes, mouth a quivering mess of blades and parts.

Cameron yelled, stumbling back.

Slowly, deliberately, the mantid pivoted, her upper body leading her abdomen. Her front legs had been resting on the tree trunk next to her, holding her body almost perfectly upright on her rear legs. The mantid's abdomen resolved into view, the wings folded along her back but not protruding past the tip of the abdomen. Cameron noted the wing length, even through her terror, and realized that it was a female. Even worse.

From behind, the mantid had blended in perfectly with the trees, the hard brown-and-green-speckled cuticle passing for a trunk in the night. Cameron had rested her forearm right across the folded wings of the mantid's back. The mantid hadn't struck only because she'd been facing away, and would surely have been detected in turning around.

Backpedaling, Cameron held the spike before her, her face drained of color. The mantid lumbered forward on her four hind legs, cocking her head, her large, unblinking eyes gathering Cameron into them. The spikes lining the raptorial legs glistened, still moist with rainwater, and the mantid snapped them once.

Cameron could not remember ever having been awed into

silence, frightened beyond words, and yet, as she gazed at the creature stretched nearly nine feet in the air before her, its abdomen thicker than an oil drum, its slender weaponed legs, she was speechless. Her mouth worked open and closed, trying to call out to Tank, or scream, or both, but nothing came.

The mantid lunged forward, feigning a strike, and Cameron raised the spike protectively across her face as she stumbled back. Her heel caught on the fallen branch and she went down hard on her back, the spike rolling off through the leaves. With a cry, she sat up, digging her hands behind her so that she could shove herself to her feet, but it was too late. She felt the shadow blocking out the moonlight even before she saw the creature looming over her.

The mantid readied herself for the strike, her arms coiled against her chest. The mouth gnashed air, and Cameron closed her eyes, thinking that the sound of wet lapping would be the last she ever heard.

Suddenly, she felt the mouth tighten around the back of her neck like a vise and she screamed, but when she opened her eyes, she was flying backward, gripped around her neck by one of Tank's meaty hands. As he yanked Cameron back, Tank swung the steel bolt with his other hand. The mantid reared up to dodge the bolt, which cut harmlessly through the empty space.

Tank backed up, dragging Cameron by the neck as her feet fumbled to find the ground beneath her.

The pain was excruciating; it felt as though Tank's fingers had penetrated right through her flesh. His thumb crunched a nerve and she screamed, but her feet still couldn't get under her as he pulled her backward. With a quick jerk, Tank flung Cameron behind him. Her whole body took flight, the pain ringing through her neck like nothing she'd ever felt, and she hit the ground on all fours, her momentum carrying her sideways into a roll.

Tank stepped forward, wielding the bolt. Like a boxer, the mantid jabbed at him, her legs flashing out so quickly he couldn't see them. The smooth back of her spiked tibia struck Tank's arm just beneath the elbow. The bolt shot within inches of his cheek, flying end over end into the forest. If the muscles sheathing Tank's arm hadn't been so substantial, the bone would have gone to pieces. The first dull wave of pain swept through his forearm and he grimaced, keeping his eyes on the mantid.

He had lost his opportunity to turn and run. Cameron rustled to her feet behind him, too far away to help. The mantid drew herself up, her arms recoiling. She stood directly over the gnarled branch.

Tank fell to his knees and lunged at the mantid's legs. Seizing the end of the branch with his good arm, he yanked with all his might, pulling two of the mantid's legs out from under her. She swayed to the side, her raptorial legs flailing to help her regain her balance.

Tank rolled to his feet and sprinted for Cameron. She stood on unsteady legs, and he grabbed her by the arm and threw her in front of him, pushing her as he ran. She prayed she wouldn't trip.

Behind them, the mantid started forward, moving with surprising speed.

Cameron felt the mantid gaining on them as they crashed through the forest, but she soon caught up to the speed at which Tank was propelling her and really started to sprint. Quickly, she was paces out ahead of him, and he opened up a bit more, and then they were pulling away, slowly but surely, from the gnashing mouth she swore she could feel behind them.

Cameron reached the field ahead of Tank and waited for him a few paces from the forest's edge. She realized it was raining again when she felt the water washing across her face. Tank was gasping when he burst into view and he staggered a bit, doubling over.

For a blissful moment, it was silent behind Tank, and then Cameron heard the mantid again, crashing through the foliage.

Cameron ran back to Tank and looped her arm around his lower back, propelling him forward. "Move, Tank, you gotta move!" she screamed.

Panic swept through her when she heard the movement among the leaves grow louder. They started to run again, their boots sinking in the grass, slowing them. With the mantid a few hundred feet behind them, they headed for the two torches lighting the hole ahead.

Chapter 64   Szabla had just laid the last of the fronds across the branches when she heard the yelling. Savage and Justin squared off with the darkness, waiting to see what would emerge. Gripping the knife handle firmly, Savage angled the Death Wind down his forearm with the sharp edge out, ready for punching or stabbing. The back of the blade pushed against his skin.

"The hole. Get the fucking hole ready!" came screaming at them through the darkness.

Savage almost instinctively swung his knife at Cameron and Tank as they dashed into the small ring of light.

"She's behind us," Cameron panted. "She's coming. Is the hole ready?"

"No, not yet," Szabla said. "We need that last branch to cover the end." She pointed to the dark strip at the edge of the hole. One on either side, the two torches still burned strong.

"We're gonna have to do without. Get behind the hole. *Now!* Behind it. Explosives ready?" Cameron spoke rapidly, frantically.

Szabla picked up the Clacker and tossed it to Savage. He stood a few paces off the lip of the vesicle, holding the unit, the wire trailing along the ground before disappearing through the covering leaves. He held it in both hands, fingers laced across the hinged end.

Behind them, the darkness was silent, save the raindrops pattering gently on the grass. Trees creaked and swayed in the breeze. About a hundred yards away, the edge of one of the GP tents flapped in the wind.

Szabla, Tank, and Cameron stood to the east of the hole. Savage waited facing the forest, toying with the Clacker.

"We can't all line up like this," Cameron said. "We'll scare it off."

"And that's a bad thing?" Justin asked.

"We don't have time, Justin," Szabla scowled. "In case you forgot, there's still another larva out there. We fuck around, we're gonna have two of these things on our hands."

Szabla stared at the rest of the squad. Cameron and Tank were still panting from their run. Szabla and Savage made the strongest team right now, so they'd have to handle it. She turned to Tank, Justin, and Cameron. "You three. Split." She pointed downslope. "Me and Savage'll lure this thing into the hole. Once you hear the blast, come running."

The shed atop the watchtower howled with the wind and they all jerked, but still nothing appeared.

"Go, Cam. That's an order." Szabla looked at them anxiously. "Now!"

Tank and Justin turned and ran into the darkness. Cameron took a few halting steps backward, her eyes on Szabla.

"*Go!*" Szabla yelled.

With a grimace, Cameron sprinted off after Tank and Justin. Szabla and Savage watched her figure fade into the night, Savage weighing the Clacker in his hand.

"How do you know it won't go after them?" Savage asked. He ran his fingers over the cut on his forearm. It had already scabbed over.

"It'll be drawn to the light," Szabla said.

"Aren't we all?" he responded dryly.

A thunderous noise nearly startled Szabla off her feet. When she looked up, Tank and Rex's GP tent floated up on the wind in the distance, trailing guy lines and strainers under it like kite tails. Something had ripped the entire thing out of the ground, sending it airborne with a single strike.

Szabla could just barely see the other tents in the moonlight, large, dark blocks quivering in the wind like slumbering elephants.

The loose canvas edge no longer flapped. Szabla looked at the tent rolling on the wind across the field and realized that the mantid had thought it was alive.

She glanced at the darkness all around, her heart hammering, her chest rising and falling visibly beneath her black tank top. The shirt was tight to her body with the rain. She thought she heard a rustling sound behind her and she whirled, almost losing her balance, but there was nothing there.

She and Savage backed around the hole. The torches only illuminated a fifteen-foot circle. They looked until they felt their eyes straining but could detect no movement.

There was a screech to their left and a flash of green, and then one of the torches was lying on its side in the grass. The flame quieted to a small yellow flare, then an orange glow, and then it was gone.

"Fuck," Szabla said. "Fuck me."

Their eyes trained on the spot where they'd seen the blur of the mantid, Savage and Szabla walked slowly back around the hole to stand nearer to the remaining torch. Szabla's chest was hammering up and down.

"Calm down, Szabla," Savage growled. "Enjoy this."

"Come on, you fucker," Szabla said to the blackness. "Come on."

Something swished through the grass. Savage stared down the length of the hole, straining to make out what he could on the far side. He undid the Clacker's safety veil, thumbing the small piece of metal aside, freeing the two ends of the detonator so that they could meet. Szabla held her ground, though her legs were shaking.

An enormous triangular head moved slowly into view, floating about nine feet off the ground. It cocked to the right, regarding Szabla intelligently. She stared into the quivering preoral cavity, the hole surrounded with grotesque living tools, and stifled a scream.

With elegance, the mantid pulled herself into the circle of light. Szabla grimaced when she saw the full length of the body, the six legs ending with hooked claws, the sheen of the cuticle.

The mantid moved forward to the edge of the hole and halted, fixing them with a predator's stare. Her eyes were large orbs, so dark they were shiny. Between them, her ocelli glittered like marbles.

Facing her across the length of the vesicle, Szabla murmured something beneath her breath, repeating it over and over like a mantra.

The mantid ran a tibia up and across her face, her antennae bristling. Her head rotated smoothly on her slender neck as she focused on Szabla again. She glanced down at the branches covering the hole, then tested one with her lead foot.

"Come on, you motherfucker," Szabla hissed. "Move forward now."

The mantid withdrew her foot and started to circle the hole rather than cross it.

Savage cursed, saliva flying from his mouth. Szabla tested one of the branches with her foot, then put more of her weight on it. She stepped out over the hole, wobbling on her feet to keep her balance. The branches bowed under her weight, stretched nearly to breaking point along the notches Savage had carved with his knife.

The mantid froze, watching Szabla with ravenous curiosity.

"What the fuck are you doing?" Savage growled.

"Live bait."

"What if you don't get off in time?"

"Dead bait."

Escaping air hissed from the mantid's spiracles, nearly scaring Szabla off her feet and into the hole, but she recovered her balance just in time.

"Keep calm," Savage growled. "Keep your movements smooth and slow."

One of the branches started to roll beneath Szabla's foot but she stayed with it, easing her weight down to nestle it back into place.

"Keep it together, Szabla," Savage said, "and get her up onto the trap."

Szabla waved her hands and the mantid darted forward a few steps, thrusting her head forward like a punch. Emitting a half-cry, Szabla stumbled back, almost falling between the branches. The mantid reared up, her front legs spread wide, revealing the eye markings on their insides. The upper part of her abdomen scraped against her underwings, screeching. Szabla swayed on her feet.

"Calm the hell down!" Savage yelled. "She's fucking with you, testing how you move. If you go into that hole, you're finished."

"Come on!" Szabla screamed. She threw her arms wide. "Come get me!" She crouched down, snapped a twig off the branch beneath her feet, and hurled it at the mantid. The twig struck the mantid between her front legs, and she reared up again, spreading her underwings. Her wingspan nearly filled Szabla's field of vision.

Szabla wondered whether Cameron, Justin, and Tank were watching right now, somewhere in the darkness. She stepped back, stammering something to herself, and Savage tried to even her out with his voice. "It's all right. Doesn't matter how big she is if we get her in the hole. Just get her to come forward."

Her raptorial legs raised hungrily, the mantid stepped onto one of the branches veiling the hole. It creaked under her weight. She pulled another leg up, easing forward toward Szabla.

Szabla turned and looked frantically behind her, gauging how far she'd have to jump when the branches started to give. She was standing on the second-to-last branch from the end, the uncovered strip of the hole looming ominously between her and solid ground.

As she glanced back, the mantid stepped forward with one of her back legs, finding and hooking the branch expertly. Her last leg trailed it, and then the mantid was standing with her full weight on the creaking and groaning branches, facing Szabla, her razor jaws mere feet away. Her front legs weren't yet coiled to strike.

"It's gonna give!" Savage said. "Get off!"

"Not yet," Szabla whispered. "Not yet."

The mantid folded her raptorial legs to her chest, pulling them up and readying them to explode. The rows of spikes meshed perfectly, like cogs in a gear. She took another step forward, directly above the explosives. With a strangely peaceful expression, she started to sway.

One of the branches cracked, and the mantid sank a few inches, but it didn't give.

"It's perfect!" Savage yelled. "Get the fuck off before it goes!"

Szabla turned to jump, but the last branch rolled under her boot, and in a moment of terror, she felt herself go weightless. Her hands flew up over her head as she fell, and she saw Savage's bearded face in a blur as she dropped into the hole.

She hit the ground hard on her back, breaking one of her elbows and sending pain throbbing through her shoulders and tailbone. She bit back a cry, determined not to make a sound. The earth smelled of clay and rot. It was astoundingly dark, but she could see glimpses of the torch's light between the crisscross pattern of leaves and branches above her, narrow slivers of gold that fell across her arms and face like cuts. The red tissue wrapping of the TNT was visible a few feet away. A broken fern tickled her cheek.

In the middle of the network of branches was an immense dark blot, the underbelly of the creature. The branches started to bow beneath her weight and then one of them cracked, held barely together by bark and pulp. Dirt was pouring in on Szabla from the sides, the ends of the branches digging jagged paths down the loose rock of the walls, and then the veil gave.

With an enormous crash, the branches split, and Szabla rolled flat against the far wall of the hole with the open air above. An explosion of bark, leaves, and dirt filled the air, refusing to settle even after the branches hit earth.

Szabla slumped against the far corner of the hole, her head bent achingly forward. With panicked hands, she wiped the dirt from her eyes and saw the mantid looming over her. The mantid had landed squarely in the vesicle on her four back legs; even so, her head was near the earth's surface. Only Savage's soldier's code stood between Szabla and death; she knew he'd never leave another soldier down.

Savage stepped to the edge of the hole, the Clacker tight in his hand. If he engaged the detonator, the blast would surely kill Szabla as well as the mantid.

In the back of her mind, Szabla could hear Savage screaming for Cameron and Tank, but she knew it wouldn't matter. She knew it was too late.

She saw a flash overhead and Savage was airborne at the thing in a dive, his body a spear ending with the tip of his blade. The mantid turned and batted him like a fly with one armored leg, striking him with the backside of her tibia. A bloody crack opened in his forehead as he flew to the wall, striking it upside down and sliding into a mound of fronds and broken branches. Unconscious, he tumbled forward, one leg sliding over the blocks of TNT.

The mantid whirled back to Szabla, her antennae erect like two reeds. She swayed once, her mouth a hole ringed with moist, sharp pieces. The legs snapped Szabla up before she had time to close her eyes, the spikes skewering her from both sides. Szabla screamed as the points tore through her ribcage, and then the mantid curled her up to her mouth and Szabla saw the cutting jaws lower out of view behind her head. She screamed again, thinking, God, oh God, what an awful way to die.

The pale faces of Cameron and Justin appeared above, and then Tank's, but she was already flailing and screaming in its grip.

The smell of the creature pungent all around her, Szabla felt the piercing jaws go to work on the back of her neck, the sharp pain of her skin being pierced like a roast. She screamed as blood spurted out on both sides of the thing gnawing on her, as the viselike jaw ripped through her bone and gristle, and then she was hanging limply in the mantid's arms as she turned her like a pig on a spit, sucking and chewing and grinding.

Szabla's arms and legs weren't obeying anymore and there was one moment of perfect silent terror as she felt, deep within her head, the vibration of the mandibles scraping the bone of her skull before she went out.

Tank picked up the Clacker where Savage had cast it aside before his dive, and stared at the hole helplessly. The explosives were nestled right beneath one of Savage's legs.

Justin was screaming and trying to jump into the hole on the mantid's back, but Cameron had her arms locked around his waist. He broke her grip and she slid to his legs, tripping him, clinging to an ankle and holding him back.

Justin was screaming and crying, the spike tight in his fist. "Lemme go! She's my fucking partner!"

"She's gone already," Cameron yelled. "Use your head! She's finished."

Justin kicked free and stood, but Tank collared him with one massive hand and pulled him back tight against his chest, wrapping his arms around him in a bear hug until his struggles lessened.

Szabla continued to twitch. The mantid's mandibles

worked on her head until she was a faceless bloody pulp above the shoulders.

Cameron lay on her stomach, her arms still outstretched from her attempt to hold back her husband. As she watched, she made no effort to rise.

The mantid paused from her nibbling to glance over at them curiously. She dumped Szabla's body on the ground where it convulsed twice, then she lumbered toward the north wall of the hole.

Cameron was up on her feet instantly. "Move out. Head for Frank's old camp!" she screamed.

"What about Savage?" Justin yelled.

"We can't do anything now!"

"We can't just leave him," Justin protested, running after Cameron and Tank. "We can't just leave him." He pulled to a stop.

Behind him, the mantid had already worked her way up the wall, her head drawing into view.

"We don't have a choice," Cameron said. "We don't have a fucking choice." Over his shoulder, she saw the mantid rising.

Justin started to say something, but Cameron shushed him, laying her fingers across his mouth. "We *don't* have a choice," she said again.

Justin looked behind him once, then followed Cameron into the darkness.

The mantid stared after them for a moment, then turned and headed back into the hole, regarding Szabla's body. Her bowels were spilled through her stomach next to her, the ground rank with blood and feces. One of her arms was twitching, the fingers scratching shallow grooves in the dirt.

The mantid moved past her to where Savage lay unconscious. Dipping her neck, she lowered her head until it was inches from his closed eyes. Blood glistened along his hairline.

She breathed his scent, waiting for a movement of any size.

Chapter 65   "What in the fuck are we gonna do?"
Justin said as they stumbled into Frank's camp. "Jesus fucking fuck what the fuck are we—"

Cameron grabbed him hard around the head, her thumbs
pressed firmly into his cheeks. She pulled his head down so
his eyes were level with hers. "Calm, baby. Calm down.
Look at me." Justin's swearing fell into mumbling. His head
relaxed in her hands and his lips stopped moving.

Cameron leaned back against the aluminum specimen
freezer, feeling its coldness through her shirt. Pressing her
hand tightly to her forehead, she tried to ease the throbbing
in her head. Every time she tried to focus, an arrow of searing pain shot up from the base of her neck, disrupting her
thoughts. She tapped the freezer door behind her with her
knuckles, her stomach roiling. The sight of Szabla was the
worst thing she'd ever seen. Thrashing around like that, still
alive—alive to the very end. She shook off a shudder.

"Jesus Christ," Justin said. "Did you see Szabla?" Panic
hid under his voice, waiting to erupt.

Cameron nodded solemnly, the image of Szabla's partially gnawed head still in her mind. She stepped into one of
Frank's tents and started digging through the abandoned
supplies to see if there was anything of use. There wasn't.

"We gotta get our hands on the explosives again," she
called from the tent. "In the meantime, we have specimen
hooks from the freezer, we have the spikes, we have canvas,
four flares left—shit, just three, Derek had one—we have
rope."

Cameron emerged from the tent, holding a battered underwater flashlight. She paused, chewing her lip. Tank and
Justin watched her intently.

"If we just had some kind of a projectile." She bolted forward, snapping her fingers. "The speargun from Diego's boat. Rex knocked it overboard—it's down in the water still."

Justin nodded tentatively. "If the currents didn't take it."

"Can you find it? Do you think you could find it in the night?"

"It'd be easier in the morning," Justin said.

Cameron tore a solar cell from Tank's shoulder and snapped it into the underwater flashlight. "We might not have till morning."

She clicked the switch on the flashlight and tapped it near the lens with her palm. A dim light flickered once, then stayed on. She handed the flashlight to Justin.

"Where are you going?" he asked.

Cameron jerked her head toward the vesicle. "Back for Savage."

"All right. I'll establish contact via transmitter as soon as I hit shore." He turned to go, but she caught him by the shoulder and spun him around. "What?" he asked gently.

"I don't . . . I don't know." She felt pressure along the bridge of her nose, tears pushing to get out, though she didn't know why. "Don't fuck up and let anything happen to you," she said.

His face softly lit in the moonlight, he reached out and moved her necklace clasp to the back. Beneath the line of her straight blond hair, her neck was bruised with dark purple blotches where Tank had grabbed her.

Justin turned and disappeared in the darkness.

JUSTIN MOVED with excruciating slowness down to the coast, making his way through the clusters of transition zone trees until he passed the watchtower, then inching down the trail through the arid zone, past palo santo trees and cacti. Finally, he reached the cliffs above Punta Berlanga, careful not to startle any birds from the masked booby nesting grounds. He hiked down the thin trail cut into the hard walls.

Casting nervous glances up the beach, he made his way to

the water and stripped to his boxers, laying his clothes in a neat pile. The breeze raised goose bumps on his arms.

The flashlight was tied to a thin braided rope that he looped over his shoulder. Though the rope was strong, he still gripped the flashlight by the handle.

He turned and faced the smooth dark bay. The water came up around him in a rush as he dipped beneath the surface. He dolphin-kicked underwater, heading toward the unbroken arc of the horizon.

WHEN CAMERON finished searching the biostation tent, she noticed Tank squatting, an elbow light on and swinging between his legs. She reached over immediately and turned it off. "No light," she said.

Tank nodded. He was holding his right arm tenderly, resting the elbow in the cup of his left hand.

"Lemme see," she said, crouching beside him. He shook his head. "C'mon, hero, you fucked it up rescuing me, the least I can do is take a look." She reached for his arm, but he pulled it away, so she slapped him lightly across the face. "Behave!"

She cuffed up his sleeve and saw that the flesh of his arm was swollen almost to the point of bursting. It was a deep bluish-black, bulging along the back of his forearm just beneath the elbow.

Tank read her face immediately.

"I think you've got a compound, kiddo," she said, trying not to sound concerned.

"Nope," he said. "Woulda felt it snap."

"Just swollen, then?" she asked. "Or a hairline?" He nodded. "Want to splint it?"

Tank shook his head. Suddenly, he leapt to his feet, pushing Cameron behind him. She whirled around but there was nothing there. Down the road, the watchtower howled.

"Sorry," Tank said.

"That's okay. Let's check on Savage. Then we should get ahold of the explosives and figure out somewhere to hole up for the night. The forest has the most cover, but the mantid's also got the advantage there." Cameron thought about how she had rested her arm right across the creature's back without noticing her. "The forest is definitely her habitat. Hopefully, she went back there with her kill." She ran her tongue along the inside of her cheek, pushing it out. "Ready?"

Tank nodded. "I'll take point," she said. She headed for the road, taking five paces before Tank followed, sliding to her right.

They eased slowly through the lines of balsas into the eastern field. The remaining torch near the hole came into view, the last flickering spot of light in the darkness. At one point, it disappeared for a moment, as if some large body had passed before it, but Cameron couldn't be sure.

They crossed the field at a laborious pace. Cameron tried to feel the ground before every step, knowing that the slightest noise, even the overturning of a small rock, could be sensed by the mantid's antennae were she anywhere near. Tank was so quiet behind her she could barely hear him. Cameron sidestepped two giant tortoises that had bedded down for the night, twinning shadows rising before her.

She had been on more missions than she could count on both hands: missions where death surely awaited several members of her platoon. And she had gone into them unshaking, unflappable. But enemy soldiers killed cleanly and swiftly. A blade across the throat, a bullet through the back of the neck, even a frag grenade in the gut and you died on the spot. If there was any, the pain was typical. If it was excruciating, at least she'd known to expect it.

What waited for them now, up ahead or in the forest, between torch-lit tents or trunks of trees, was unlike anything she'd ever thought she'd have to contend with. A clawing, biting, grasping death, an awareness even as something began to feed on your skull.

She thought about Szabla twisted in the arms of the creature—her mouth open in a scream, her eyes rolling, her arms dangling from her hunched shoulders like those of a mannequin.

The three remaining tents quivered in the wind. The dark curve in the ground where they had built the fire looked like a crater. When Tank passed the log near the fire ashes, he picked up the spike that was leaning against it. She was glad to see him with a weapon back in his hands. With cautious steps, Cameron circled the base camp once. No sign of the mantid. With two fingers, she signaled to Tank that she was moving forward. They eased along the grass toward the vesicle on their toes, the heels of their boots never touching the ground.

The torch waned, flickering dimly across the yawning mouth of the hole. A few broken branches protruded, flared like the feathers of a peacock. The torchlight played sharply off the woven mat of leaves and fronds that had covered the hole, outlining the waving foliage on the field. The shadows bounced and dipped on the grass like puppets.

Leaning forward, Cameron inched to the edge. She peeked over, pulling back quickly in case the mantid was waiting there. Among the broken branches and fronds, Savage lay, his arms and legs bent at unnatural angles, one hand still tightly gripping his knife. The whites of his eyes flashed as he blinked. She knew right away that he was paralyzed. He did not cry out.

There was a mound of fresh rock at the base of the northern wall. Cameron signaled Tank to stand guard and used the knotted rope to climb down. Tank stayed close to the edge, his head and shoulders visible from the bottom of the hole.

The ground was moist on the far side. In the corner, there appeared to be a pile of clothing, but Cameron couldn't quite make it out in the darkness. When she realized that it was a heap of Szabla's bowels, she almost retched, her stomach rising until she felt a pushing at the back of her throat.

Savage's eyes followed her as she approached him.

"Hey there, soldier," she said.

He smiled but it turned into a grimace. Cords stood out along his neck as he tried desperately to move his limbs. Cameron watched him and felt her breathing intensify.

Savage relaxed, then cracked a smile. "Ain't life a bitch?" he said.

Cameron started to talk, but her throat was gummed up with mucus, so she cleared it and tried again. "You're gonna be okay. We're gonna get you out of here."

The red blocks of TNT peeked out from beneath his stiffened leg. He shook his head, nearly imperceptibly. "No, you're not. You're not gonna do that to me."

"I can—"

He laughed quietly, but it ended like a sob. "I done a lot of shit," he said.

Cameron crouched, then stood again.

"I done a lot of shit, but I never left a man down." His eyes moistened. "I *never* left a goddamn man down."

Cameron had to wait a moment before speaking. "I was responsible for Tank and Justin. I had to make a choice."

"Well, now you have to see that choice through." His eyes were neither angry nor accusatory; they were pitiless.

She glanced up the steep wall of the hole. "We can make a stretcher, maybe haul you up with rope." Her voice sounded hollow, even to her.

Savage's snicker tangled in his throat. "Yeah. Good thinking. Sit around and nursemaid me so we all die."

They faced each other, breathing together, though even this was a struggle.

"I was knocked out, so I didn't see where the bitch went," Savage said. He tried to turn his head to the mound of rock the mantid had left when she'd scrambled out, but he couldn't. "I'd bet back up to the forest." Cameron nodded. "You're gonna kill her," he said. It was not a question.

"Yes," she said. "I know."

He faced her, unflinching. "Take my knife."

She shook her head. "I can't."

"My knife." He gazed at the knife still clutched in his use-less hand. "Take my knife."

She felt her face trembling.

"You're not gonna leave me down again," he said. A drop of sweat rolled from his temple and lost itself in his beard. Another clung to his ear, stubbornly refusing to fall. "Come on. Let's get this done." He licked his lips. "Take my knife."

Cameron felt her eyes moistening. "I can't. I don't . . . I can't." She looked back to Tank, as if in appeal, but he held his ground, his eyes scanning the dark outskirts of the field.

Savage's forehead wrinkled with his scowl. "No, god-*damn*it," he said, the veins on his neck standing out. "Don't look to him. *You. You* need to do this."

Her face felt hot. She raised a hand and brushed a wisp of hair from her eyes.

"Take my knife."

"I can't."

"Cameron. Take my knife."

She stared at him for a long time, until she felt something inside her die down. As she leaned over Savage, she pressed her lips together to keep them from shaking. He held the knife in a death grip; it took all her strength to pry it from his hand. She stood and faced him. Without his knife, he seemed naked. He lay there, sprawled and broken.

He looked up at the dark figure towering over him. "You sure you want this?" it asked.

He strained with all his might to nod his head. The figure stood there, tall and unmoving. "What the fuck," he rasped. "You gonna take all night?"

The figure bent, crouching over him. He refused to close his eyes.

TANK TOOK a few steps away from the edge of the hole and waited patiently, keeping his eyes on the forest. After a few minutes, Cameron emerged holding the blocks of TNT, Savage's knife sheathed and stuck in the back of her pants.

"All right," she said, moving slowly next to Tank. Her voice was husky, her hands stained to the wrists with fresh blood. "Let's hit base, grab the flares and some more of the explosives."

Her stride was different as she led across the field toward base camp—more purposeful. She set the blocks of TNT on the ground by the fire pit and headed for Diego's old tent, where they'd left the rest of the explosives. The flap was unzipped, and she whispered loudly back over her shoulder as she ducked through. "We should grab a change of clothes so we can burn our—"

Her voice stopped so sharply it sounded as if she'd been swallowed. Crouched awkwardly, bent at the legs, the mantid filled nearly the entire space of the tent, her enormous abdomen curled to fit inside. She stood over the cruise box in which they'd kept the larva. Probably drawn by the scent.

The breadth of her body almost touched the opposing walls of the tent. Both of the sleeping pads had been pushed aside to allow her ample room. She'd stretched the wide entrance flap of the GP tent to pull herself inside.

Cameron's upper body leaned through the opening of the tent, her legs and waist still outside. She didn't dare to exhale. The mantid had not yet noticed her; the amplified sound of the wind against the canvas walls had evidently drowned out the vibrations of her and Tank's approach.

The mantid's head was at the far side of the tent. Cameron was no less than two feet from the back of the creature's abdomen; she could have reached out and stroked the shiny cuticle had she wished.

She bit her lip to keep the panic from spilling through her, curling her shoulders into a hunch as she eased back out of the tent. Any sound could attract the creature—the rubbing of her shirt against the zipper around the flap, the slightest click of her teeth.

It was a miracle that the mantid hadn't sensed her coming through the flap. Cameron stepped back, keeping her torso bent, hoping to extract her shoulders and head with the movement of her legs alone. She was aware of every noise she made—her shirt folding against itself as she doubled at the waist, the beating of her heart, her tongue scraping along the roof of her mouth. In a heart-stopping moment, the heel of her boot ground against a rock, but the mantid didn't sense the vibration.

The mouth of the tent passed her ribs, then her shoulders. It was just around her neck when she felt something behind her. She gasped with fright.

The mantid's head turned nearly 180 degrees on her neck, swiveling like a periscope. Her mouth opened as if in a scream, but there was only a horrid silence. Cameron shoved back hard into the thing behind her, knocking it over. She turned, fist raised, to see Tank lying on his ass.

"Get up!" she screamed. "She's in there!"

The GP tent reared up off the ground behind them. One of the strainers flew at Cameron's head, trailing a sharp stake, and she ducked it just in time.

The tent rattled and screeched, then split down the sides as two long deadly legs burst through it. The sharp spikes sliced through the canvas like razor blades, and the mantid's head emerged from one of the holes. She struggled to free herself from the tent, swinging her legs wildly at Cameron and Tank.

"Back to Frank's camp!" Cameron screamed. She grabbed Tank, hauling him to his feet. One of her hands closed on his wounded arm and he cried out in pain.

Wriggling her body as if she were molting, the mantid freed her thorax from the tent. She lunged forward and swung at Tank, the hook on the end of her leg slicing through the back of his shirt. His grunt sounded like a bark. The slit immediately began gushing blood, but Tank didn't stop moving.

The mantid leapt after them, but the tent had fallen around

the base of her abdomen, tangling her legs. She fell to the ground, air rushing through her spiracles with a screech, her front legs bearing her weight.

Tank glanced back over his shoulder. The creature's raptorial legs were pushed into the grass, unable to strike. He ran toward her, raising the spike behind his head in his left hand, winding up for the swing with his entire body.

He yelled something Cameron couldn't make out, braced with his right leg, and threw his entire weight into the swing, aiming for the mantid's eye.

At the last moment, the mantid ducked and his blow glanced off the top of her head. The force was great enough to snap her head to the other side, but her strong cuticle didn't even crack. The spike fell from Tank's hand to the ground. The mantid kicked free of the tent and rose, but Tank was gone before she had regained her raptorial legs.

Cameron reached Frank's camp before Tank, almost losing her footing as she ran between the tents. Tank appeared a moment later. They could hear the soft swishing of the mantid's approach as she crossed the road and headed onto the western field.

"Where are we gonna go!?" Cameron gasped, a line of drool spinning down her chin. "Where the fuck are we gonna go?"

She looked around frantically. The forest, two canvas tents, the dark open expanse of the field. There was nowhere safe to take cover. The rumbling in the darkness was getting closer. She could have sworn she smelled the creature approaching. She spun around, looking for somewhere to hide, then fell to her knees. "Fuck!" she screamed.

Her hand closed on a cyanide jar and she hurled it into the darkness. It shattered against something with a metallic ring. She rose, her eyes wide with realization. Tank hesitated, but she pulled him forward.

They had no choice.

Chapter 66   The smell when she swung the specimen freezer door open was overpowering. Since they had burned through the lock, the freezer had not been properly sealed, and the mangled bodies were rotting in the heat. The odor pressed into their noses and pores, making their eyes burn. The air inside was so humid it felt liquid. Cameron took a deep breath of the fresh air outside and pulled the door shut behind them.

The blue light from the compressor barely lit the inside of the freezer, but it was enough for her to make out the shadowy outlines of the mutated bodies swinging overhead. Because the heat had softened the bodies, the hooks were tearing through the rotting flesh.

The canine-headed creature dangled from its jaw like a fish, the hook having pulled through its neck. Puddles of dark viscid liquid lay beneath each of the bodies, spotted with floating chunks of flesh and tangles of vessels. Another body had rotted right off the hook; it slumped on the ground as if sitting upright. The meat of its face had slid down, hanging loosely inside the translucent cuticle like water in a sac. One of its limbs had come off when it struck the ground and was lying beside it like a discarded toy.

Cameron's stomach rose immediately at the thought of the virus running through the bodies around her, its presence thick in the air. An icy terror trickled through her when her mind turned to the child she was carrying, and to the ways the virus could alter and distort the fetus. She thought of the gnarled little creature that had split Floreana open when she birthed, and felt herself go weak with fear.

She raised her hands to her watering eyes and choked down another breath, feeling the rank odor fill her chest. She turned and vomited twice into the corner. Behind her, Tank looked as though he were fighting to keep his stomach where it should be.

She wiped her mouth and went to lock the door. The two empty braces, one on the door and one on the freezer wall, protruded in parallel curves. But there was no bolt.

A chill ran from the base of her skull down her spine when she remembered that Tank had removed the bolt to use as a weapon. Now it was lying somewhere in the forest. She glanced over at Tank and a look of resignation passed between them.

She grabbed a specimen hook from the corner and tried to get it through the braces, but since it was curved, it wouldn't fit through both of them. Setting the hook down quietly, she pressed her ear to the door; she heard nothing over the hum of the compressor and the wind outside.

Without speaking, she turned Tank around and examined his cut as best she could in the bad lighting. It was deeper than she would have guessed from how well he'd been moving, but Tank was tough like that. She pressed down on the cut with her hand and he winced a bit, the muscles in his back tightening into a plate. Her hand came away drenched with blood. She'd have to do something to stop the bleeding.

She unbuttoned her shirt quickly and pulled it off. She wore an army-green tank top beneath, the kind Szabla used to wear. She held up the shirt, finding the seam. The sound of the material ripping filled the freezer.

It was when she pressed the strip of cloth to Tank's back that they first heard the scraping. Cameron froze, keeping her fingers on Tank even as the blood seeped through the fabric. The noise was agonizing—a delicate scraping against the outside of the freezer door, like fingernails on a chalkboard. Cameron and Tank shivered at the sound, stepping back although there was nowhere to go.

If only they had the bolt.

The scraping started again—probably the mantid's climbing hook screeching down the aluminum. Cameron's whole body went damp. She was breathing as quietly as she could—short inhalations and exhalations that didn't even expand her chest all the way.

She glanced over at Tank, but his eyes were on the door, glued to the empty braces. He chewed his lip, a thick trickle of blood spilling over his stubbled chin. He watched the door, working his lip.

A deafening bang echoed through the freezer and Cameron couldn't help but gasp. She could see the beginnings of a dent in the thick door. They braced themselves for another bang, but there was nothing, only the compressor's labored hum.

Then the scraping started again, seeming to come from higher up. The freezer shifted a bit and then there was the sound of claws on the solar panels above, scrambling to take hold of the slick surface. Terror flooded through Cameron, but she blinked hard, pushing it away. The next strike set their ears ringing—small dimples appeared toward the top of both metal walls simultaneously as the mantid clawed around the freezer in a bear hug. Cameron noted with terror the span of the deadly front legs.

They heard a screech and then the freezer jumped, rocking in its foundation. It was all Cameron could do to keep her balance. In the corner, one of the rotting corpses fell from its hook and went to pieces on the ground.

There was a scrambling sound, like a person running on ice, and then a dull thud as the mantid fell from the freezer roof onto the grass. "She can't grip," Cameron whispered.

The silence that followed seemed endless. Tank and Cameron tried to regulate their breathing, standing side by side among the bodies swaying crazily on the hooks. Cameron no longer noticed the smell, only the rank humidity against her face. She exhaled sharply through her nostrils, expelling the virus-laden air from her body.

The mantid's hook clicked against the metal. It slid down the freezer door, stopping when it encountered the handle. It grinded around the handle, and Tank lunged for the door just as it yanked open with tremendous force. He grabbed the empty brace on the door with both hands, yelling as the cut on his back split open like a burst seam.

Blood splattered across Cameron's face. She grabbed Tank around his waist and held onto him, pressing her cheek to his hot, sticky back.

The mantid's head appeared for a moment in the gap of the door, her mouth spread open, silent and wild with movement. Tank grunted and yanked back on the brace, crying out in pain. The mantid's hook slipped from the handle, and the door banged shut.

Tank fell back on top of Cameron and they lay there for an instant, collecting themselves before standing. Tank stared at the empty braces, his breath coming as if he were sobbing, though he was not. Beads of sweat stood out all through his crew cut. His neck looked raw and red, even in the dim light.

Let her go away, Cameron thought. Just let her go away.

The specimen hooks creaked as they rocked, the bodies dripping hemolymph into the puddles beneath them.

There was a gentle tap on the freezer door. The mantid's hook screeched as it drifted down toward the handle again. Tank and Cameron stared at the door, their eyes lowering with the hook as if they were watching it through the metal.

It ticked against the handle and stopped.

Tank looked over at Cameron, his eyes moist with fear and affection. "Back vent," he said. "Go."

He stepped forward and rammed his bloated arm through the two braces. The door yanked, the braces tearing his arm in opposite directions. He roared as the swelling popped, sending a spray of watery blood across the back of the door.

Cameron screamed and lunged forward to grab Tank, but he placed an enormous hand over her face and shoved her backward. She skidded on her ass, sliding through the sitting corpse, and it came apart beneath her, drenching her backside with viscous juices. She tried to push herself to her feet, but her hands slipped on the hemolymph and she went flat on her back, its parts all through her hair and warm against her neck.

The door banged again and Tank's scream was high, piercing. His body flapped against the back of the door and Cameron realized he was sobbing with pain.

Jesus, pass out, why don't you pass out? she thought, but she knew it was too much to hope for.

With Tank's cries in her ears, she scrambled through the smeared remains of the body to the humidor vent, barely gaining traction on the guts and the slick metal. Sliding on her ass toward the humidor, she kicked it with both feet. The duct connecting the vent to the humidor unit came loose, swinging to the side and laying the vent bare.

She knew she'd have to be careful; there were sharp metal teeth lining the vent to catch it if pushed in from the outside. She banged her feet against the vent, straining through her thighs, but it budged only slightly. Even if she could kick it out, she didn't know how she was going to distract the mantid long enough to drag Tank through the hole.

Behind her, Tank's scream was unbelievably high. The mantid hooked the handle again, throwing her weight back as she snapped her front leg to her thorax. As the door yanked open, Tank's arm tore from his body, right in front of his face. He went limp for a moment, and then his legs straightened under him again.

The mantid collected herself from the ground and lunged for him, wrapping him in the tines of her legs. Tank yelled, struggling in her grasp. Cameron turned from the vent, scrambling across the slick floor to the specimen hook pile. Her fist tightened around a hook, and she rose and charged the mantid.

Tank's legs were crushed nearly flat and the ripped stump of his arm was pressed to his side, but his left arm was still free. He drew it back, forming a hammer of a fist, and drove it through the creature's eye to the wrist.

The mantid reeled, air rushing through her spiracles and creating a shrill, awful screech. She jogged Tank once to get a better grip and snapped her legs around him, severing him through his massive chest. His shoulders, head still intact, fell to the ground, landing upright like a bust.

Crying out, Cameron swung the hook, aiming for the mantid's other eye with the barbed point. The mantid jerked to the left, and the hook struck the hard cuticle above her eyes but did not stick. It clattered to the floor, ringing against the metal. Cameron leapt for the back of the freezer, sliding toward the vent. Beating against the vent with both feet, she smashed it outward. It bulged against the screws, the middle bowing.

The mantid stepped into the freezer, evidently confused by the twirling bodies all around. She snapped a dangling body from a hook with her legs, then dropped it. Another body spun to her right and she leaned back and seized it, the hook tearing into her leg. She ripped the corpse, specimen hook and all, from the ceiling, biting into the rotting flesh before discarding it on the floor. Her trembling antennae snapped upright and she turned, her good eye finding Cameron. The mantid started forward.

Cameron felt the vent about to give and she reared back and hammered both legs into it. One of the metal guard teeth ran a slit up her calf and she grunted with the pain but pushed through the end of her kick nonetheless. The vent left the back wall of the freezer, flying out onto the grass beyond.

Cameron felt the shadow of the mantid fall across her, and she dived forward through the toothed gap where the vent had been, the creature's raptorial legs snapping shut inches behind her. She curled up as she flew through the vent hole, dodging the teeth surrounding it. Tucking as she hit the grass, she rolled over her shoulders, still guiding her legs through the metal teeth behind her. One of the teeth caught her boot, swiping a section of rubber from the sole, but then she was on the grass and free.

The mantid rammed her head through the hole, her gaping mouth straining to reach Cameron. The metal teeth scraped into her cuticle and she expelled air in a breathy hiss, backing up and struggling. Her head stuck on the teeth for a moment before pulling free.

Cameron finished her roll, coming up and onto her feet immediately, and sprinted around the freezer. She kicked the front door closed as she passed, trapping the mantid inside. With its missing lock, the freezer wouldn't hold her, but Cameron hoped it would confuse her, buying time to escape.

She heard the mantid smash against one of the walls before she was more than ten yards away, a screech echoing in the cold aluminum walls. The wind picked up, howling through the watchtower and drowning out the fierce banging within the freezer.

Ignoring the burn setting in through her legs, Cameron sprinted for the forest.

Chapter 67 Even with a mask, Justin's visibility underwater would have been extremely low. Hiding sea-urchin-dotted stretches of coral and sharp lava ledges, the inky water enveloped him. He progressed steadily toward the tuff cones, his strokes regular, his breathing calm. He surfaced frequently, the cloud-hazed moonlight seeping across the waters and his own wan face.

His foot tangled in a strand of seaweed and he doubled over underwater, calmly freeing himself. He resurfaced and swam slowly in circles, glancing around through the darkness. He felt for the flashlight but did not turn it on.

Turtlebacking slowly, he floated on the ripples and looked at the stars above. Orion was clearly lit, the point of the arrow like a beacon. As he headed back through the darkness, the near-full moon broke clear of the clouds. The first of the tuff cones was about fifteen feet away from him. He would have swum directly into it had the moon not made its fortuitous appearance.

He gripped the side of the tuff cone, breathing hard, then eased his way around it, kicking gently to the next one in the chain. He swam quietly, the dark slumbering forms of the sea lions dotting the nooks of the rock. When he reached the third cone, he swam about five yards west, then dived beneath the surface and kicked to the bottom. He hit sand in seven strokes. The moonlight filtered beneath the surface for the first several feet, but down at the bottom, it was pitch black.

He drifted for a moment, his body limp, suspended in perfect blackness. Once his torso had oriented toward the truest angle upward, he kicked, paddling fiercely until he broke the surface. He was barely winded.

His fingers were white when he released the flashlight. He clicked the switch and headed down, following the yellow-white shaft of light. He followed a sharp slope, the sea bottom about ten feet deeper at the far end. He paused when his feet struck sand, the flashlight illuminating a band of water across the bottom.

Tightening his grasp on the flashlight, he bent his legs beneath his body on the sand, raising the flashlight as he started to push off from the bottom. It shot a beam of light in front of him and he jerked back, his breath billowing out in a burst of bubbles.

Directly in front of him, no more than an arm's length away, was the head of a large blacktip reef shark. Its mouth opened, revealing row upon row of razor-sharp teeth, and Justin threw himself supine as it glided above him, knocking his face with the leathery bottom of its jaw.

Before shoving off for the surface, he followed the shark with the light until it glided up the slope and out of view. Then, he kicked up hard, pushing a few meager bubbles from his nose.

He gasped when he broke the surface, sucking in a mouthful of water. He swam to the nearest tuff cone, ignoring the barking sea lion he'd awakened, and gripped it tightly as he regurgitated a mix of salt water and mucus.

He clung to the tuff cone for a few minutes, breathing

steadily until he calmed. Kicking west again about fifteen yards, he swam to the bottom, scanning with the flashlight. He returned to the surface more quickly than he had before.

The second and third dives were equally fruitless. He was breathing heavily again by the time he surfaced from the fourth.

CAMERON RAN into the forest until the searing pain in her lungs became too much, then she collapsed. Since it was night, the mantid could roam anywhere on the island; the forest, with its myriad hiding places, was probably Cameron's best bet.

She was heavily scented with her sweat, Tank's blood, and the rotting flesh of the body from the freezer. She stared at her damp, stained shirt, soaked with the Darwin virus, and knew she'd have to wash off as soon as she could get back to the water. There was no way she was going to risk another trip to the beach, though. Not until sunrise. She thought of the antibacterial gel at base—that would be her first priority in the morning.

She resisted the urge to page Justin given they'd agreed he'd contact her once he reached shore. She'd just have to trust that he'd be okay on his own for now.

She searched among the *Scalesias*, trying to find one tall enough for her to scurry up and hide. The mantid could reach her in a tree, but if Cameron was up off the ground, she'd at least have more warning of the creature's approach, and be out of her probable line of sight and scent. Finally, Cameron came upon a tall, skinny quinine tree, towering feet above the smaller *Scalesias*. It was perfect, though the lowest branches thick enough to support her weight were at least thirty feet up.

Shinnying up the trunk, she rested about ten feet off the ground, clutching the trunk with her thighs and arms. The bark felt harsh through her thin tank top. She humped her way farther up until she reached the lowest limb, which she grabbed like a pull-up bar, letting her feet swing free. Tucking her knees to her chin, she rolled upside down, hooking her legs over the branch and using the trunk to pull herself upright.

She looked around, noting that the branches of the other trees were not as close as they had seemed from the ground. Her escape route was questionable; if she got sighted, she'd probably be pinned down. For the time being, she was too exhausted to move, but she would force herself to stay awake.

Straddling the branch, she leaned against the trunk, pressing her forehead to the rough bark.

For the first time in nearly eighteen hours, she let her muscles go limp.

JUSTIN MOVED over two strokes west, as he had before each dive, and tried again. When his feet hit bottom, he gazed along the column of light. Something glimmered in the sand, a bright yellow streak. Swimming over to it, he uncovered the fluorescent stock of the speargun and pulled the weapon free. Sand swirled around him like confetti, and he held the long, slender speargun before him for a moment, as if admiring it.

Surfacing, he swam to the tuff cone and rested. He pressed his cheek to the rock as he bear-hugged it, twisting his hips to protect his groin. Breathing deeply and evenly, he rose and fell with the water against the tuff cone.

The spear gun had no sling, and he tried unsuccessfully to secure it tightly to the flashlight sling. Finally, he struck out for the island, holding the speargun and paddling mostly with his other hand. The speargun lopsided his stroke. He switched hands, shaking out his biceps as he propelled himself forward with both legs. The rhythm of his kicks and breaths was almost hypnotically steady. To his left, a sea lion shadowed him, watching his progress with what appeared to be amusement.

Each time he surfaced, his breath came harder, and soon

he was coming up for air every other stroke. After a while, the hazy outline of the island up ahead became visible. The sea lion dipped beneath him and popped up on his right, barking playfully.

Justin's pace was painfully slow by the time he was within a hundred yards of shore. A glow was already lighting the sky, the gray edge of morning.

He looked for the sea lion, but it had suddenly vanished.

Stopping to tread water, he wheezed until his breathing had some semblance of regularity. He breaststroked a few yards quietly, careful to dodge the jagged edges of the broken reef.

His head snapped up suddenly, and he expertly pivoted in the water, staring behind him. He continued to tread water silently for a few more moments, watching the surface closely. Something large swept by him about fifteen feet away, sending a ripple in his direction. An eddy sucked at his feet. Then the water around him stilled.

His hand tightening on the speargun, he gazed for shore, which was about seventy yards away. The sand sloped gradually; at thirty yards out, it was only five feet deep. Despite the glow along the edge of the island, the waters were still dark.

Something broke the surface, but by the time Justin whirled around, there was nothing but a spiral of ripples and a sinking fin. He raised the speargun defensively but gazed at the sole spear for a moment, then lowered it. Pulling the sling free from his shoulder, he palmed the flashlight, flicking the switch with his thumb.

There was a sudden movement in the water, a wake headed directly at him. The furrow of water was about ten yards away when he heaved the flashlight as far as he could to his left. He folded his arms around the speargun and sank with it, motionless.

The wake had nearly reached him when the shark switched directions, veering off after the flashlight. Underwater, Justin caught a glimpse of movement and then a wall of water struck him as the shark turned.

He kicked to the surface and swam as quickly toward the beach as he could without splashing, sidestroking and keeping his eyes on the waters behind him. When his feet hit sand, he crept forward, still keeping his splashing to a minimum. Sunrise was a good half hour away, but the lines of the beach and the cliff were visible. He continued wading until his chest was clear of the ocean, and soon the water was down around his stomach.

He froze, eyes trained on the shadowy form on the beach ahead. Fat, round, and lifeless, it could have been a segment of log. Focusing on the form, waiting for the beach to lighten, he inched forward. He held the speargun above his head, wincing each time water dripped from it and made a vibration in the water. His lips trembled as he stepped . . . waited . . . stepped.

His arms and his knees were starting to wobble slightly when he paused. He stepped forward once more, easing his bare feet onto a rib of lava.

The beach lightened infinitesimally, and large footprints came into view, leading from the top of the trail to the form on the beach. They were the tracks of a four-legged animal, each one forked at the top where the bifid claw had pressed into the sand. He looked back at the form on the beach, now visible—it was a grown sea lion, viciously halved, its tail and rump missing. Fresh blood leaked from the wound, staining the protruding plugs of blubber. The eyes were black and glossy like dark marbles.

The sand around the body was kicked up, but the footprints became clear again a few feet over, continuing down and disappearing into the ocean. Justin's eyes immediately went to the waters around him. He pivoted slowly, silently, lowering the speargun.

Behind him and to the side, mere feet away, the mantid pulled her body from her underwater crouch, the water draining from her head and gathering in her broken eye. The spray from the splash covered the back of Justin's head.

He lowered his chin to his chest, teeth clenching. "Cameron," he whispered, just as the mantid tore into him.

CAMERON'S TRANSMITTER vibrated once, startling her from sleep, and she shifted her weight, nearly falling from the tree. She activated the unit, and the air immediately filled with the sounds of thrashing. She heard her husband's screaming, and she knew she had lost him.

She leaned back, trying to block out the horrible sounds. Her entire body started shaking, her arms quivering so severely she almost lost her hold on the trunk.

Justin's cries lessened, and then she heard an awful rasping noise, splashing, and what sounded like flesh tearing. The transmitter clicked off.

THE MANTID attacked Justin even before he could turn to face it, but her legs were unaccustomed to the water, and she mistimed her strike. Hitting Justin with the outside of her femur, she sent him tumbling over himself in the water. He yelled, sucking salt water into his lungs, his shoulder scraping against lava. When he surfaced, the mantid hovered over him. The smooth backside of a flying leg struck him on the jaw before a hook swiped a chunk of flesh from his left shoulder.

Stumbling, he spit hard as if clearing vomit from his throat. The blow had cracked his tooth and spilled blood through his mouth. He gagged against the thick fluid, staggering on his feet in the water. The spines of a sea urchin sank into his feet, but he did not respond to the pain.

The creature loomed before him, nine feet of spikes and armor. She lowered her head, regarding him for a moment as her jawlike legs scraped together and then apart.

He dived to his side, rolling over his right shoulder and readying the speargun for when he surfaced. He fired as soon as he came up, aiming for the broken black hole of the eye. It hit the edge of the cuticle around the socket and stuck. The mantid's body contracted, air screeching through the spiracles and bubbling the water as her legs flailed. She stumbled back, shaking her head from side to side, the spear protruding ridiculously.

Justin dragged himself toward the beach on weak legs. He was losing blood at an alarming rate from his shoulder, and he blinked hard, as if trying to clear his vision. The water splashed around his thighs, slowing his pace. Behind him, the creature thrashed in the water, but he didn't turn around; he plodded heavily toward the beach.

Stumbling onto the sand, he went down on a knee. He tried to rise again but could not. He fell flat on his chest and stomach, sand pressing into his nose and mouth. He turned his head and fought to stand up, as the mantid lumbered to shore behind him, but went limp on the sand.

With all her thrashing, the mantid finally snapped the spear against a raised leg. The spear stock sticking out from her head, she made her way slowly to shore, pausing above the still, sprawled body. A chunk of flesh slid from her claw, thunking on the sand. Embedded in the soft pink underside was a small metal disk, Justin's transmitter. The mantid watched the body for another moment, but it did not stir.

Stepping heavily around Justin, she began the long walk back to the forest.

31 DEC 07
MISSION DAY 7

Chapter 68   Cameron's trembling subsided as suddenly as it had started, though she was still breathing so hard and fast that she thought she might hyperventilate. She stared at the small black squiggles of the graffiti lichen on the bark before her, tracing them with her eyes and waiting for her breathing to slow. Though it was still quite dark in the forest, the sky was just beginning to draw light from the still-unseen sun.

Life was so far from her here in the forest, as far as it had ever been. She couldn't remember ever driving a car, cooking dinner, getting dressed. A line of ants crawled across her thigh and she let them.

Grief came not as a sharp stab but an ache. It spread itself inside her like a deadly flower. Her eyes glazed over; her tongue went numb against her teeth.

She pressed her face to the tree and wept. She gave herself time to cry, relearning as she went. It was an indulgence of sorts, a dark undercurrent that carried her soothingly even as it drowned her. Her pain was bottomless and calm, and chilling for its purity. She cried softly until her throat went hoarse, cried until it seemed as though the burn in her eyes would never subside.

She had been widowed here, in this tree; everything had changed since she'd shinnied up the trunk. Part of her didn't want to go back down. The loss and defeat weren't entirely real as long as she stayed up in the tree, as long as she didn't have to walk, or speak, or eat.

Death had always been the third member of their marriage, with the work they did, but she'd never thought it would come down like this. It wasn't as if she hadn't prepared herself mentally—she'd never let herself think about rocking chairs and grandchildren, she didn't look older couples in the eye, and it seemed she'd gone through what life would be like without Justin or for Justin without her a thousand times—but still it felt like a blind side punch.

And his cries, Jesus, his cries. They still rang in her ears.

Maybe she could stay up here until she died. Maybe she'd waste away, her skin rotting from her bones until she was just a skeleton perched on a branch, arms wrapped around the trunk. Her resolve to live drained away with her tears;

she felt weak, deflated. It was an effort just to wipe her cheek—she couldn't even comprehend continuing the battle against the thing that waited for her in the forest.

Her head throbbed from the base of her skull through her forehead. The dark purple bruises around her neck stood out, dead flowers against her pale skin.

The creature was out there still, Cameron knew.

And there was still another larva unaccounted for. For all she knew, it had already slid into the cool sea and made its way to open waters, its body brimming with virus. If it was on the island, it would be metamorphosing soon.

Cameron imagined being trapped on the island with two creatures. If only she could survive another sixteen hours, she could escape in the helo. But there was no way she'd make it from nightfall to her 2200 extraction, not alone. She imagined the death that almost surely awaited her.

She thought of her father-in-law's gentle hands and white hair, a Christmas table fully set, the slope of Justin's shoulders, the smell of him right before she kissed him, the grocery store, cold fall mornings, the blue sheets on their bed back home, and the reddish glow of their alarm clock. She thought of these things and began to sob.

The agony compounded wherever she tried to turn her mind—Tank's swollen arm laced through the braces, Derek's wobbling voice through the transmitter, Szabla's body shaking as if she were having a seizure, Juan, Savage, Tucker.

There were no tears left. She opened her mouth, expecting something to come out, but nothing did. Snot ran down her upper lip and she tasted its saltiness before wiping her nose with her forearm. Her shoulders curved forward as she slumped into the trunk, spent. She wasn't sure how long she sat with her face pressed to the tree, but when she leaned back, her cheeks felt raw.

Her voice was throaty and uneven, and the operator at Fort Detrick barely understood to patch her through to Samantha Everett's room.

"Yes, Samantha here. Everything all right? Cameron? Cameron?"

Just hearing a familiar voice reduced her to tears again. "Samantha."

"Yes. Are you all right? Cameron, talk to me. Tell me what's going on."

Cameron tilted back her head to prevent more tears from spilling. "It's down to me," she said. "It's just me. And it."

"Everyone's gone? Even your . . . Even Justin?"

"Yes," Cameron said. Samantha could do nothing to help, and they both knew it, but Cameron didn't want to let her go, because then she'd be alone floating up in a tree in the middle of a forest on this godforsaken island. Now, she at least had a connection to the world, to another life, to another person she could hear breathing in the darkness. She pressed her forehead again to the rough bark and let it scrape against her cheek. "Are you married?" she asked.

"No. But I have kids."

Cameron was winded, as if after a long run. "You hold on to them. You hold on to everything you can as tight as you can because there's a time . . . " Her lower lip wavered a few times before she caught it. "Because there's a time you can't anymore."

"I will," Samantha said. "I will."

More silence. Something chirped.

"There's nothing I can say or do that will be useful, and I'm not gonna fake it," Samantha said.

Thank you, Cameron thought. Thank you for knowing and admitting.

"And things are going to get worse, probably, before we can get you out of there," Samantha continued. "But you make me one promise. When you hit bottom, you keep going. You find that small part of yourself that's unbreakable and grip it until your fingers bleed. It may not seem worth it to keep fighting, not now, but it is and someday—in a month, in a year, in five years—you'll know that again." She paused, and when she spoke again, her voice was filled with intensity. "Don't you give up. Don't you roll over on me."

"Don't worry," Cameron said, her voice edged with a rasp. "I don't know how." Her eyes stayed shut when she blinked, and she let them.

CAMERON WAS in another state of consciousness, though it was not sleep. A swarm of gnats circled her head, and she grew drunk on their whirring. She was trying to fight her way back to alertness, but it was like swimming through mud. Her eyelids felt leaden.

The morning light was finally filtering through the leaves. She had not gotten any true sleep. Her face was swollen, her lips parched and sore. Her contacts felt as if they were glued to her eyeballs; she was amazed she hadn't lost them.

Sorrow struck her from all sides, like a talon closing. She braced herself against it, closing doors in her mind, containing the damage. She could count her breaths, that much she could do. If she counted her breaths, she'd know she was still alive. Pushing away from the trunk and holding it between her hands, she began to regulate her breathing, focusing on her knuckles. She lost count around 190, so she began again, listening to the breaths rattling through her chest, wiping her mind as clear as a pane of glass.

She fought against the weariness, her lips still moving even as she started taking longer and longer blinks. Her head bowed, then snapped back up. She had been trying not to rest it against the trunk, but finally, she gave in. Her eyelids shut, her forehead pressed to the tree, and sleep washed over her like a salve. If she wasn't aching so much, it would have felt divine.

The rhythm of her counting continued, though the numbers were no longer there. Instead of numbers, there were knocks, even and firm, like a blacksmith's hammer. The knocking pulled her up through the layers of sleep, through grief and fear and hunger, and then she felt the tree bark against her cheek.

She opened her eyes.

The knocking continued, continued from below.

Cameron glanced down and saw the mantid halfway up the tree, pushing the hooks of her front legs into the bark, pulling herself up using her claws. Cameron's mouth opened to yell, but her vocal cords were raw, so her scream came out as a rush of air.

She popped up to a crouch on the branch, glancing around. The trees nearby were much shorter, the closest branches a good twenty feet out and below. She had only about five more steps out before the branch would give under her weight. Even with her strength, she could never make that jump.

The mantid pulled herself toward Cameron, each knock of her hooks against the bark followed by the drag of her body up the trunk. Cameron could hear her breathing, feel the air from her spiracles. About ten inches of the spear protruded from the mantid's cuticle, just above the broken eye—Justin had gotten off the shot. The eye was out, shattered through the middle in a run of ooze, and Cameron looked frantically for anything to plunge into the other. The twigs were all too small.

There were no bushes on the ground to break her fall, and the thirty-foot drop would certainly leave her wounded. About fifteen feet to her right was another quinine with a long, thin trunk. It had been snapped in an earthquake, so it was missing its conspicuous crown. She might make it in a fully-extended dive, but if she misjudged her leap, she could be impaled by the sharp, broken trunk. She looked around at the other trees, but they all seemed much farther away.

When she edged farther out on the branch, it started to bend under her weight, so she shuffled back toward the trunk, her heart rising in her chest as the mantid's head pulled into view. A long leg shot out and hooked onto the branch.

With a cry, Cameron scurried forward and kicked the mantid's leg away, jabbing with her heel. She wobbled like a

performer on a high wire, sensing the curve of the branch
beneath her arches. The mantid reeled as the hook came
loose, but swung right back into place. Cameron knew she
would be up and on her in seconds.

She had to move or she was going to topple over, and she
couldn't step to the trunk for support because she'd be
within the creature's grasp. The mantid wrapped one leg
around the branch, the other around the trunk, and began to
pull herself up. Her back legs found their footing.

Cameron inched away from the mantid, her boots scraping off bits of bark, sending them spiraling to the ground.
She stared at the nearest *Scalesia* branch. At least twenty
feet away. There was no chance.

Behind her, she heard the mantid slide up onto the branch,
mere feet away from her. The branch dipped under the
weight. Cameron almost fell but regained her balance by
doubling over at the waist and waving her arms.

A raptorial leg snapped shut less than an inch from her
skull as she pulled herself upright. Having been meticulously cleaned, the spikes were perfectly smooth, the chunks
of flesh removed. Cameron saw a tuft of her blond hair dangling between two of the spikes.

She glanced at the narrowing branch, the step and a half
she had left, and the drop beyond. The broken quinine was
her only realistic option. She'd have to jump far enough to
make the trunk, and pray she hit it safely below the jagged
end. Whether she could hold on or not was another question,
but she didn't have time to debate it.

The mantid was wrapped around the branch and trunk like
an odd growth. Having stabilized herself, she was readying
her raptorial legs for another strike. They jackknifed in,
folding to her chest.

The massive eye stared through Cameron, the antennae on
end. The creature's mouth was a fearful hole; the mandibles
glistened with digestive fluid, and the labrum looked soft
and spongy, though Cameron knew it was not.

The mantid tilted her head to the right. There was no more

time. Bending deep at the knee until her ass brushed her heels, Cameron uncoiled like a spring, flying from the branch in a horizontal dive. Though she couldn't see the legs snap shut behind her, she heard them.

Her shoulders led her body as she began to descend, and her stomach left her in a rush. The air whistled in her ears; the ground blurred beneath her; her eyes watered. The trunk approached.

For a moment, she was sure her momentum wouldn't carry her, that she'd fall short and wind up a tangle of bones and limbs at the base of the tree, but she kept moving forward even as she plummeted down.

The trunk struck her shoulder with the force of a major-league swing. She hit it in a flying tackle, clenching it in the circle of her arms as she jarred to a halt, feeling the transmitter in her shoulder go to pieces beneath her flesh. The bark scraped along her cheek, drawing blood. Her torso and legs swung down into the tree beneath her, her breasts and crotch smashing into the trunk. Pain seared through her, her muscles contracting all at once.

Losing her grip, she slid down the trunk, clawing and digging at it with her ankles and hands. Twigs broke off beneath her as she fell, and she squeezed with her arms, trying to pull her chest tight to the bark even though it was flying past like a belt sander.

A knot protruding through the bark miraculously flew between her legs, but it nicked her chin, knocking her torso away from the trunk. The brilliant green of the canopy zoomed overhead and she spread her legs, then clenched them around the trunk, flexing so hard through her thighs and calves she thought her muscles would snap like pieces of twine. Her heels dug like spikes into the trunk, stripping away sections of bark.

Her arms were extended back over her head, bouncing with her torso as she ground to a halt. Though her thick cammy pants provided some protection, the burning through the insides of her legs was excruciating. She winced as she pulled herself upright, flexing through her stomach to bring her chest to the trunk.

She was fifteen feet above the ground.

Immediately, she tried to locate the creature on the branch but could not. Then she saw the bulge of the abdomen behind the trunk, the legs wrapped around the bark. The mantid was moving down already, down to the ground.

In something of a halting fall, Cameron slid down the remaining fifteen feet of the trunk, squeezing occasionally with her arms and legs to slow herself, trying to ignore the pain. Her teeth knocked together when she hit the ground and she sprawled flat on her back for an instant before rolling onto all fours.

The mantid sprang from the other tree, dropping to the ground. Her wings fluttered for a moment but did not spread wide.

Cameron found her feet before the mantid drew herself up, and she turned and sprinted into the foliage, praying she could remember the correct direction. Her arms were a blur of motion as she knocked vines and fronds out of her way. Kicking through bushes and leaping over fallen trees and boulders, Cameron moved as quickly as she ever had. She didn't know how she was running so fast, especially after the slide down the tree, but her body was feeding off adrenaline, hurtling forward through the forest on autopilot. She should have been weak and tired—she couldn't even remember the last time she'd eaten—but she felt a second wind sweeping through her.

Not far behind, the mantid crashed through the undergrowth. Cameron rolled under a fallen tree with one end propped on a boulder and counted the seconds until she heard the mantid smash through it. Six. There were six seconds between her and the jaws.

The rumbling neared, a semi truck bearing down. Praying she'd see the low grass of the fields, Cameron pushed through bush after bush, slid between tree trunks, leapt across creeks, but there was only forest and more forest.

Just when she was convinced that she'd been running the wrong way, the ground went out from under her and she was enveloped in blackness. She slid down a slope and found herself lying flat on her back about ten feet beneath the earth's surface, staring up at the small circle of sky above.

She turned her head and pain shot down her neck. The realization dawned slowly on her; she'd fallen into the lava tunnel. She searched overhead for the remains of the ootheca they'd found earlier, but it was nowhere to be seen. A few roots had made their way through the entrance along the roof; they curled against the rock like enormous maggots—crawling things fat with life.

The lava tube was smaller than she'd remembered; it was only about two and a half meters high, and two wide. She realized she must be on the other end—the northern end closer to the heart of the forest.

The tube curved back out of sight, running horizontal to the ground, the top of the tunnel a few feet beneath the surface. Calcium carbonate textured the walls like coral, and stalactites hung from the ceiling like lone fangs. Iron had oxidized on the lava in yellow-reddish patches. Long and slender, the lava tube looked like a corroding subway tunnel, or the intestines of some immense beast.

A shadow fell across Cameron's face, and she looked up at the mantid's head, a dark silhouette framed perfectly in the lava tube's entrance. She rolled to all fours, pain screaming through her, and limped a few steps down the corridor. The mantid tried to navigate the drop through the narrow entrance but could not. She backed away, seemingly frustrated.

She would just have to wait.

Cameron's bloody knee was visible through the leg of her ripped cammies. A deep sob shook her as she realized that, if it had survived on her clothing, the virus could have leaked through the cut into her bloodstream. Her mouth loose and wavering, she looked up at the mantid's head waiting within the small patch of light.

She remembered Diego saying that the lava tube was about 350 meters; she'd just have to walk its length and emerge through the southern opening, closer to base camp.

The flesh over her broken transmitter was bruised, raised in a few hard edges from the metal pieces. She whispered a test command into it, but she knew it was dead even before she was greeted by silence. She couldn't remain in hiding here in the lava tube; she'd have no way to contact the helo when it arrived. She had to make it back to base camp and the dirt road, and set the infrared strobe to guide the helo in.

She turned and limped a few steps farther down the tube; when she glanced behind her, the creature was gone. What appeared to be burrows potholed the ground, worn into the rock from the unremitting drip of water from overhead. Her shoulder brushed a fragile stalactite, sending it crashing to the ground.

She walked a few more steps, surrounded by the echo of her breathing and dripping water. A trickle of dirt landed on her shoulder. She thought at first that it was an earthquake coming on, and she was sure she'd be buried here, beneath the earth's surface, but the trickling dirt stopped. She took another step and felt a tiny vibration, then another trickle of dirt fell from the roof, clouding into dust around her head.

The mantid was shadowing her overhead, sensing Cameron's movements with her delicate antennae, even through the earth.

Cameron stepped and paused, and sure enough, a moment later, another thin stream of dirt dropped from the ceiling. She leaned against a wall, the lava moist and claylike against her back. Sobs rose in her chest, but she choked them down. She dropped to all fours, wincing as her tender knee struck lava, and crawled forward as quietly as she could. She froze, waiting to sense the small vibration overhead.

There was none.

She continued at that tedious pace for what seemed days, crawling slowly forward and pausing, listening for the vibration of footsteps overhead.

It was pitch black now that she was a good distance from the northern entrance; for all she knew, the lava tube would drop off at any point into a bottomless cavern. The humidity made it difficult to breathe, but she fought to control herself, inching forward, regulating her inhalations and exhalations.

Finally, she rounded a corner and saw a dot of light ahead. Another endless stretch of time as she pulled herself, slowly crawling, to the northern opening. She saw the ootheca overhead, the shriveled cords still dangling from it like wood shavings. When she stood, her legs immediately cramped and she took a few silent moments to get the blood running back through them.

She peered cautiously around the entrance of the lava tube, but there were no signs of danger. Tentatively, she stepped through the partial curtain of ferns into the forest. There was nothing waiting for her.

She glanced quickly behind her just as the mantid pivoted atop the lava tube's opening, seemingly surprised that Cameron had emerged behind her. The mantid scrambled down from her perch, the wind from her snapping legs rushing across Cameron's face. Because of her pierced eye, the mantid's strikes were slightly imprecise.

Cameron screamed, adrenaline shooting through her body, and hit a dead sprint in four steps, heading for camp. The mantid pursued, leaves and branches shushing around her cuticle. Her remaining eye was still acutely sensitive; it wouldn't be long before she adjusted her movements.

The knotting in Cameron's legs intensified, and just when she was sure she could sprint no longer, she burst through a line of trees onto the field about fifty yards west of the road, her feet skidding on a wash of rocks. A few scattered *Scalesias* still studded the ground, and together with the tall balsas that lined the road, they provided irregular shade.

She barely had time to look back at the forest's edge before the mantid flew into sight, a whirlwind of legs and spikes and mandibles screaming down on her. Cameron got her feet under her just as the mantid slid on the rocks, and she was two paces toward base camp when the mantid lost her footing, screaming and flailing.

When Cameron saw her husband stumbling up the road toward her, bare-chested, weak, and bleeding, she thought at first that she was hallucinating. Her chest heaved as if her heart had flipped over in her ribcage, and she sprinted toward him, wanting to fall into him with an embrace. But there would be no time for that, no time for relief or joy or affection.

Justin leaned heavily on the trunk of a balsa at the road's edge, almost falling over. A thick stream of blood ran from his shoulder, crusting across his chest and abdomen. His mouth moved weakly and she knew, somehow, that he was trying to say her name. He was still a good thirty yards away, though Cameron was running to him as fast as she could.

Behind Cameron, the mantid popped up, her head rocking on her long neck. She started after Cameron. Lowering her head, she closed the space quickly, turning the ground over beneath her legs.

Cameron had not even reached her husband when she realized there was no way, in his weakened state, that he could possibly escape. Perhaps she could outrun the creature if she only had herself to worry about, but she could see even from a distance that Justin was barely holding on. He didn't stand a chance.

Behind her, the mantid was picking up speed. Cameron reached back and yanked out Savage's knife, twirling it once so the butt protruded from her fist. She closed in on Justin and he stretched out an arm to her, his eyes loose and rolling. He managed to call her name once before she shoved him, spinning him face-first into the tree trunk. She brought the butt of the knife down squarely on the back of his skull, and he crumpled to the ground. The mantid was no less than ten yards away from her and moving fast.

Shoving off Justin's body, Cameron sprinted up the road. She felt the creature bearing down, sensed the spikes only feet, then inches from her back, and she pumped her arms as hard as she could, sprinting for the watchtower and panting so hard the air almost choked her. She broke from the shadow of the trees, then the mantid screeched and Cameron ran toward the watchtower screaming and swinging her arms wildly, knowing the creature was upon her.

But she wasn't.

Cameron turned and saw the mantid watching her from the edge of the shade, her legs snapping reflexively. The dirt felt hot even through Cameron's boots.

Cameron sank to her knees, throwing her arms wide and looking up at the sun. As Rex had said, the mantid wouldn't expose herself directly to the baking sun during the day; it would dry out her cuticle. Though she owned the whole island at night, she was limited to the forest's cover during the brightest daytime hours, needing the protective cover of the canopy.

Justin's body lay in the road just behind the creature. Cameron had swung the butt of the knife so that it would strike him between the ear and the back of the head, a region where the skull plate was solid, so it wouldn't crack, and strong enough to absorb a blow that could knock a man unconscious. The mantid only attacked moving prey; she'd left Savage in the ditch earlier when he was unconscious.

The mantid turned and examined Justin's body, lying still in the shade provided by the balsas that lined the east side of the road.

"Don't you touch him!" Cameron screamed. "Don't you fucking touch him!"

The mantid leaned over Justin, scanning his body with her massive head, the spear stock sticking up like a black feather. She paused over his face, her mouth inches from his cheek. Justin's eyes remained closed, but Cameron noticed one of his fingers twitching. The mantid's legs snapped, as if she were debating picking him up for a closer look.

"Oh, Jesus," Cameron whispered. "Don't wake up. Oh, baby, please don't wake up." She shook her head, her lips moving quickly, as if in prayer.

Justin's hand rose an inch above the ground, then fell. The mantid was too intent on his face to notice.

Cameron stood up, waving her hands to get the creature's attention. The mantid raised her head to Cameron as Justin stirred on the ground beneath her. "Justin!" Cameron yelled. "Just stay perfectly still! Play dead and she'll leave you alone!"

She thought she saw the flash of Justin's eyes, and then he seemed to be agitated, fighting off panic. His body trembled, his head rocked side to side.

"Don't fucking move!" Cameron screamed.

The mantid's head snapped down, but Justin lay perfectly still. Cameron felt herself go limp with terror, and she collapsed on the ground. She'd never felt so helpless.

"Stay still, baby! God, please stay still!" Justin wasn't stirring; either he was still out cold or had registered what she was shouting to him. The wound on his shoulder glittered.

Cameron sat on the road, her legs curled beneath her, the sun blazing down, and watched the mantid at the edge of the shadows. The mantid met her stare. As the sun rose, shortening the shadows the balsa trees threw across the road, the mantid was forced to step back off Justin's body. Cameron began to sob with relief, continuing to call to her husband, reassuring him and telling him not to move.

Every few minutes, the mantid had to step back to remain in the shade. Her front legs remained just at the edge of the shadows, and she moved back only when forced to by the sun, her remaining eye never leaving its focus on Cameron.

Finally, when the heat grew too intense, the creature turned and scurried back to the edge of the forest proper.

Cameron ran forward to her husband. He stirred under her touch.

"The speargun," Justin said. "I lost the speargun." He was trembling and sweating. The wound on his shoulder was deep and bleeding freely.

"That's okay," Cameron said. She pressed her cheek to his, helping him sit up.

When the mantid saw Justin move, she stepped forward into the sunlight, air issuing from her spiracles, but quickly withdrew again from the heat.

Cameron looped Justin's good arm around her neck and half-carried, half-dragged him across the eastern field to base camp. To the north, the creature shadowed them, moving among the trees at the edge of the forest.

Justin was delirious, mumbling to himself. "Gotta go into the forest," he muttered. "Gotta find my wife."

"It's okay, baby. I'm here. I'm right here."

When they neared the tents, Cameron's legs gave out. Justin grunted in pain when he hit the ground, then he passed out.

The mantid watched them from among the waving trees, then turned and lumbered back out of sight. Cameron collapsed on top of Justin.

They had survived the night.

Chapter 69   They were down to their last fuel can when the Zodiac puttered up to the blue-and-white painted dock behind the Bio Mar building. A few marine iguanas labored to get out of the bow's way, their heads and the top ridges of their tails protruding from the water as they swam. The morning light spilled across the water, lighting it a twinkling green.

Save a stop directly over the location of the deep-sea core holes to gather three more water samples, they hadn't slowed their pace for the last seventeen and a half hours. The sea had been choppy, which had stretched their voyage an hour and a half longer than they'd anticipated. Diego's hands were chapped and raw from the salt water and the whipping wind, and Rex's back was so sore he could barely straighten up when he stood. Ramoncito was in surprisingly good shape, having passed the time sleeping beneath the edge of a tarp, Rex's Panama hat protecting his sun-chapped face.

Diego was out of the boat in a flash, Rex right behind him, struggling to be careful with the bag full of water samples. He stumbled on the dock and the jars clicked together dangerously, but none broke. They jogged for Diego's office in the Plantas y Invertebrados building, ignoring the overturned furniture and shattered glass inside. Diego pointed down the hallway. "The lab," he said. "I'll grab a few things and meet you there."

Rex entered the lab and arrayed the water jars, seventeen in all, on a countertop. He began to centrifuge the samples, spinning them to isolate the denser dinos from the rest of the seawater. Accustomed to fieldwork, he was a little hesitant in the lab.

Diego entered, holding a test tube filled with dinoflagellate DNA, a wild type sample known to be normal and uninfected; he could use it as a control against which to test the seventeen samples from around Sangre de Dios.

"I'm pelleting at two thousand g," Rex said.

Diego picked up a sample jar and weighed its heft in his hand. "Fine. Next we'll need to do genomic preps to pull the DNA away from the rest of the dino molecules." He headed for a storage closet and removed a stack of kits.

"How long do those take?"

Diego shrugged. "One and a half, two hours. Let's fly through them, get as many as possible running simultaneously."

Diego walked over to the minus-twenty freezer and checked

inside, locating the test tubes containing the enzymes they'd use to do restriction digests, which would cut specific sections of the dinoflagellates' code once they got the DNA separated.

Working at a furious pace, they began to set up the genomic preps. Rex glanced at his watch. It was already 9:20, and they still had so much work to do.

Out on the empty boat, Ramoncito stirred beneath the tarp, Rex's Panama hat crooked over his face. He pulled it back, squinting into the morning light. Looking around, he realized they had arrived back at Puerto Ayora, and he pulled himself stiffly to his feet and stretched.

Pressing his fingertips to his sunburnt cheeks, his head still spinning with all that he'd been told earlier, he headed for the lab, where he knew Diego would be needing his help.

Chapter 70   Cameron raised her head from Justin's back and peered around. The base camp stood deserted twenty yards to their right. For the time being, they were safe. She rolled her husband onto his back and examined his wound. He opened his eyes, blinking hard. Some of the haze had lifted from his eyes.

"Hey, baby," he said. "Did I rescue you?" He tried to smile but couldn't. "I seem to remember taking out the butt of your knife with my head."

"Stay still," Cameron said. She noted that he didn't ask about Tank; she must have looked worse than she thought.

The mantid's hook had swiped a chunk of flesh from his left shoulder. His collarbone was exposed and shattered, but it had managed to absorb the brunt of the blow, protecting the subclavian artery beneath. The mantid had not cut deep enough to reach the axillary artery.

Staring at the exposed muscle and tissue, Cameron realized that Justin would be unable to help her. The plexus of nerves on his left side was compromised; his arm would be useless until he received real medical attention. Plus, his transmitter was missing—they had no way to contact anyone. She was on her own against the creature.

Justin read her face. "I know. I've lost so much blood, I'm probably hypovolemic." He tried to raise his arm but could not. "Check my heart rate."

Cameron took his pulse, pulling back the top lip of her pants so she could time it using the small digital clock face sewn into the material. Her lips tightened when she saw the reading. "One twenty-four."

He cursed. "My resting's fifty-five. I'm tachycardic." He blinked hard, focusing. "You're gonna have to clean the wound for me. Apply pressure."

Cameron retrieved an old cammy shirt from Szabla's tent and ripped it in half. She poured two salt packets into her canteen and shook it, then poured the water from the canteen over the rags. Returning to Justin, she leaned over him, the rag dripping salt water. It would help clean the wound. Justin blocked the open wound on his shoulder protectively with his good hand.

"This is gonna be bad," he said.

She nodded.

He moved his hand and grimaced. "All right, Nurse Ratched."

Cameron pressed the salty cloth to the open wound, and Justin's breath came in hard gasps, though he didn't cry out. Once the wound was clean, she ripped strips of material from the remainder of the cammy shirt and tied them tightly to secure the makeshift pressure dressing over the wound. Beads of sweat stood out along Justin's hairline. His forehead was red and peeling. For once, he didn't even attempt to joke.

"There," she said, standing back to examine her work. "Hopefully it'll clot. Justin. *Justin.*"

Justin's head lolled back, and Cameron caught it. He

blinked once, lazily. "It's all right," he said. "I'm all right. You're gonna have to stick me now. I think I threw some Lactate Ringer's in my kit bag."

She retrieved the IV bag, then tied a strip of cloth around his arm as a tourniquet. Justin flexed his right fist, trying to swell his antecubital vein at the crook of his elbow. She inserted a large bore needle with his guidance, then spiked the IV bag. He lay back as she stood over him, squeezing the bag to push the fluids.

Twenty minutes later when the bag was drained, she removed the needle. Justin tried to struggle up to a sitting position, but she pushed him back down. He grunted in pain.

"You're a liability, Justin. The minute I leave your side, the mantid will come after you, because she'll sense you're easy."

"I am not easy," Justin said. He tried to move his injured arm and cried out. Scrunching his face up, he rolled on the grass, waiting for the pain to subside.

Some blood had seeped through the cloth. Cameron pressed down on the bandage and Justin winced. "We need to get you out of the mantid's sight. If she sees you as vulnerable prey, she might brave the sun to get you."

"Okay. I'll just hide out in the ambulance." His lips were moving less and less when he spoke. His moan sounded like a door creaking open. "What do you want to do?"

"Bury you."

SHE COULDN'T help but notice that the hole she was digging for her husband looked like a shallow grave. It was about ten yards behind the base camp, the remaining tents blocking it from view of the forest in case the mantid was watching. Cameron held the pain at bay while she worked, refusing to let it set in until she finished. Her arms ached so much they finally went numb.

Justin lay on his stomach, watching her work and doing

his best to remain conscious. Cameron had already hydrated him as best she could. He would be going into the hole for a long time, until their 2200 pickup.

If they lived that long.

When she stepped aside, Justin rolled into the hole, lying on his back so his face was nearly level with the ground. His breath quickened as Cameron packed dirt over his legs, his stomach, his chest, obscuring them from view. Finally, only his face remained, an oval of flesh sunk in the dirt.

"You gonna be all right?" Cameron asked.

Justin nodded weakly. He glanced at the side of her shirt, moist with rotting hemolymph. "Good color for you." He closed his eyes and Cameron felt her heart quicken.

"Don't you fucking die on me."

"Please," Justin managed. "I have dry cleaning out."

Cameron leaned over her husband and kissed him tenderly on the lips, then fitted into his mouth a short length of camel bak tubing she'd found in Savage's kit bag. She smoothed dirt over his face until it was gone from view. The tubing protruded from the dirt a few inches, but aside from that, the ground above Justin was perfectly flat.

Since the gash hadn't compromised any major arteries, he would survive if he didn't lose any more blood. And she'd made a point of digging deep enough so that he'd be buried in cool earth, protected from the pounding sun.

Cameron rose and stood near the overturned soil for a moment, then placed her hand near the top of the tubing, wanting to feel Justin's breath on her palm. The person whom she cherished most in the world was buried alive at her feet, and she would have to leave him there for a good long time.

Turning, she headed back to the base camp. She changed her cammies, rinsed with water from the canteen, and applied the last of the antibacterial gel, smearing it liberally over her cuts. She didn't want to waste time now hiking down to the beach for a more thorough washing—it would have to wait until she figured out a plan.

She ripped a blank sheet of paper from a logbook and jotted a note explaining that Justin was in fact alive, and that she'd buried him. Beneath, she scribbled a diagram showing where he was buried. She pinned the piece of paper on the front of one of the remaining tents, where it flapped conspicuously. She stood and stared at the note for a few moments before turning to find her kit bag.

She dug out her IR strobe, turning over the rounded, cigarette pack–sized unit and clicking the waterproof button on the bottom. A soft whirring indicated that it was strobing, though the infrared cover ensured it could only be seen with night vision. She set the strobe in the grass a safe distance from Justin, about midway between base camp and the air vesicle they'd used for the trap.

She returned to her kit bag, finding a bottle of multipurpose solution encased in a Ziploc bag, and cleaned and reinserted her contacts. Pressing her fingers to her temples, she ran through her options in her head, trying to come up with a plan to survive until the helo arrived.

Pulling back the top lip of her pants pocket, Cameron glanced at the small digital clock face. A couple minutes past eleven. For now, the mantid was trapped in the forest, needing shade. Dusk would hit at about six o'clock, which gave Cameron seven hours. In seven hours, the creature could travel wherever she wanted.

Cameron couldn't swim out to the tuff cones for the night because the mantid might discover Justin's hiding place or fly off in search of food, taking the virus with her. And if Cameron couldn't find the remaining larva, which seemed quite likely, there was a good chance she'd have two of the things on her hands at nightfall.

Given Justin's vulnerability and the creature's advantage at night, Cameron would have to take the offensive. The speargun was lost, but she still had three flares, and two crates of TNT. She tried to think of different traps that she could rig, but her mind came up blank. She'd never realized how much they'd counted on Tucker for demo.

Virtually alone on an island, no gun, tracked by one of nature's most advanced predators in its own habitat. Her husband's and the island's life dependent not just on her surviving, but triumphing over the creature. Things looked bad.

Covered with blood, hemolymph, and sweat, Cameron rose and stood on unsteady legs. She needed to eat. If she had food in her stomach, she'd be able to think more clearly.

She staggered toward her old tent, her arms sore, cramps setting in through her legs. The insides of her thighs brushed with each step, sending waves of pain through her lower body. Her head felt close to exploding, her shoulder throbbed incessantly, and the cut on her calf from the freezer vent was deeper than she'd thought.

In all likelihood, she had seven hours to live.

She drank from the canteen until she vomited, the water tasting pure and fresh on the way back up. After that, she regulated how much she hydrated, even though the pork and rice from the MRE felt as dry as sand in her mouth. If she threw up again, she'd lose the nutrients from the meal.

Ravenously devouring the oatmeal cookie bar, she glanced out along the edge of the forest. It took her a long time to pick out the mantid from her hiding place among the foliage. With her motionless, alert stance, she protruded just barely from the last line of trees like a gargoyle, her head swiveling ever so slightly, keeping Cameron in view.

Cameron lay back on the grass, propping her head up on the log so that she could keep an eye on the mantid. It was not long before she began to doze off, and when she snapped awake, she saw that the mantid had broken from cover, taking a few steps toward her.

With a choking gasp, Cameron jumped up, waving her arms and yelling, and the mantid scrambled back to the trees. Evidently, the mantid would risk going out in the direct sunlight only if she was assured an easy kill. Cameron's display of liveliness had saved her—the mantid couldn't afford a chase, since her energy would drain quickly in the hot sun. She knew she could just wait until dark.

The incident reinforced Cameron's relief that Justin was buried, hidden safely from view. It would not have taken long for the mantid to work up the courage to go after wounded prey. The adrenaline from the scare kept Cameron wired for a while, but physical exhaustion, coupled with emotional fatigue, made it hard for her not to think of napping. Sleep called her like a siren's song. She chomped down on her cheek until it bled; she bit her fingers as hard as she could across the nails; she even forced herself to stand, but still, she drifted off.

A jolt of images thrashed through her mind—deformed babies choked and burnt and flaming, piled up in pyres and slaughterhouse mounds, twisted eyes and mouths spread in wordless, thoughtless terror. A mutated baby pulled itself from the melting mound of infant flesh, crawling on distorted limbs though it sank to the wrists. The baby's mouth stretched wide, a clown's screaming frown.

Listing to her left so she had to stumble to recover her balance, Cameron realized that the scream was her own. Her hands struck at her face, trying to wrench the images from her eyes. Remembering where she was, she turned frantically to locate the mantid in the forest. She was gone.

With alarm, Cameron glanced down along the forest's edge. Instinctively, she stepped back toward base camp, then she finally saw her, blending in among the balsas along the side of the road, swaying slightly in the breeze, her one good eye staring at Cameron.

Cameron waved her arms and screamed, "I'm not asleep, you bitch. I'm awake. I'm fucking awake!"

Cameron's wild movements again made it clear that she

was not sluggish prey. The mantid scurried back to the forest, using the trees for cover, moving with surprising speed. Cameron plucked a rock from the ground and hurled it at the mantid, but it careened harmlessly off a tree trunk several yards behind her.

"Fuck you!" Cameron screamed. "Fuck . . ." She fell to her knees.

When she closed her eyes, the deformed babies crowded her, soft-fleshed and innocent and screaming all the screams of hell. She shook her head, trying to clear the haze from her mind, then watched the mantid fade back into the forest, the razor spikes flashing in the sunlight.

She was going to die a slow, painful death and no one would ever know about it. She felt tears filling her eyes beneath the lids, and her chest closed in a mix of panic, frustration, and grief. She pulled Savage's knife from the back of her pants and hurled it at the log. It stuck with a thunk. She broke down sobbing for a few minutes, rocking and pressing her hands to her eyes.

She sat for a long time before the fear started to fade, and then she started muttering to herself, running her fingers through the grass. The fear burned away, leaving only hard, hot embers of rage. Her fist snapped shut around a handful of grass.

When the babies flashed through her mind again, she greeted them, refusing to flinch from the image. She stared at them shrieking and whining until she felt nothing, just a numb tingling across her face.

A part of her had died. She could feel it hanging, loose weight around her heart.

Even though Cameron remembered right where the mantid was, it took her a few moments to distinguish her from the trees. The creature came slowly into view—the angled head, the greenish-tan good eye, the smashed hull of the other. Cameron stared at the mouth that was always slightly open, a collection of protruding parts, and felt the closest thing to pure enmity she had ever felt—not a hatred fueled by emotion, but a cold, dispassionate antipathy.

She rose to her feet and walked to her discarded MRE envelope, digging out the coffee package. Ripping the top open, she poured the grounds into her mouth and chewed, taking a sip from the canteen when they started to gum up. She opened two more MREs and ate the coffee grounds from them as well.

By the time she finished, the thin skin over her temple was pulsing with her heartbeat. She was badly burned across her shoulders and cheeks, and the insides of her ears were so sun-raw they throbbed even in the absence of touch. Through the soreness, she tested her muscles one by one. They still worked, all of them, without enough pain to debilitate her, though her thighs were pretty badly ripped up from her slide down the trunk.

She laced her fingers together and brought the backs of her hands across her forehead, pushing until her knuckles cracked. Ducking, she practiced two hard jabs and a right, grunting with the movement. She pulled her shoulders forward, flexing them, then settled them back. They were broad, as powerful as they'd ever been.

The creature met her glare from the forest.

Cameron was wide awake, so alert her leg was hammering up and down at the knee. Right now, she felt as if she could take the mantid with her bare hands and a blade, as Savage had before. Her eyes halted on the fallen balsa tree near the road. It was propped up off the ground by the boulder on which it had landed. The force of the massive trunk smashing down had been enough to send a crack through the rock.

It had been there all along, right in front of them. The earthquake had practically shown them how to do it, how to take care of the creature.

Cameron charged over to the explosives crates. She threw open a lid and saw the dull red tissue paper of the TNT wrap staring back at her. She picked up one of the two-pound blocks, turning it over before her eyes. The three blocks from the air vesicle were outside near the fire pit, taped together and not yet detonated.

The Death Wind protruded from the top of a log like an arrow, glinting in the sunlight. Slowly, she walked over and pulled it out, holding it up for a moment to see her wavering, silver reflection. She sheathed it, ramming it into the back of her pants again like a gun. With the sheath pressed against her skin and the sorrow in her heart turning to a leaden frost, she understood a part of Savage now that she had not before. She felt hard, ruthless. The mantel had been passed.

She pulled Tucker's kit bag from his tent, digging through it and tossing his clothing and supplies over her shoulder as she searched for the manual she needed. She couldn't find it.

The mantid watched her work.

The other manuals were flapping along the grass and Cameron ran them down frantically, fearful she had overlooked the one she needed. She stepped on one just before it blew across the field, and when she glanced down at it, her face lightened with relief. In large stenciled letters across the front cover, it said: *Tactical Demolitions Training Manual.*

Cameron ran her finger down the table of contents, flipping to the page labeled *Abatis*. A rough sketch showed two rows of trees felled in a crisscross pattern, blasted but still clinging to their stumps.

The wind picked up, howling through the watchtower.

She was ready to get down to business.

Chapter 71   Cameron had five hours until dark and a lot of work to get done.

As she unwound the tape from the TNT blocks she'd retrieved from the hole, she prayed that the other larva had died somehow or that it would not emerge from metamorphosis until tomorrow. She stood a chance, however small, of surviving until 2200 with only one mantid on the island, but with two, there was no way she'd make it.

And two could mate.

Cameron had rigged an Abatis tree trap only once, in Iran in '03, but between her memory and the demo manual, she'd be fine. She retrieved the previously rigged TNT blocks from where she'd set them beside the fire pit and threw them in one of the explosives crates. The crates left furrows in the grass as she dragged them across the field toward the road, ignoring the pain spreading through her body like a fever.

The mantid watched her with interest, then pulled back into the forest, disappearing. As Cameron struggled with the heavy crates, the mantid appeared at regular intervals, craning her neck out from different spots in the foliage along the forest's edge. She wouldn't dare come down here in the heat, not now with the sun near its peak.

Cameron would have to hurry to get all the trees wired before dusk. She still carried the scent of the body from the freezer, carried it on the bottom of her pants and in the hardened smear on the back of her tank top. After she finished setting the Abatis, she'd have to wash all the virus-laden secretions off herself.

She finally reached the middle of the road and dropped the end of the cruise box. It thunked to the ground, kicking up a cloud of dust.

Carrying the blocks of TNT two at a time, she laid them beside some of the balsas lining the road. She selected ten of the taller trees on each side, including the slender quinine toward the middle of the row, spacing them out so that they were roughly five yards apart. Diego would approve of the fact that she was only blasting introduced species, she realized with mild amusement.

Despite her aching arms and back, she went to work immediately on the twenty trees she'd chosen, aware all the time of the creature leering at her from the cover of the forest at the road's end. Whenever Cameron looked up, it took her several minutes to actually see the creature, but she could *sense* her immediately and instinctively.

If she used too much TNT on a tree, she was liable to blow it straight off the stump, and she'd have much less control over which direction it fell. If the charge was too small, then the tree might not go over at all, in which case she'd be a sitting duck. In the manual, she'd found the conversion chart that calculated the size of the charge to use. The trees she'd chosen were old and sturdy, with diameters that she estimated at three feet; according to the equation, she'd need roughly twenty-four pounds of TNT per tree.

She fit the TNT blocks with nonelectric blasting caps, smearing the puttylike booster around their bases. Technically, TNT didn't require booster, but she used it on each charge anyway. She wasn't going to fuck around and have something not blow at the last minute.

There were no tools to make bore holes in the trees, but the blocks of TNT could be easily fastened to the trunks and used as untamped concentrated external charges. The manual, she recalled, had said to set the charges five feet above the ground to ensure the trees would remain attached to the stumps when they fell. But Cameron wanted them low to the ground all the way across, so she primed the timber at three and a half feet, notching the bark with the peen of the hammer Szabla had brought back from one of the farmhouses.

The work was hard and tiresome, and it took her even longer because she kept glancing nervously at the forest. Now, the creature was nowhere in sight.

Using the thick tape that was stored in the underside of the explosives box lid, she adhered the TNT blocks to the trees—two rows of six blocks for each trunk. The tape stood out in shiny bands. She used one strand of det cord, with small extensions, for the charges on each side of the road, carefully crimping the aluminum ends of the blasting caps around it. It looked pretty when she was done; Tucker would've been proud.

The TNT would blow out a chunk of tree beneath it when it detonated. Because of the placement of the blocks, the trees of each side would fall parallel at a forty-five-degree angle to the road, crashing down on the dirt in the middle. Cameron would have to set two trip wires so that one side would detonate before the other, or the trees would deflect each other on the way down. She dug through the explosives box for eyelets, then started to run wire off the spool. She decided to set the trip wires about ten yards apart, each of them four feet off the ground so that the mantid wouldn't unwittingly step over them.

The sun had already peaked and begun its descent. Cameron checked the watch face and saw that it was already three o'clock. Only three hours remained until dusk.

The air was already starting to cool across her shoulders.

DIEGO PLACED the dino DNA segments from the seventeen water samples into separate wells of the ethidium-bromide-soaked agar and plugged in the gel box, a voltage machine that would draw the negatively charged DNA downward. The DNA's progress through the viscous agar would form distinct banding patterns visible under UV light, which he and Rex could compare to the control dinoflagellates' banding pattern to determine if the samples were infected.

Rex drummed his fingers on the countertop, checking his watch. "How long will this take?" he asked.

Diego settled back on the high metal stool, fished for a joint in his shirt pocket, and lit it. Ramoncito watched him, shaking his head.

"An hour," Diego said.

Rex tapped the gel box. "Can't we speed it up?" he asked. "It's only at one hundred fifty volts."

Diego shook his head; his chest expanded with a toke. Smoke wafted from his mouth when he spoke. "It'll melt the gel. Fuck up the resolution."

He pointed to Rex's knee, which was vibrating up and down in a nervous tick, then held out the joint. Rex stared at the joint, at Diego.

"There's nothing more we can do now," Diego said.

Rex reached out and took the joint.

THE MANTID'S legs moved her back into the forest, the cuticle scraping loosely around her body as she walked.

She crawled up the trunk of a tree and secured herself upside down, her slightest movements causing her to swing. Dangling like a bat, she began to push through her old exoskeleton. It split first along the seam of the thorax, and she wriggled her head and raptorial legs from the gash, squirming. The spear stock was deeply embedded in her head; the old cuticle had disintegrated around it. Her abdomen remained encased in the old cuticle and she flailed back and forth, screeching, until it popped free. Then, she hung from the exuvia for the better part of an hour, which gave her new cuticle a chance to begin hardening. When she finally dropped to the ground, she landed in a heap, her new cuticle still moist and tender. She rose quickly; the dirt could crumple up her new wings and dry out her exoskeleton. Her anomalous post-metamorphosis molt was complete.

Her protective tegmina were a deep brown, attached to her body at the second link of her thorax and overlaying her light-green speckled underwings. Sprouting from the third section of her thorax, the underwings stuck out a bit, forming green stripes along her sides.

The mantid crawled back up the tree, past the branch to which her old cuticle still clung, past the other branches that spread like balconies from the core of the trunk, and when she reached the top of the canopy, where the foliage of all the *Scalesias* wove itself together, she pushed through and stood on top of it, her four back legs taking hold of the uppermost branches and leafy boughs.

She was standing atop the forest.

The water circling the island was visible all around, the sky stretching clear and blue for as far as the eye could see.

Unfurling her wings from her sides like massive capes, she spread them wide. Their span was enormous, and as they dried, they would continue to stretch and grow; only this benefit had driven her to brave the sun. Already, the new cuticle stiffened around her, a living suit of armor. Her body unfolded to the air, the mantid rested, growing stronger and harder in the sun.

Soon, it would be nightfall.

Chapter 72   As Cameron finished setting the trip wire, a shriek echoed up the road. She wasn't sure whether it was the mantid or a wounded animal, but it sent a chill from the depths of her bowels all the way up her spine.

Using herself as bait, Cameron would attract the mantid. The mantid would be drawn from the forest, heading for Cameron along the open stretch of the road. About a third of the way down, the mantid would trip the first wire. The det cord would explode, detonating the blasting caps and, in turn, the TNT. All the trees on the corresponding side would fall simultaneously. The explosion would either freeze the creature or startle her forward. If she froze, she'd be crushed by the toppling trees, and if she started forward, she'd trip the second wire and the whole trap would go. The trees would fall from both sides, pounding the ground along a hundred-yard segment of the road.

There would be gaps—that was certain, since the Abatis was generally used as a roadblock, not a killing trap, but that was a risk Cameron would have to take. She was fairly confident that the trees falling at crisscrossing angles would crush anything beneath them. Once the wire was tripped, no matter which direction the mantid moved she didn't stand a good chance.

The trap had a number of situation-specific advantages. Most important, it expanded the danger zone drastically; if the mantid moved anywhere along the guessed route, she stood a good chance of getting killed or maimed. A compact little boar might find its way through an Abatis, but not the long, wiry mantid. If Cameron had elected to rig a smaller booby trap, she would have had to predict exactly where the mantid would step, and that had already proven difficult. The Abatis also had the advantage of drawing the prey into a known area, cutting down the variables one faced when dealing with a free-roaming adversary.

Cameron walked the path she hoped the mantid would take, careful not to get too close to the forest at the northern end of the road. She saw the first thin trip wire gleaming in the sunlight and stopped, letting it rest across her stomach. Ducking under, she counted ten steps to the second trip wire, which she also cautiously avoided.

The Abatis was ready.

She strode down the road to the trail just beyond the watchtower. She still had time to wash off.

THE WATER reminded her of Justin. It always had. When he swam, his entire body moved with a grace usually reserved for porpoises and rays. For fear of revealing his hiding place to the creature, she had resisted the urge to go and check on him, though she wanted to desperately. As long as his heart rate stayed low, he shouldn't bleed out. And he was resting, maybe even sleeping, cool beneath the surface of the earth. He'd have to wait until after the Abatis was detonated.

Cameron sank all the way beneath the surface, the water closing over her head with a gulp, and then she was drifting, alone and lifeless and free. The teal water was so clear that when she opened her eyes, it was as if she were looking through a mask. She rinsed herself off, wiping the virus-laden smudges from her clothes and skin.

The sand on the bottom was brilliantly white, ribbed like

desert dunes. Mini-cyclones swirled, the white grains glimmering as light swept through them. Ahead, a series of vesicular lava rocks unfolded like the vertebrae of a sunken creature.

Just beyond them, Cameron saw an outline of something large, majestic. She swam toward it in awe, breaststroking underwater. It rippled into view, a magnificent and rare coral head, standing alone before the wall of the reef. As Cameron approached it, she saw that it curved around, encircling an underwater lagoon. The walls would keep growing upward, eventually forming an atoll.

Small patches of the coral were bleached, destroyed by UV sunlight, but for the most part the underwater life had rejuvenated since the last El Niño. Within the ring was a fantasia of color and movement. Shiny green sea urchins dotted the white surface of the walls, flicking into view behind drifting strands of seaweed. A jewel moray shot from a dark hollow, narrowly missing a darting minnow. A blue parrot fish grazed, its small mouth emitting bubbles as it nibbled along a notch of coral. A marine iguana tirelessly navigated the surface, its small legs churning, tail undulating.

The water within the reef was tinted green from the minuscule bits of floating algae, but still it retained a near perfect clarity. Cameron watched a yellow damselfish chase the parrot fish off the coral wall, flicking its tail as it shot forward. The parrot fish swam away, though Cameron could see it for several yards before it disappeared from sight. Triumphantly, the damselfish banked in a fighter jet's wide turn before returning to the inner sanctum of the reef, its bright yellow tail and lip contrasting sharply with the sleek black of the rest of its body. With wonder, Cameron watched it slither through the water, her lungs beginning to burn.

As Cameron started for the surface, the damselfish swerved sharply to avoid something rising from the depth of the ring. Startled from her reverie, Cameron waited to see what would emerge.

Her arms flared in shock when she saw the distinctive green head, the rings of the abdominal segments. Rising like steam from a grate, the larva drifted into view, its back to Cameron. Moving its body side to side like a sea snake, the larva coasted forward, its shadow rippling along the bottom of the sand like a strange, dark organism. It broke the surface a few feet behind the marine iguana, which was still clumsily churning the waters. The larva's mouth opened wide, mandibles spreading. The iguana was gone and the larva dipped back below, mouth working. It slithered through the inner ring of the atoll, heading for the open waters beyond.

Cameron kicked to the surface, pausing only to fill her lungs once, and then she swam toward the larva, taking long, fluid underwater strokes. Her hand went to the knife tucked into the band of her pants and slid it from its sheath. She moved without hesitation.

The larva did not sense her approach. Its head rotated as it tracked a brilliant moorish idol swimming before it, and its gills rippled as they expelled water.

Arcing her arm like a javelin thrower, Cameron guided the knife, releasing it gently so as not to upset its course. It sent silvery disks of light through the water as it coasted, seeming to vibrate as it caught the sun.

It approached the unsuspecting larva from behind, nearing its head. As the larva's gills flickered wide, the blade disappeared through one of the slits, burying itself in the larva's head to the hilt. The larva jolted as if it had been shocked, bubbles steaming from its spiracles. A gorgeous cloud of hemolymph spread from the three gills like a blossoming rose, and Cameron tried not to think of the virus moving through the waters around her.

The larva's mouth opened, the tip of the blade visible between its mandibles. Even underwater, Cameron could hear the screech emanating from its spiracles. The larva bent to face Cameron, too stunned to thrash about, though its prolegs squirmed in slow circles. The greenish liquid continued to pour from the slits of its gills.

Cameron's eyes narrowed as she closed in on the larva, her teeth clenching until she felt the grind deep in her head. She fisted the knife stock and turned for shore, the impaled larva turning with the blade. The larva snapped along her side as she kicked back to the beach, surfacing occasionally for air.

She pulled herself from the water, the knife still embedded in the larva's gills. The larva's terminal segment skimmed along the surface of the waves as she sloshed to shore. The larva emitted squeals, still strong, though it had lost so much of its fluids. It bucked and kicked, bouncing along her side, its head twisted by the blade's intrusion. Cameron kept its body tilted so that the infected hemolymph would run off the body rather than down the knife onto her hand.

Cameron headed up through the cliff and then along the trail that led to the road. She passed the watchtower and went directly to the specimen freezer, dragging the larva as it shrieked and struggled. Yanking the door open, she ignored the fetid air, the puddles of ooze, the rotting corpses. Her boot struck Tank's head as she stepped forward, knocking over his bustlike remains. She angled her knife hand and the larva slid from the blade, thumping to the floor.

She seized the empty hook dangling from the ceiling and impaled the larva on it, jerking the barbed end through the bottom of its chin until it curved from its mouth like a pointed tongue. Squealing emanated from its whole body.

Gripping the end of the hook in a fist, Cameron raised it above her head like a fisherman, holding the shaking larva right before her. She viewed it neither with anger nor with the pleasure of vengeance; it was merely a tool to be used as she'd used Savage's knife and the TNT.

The sun was low in the sky as Cameron stopped by base camp and scooped up the three flares, ramming them into her back pocket where they protruded like a rolled newspaper. Swinging the larva at her side, she started down the road, the trees rising on each side of her. Ahead, the howling watchtower continued its laments.

The splintering wood of the ladder hurt her sore hands, but she pulled her body up, paying no attention to the larva as it dragged along beside her, shaking and squealing. The shed was a dark, gaping hole atop the watchtower, a screaming mouth. She swung the hook up into the shed first, using it to pull the rest of her body up. Impaled on the hook, the larva crashed against the floor, leaving a wet stain. The squealing grew even louder.

As Cameron pulled herself onto her feet, the wind resonated within the shed, and she felt the sounds as vibrations in her bones.

A ruler-thick strip of wood had come free from the plywood of the roof, and Cameron threaded it through the eyelet at the top of the hook. It wedged deep and firm, the larva swinging from the ceiling like a tortured chandelier when she let go.

She yanked the flares from her back pocket, holding one in her mouth as she ripped the strikers from the other two. They fizzled with a bright-red glow. Cracking the top of the third flare, she lit it also, the red lights dancing in the walls of the shed.

Her front pocket held the last inches of tape from the demo box, and she looped it around the flares as the larva dangled and squirmed behind her, trying to free itself from the hook. The hook had torn through the cuticle of its chin, stopping at the firm line of its jaw.

Cameron tossed the flares to the floor beneath the larva and walked past it without so much as a look. She had to return to base, rinse her hands with canteen water, and see if she could squeeze a bit more antibacterial gel from the bottle. The sun had dipped to the horizon, casting an orange glow through the tops of the trees and turning the forest to a sea of waving flames.

It was dusk, she noticed, as she started the climb down. The creature would soon appear.

Chapter 73   Fourteen of the water samples were clean. Only the three that had been taken from directly over the deep-sea core holes remained. They'd saved them for last, since they were the most likely to show traces of the virus. Polaroids of the DNA bands in the agar lay on the counter-top, including a control shot from the wild type sample that they knew to be normal.

"All right," Diego said. "We'll each check one result."

Ramoncito looked first, comparing the sample Polaroid to that of the control and checking for differences. There were none. "Clean," he said. Diego glanced over his shoulder, double-checking that the banding patterns of the sample and the control matched.

Steeling himself, Rex took the control Polaroid from Ramoncito and raised the second sample photograph up beside it. He exhaled deeply. "Clean," he said.

The final Polaroid sat in the middle of the counter, hold-ing the key to Sangre de Dios's fate. Diego gazed longingly at the joint, snubbed out in a beaker. He picked up the photo and held it before his face, his eyes closed. He opened his eyes. Looked from one photo to the other. Slowly, he set them down, his cheeks trembling.

"What?" Rex asked, trying to contain his panic.

"Clean," Diego whispered. "Clean, clean, clean."

He lowered his head to the countertop and they all stayed quiet for a few moments. "Well," Rex said. "That's step one. We still need to check in with Everett to see if the squad has taken care of the accountable virus reservoir."

He pulled the transmitter from his pocket and placed it on his open palm, leaning toward it as he asked to be put through to Slammer Two at Detrick.

Samantha's voice came through clearly. "Yes?"

"It's clean," Rex said. "The water system is clean. Every last sample."

There was a silence.

"That's good news," Samantha said slowly. "But we've been unable to contact Cameron. Either her transmitter is down or she's . . ." She declined to finish the sentence.

Rex noticed that she'd only mentioned Cameron. He closed his eyes, pushing away his concern, fighting to stay focused.

"What does that mean?" Diego asked. "About the bombing?"

"Without confirmation that the virus reservoir is exterminated, there's not much we can do," Samantha said. "Unfortunately. They're going to send a medevac at 2200 to look for survivors."

"And the B1 departure is 2300?" Rex asked.

"Yes."

"You keep trying to contact them via transmitter," Rex said, "and we'll haul our asses to the airport for when the medic unit returns. With the soldiers, let's hope."

By the time Rex had shoved the transmitter into his pocket, Diego was already out the door. Rex and Ramoncito ran after him through the Darwin Station and down the winding dirt road that led to Avenida Charles Darwin, having a difficult time keeping up. Rex was surprised to realize that it was already nightfall.

When they reached the street, Diego was sitting in the driver's seat of a huge blue truck that was parked near the path to Hotel Galápagos, his hands working beneath the steering column. A pair of handcuffs dangled over the rearview mirror.

"You run fast for a stoner," Rex said, panting.

Diego jerked his head toward the passenger door. "Shut up and jump in," he said. He twisted two wires and the engine roared to life.

Chapter 74 Cameron sat patiently, legs folded Indian-style beneath her at the south end of the road, about twenty yards north of the watchtower. The wind whipped over her shoulder, blowing to the forest. She gazed up the road into the *Scalesias*, watching the trip wires blend into the air as the sun sank from view. The air tinted with shadow, turning dusty gray, then black, but still the mantid did not appear.

The glow of the red flares in the shed became more pronounced as the light drained from the sky. Soon, the watchtower behind her was the only point of light in the dark landscape, a shining devil's eye. The squeals of the larva should have been horrifying to Cameron, yet she found them almost pleasing, riffs of a symphony she had composed. The watchtower's howls joined the larva's squeals, sometimes even overpowering them.

Underlit with the red glow of the flares, the larva continued to struggle against the hook, its head cocked back at an excruciating angle, its figure shadowed on the shed's inside. Cameron hummed to herself, the tortured outline writhing behind her.

She didn't understand what was delaying the mantid. The wriggling larva, in combination with the bright artificial light of the flares, surely should have drawn her attention by now.

Cameron sat in the dead center of the road, completely unprotected. Whether the mantid was attracted to the larva or to Cameron, she'd be heading down the road toward the watchtower. Cameron would stand and wave her arms once the creature appeared by the edge of the forest, drawing her forward across the trip wires. The two minuscule wires would be all that stood between Cameron and certain death.

Cameron was growing impatient, anxious about the mantid's delay. She stood, letting the wind carry her scent up the road to the dark leaves of the forest.

The moon cast the road in a pale yellow glow. Cameron stared hard at the dark mass of the forest, as if she could will the creature to appear. She expected to see her at any moment, the wide insect head leering on the thin neck, the legs pulling her forward, graceful and ungainly at the same time.

The howl of the wind rose to a pitch that for an instant drowned out the larva's piercing squeals. And then a shadow fell across the road.

Cameron whirled around, trying to figure out how the dark night could have gotten darker, and then she saw her, stretched wide across the watchtower. The mantid clung to the walls around the shed's mouth with her legs, spread wide like a spider in a web.

The mass of her body nearly filled the shed's entrance, blocking out most of the reddish light. Cameron stumbled back, surprised. It hadn't occurred to her that the mantid would circle around to the watchtower. For some reason, she had assumed that she would come directly down the length of the road.

For an awful instant, Cameron thought that it was a different mantid—a new creature that she had not yet encountered—but then she recognized the shattered eye and the black stock of the spear. She realized why the mantid was so much larger; she had molted. She'd taken so long to appear because her new cuticle was hardening.

Cameron glanced nervously down the dark road, trying desperately to recall the location of the trip wires. She'd have to get the mantid to run up the road toward the forest in order to trip the wires, opposite the direction for which she had planned.

The mantid pulled herself into the shed and stood in profile facing the larva. The red light outlined her dark figure, shining around her with a glow that looked almost divine. The rows of spikes on her raptorial legs glistened like fangs. Cameron could see exactly how they fit together, like the teeth of a bear trap.

Cameron started moving quietly up the road, backing up into the Abatis trap. She'd try to sneak under the trip wires and get the mantid's attention when she was on the other side. She hoped the creature would charge her, tripping the wires on the way.

Cameron would be all right if she could just get to the other side undetected.

The mantid leaned forward, her massive head angled. Through her unbroken eye she regarded the larva, her last dying hope for procreation. The larva writhed in pain, shaking its head back and forth, attempting to rip the hook free. The squeals from its spiracles reached a pitch rife with nearly human agony. Its posterior end plopped across the mantid's head, but the mantid did not flinch.

Cameron felt viciousness emanating from the creature like waves of heat. A drop of digestive fluid slid down one of the mantid's mandibles and dripped to the ground. The light of the flares reflected in the creature's eye, which had again gone black with the night.

With one swift motion, the mantid lashed her legs at her squirming sibling, raking it from the hook. Clenched in her spikes, the larva screeched, the sound continuing even after its head rose into the creature's mouth and was severed with a single bite.

Cameron felt her stomach churning, but she continued her slow pace, careful not to disturb the occasional rock on the road. As she backed up, her heel caught on a lip of the road raised in the recent earthquake, and she went down softly on her ass.

But not softly enough.

The mantid's antennae snapped erect, and she rotated her head and front legs, peering into the night. Cameron felt her stare, felt her locate her in the darkness. The creature's head split in a gargantuan soundless scream, the pieces of her mouth flailing in the cavernous rictus. The larva's head fell from the mouth.

Panic rose like vomit through Cameron's chest and she tasted it at the back of her throat. The road dug into her chafed palms as she watched, frozen.

The mantid's legs snapped once, discharging the larva's small, limp body. Moving to the edge of the shed, the mantid extended her slender neck, sticking her head out into the open air and fixing Cameron in her stare.

Relax, Cameron thought. You still have time. She's gotta climb down the watchtower. You can still make it past the trip wires.

The mantid stepped forward, her four back legs crowding the edge of the shed's entrance. Folding her raptorial legs to her chest, the mantid leaned forward even farther into the open air. Slowly, her enormous inner wings slid out from beneath the tegmina, fanning behind her and spreading across the expanse of the watchtower. The red light shone through them, casting a bloody glow over the road.

Cameron tried to swallow, but her throat had tightened into a ball.

The mantid tipped forward from the edge of the tower, drawing her massive wings up behind her like the sail of a hang glider. Their span was so wide it dwarfed her body. She stepped from the watchtower, her sharp front legs hanging beneath her like missiles.

She was gliding. She hurtled up the road at Cameron.

Cameron screamed and started sprinting for the forest. She had nothing by which to gauge the creature's progress, no sound of footsteps, no crunching foliage. Blindly, terrified, she ran, the trees watching solemnly over her from both sides like spectators at an execution. Her legs seemed to move in slow motion; her boots felt as if they were made of concrete. The hammering of her breath filled her entire body. Her heartbeat pounded in the tips of her fingers and the backs of her knees.

The mantid was at her back; Cameron could sense her closing in. If she could have died instantly, simply melted into the ground before the creature seized her, she would have.

The mantid screeched, sending a fresh wave of terror through Cameron. She chanced a glance behind her. The mantid was about twenty yards back, swooping down fast.

Cameron whirled back around and saw the first trip wire right in front of her. With a yell, she hurled her body in the air over it, rolled once sideways across the road, and was up running, having barely slowed down.

The explosion should have come right behind her, but Cameron realized that the mantid was up too high, that she had glided right over the wire. Cameron would have to trip the last wire herself. But if she ran into it, it would slow her down, and she'd never make it off the road before the trees crushed her. If she tried to roll under the wire, the creature would be on her instantly.

She had ten walking steps until the next trip wire, that much she remembered. Her body flew forward, her mind racing. Air from the plummeting mantid blew across her shoulders. She had no time to think. The thin wire gleamed in the moonlight, mere feet away.

Reaching behind her, Cameron yanked the knife from the back of her pants, pulling it from its sheath. It slid smoothly out. She twirled it in her hand, never slowing, angling it down her forearm with the blade out, just as Savage used to do.

The blade met the wire with a click and bent it forward as she ran through it. The explosives went off with a deep roar, sending fragments of bark and tree chunks flying. A plug of pulp whistled just over her head. The blasts were blinding, flashing one after another and illuminating the road like a strobe light.

The mantid was momentarily startled, but she kept her eye on her prey below, trained on the kill.

The wire stretched to its limit against the knife and then broke with a twang, whipping off to both sides. Cameron's legs didn't stop pumping for an instant.

Above her, the mantid drew her raptorial legs up under her chin. They were coiled, ready to flash out like the talons of a hawk.

Higher still, the balsa trees started their downward crash, sporadically lit by the explosions. The twelve blocks of TNT had been too much for the quinine trunk, blowing it straight off the stump. It went horizontal almost instantly. Heavy with branches, the top end of the tree clubbed through the air.

The mantid sped down at Cameron's back. The raptorial legs flexed, pausing a split second before the lightning-fast strike.

Cameron felt the whole island closing in on her, the falling trees blocking out the sky, the flying predator at her back, and it seemed her blood itself was adrenaline as she raced toward the end of the constricting road.

The quinine tree struck the mantid across the back, knocking air through her spiracles with a screech and sending a splattering of digestive juice across Cameron's shoulders. Knocked off balance, the mantid careened upside down, one wing crunched to a worthless flap. The momentum from the blow shot her ahead of Cameron on the ground, and Cameron leapt over her gnashing head, dodging the snap of a leg midair. The mantid rolled once and began a fast limp after Cameron.

The airborne quinine smashed the ground behind them, tripping the second wire. The road lit with another blaze of light. The air filled with flying wood, the fragments zooming overhead. The other trees crackled on their stumps as they tipped in on Cameron and the mantid from both sides.

The tree closest to the forest, right at the end of the trap, was falling ahead of the others. The TNT had blown out a huge section of the trunk, hastening its plummet.

Cameron sprinted at the shrinking space beneath the final tree, the mantid dragging herself rapidly after her. If Cameron didn't squeeze under the tree before it hit the ground, she'd either be caught by the creature or crushed by the other trees. Overhead, the air was filled with falling timber, flash-lit, so it appeared to crash down in great jerks.

Gasping, Cameron threw herself under the last tree as it closed to the ground like a guillotine. Her shoulder barely glanced off the trunk as she skimmed under, but it was enough to send her flying. Pain clawed through her back, tempered only by her relief that she hadn't been crushed. She spun in the air 180 degrees, landing flat on her stomach and chest, facing the imploding road.

Above the fallen trunk of the last tree, she could see the mantid reared up to her full nine feet, hurtling forward even with the left side of her body crushed. A tree smashed to the ground behind her, barely missing.

Oh God, Cameron thought, what if they don't hit her? What if they all miss?

The mantid leapt forward, screeching as she barely outran another falling tree, and Cameron tried to get up and run, but she was limp with fear and exhaustion. Her body had nothing left.

No images flashed before her eyes, no childhood memories, no thoughts of Justin—there was just the charging creature, the road digging into her chin, her mouth full of dirt.

She had resigned herself at last to death, when the last falling tree smashed across the mantid's back, pounding her into the ground with such force that Cameron's eyes couldn't even track her movement down.

A large tree trunk blocked the creature from view, but Cameron heard her screech turn into a rasping whistle. The air filled with settling leaves and dust and a magnificent silence, broken only by an occasional rustle from the mantid, which she heard even over the ringing in her ears.

Cameron slid the knife back into the sheath behind her pants and tried to rise, but pain raked through her back and she crumpled up with a yell. Her hip was completely numb, and her leg did not respond when she tried to move it. Pulling herself forward, her fingers clawing holds in the dirt, Cameron scraped along the ground toward the fallen tree trunk that was blocking the mantid from view. The dirt felt like steel wool across her stomach, and a few sharp stones stung her through her ragged tank top.

As she neared, the rasping grew louder. She used a knot to

pull herself on top of the trunk. The mantid was lying on her back, the massive trunk having crushed her abdomen nearly flat. Though her head and prothorax still extended from beneath the tree, her raptorial legs were pinned beneath it, the razor spikes smashed somewhere in the mess of tree, guts, and earth. Her head moved slightly back and forth, her mouth opening feebly.

She was dying.

Cameron tried to climb down the other side of the trunk but ended up falling. She landed on her hip and screamed, the pain watering her eyes. Her vision dotted, then cleared, and she pulled herself toward the creature.

The mantid couldn't lift the back of her head from the dirt. Her mouth gnashed at Cameron, moving as if trying to free itself and attack her on its own.

The smell of the rotting mouth rising to her, Cameron lowered her face right above the mantid's, her reflection clear in the creature's remaining eye. Glaring into the black eye, she knew, somehow, that the mantid sensed her life draining away.

The mantid struggled, trying desperately to lift her head so she could crush Cameron's face in her jaws. But she was too weak; she succeeded only in turning her head meekly from side to side. Cameron reached for the protruding spear stock, the movement causing her to lean over the mantid. Her blond hair fell in neat curves around her cheeks. Her chin was awash with saliva and blood; she inadvertently drooled a thick cord into the quivering maw. Cameron grabbed the stock of the spear with both fists. The whole head lifted when she drew back her arms. She smashed the head back against the ground, driving the spear stock deeper through the cuticle. The mantid's mouth gaped in its awful silent fashion. The spear tip continued to press through the creature's head, which yielded with a moist crackling.

The mantid shuddered beneath Cameron's hands, then convulsed, her cuticle rattling against the tree trunk that was now part of her abdomen. Her mouth still spread wide, the mantid stopped shaking and her head rolled up and to the side.

Spitting a mouthful of blood down the front of her chin and onto the ground, Cameron started to sob. She wept lying flat on her stomach, tears cutting through the dirt on her face, her fists still gripping the last protruding inches of the spear.

Cameron lowered her head, resting it on her forearm as she fought for control, pushing her lips together until they stopped quivering.

Savage's knife was lying where it had fallen in the dirt nearby. She closed her fingers around the black Micarta as if to draw strength from it. Raising her aching arm, she plunged the Death Wind into the top of the tree trunk that lay across the creature's chest. The knife rose vertically, like a cross from a grave.

She thought of Justin and tried to rise, but could not. A few dry sobs escaped her, shaking her shoulders. She rolled onto her back, the stars above blurring into a fantasia of pinpoints and yellow streaks.

Darkness claimed her.

Chapter 75   La Carretera al Canal, a poorly paved highway that led over the highlands of Santa Cruz to the northern side of the island, was forty-two kilometers of mess. Scarps and cracks slowed the truck to a cautious crawl in the night. A few times, Diego had to stop before driving across a fissure, and wait for Rex and Ramoncito to remove the two planks from the bed of the truck and lay them across the gap. They hit one scarp particularly hard and Rex was convinced they'd blown a tire, but the truck rattled on, undeterred.

After what seemed a lifetime, they drove down the far side of the hill, coasting to the dock at the Itabaca Channel and gazing across the dark stream of water at the airport lights on Baltra.

The truck skidded to a halt, and they hopped out.

Rex looked at the stretch of water and cursed. "I forgot

about that," he said. "There's no boat. What are we going to—" He glanced over, but Diego had already stripped down to his boxers.

Diego leaned back in the truck, grabbing the handcuffs from the rearview mirror. "I'm going to stop that plane if I have to handcuff myself to it," he said. He ran a few steps and hit the water with a graceful dive.

Ramoncito groaned and began to strip down. Rex watched him for a few moments before following suit.

CAMERON AWAKENED with the helo blowing sheets of wind across her body. Guided by the IR strobe, it flew low over the road, landing in the grassy field between base camp and the air vesicle. A soldier sat crouched behind the M-60 mounted in the door.

Three figures scurried from the helo, running to her body under the yellow blanket of the spotlight, white bands with red crosses standing out on their arms. They stopped dead in their tracks, Berettas drawn, when they saw the mantid's body beneath the tree. One shouted back to the gunner and two men emerged with flamethrowers. Cameron coughed, her throat lined with dirt and blood.

The flamethrowers burst to life with sporadic belches, obliterating the remnants of the virus from the base camp. Cameron raised a weary hand and held up two fingers, then pointed in the directions of Ramón and Floreana's house and of the specimen freezer—the two additional sites that needed to be sterilized by fire. One of the soldiers nodded and jogged off down the road, flamethrower in hand. This was all relevant, she realized, only if the water samples had come in clean.

Two figures moved in cautiously, eyes on the creature, and lifted Cameron onto a stretcher. Cameron tried to speak, to tell them where Justin was buried—that despite her last correspondence with Samantha, he was still alive—but her throat was caked with dust and no sound came out. Despite her protestations, they carried her briskly but carefully back to the helo. Behind her, the flamethrower claimed the mantid's body.

Cameron thrashed on the stretcher. "Stop, we have a man down," she managed to croak, but her voice was barely audible over the burst of the flamethrowers and the whir of the rotors. She pointed to the mound of upturned soil under which Justin was buried, but they moved right past it. Her and Derek's old tent was ablaze, along with the note she'd pinned to it.

She threw herself from the stretcher, grunting when she hit the ground. Justin's body was buried about ten feet away. The figures stopped, concerned, then leaned over her. She saw a needle flash in a gloved hand—a sedative. She rolled on her back, swinging roughly, and the figures backed off.

She turned and pulled herself toward Justin's grave, feeling the pinch of the needle in her ass. The world blurred and swam. She fought off unconsciousness, dragging herself forward with bloody fingernails. The figures waited for her to pass out.

Grunting, she yanked herself toward the plastic tube that protruded from the ground. Spots dotted her vision. She finally reached it and swiped away a handful of dirt, revealing the edge of Justin's cheek. One of the figures crouched over him, checking his neck for a pulse.

Cameron felt her body floating away.

STRAPPED TO the stretcher, she came to when the Blackhawk struck pavement at Baltra. One of the corpsmen fiddled with an oxygen line. She leaned over Cameron and checked her pupils with a penlight, first pulling on a second set of latex gloves.

Resting in the tangle of an oxygen tube on her chest was a transparent Ziploc bag that held her necklace and wedding ring. The corpsman must have removed them from her neck to get a clear line to her pulse. Afraid the ring would get lost with all the activity, Cameron reached out weakly and fought the bag open, pushing the ring onto her finger. The necklace slid from her chest, falling to the helo floor. She wasn't used to wearing the ring properly—it felt large and unwieldy, yet comforting.

Cameron rolled her head limply to the side. Justin lay on the stretcher across the helo, his glassy eyes staring up at the roof. His face was pallid, like a corpse's, and awash in sweat and dirt. Cameron's eyes traveled down to his fingernails. They were blue; he was shunting blood to his heart and brain. A single tear rolled from the corner of his eye, but he did not blink.

"Baby," she said, her voice choked and broken. She sniffed and wiped the mucus roughly from her upper lip. Justin's body stiffened as a wave of pain wracked him, his thighs straining the vinyl straps, his back arched and contorted. His eyes seemed drugged, insensate, and for a moment Cameron thought she'd lost him already despite the steady blip of the monitor.

The soldiers disembarked, hardly taking note of them.

Cameron cleared her throat and fought to enunciate, but her words still came out a scratchy drawl. "Baby," she said. "Baby, look at me. Look at me."

A glimmer of recognition rippled through his eyes, and Cameron bit her lip, fighting not to sob from relief. He turned, his eyes finding hers. A thin line of drool dangled from the side of his mouth.

"That's right," she breathed. "Just look at me. Look at me."

He watched her, his eyes lit through with pain. Weakly, he raised a trembling hand. It hovered in the space between their stretchers, reaching for her. Despite the excruciating pain in her shoulder, she reached for him too. For an instant, there was nothing else—no noise, no pain, no hammering rotors overhead, just the feeling of her husband's hand in hers, his eyes on her face.

The door swung open, and she saw a montage of images in the night—Rex sprinting for the open helo door, the B1 bomber on the tarmac ready for takeoff, Diego lying down before the plane, his wrists handcuffed around the forward landing gear. It seemed as if Rex and Diego were wearing only boxer shorts.

Cameron blinked lazily, trying to make sense of everything. The bomber should already have taken off; it should have been heading to Sangre de Dios by now, bearing the neutron bomb in its belly. Diego must have delayed the takeoff by handcuffing himself to the wheel. A UN soldier pinned down Diego's arms with his knees as another struggled to undo the cuffs with a key. They came free, and the soldiers dragged Diego away struggling and shouting. A button popped from the soldier's shirt, pattering on the tarmac. Ramoncito, wearing a dirty pair of underwear, ran forward from seemingly nowhere, pounding one of the soldiers' backs weakly with his fists.

The bomber rolled forward, engines revving for the takeoff.

Rex stumbled up to the door, shoving the corpsman aside. Water dripped from his hair. "The water samples are clean," he said. "All of them."

Cameron tried to smile but couldn't.

"Did you exterminate the carriers?" he asked.

Cameron fought against the haze. She raised a pale hand and flashed a weak thumbs-up. Behind them, the B1 roared into its takeoff, engines screaming, cutting through the night air like a scythe. Justin mumbled something, but it was lost in the noise.

Diego kicked free from the UN soldiers and ran for the helo, his sleek ponytail bouncing, Ramoncito at his heels. "Did you do it?" Diego screamed. One of his elbows was bleeding, scraped by the tarmac.

Rex pulled out his bottom lip and removed the small disk of the transmitter from where he'd wedged it against his gums. Holding it in the palm of his hand like a jewel, he activated it, telling the operator to patch him through to Samantha. His leg hammered up and down nervously as the B1 grew smaller over his shoulder.

On the runway, the *Minutes to Burn* electronic billboard sat blank, awaiting another morning, another reading. Diego muttered Spanish curses under his breath as they waited. Finally, Samantha's voice clicked through.

"They're back," Rex said. "The virus reservoir was exterminated. We're clear."

The phone rustled against Samantha's shirt, but they could still make out her yelling through the window at Secretary Benneton.

The B1 faded in the night, the blinks on the wingtips almost out of sight. Diego watched it go, clearly fighting off panic.

"He just issued the order to abort," Samantha said.

Diego's face went limp with relief. He began to sob with a slow urgency. Ramoncito leaned against him, burying his face in his side.

"I want you, Dr. Rodriguez, the boy, and Cameron to come straight here for tests. The C-130 is standing by."

Rex turned. "Yes," he said. "I see it."

A corpsman jogged over from the C-130. "How many cots should we prepare?"

Rex looked inside the helo, noticing for the first time how empty it was.

When the corpsman asked again, his voice was full of dread. "How many cots?"

Cameron nodded weakly.

"Two," Rex said. When he spoke again, his voice was little more than a whisper. "Just two."

In the distance, the sound of the B1's engines shifted, rising to a sharper pitch. The plane banked high and hard, a broad sweeping arc in the night, and headed back for the airport. Diego fell to his knees, his hair wet and hanging across his eyes in the front.

It was the most beautiful sight he had ever seen.

RECLINED ON carefully secured cots, Cameron and Justin were out cold before the C-130 even took off. The acceleration caused Rex to lean in the cargo seat, but he quickly adjusted. The plane climbed rapidly and circled the island before heading northeast toward Maryland.

Wanting one last look at the islands, Rex rose carefully and crossed to the small round window near the propellers.

One of the corpsmen tending to Justin urged him to sit down, but Rex waved him off. He peered outside, then turned and smiled at Diego and Ramoncito. "Come here," he said. "You've got to see this."

Diego was careful to keep his balance as he joined Rex. He reached out a hand, helping Ramoncito navigate his way from the seat to the window. The boy's wonder at the plane was evident.

Down below, the black mass of Santa Cruz was visible on the dark waters. Above the southern edge of the island, right near the heart of Puerto Ayora, the air was lit with dozens of fireworks, the bright sparks coasting to the ground like settling embers.

Diego instinctively reached out, ruffling Ramoncito's hair. The three of them stood and watched the brilliant flashes of light until the island passed from view. Diego's eyes moistened when he looked down at the boy at his side.

"Happy New Year," he said.

1 JAN 08

Chapter 76 Samantha was ready and waiting when an irritable male nurse arrived to unlock her from the slammer at nine in the morning. She stepped out into the hallway and took a deep breath, stretching her arms. It felt odd to be out of the confines of the room; it usually took her a few hours to adjust.

The nurse handed her that morning's test results—viral count: 0. Samantha rested her hands on his shoulders. "I'll always remember you," she said.

He did not smile.

She received a standing ovation when she passed the staff room and she clenched her hands above her head like a heavyweight champ. As she passed reception, one of the secretaries stood up, holding out a pink message slip. "NIH called this morning, girl," she said. "Heard you were available."

Without slowing her pace, Samantha snapped up the message slip, heading for the entrance.

Colonel Strickland caught her at the door, placing a firm hand on her elbow. Samantha had to tilt her head way back to look him in the face.

"Secretary Benneton was quite impressed with your efforts," he said. "He strongly recommended that we extend to you an offer to return as Chief of the DAD."

Samantha ran a hand through her messy brown hair, scratching her scalp. "You're not gonna much like my proposal for what you can do with your offer. Sir."

"I imagined you'd have ... reservations." He raised a neatly-trimmed eyebrow. "Retiring?"

She laughed and pushed through the door. "Yeah," she called over her shoulder. "I thought I'd take up needlepoint."

Though she didn't see it, Colonel Douglas Strickland actually smiled.

"HELLO THERE," Samantha said when Maricarmen picked up the phone. "Where are my children?"

"Iggy and Danny are watching cartoons," Maricarmen said. "And Kiera is pretending not to."

Samantha tapped the sat phone against her ear. A few lanes over, a car honked.

"What is that? Are you out?"

"Free at last."

"I should get the children. They'll be so excited."

"I'd rather surprise them in person. But I'm taking a quick trip to Hopkins first."

"Johnny Hopkins Hospital? In Baltimore? What for?"

Samantha smiled. "To visit a friend."

"A friend?"

"Dr. Martin Foster. Don't worry, I'll be home soon."

Hanging up, she fiddled with the radio until she found an

oldies station. The Carpenters came on, and she sang along with them, zoning out and watching the trees fly by at the edge of the highway.

Finally, she reached the hospital, parked the van near the Ross Building, and found her way to the Infectious Disease Offices. She stopped outside the door, suddenly nervous. Looking down, she realized she was still wearing scrubs, and she cursed herself for not going home first to shower and change.

She entered and greeted the receptionist, a heavyset woman whose computer was framed with family pictures. "Hello, Samantha Everett here to see Dr. Foster."

"Is he expecting you?"

"No," Samantha said. "Not at all."

"Well, he's in with a patient right now. He's booked pretty solid for the next few hours."

"That's all right," Samantha said. "I'll wait."

She sat down and picked up a *People* magazine. She tilted a brass lamp over so she could fix her hair in the reflection.

"Ms. Everett," the receptionist said, trying not to smile. "Or is it Dr.?"

"Either," Samantha said. "Whatever."

"I think I can free him up for a few minutes at the end of the hour." She scanned the appointment book. "But I'm not certain. Maybe you'd like to wait somewhere more comfortable?"

"Sure." Samantha shrugged. "Where would you suggest?"

The receptionist smiled shyly. "Maybe it's the mother of four in me, but I always like the nursery."

"Huh," Samantha said. "Actually, that sounds nice."

She left the office and crossed the street to the Nelson Building, riding the elevator up to the second floor. A row of chairs was arrayed outside the long window where expectant mothers and fathers could see their infants for the first time. Samantha sat in an orange plastic chair, tilting it back on two legs. She stared at the rows of gorgeous, smiling babies.

Closing her eyes, Samantha thought of the Darwin virus, safely frozen in the Revco freezer back at Fort Detrick. There were still many tests to be run so that they could better understand its etiology and pathogenicity. Maybe some of the infected dinoflagellates had survived and were out there now, floating around in the ocean, the virus ready to find its way into another species if circumstances allowed. She prayed silently that it wouldn't again rear its head. In her mind, she sorted through the events of the past week, searching for any mistakes she may have made, any errors in judgment. It was the heaviest burden of her job—making tough decisions when lives hung in the balance. Complete accountability was difficult, but she wouldn't have had it any other way. She wondered how long she had before another deadly virus found its way to her from the Kenyan jungles, the Amazon basin, the scrubby plains of Australia.

She felt a hand on her shoulder and she opened her eyes, seeing Dr. Foster's reflection in the nursery window. He stood behind her quietly. She felt the warmth from his hand. They stayed silently like that for a few moments, Samantha sitting and Martin Foster standing behind her. Without turning around, she reached up and took his hand.

The peace was broken by a tray clattering to the ground somewhere out of sight. Iggy's voice sailed loud and clear around the corner. "Is this where the fat lady said mommy was?"

Kiera's voice followed. "It's not nice to say *fat*, you idiot. She was big-boned."

Samantha heard Danny laughing and Maricarmen trying to shush all three children, and a broad smile spread across her face. She leaned back in the chair, admiring the healthy newborns laid out before her, the warmth of Martin Foster's hand on her shoulder, the noise of her children growing closer. This is how it's supposed to be, she thought. This is really how it's supposed to be.

For the first time she could remember, she reached down and turned off her pager.

Chapter 77   Gorged with fruit, the wicker cornucopia seemed to stare back at Cameron and Justin from its perch on the table in the waiting room. The glass tabletop had broken in a recent tremor; it had been replaced temporarily by a piece of plywood. Next to them, a new mother bounced her baby on her knee, its little hands opening and closing, grabbing at nothing. The baby hiccuped and giggled as the mother leaned forward. They rubbed noses.

Justin held Cameron's hand as they waited side by side, his shoulder bandage bulky under his shirt. Cameron shifted a little in the chair, ignoring the pain in her hip. Toying with her necklace absentmindedly, she noticed that the clasp had worked its way around to the front. Justin extended his hand, wiggling his fingers and flexing, testing out his muscles. The reconstructive surgeries had restored to him full control of his arm. Using cutting-edge technology, the doctors had even managed to repair the plexus of nerves that ran down the arm.

Fiddling her wedding ring on her finger with her thumb, she gazed blankly at a *Child* magazine sitting under the curved brass reading lamp. On the cover, a pudgy, grinning boy of about two sat with his legs kicked wide out in front of him. He smiled proudly at the tower of colorful blocks he had stacked between his legs.

Despite her apprehension, Cameron forced herself to stare at the dark, solid door to the right. The door without a peephole. She thought of the choice before her should the fetus turn out to be healthy. When she turned back to the yellow door, she felt better, almost empowered.

The Darwin virus had not appeared in her or Justin's bloodstream, and Rex, Diego, and Ramoncito had been cleared as well. Because Cameron was pregnant, Samantha had asked that she have a full workup six weeks after the end of the mission, including a prenatal intake, chorionic villus sampling, and a set of ultrasounds. The results awaited.

Diego had returned to Sangre de Dios, further sanitizing everything that had been in contact with the virus—the specimen freezer, the vestiges of the two camps, the areas where the mantids and larvae had been burned. He'd also set three more GPS units, finally completing the network.

Next to Cameron, the mother whispered lovingly to the baby as she burped him. Evidently he had spit up, because she dabbed at her blouse with a little white towel. The towel was decorated with cabooses.

Some footsteps sounded down the corridor, shoes clicking on tile.

The mother gazed at the cheerful yellow door ahead, then turned a kind smile to Cameron.

"So exciting, isn't it?" she asked.

Cameron looked at her, expressionless.

The door swung open, and the stocky Italian nurse filled the doorway, hunched slightly at the shoulders. The rings under her eyes looked dark, even darker than Cameron had remembered. Her hair stood out in graying wisps.

"Kates," the nurse said, her teeth discolored and crooked. "Cameron Kates. Your results are in. The doctor would like to discuss them with you."

Cameron felt Justin squeeze her neck reassuringly. She rose calmly. Justin kept his hand on her back to steady her as they followed the nurse back.

The room was small and claustrophobic. Cameron slowly undressed, put on the gown, and slid up onto the exam table, crinkling the paper. A small notch of a scar crested her deltoid where her transmitter had been removed.

When she heard the doorknob turn, Cameron felt panic spreading through her, but she fought to quell it. Dr. Birnbaum entered, a bearded man with kind blue eyes. He glanced down at a chart, scratching his cheek with a pen. Cameron and Justin stared at him, eyes wide, too nervous to speak.

"I just got off the phone with Dr. Everett at the NIH," he said. "And together we concluded that your results are totally normal. It looks like you have a healthy baby on your hands." His smile lessened when he looked at Cameron. "Should you elect to keep it."

Cameron had thought she'd feel nothing, so she was completely unprepared for the wave of emotion that swept through her. Her mind danced across a landscape of memories, spinning with images. She thought of the larva, bucking and squealing and dying. She thought of the gnarled little creature on the floor of the Estradas' house. She thought of Derek and Jacqueline and their baby girl. She thought of all the frightful things she had seen—so many reasons to be afraid, so many reasons to pull back into herself where everything was neat and safe.

"Baby?" Justin was asking. "Do you want to? Do you think you're ready?" His eyes were as soft as they'd ever been—brave yet intensely vulnerable.

She could barely hear him because she was so far down in herself, swimming in fear and excitement and sheer elation. The answer was there like a bright beam of light, and with it came tears, hard and unremitting. She was pressing her face against his chest, weeping with joy, and from somewhere far away she heard herself saying yes over and over like a prayer.

Chapter 78   The island's last remaining feral dog nosed through the ash and debris of the base camp, looking for food. Her paws were ragged, one of her nails torn off from a fight with another bitch. She'd caught a masked booby chick the previous day, which she'd eaten right in front of its squawking mother, sliding down to her belly and savoring the meal. But the hunger had returned again quickly, greeting her in the morning with the rising sun.

Maybe it was because she was pregnant.

She tugged on a scorched edge of canvas, searching for something edible beneath, but there was nothing, just a warped cruise box and a dented canteen. Finally giving up, she trotted toward the road, her head barely protruding from the high grass.

Leaping gracefully among the fallen balsas, she nosed her way through the cracks of the trunks, but again there was nothing. She was just about ready to head to the forest when she caught a whiff of something faint, lining the southern wind.

She jogged up the road toward the source of the smell, her nose elevated and twitching. Stopping at the base of the watchtower, she sat, peering up its length.

In the shed at the top, the desiccated body of the larva lay beneath the dangling hook, protected by the shade of the shed. The abdomen and thorax had long rotted away in the sweltering heat, but the sclerotized head had just begun to crack. Green hemolymph oozed out, working its way slowly down the side rail of the dilapidated ladder, its pungent odor thick in the air. The bitch sat, head cocked, watching the ripe fluid slowly descend.

In the distance, the dot of a boat appeared on the horizon, Diego on the deck, Ramoncito laughing and swinging from the boom. It was still a good few hours away from shore.

The hemolymph pooled momentarily above a crooked 2 x 4 that served as one of the ladder's steps before spilling over and snaking the rest of the way down the side rail.

The dog stepped forward and began lapping.

FACE white and blistering, eyelids swollen nearly shut, hair falling from the front of her scalp in thin clusters, the nurse stumbled blindly through the UCLA Medical Center Emergency Room doors, both hands waving in front of her. Her cries came from deep in her chest, rapid animal sounds that twisted into raspy moans by the time they left her mouth. A half-moon darkened the V of her scrub-top collar, and the skin along her clavicle had whitened and softened.

She tried to say something, but it came out a guttural bark.

A Hispanic gardener leapt up from his seat before the lobby's check-in windows, cradling the bloody bandage wrapping his hand and knocking over his chair. He circled wide as the nurse advanced, as if afraid of attack or contamination. A mother holding her five-year-old stepped through a set of swinging doors, shrieked, and beelined to the safety of the waiting room. The guard at the security desk rose to a half crouch above his chair.

A blister burst near the woman's temple, sending a run of viscous fluid over the mottled landscape of her cheek. Open sores spotted her lips, and when she spread her mouth to scream, her Cupid's bow split, spilling blood down her chin.

She groped her way along the wall, her shoulders racking with sobs, her mouth working on air.

An expression of horror frozen on her face, Pat Atkins circled her desk in the small triage room, knocking over her first cup of morning coffee, and ran into the lobby toward the woman.

The woman retched, sending a thin spray of grayish vomit across the vivid white wall. She lunged forward, her shin striking the overturned chair, and tumbled over, breaking her fall with the heels of her hands.

Pat sprinted over, shouting at the security guard, "Tell them to get Trauma Twelve ready!"

She reached for a pulse as the nurse rolled onto her back, sputtering and gurgling, leaving a hank of hair on the clean tile floor. When Pat saw the nurse's ID badge, she inhaled sharply, running a hand over her bristling gray hair.

"Jesus God," she said. "Nancy, is that you?"

The swollen head nodded, the whitish raw skin glistening. "Dr. Spier," she rasped. "Get Dr. Spier."

NEARLY KNOCKING over a radiology resident with an armful of charts, David Spier sprinted into the Central Work Area bridging the two parallel hallways of exam rooms that composed his division. He pointed at an intern and snapped his fingers. "I need a urine on Mitchell in Eight."

He stepped across the CWA, patting his best resident on the shoulder. "Diane—let's move."

Diane handed off the phone to a nurse and pivoted, her shoulder-length straight blond hair whipping around so the nurse had to lean back out of its way. Grabbing the pen from behind her ear, Diane slid it into the pocket on her faded blue resident scrubs. David rested a hand on her shoulder blade, guiding her into Hallway One. They both shuffle-stepped back as the gurney swept past them and banked a hard left into the trauma room. They followed behind, David resting his hands on the back of the gurney. The nurses folded in on the patient's writhing body, a wave of dark blue scrubs. Pat leaned over, slid a pair of trauma shears up the moist scrub top, threw the material to the sides.

"What do we have?" David asked.

A nurse with shiny black hair glanced up. "Caucasian female, probably midtwenties, some vomiting, erythematous blisters on face and upper chest, eyes are opaque, moderate respiratory distress. Appears to be some kind of chemical burn." She reached down and untwisted the ID badge from the mound of fabric. Her face blanched. "It's Nancy Jenkins."

The news rippled visibly through the nurses and lab techs. Though they were accustomed to operating under duress, having a colleague and friend wheeled into the ER in this state was beyond even their experience.

David glanced at Nancy's blistering face, her pretty blond hair lying in loose strands on the gurney, and felt a chill wash down his chest to his gut. He recalled when they had wheeled his wife in here two years ago, the night of his forty-first birthday, but he caught himself quickly, checking his thoughts. Instinctively, his physician's calm spread through him, protective and impersonal.

He quick-stepped around the gurney so he could examine Nancy's face. Her eyelids and lips were badly burnt. If the caustic agent dripping from her had gotten into her eyes and down her throat, they were dealing with a whole new host of problems.

"Get me GI and ophtho consults," he said. "And someone contact the tox center. Let's get the offending agent ID'd."

Pat glanced up from her post behind Nancy's head. "Some nasal flaring here, and she's stridorous." She chewed her lip. "Hurry with that monitor."

"Find me some pH strips," Diane called out. "And let's get saline bottles in here stat."

A clerk ran from the room. Two nurses dashed in, pulling on latex gloves and snapping them at the wrists. "Was it an explosion?" someone asked.

"Doubt it," Pat said. "Nancy walked in herself—it must've happened right outside. Security's already contacted the police."

"She's working hard," David said, glancing at the skin sucking tight against her ribs and around her neck. "Supraclavicular and substernal retractions. Let's get ready to tube her."

Nancy tried to sit up, but Pat restrained her. Nancy's breath came in great heaves. "Dr. Spier," she said. Her voice was thick and rough, tangling in the swell of her throat.

David leaned over Nancy's face. The skin around the blisters was whitening, contrasting sharply with the red bulges. She appeared to be trying to go on speaking.

His hands fluttered near her jaw, ready to check her airway, "I'm right here, Nancy. We're gonna get you taken care of. Can you tell us what substance we're dealing with?"

IVs being hung, pulse ox sliding on the finger, scrubs cut free from her legs and tossed into a trash bin. Cardiac leads plunking down across her chest like bullet holes.

Nancy coughed, contorting on the gurney.

"Heart rate's one forty," someone said. "O-two saturation's low nineties and dropping."

David leaned closer. "Nancy, can you tell us?"

The green line on the EKG monitor showed tachycardia, the peaks and valleys getting mashed closer and closer. Her arm rose, a hand pawing limply at air.

No more time. He pulled her jaw open and peered down her throat. Ulceration of the oropharynx, subacute airway compromise from edema. Whatever had gone down her throat had irritated the tissue, causing massive swelling. He needed to secure an airway quickly before her throat closed off.

David tilted her head back to give her throat maximum patency. "Push twenty mgs of etomidate and one hundred of rocuronium," he said, his voice ringing sharp and clear. The drugs would sedate and completely paralyze Nancy. She'd be unable even to breathe unless they could get a tube down in her to do it for her. "Laryngoscope," he said.

The L-shaped tool slapped the latex covering his palm. Positioning it in his left hand, he then slid the blade down along her tongue, using the small attached light to guide it past the epiglottis. The laryngeal swelling was bad, even worse than he'd noticed at first glance. He couldn't see the vocal cords between which to guide the endotracheal tube.

He glanced up at Diane, who was performing the Sellick maneuver, applying pressure to the cricoid membrane beneath Nancy's larynx, trying to bring the vocal cords into view for him. It wasn't working, and they didn't have time to get a fiberoptic scope down from anesthesia. He repositioned Nancy's head and tried again, but still couldn't make out the vocal cords behind the swelling.

"Crich her?" Diane asked.

David pulled the endotracheal tube from Nancy's mouth; it swayed beneath his fist like a bloody snake.

"Her O-two sat's dropping. . . ." Pat said, a note of panic creeping into her voice. Nancy's flesh was going from white to blue.

David reached for a scalpel, fingering beneath Nancy's larynx for the cricothyroid membrane with his other hand. He cut lengthwise along the membrane, opening up a surgical airway in her throat. Diane had the three-pronged retractor in his hand immediately; he slid it into the cut and it opened like a tripod, spreading the hole. Feeding a 4.0 ET tube into the hole, David plugged the other end into a ventilator hose. The ventilator breathed for her, pushing air through the tube into her lungs.

Her chest started rising and falling, and her oxygen saturation climbed slowly back up past ninety. Airway secured. Now he'd have to identify the offending agent.

He glanced up at the nurses. They were moving a little slower than usual, still shell-shocked. A lot of looks to Nancy's face.

"I know this is hard," David said, gently yet firmly, "but right now we're just dealing with an injured body, like any other body. Have you drawn blood?"

Pat nodded.

"Send off a CBC, a chem panel, type and screen, and get a rectal. Does someone have my pH strips?"

The black-haired nurse slid a gloved hand between Nancy's limp legs.

Someone handed David a yellow pH strip and he laid it across Nancy's cheek. It dampened quickly, but did not change. He threw it aside. "Not an acid," he announced. Pat was ready with the red strips; he laid one on Nancy's forehead and one just beneath her eye. Almost immediately, they turned a glaring blue.

David cursed under his breath. A base. Probably Drano. Acids are nasty, but they attack tissue in such a way that the skin scars quickly, usually protecting healthy underlying tissue. Alkali, on the other hand, produces a liquefaction necrosis, saponifying fats, dissolving proteins, penetrating ever deeper into the tissues. Unlike acid, it keeps burning and burning, turning flesh to liquid. Same way it opens clogged drains.

Diane glanced at the blue pH strip and immediately began dousing Nancy's face with saline.

"Follow her lead," David said. "Irrigate the hell out of her." He raised one of Nancy's lids with a thumb and stared at the white cloudy eyeball. Corneal opacification. More bad news. He picked up a little 250-cc saline bottle and flushed the eye.

The blistering lips and swollen throat indicated that the alkali had gone down Nancy's throat. If it had burned through her esophagus, letting air escape into her chest cavity, he would have to get her to the OR immediately. If it hadn't fully penetrated, then the alkali remained on the esophageal walls, eating through additional tissue, and there was very little they could do about it.

He slid an X-ray cassette, encased in a dull silver case, beneath Nancy's body. "Everyone in leads!" Everyone present threw on lead aprons as Diane positioned the X-ray unit over Nancy's body and threw the switch. Quickly, they repeated the procedure until they'd completed serial chest and abdominal films. A lab tech slid the final cassettes out from beneath Nancy and handed them off to the radiology tech, who scurried from the room.

"Check for free subdiaphragmatic air, mediastinal emphysema, and examine lung parenchyma for signs of aspiration," David yelled after the tech. "Did he hear me? Someone make sure he heard."

Several nurses and lab techs were spraying down Nancy's face with saline bottles. Water and runoff drenched the gurney sheets. David's bottle spat air, so he tossed it into the bin, grabbed another, and continued irrigating the eyes.

Pat switched IV bags, then checked Nancy's blood pressure cuff, her face stained with grief and shock. With twenty-three years as an RN under her belt, Pat was the den mother of the ER nurses; that's why she'd followed Nancy in here, probably sending one of the more junior nurses out front to triage. Her crew cut was shot through with sweat.

David glanced around the small room bustling with people. A few other faces looked upset, and a lab tech was holding one of Nancy's limp hands. "We have a damn sharp team here," he said. "Don't worry, and stay focused."

The telephone behind David emitted only a half ring before he grabbed it, first handing off his saline bottle to a nurse and pivoting to miss an IV pole a lab tech pulled around. "Dr. Jenner, just in time. We need you down here, got a bad alkali exposure to the eyes."

"Was the skin around the eyes burnt?" The ophthalmologist's deeply textured voice was low, rolling, authoritative.

"Everything's burnt. The cornea's cloudy white."

"So the endothelium's already not functioning. You're irrigating copiously?"

"Yes. Saline."

"Good. Osmosis advantage. Once the eyes are better cleared, give her a drop of Pred Forte to stop the inflammation and a drop of Cipro for infection. I'm on my way."

Diane glanced up at David as he hung up the phone. He chewed his lower lip. "Pat, can you call GI again, ask what's taking so goddamn long on our consult?"

The radiology tech poked his head into the room, fresh back from the X-ray suite in the rear. "No free air," he said.

That was good—at least the alkali hadn't eaten through the esophagus, allowing air to escape into the body. Yet.

Diane leaned forward over Nancy's body, and she and David brushed foreheads. Her eyes jerked quickly away. "Sorry."

"How are you doing on the eyes there?" David asked.

Diane nodded. "Okay. But I think she's gonna need a corneal transplant." She leaned over, examining the other eye. "Two."

"We're going to apply some Cipro and Pred Forte drops. Can you get them ready?"

A uniformed UCLA Police Department officer strolled in; David was immediately irritated by his casual gait. The cop cleared his throat. "I have some questions I need to—"

"This patient is unconscious and can't answer questions."

"Well, I'll need to take a—"

"Not right now," David said. "Out, please. *Out*."

The cop shot him a good glare before retreating.

The nurses and techs continued to irrigate Nancy's flesh, lined on both sides of her body like feeding pups.

"Good, good," David said. "We're gonna keep irrigating her for hours."

Pat looked up, a little moist-eyed, and nodded. "We'll be here."

The wall phone rang, and a tech grabbed it, then held it out to David. "Dr. Woods."

David shot a latex glove into the trash bin and fisted the phone. "We have an alkali burn, some ingestion. No free air on the film."

"Ulceration of oropharynx?"

"Yes. And acute laryngeal swelling. We had to crich her."

"We like to have them swallow a little water, push the alkali down the esophagus into the stomach. Greater area, protective acids." Dr. Woods's voice was slow and droning. It reflected his personality.

"The swelling was already acute, and I didn't want to run the risk of her vomiting it back up," David said, a note of impatience creeping into his voice.

"Smart . . . smart. Unfortunately, there's little you can do to mitigate esophageal damage. Liquefaction necrosis happens almost instantaneously. Fever? Whites are normal?"

"No. Yes."

"I'm going to need to get down there and take a look. Give her one-fifty of Zantac IV stat to reduce the stomach acid. That should prevent stress bleeding and ulcerations as well."

"We'll see you shortly." David set the phone down on the cradle and relayed the order. He glanced at the monitor, admired the healthy baseline rhythm. Blood pressure 160 over 100. Respiratory rate at eighteen. Pulse 120. Oxygen saturation 99 percent.

He pulled a deep breath into his lungs and exhaled loudly. It took a conscious effort to relax his muscles and let his shoulders sink. Diane leaned forward over Nancy's face, continuing to irrigate her eyes. A wisp of hair arced across her cheek, finding the corner of her mouth.

An intern skidded on the floor, accidentally sliding past the door. She hooked the frame with a hand as she leaned in. "Golf cart versus Buick. Two forty-three-year-old males with penetrating head wounds. ETA two minutes. We're prepping Procedure Two."

David shot his other latex glove at the trash bin and headed for the door.